Joan Jonker was born and bred in Liverpool. She is a tireless campaigner for the charity-run organisation Victims of Violence, and she lives in Southport with her son. She has two sons and two grandsons.

Joan is the author of *Victims Of Violence*, and a trilogy, *Man Of The House*, *When One Door Closes* and *Home Is Where The Heart Is*, the heartwarming story of an engaging group of Liverpool friends. Her affectionate and humorous tales have already won her many fans in her hometown and they are sure to delight readers everywhere.

Stay
In Your Own
Back Yard

Joan Jonker

headline

First published in 1995
by HEADLINE BOOK PUBLISHING

First published in paperback in 1996
by HEADLINE BOOK PUBLISHING

20 19

ISBN 0 7472 4916 4

Typeset by
Letterpart Limited, Reigate, Surrey

Printed and bound in Great Britain by
Clays Ltd, St Ives plc

HEADLINE BOOK PUBLISHING
A division of Hodder Headline PLC
338 Euston Road
London NW1 3BH

To my darling husband Tony
who was my prop, my friend
and my love

Chapter One

'I wish I knew what she wants me for.' Molly realised she was talking aloud and turned her head quickly to make sure there was no one around. 'I'll be getting locked up one of these days, talkin' to meself.'

She gripped one of the round iron end posts of the railing before her and surveyed the single-storey council school. Since her daughter, Jill, had come home yesterday with a note saying the headmistress wanted to see Molly, she had been a bag of nerves. If it had been her other daughter, Doreen, or her son Tommy who'd brought the letter home she'd have known it meant bad news 'cos they were a right pair of scallywags. Always in trouble for one thing or another, getting the cane in school for being cheeky or fighting with the other kids in the street. But Jill was different, never caused her a moment's worry. Her school report was always good, and she never fell out of friends with anyone. So what the headmistress wanted to see Molly for was a mystery.

She looked down at her old coat which was frayed around the button holes and cuffs. It had been blue when she bought it, but now it had faded so much it was hard

1

to tell what colour it was supposed to be. And when her eyes travelled down to her scruffy shoes, she let out a deep sigh. For all the polish and elbow grease, they still looked like something the rag man would turn up his nose at. Still, they were all she had so it was a case of Hobson's choice.

Her gaze moved to the hand gripping the railing, and the ring of white skin on the third finger of her left hand. For the first time in her married life, she'd pawned her wedding ring. If Jack found out, there'd be merry hell to pay. But what else could she have done? She didn't have a pair of stockings to her name, and she certainly wasn't going to let her daughter down by turning up with bare legs. Being poor didn't mean they had no pride.

Reminding herself to keep her ringless finger out of sight, Molly took a deep breath, muttering, 'Don't know what I'm gettin' all worked up about, she can't eat me.'

Straightening her shoulders and holding her head high, she marched through the school gates and across the playground. Molly had a bonny figure, not fat but padded in all the right places, and she moved now with an easy grace that belied the apprehension she felt.

The corridors were empty when she entered the building but she knew where Miss Bond's office was, and made her way towards it.

'Sit down, Mrs Bennett.' The headmistress waved her to a chair on the other side of her desk. She was a tall angular woman with steel grey hair combed back from her face and coiled into a bun at the nape of her neck. She had a stern face, and looking at her beneath lowered lids, Molly thought, it's no wonder all the kids are scared stiff of her. Her face is enough to frighten the living daylights out of anyone!

Miss Bond took some papers from a side drawer of her desk and laid them in front of her. 'I wanted to talk to you about Jill.'

'Why?' Molly sat forward. 'What's she been up to?'

The ghost of a smile crossed Miss Bond's face. 'Nothing wrong, I can assure you. Jill is one of the best pupils we've ever had. She's always polite, pleasant, and very diligent.' She picked up the top sheet of paper from the pile and handed it to Molly. 'This is her school report, which you'll be getting when she leaves school next month. As you will see, she came top of the class in every subject.'

The words on the paper swam before Molly's eyes. She looked at them because she knew it was expected of her, but her mind was still asking why she was here. She raised her head. 'Our Jill's always been bright, right from when she was a toddler.'

'She's more than bright, Mrs Bennett, she's a very clever girl. That's why I wanted to talk to you. I think Jill should go on from here to a high school.'

'A high school!' Molly's jaw dropped. 'But she'll be fourteen! Everyone goes to work when they're fourteen.'

Miss Bond leaned forward, her elbows on the desk. 'Not everyone has Jill's brains. She's a very intelligent girl, and with the right education she could go far. It would be such a waste to send someone as bright as she is to work in a corner shop or a factory.'

'A factory job was good enough for me,' Molly said,

3

her face red. 'It didn't do me no 'arm. An' her dad works in a factory.'

'I didn't mean to sound patronising,' Miss Bond replied. 'But I don't think you understand how gifted your daughter is. I've been teaching for thirty years now, and Jill is one of the most promising girls I have ever taught. With the right education, she could go far.'

'And where's the money comin' from?' Molly asked, thinking the woman must have lost the run of her senses. Did she think they were millionaires or something?

'If you agree, we could try to get her a free scholarship. She would have no trouble passing the entrance exam.' Miss Bond knew she was asking a lot from a family who were hard put to make ends meet, but she had to try. Jill Bennett had it in her to make something of herself, to get out of the poverty trap that her parents and all their neighbours were in. 'The only money you would need to provide would be for her uniform and books.'

'Is that all?' Molly couldn't keep the sarcasm from her voice. Then she lowered her head, and gazing at her clasped hands told herself to keep that quick temper of hers in check. 'Miss Bond, we don't 'ave money to spare. My 'usband brings in two pounds fifteen shillings a week, and that's with workin' all the hours God sends. Out of that I 'ave to pay the rent, gas and coal, and feed and clothe the six of us. I get me money on a Saturday, an' by Tuesday I don't 'ave two ha'pennies to rub together. We live on tick from the corner shop until pay day, then we start all over again.'

'Will you at least think about it, and talk it over with

your husband? It would be such a waste if Jill weren't given the opportunity to make use of the talents she's been blessed with.'

Molly's eyes narrowed. 'Does our Jill know about this? I don't want yer fillin' her head with impossible dreams, an' then 'er blamin' us for keepin' her back.'

Miss Bond shook her head. 'I haven't spoken to Jill about it. But I beg you to give it some thought, talk it over with your husband and see what he says.'

Molly put her hands on the arms of the chair and levered herself up. 'All the talkin' in the world won't change things. I've been waitin' for our Jill to leave school, lookin' forward to havin' an extra few bob comin' in.'

Molly looked at the headmistress's good quality warm dress and sturdy shoes, and wondered if she had any idea what it was like to try to feed and clothe six of them on the money Jack brought home. She didn't look as though she'd ever known hard times.

Miss Bond held the door open. 'I know it's a lot to ask, but please think it over.'

'I could think about it until kingdom come, but it wouldn't make any difference.' Molly gave a deep sigh. 'I know yer've only got Jill's interests at heart, an' I thank yer for that. If our circumstances were different I'd be only too happy to do anythin' to help 'er and me other children, 'cos they mean the whole world to me an' my 'usband. But as things are, we've barely enough money comin' in to put clothes on their backs an' food in their stomachs. I need Jill working and bringin' in a wage every week, not for luxuries but for survival.'

5

Molly could feel the headmistress's eyes on her back as she walked down the corridor and forced herself to move slowly. But as soon as she was through the main door she took to her heels and ran across the play-ground, tears streaming down her face. She kept up the pace until she was out of breath and pains in her chest forced her to slow down. Her tummy was churning with a mixture of despair and humiliation, and she felt like being sick.

Molly dashed a hand across her eyes. She'd never felt so worthless in her life. When she'd told Miss Bond they were too poor to send Jill to high school she was only telling the truth. But it didn't stop her feeling guilty that their circumstances were going to prevent her daughter from having the start in life she deserved.

Then the anger in Molly answered back. I should never have been put in that position! As though I was to blame! Surely to God the woman should be more understanding, seeing as all the kids attending that school are from working-class families, some of them without a decent pair of shoes on their feet. Perhaps she hadn't meant to sound as though she was blaming Molly for holding her daughter back, but to Molly's ears that's just the way it did sound. As she walked in the direction of home an argument raged in her head.

'Bein' poor isn't somethin' to be ashamed of,' she muttered aloud, bringing a startled look to the face of a woman passing in the opposite direction. 'Half the people in the country are as poor as we are . . . some are even worse off! She 'ad no right to make me feel guilty, as though I don't want what's best for me own daughter.

As if I wouldn't give 'er the world if it was in me power! But I can't just pluck money out of thin air. And I don't 'ave a magic wand to wave, or a fairy godmother to grant me three wishes, so it's no good me cryin' me eyes out and gettin' all upset. Fate deals the cards and we didn't get a winning hand, that's the top an' bottom of it.'

'Has she been behavin' herself? Not givin' yer any lip?'

'She's been fine.' Mary Watson had been minding Molly's four-year-old daughter, Ruthie. 'We've been playin' snap all afternoon.'

'I won, Mam!' Ruthie threw her arms around Molly's waist. 'I won nearly all the games.'

'Yer cheated,' Bella Watson said, her tiny mouth pursed. She was the same age as Ruthie, and when they weren't fighting they were the best of friends. 'Yer hid cards under the table.'

'Don't be tellin' tales out of school,' Mary laughed. 'Yer both as bad as one another.' She looked hard at Molly, noting the red-rimmed eyes. 'How did yer get on?'

'All right!' Molly wasn't in the mood for confidences. 'It was just to tell me our Jill's done very well, top of the class in everythin'.'

Molly turned to her daughter and was just in time to see her raise her hand and smack Bella across the face. 'You little faggot!' She bent and delivered a resounding slap across Ruthie's legs. 'Honest, I need eyes in me backside with you.'

'That's not fair!' Ruthie hopped up and down, rubbing her leg. 'She 'it me first.'

Molly groaned and raised her eyes to the sky. 'Flippin' kids! Who'd 'ave 'em?' She grabbed her daughter's hand. 'Say yer sorry to Bella, and thank Auntie Mary for mindin' yer.'

Ruthie lowered her head, her toes scuffing the pavement. 'She 'it me first.'

'Skip it, Molly,' said Mary. 'They're both as bad as one another.' She folded her arms. 'Yer haven't seen anythin' of Miss Clegg, have yer?'

Molly looked puzzled. 'No, why?'

'I haven't seen hide nor hair of 'er for three days and I'm gettin' worried. Usually I see her a couple of times a day, either standin' at the door or in the yard, but for the last three days I haven't set eyes on her. I've tried knockin' on her door, and on the wall, but there's no answer.'

'Have yer tried the back door?'

Mary nodded. 'It's locked.'

Molly walked the few steps to next door and banged hard on the knocker. Then she lifted the letter box and yelled, 'Miss Clegg!' After a few minutes she walked back to Mary. 'Yer've got me worried now.' Mary's neighbour was eighty-two, a lovely old lady who was popular with everyone in the street. 'We'd better do somethin', 'cos at her age anythin' could 'ave happened.'

'I've thought of everythin', Molly, and don't know what more I can do.'

'Well, we can't just stand by an' do nothin'.' Molly was feeling uneasy. She was very fond of the old lady who was like a grandmother to all the kids in the street. 'When our Tommy comes 'ome from school, I'll get 'im to climb over 'er yard wall and open the entry door for us. With a bit of luck 'er kitchen door might be unlocked.'

Tommy gazed at the wall, a gleam of excitement in his eyes. 'I'll easy get over there.'

Molly and Mary gaped as he pressed his back against the opposite wall, then with his arms high above his head, took a running jump. Before they had time to take in what was happening he was sitting astride the top of Miss Clegg's wall, then he swung his body round and jumped down.

'My God, he's done that a few times,' Molly said. 'No wonder he's never got an arse in 'is kecks or soles on 'is shoes.'

Tommy opened the entry door with a flourish, a look of triumph on his face. 'Easy-peasy.'

Molly didn't know whether to kiss him or give him a crack. Then she remembered she was the one who'd asked him to do it, so she could hardly blame him. 'Come on, Mary, let's see if the door's open.'

But the kitchen door was locked, and they looked at each other questioningly. 'What now?' asked Mary.

Molly was already peering through the net curtains on the window, but the material was heavily patterned and she couldn't see anything. 'Tommy, come and stand on this sill an' see if yer can get the top of the window down.' He hopped on to the sill, thinking it was getting more exciting all the time. With his mother's hands supporting him, he looked through the glass pane. 'The window's not locked, I can see the catch.'

'Then pull it down,' Molly said. 'Gently though, I 'aven't got no money to be payin' out for a new window.'

But the window hadn't been opened for years and it refused to budge. Tommy grunted and groaned as he pushed and pulled, but to no avail. 'It's no good, Mam, it's stuck.'

'I wish Harry was here,' Mary wailed. 'He'd know what to do.'

'Well, he's not 'ere, so forget it.' Molly stroked her chin. 'The flamin' window's probably been painted over while it was closed and now it's stuck fast.' She thought for a few seconds then patted her son's bottom. 'Tommy, give a few bangs on the side of the frame, that might do the trick.'

He banged and pulled until his hands were sore. 'Ah, ray, Mam, I've got splinters in me 'ands!'

'Just once more for luck,' Molly coaxed. And when the window dropped an inch she had reason to smile for the first time that day. 'Ooh, yer clever kid! Now see if yer can get it down lower.'

His fingers in the narrow gap, Tommy put his full weight behind the next pull. He was rewarded when the frame rattled, then shuddered down a further twelve inches. After that, though, no amount of coaxing or pulling would shift it.

'Could yer get through there, son?'

Tommy eyed the narrow aperture. 'Yer won't blame me if I break anythin', will yer?'

Molly watched his head and shoulders disappear before closing her eyes. 'I can't look, Mary, tell us what's goin' on.'

10

Mary's hand was over her mouth as she gave a running commentary. 'His legs are goin' in now. I can see 'is hand on the inside of the window. There's a lot of clatterin' goin' on, like pans and dishes, but I can't see anything.'

Molly opened her eyes when she heard the bolt being drawn back. Then the door opened and Tommy stood there grinning from ear to ear. The last half hour had been more exciting than going to the Saturday matinee to see Tom Mix. He wished his mates had been there to see him 'cos he knew when he told them on Monday they wouldn't believe him.

'Good work, son.' Molly ruffled his hair. 'Now wait 'ere while me an' Mary 'ave a look-see. Don't go away in case we need yer.'

Mary was so close on Molly's heels she collided with her when Molly came to an abrupt halt. 'Oh, my God!' Molly rushed across the room to where she could see Miss Clegg stretched out on the couch. The old lady's eyes were closed and her body was so still it caused the blood in Molly's veins to run cold. She bent down and put one hand to the cold forehead while feeling for a pulse with the other.

Behind her, Mary cried, 'She's dead, isn't she?'

Molly silenced her with a withering look. Then she knelt down and stroked the thin, snow white hair. 'Miss Clegg, it's Molly.'

The old lady's eyelids flickered briefly, then her lips moved. Molly bent closer. 'What was that, Miss Clegg? Yer want a drink? I'll make yer one right now.'

Molly scrambled to her feet, grabbed Mary's arm and

11

marched her through to the kitchen. 'Run up to the corner shop an' ask Maisie to phone for the doctor. Tell 'er it's urgent, then get back 'ere quick.'

'D'yer want me, Mam?' Tommy asked.

'Yeah, run 'ome and get me a cup of milk.' Molly held the kettle under the tap. 'And don't hang around, d'yer 'ear?'

The tea was made when Mary returned to say the doctor would be there as soon as he could. 'Maisie said if yer need a hand, let her know.'

'Raise Miss Clegg's head while I give 'er this drink,' Molly said. 'I'm frightened to move 'er until we know what's wrong.'

She held the cup to the parched lips and nearly jumped out of her skin when a thin hand covered hers to stop the cup being taken away. Within seconds it was empty. 'Well, I never! Yer must 'ave been thirsty, Miss Clegg.'

The old lady dropped her head back. 'Three . . . days.' The words were as soft as the rustle of a leaf. 'No . . . drink.'

'I'll make yer another one, then.' Once again Mary was marched through to the kitchen. Molly opened her mouth to speak then realised her son was watching and listening, taking in everything. 'Tommy, go 'ome an' put a match under the pan of scouse. Leave it on a low light so it doesn't burn.'

She waited till her son was out of earshot. 'We'll 'ave to clean 'er up before the doctor comes. The poor thing's wringin' wet, an' she's dirtied 'erself. The couch is soakin', too, but we can't do much about that.' Molly gave a deep sigh. 'Now yer not goin' to go all weepy on me, are yer, Mary? 'Cos if yer are, yer'll be neither use nor ornament.'

Mary squared her shoulders. 'I'll be all right. What d'yer want me to do?'

'We'll 'ave to see what's wrong with 'er first, she seems to be in a lot of pain. But if we can, we'll change all her clothes 'cos she smells to high heaven.'

Molly knelt down by the side of the couch. 'Miss Clegg, can yer tell us what's wrong with yer? The doctor's comin' an' we'd like to clean yer up a bit before 'e gets here.'

'My foot . . . terrible pain.' The words came slowly as though the old lady didn't have the energy to talk. But with a bit of coaxing from Molly they heard that she'd been standing on a chair cleaning the inside of the windows when she fell. She'd managed to crawl to the couch before passing out with the pain. When asked by Mary why she hadn't knocked on the wall for help, Miss Clegg said it was dark when she came to, and she didn't like to knock in case they were in bed. After that she'd been too weak even to try to move.

'It's too dark in 'ere to see anythin', we need some light on the subject.' Molly stood on a chair before striking a match and pulling on one of the chains hanging either side of the gas fitting. She held the match to the gauze of the gas mantle and the room flooded with light. 'That's better, we can see what we're sayin' now.'

As she was stepping down from the chair, Molly heard Mary's gasp. 'Just look at the state of 'er leg.'

'Oh, dear God!' Molly gazed with horror at the old

lady's leg. The foot and ankle were swollen to three times their normal size and the swelling reached halfway up her leg. 'Yer don't do things by half, do yer, sunshine?' Molly forced a smile to her face. 'It probably looks worse than it is, so don't be worryin'. We'll get yer changed an' lookin' pretty for the doctor comin', okay?'

The old lady's embarrassment was obvious as she tried to say she was sorry for putting them to so much trouble, but Molly brushed her words aside. 'What are neighbours for, eh? Yer might 'ave to do the same for me one day.'

There was a sad smile on Molly's face as she collected clean clothes for Miss Clegg. Everything was exactly where she said it would be. Knickers and stockings neatly folded in one drawer, nightdresses and vests in another.

'It's to be hoped she never 'as to do the same for me,' Molly chuckled to herself. 'If she saw the state of my drawers she'd 'ave a duck egg.'

'Shout out if I hurt yer.' Molly gently removed the garter, stretching it as wide as she could to avoid touching the swelling. Next came the stockings. 'There, that wasn't so bad, was it?' She could see the shame in the faded eyes and had to bite on the inside of her lip to keep the tears at bay. She was such a proud old lady, this loss of dignity must be tearing at her heart. 'I'll close my eyes if you close yours,' Molly said as she reached under the sopping wet dress for the equally wet knickers.

Twenty minutes later Miss Clegg had been washed down and dressed in fresh clothes. And they'd managed to get a thick blanket under her to save her clean nightdress getting wet. She'd had two cups of tea and a slice of bread and butter. Her face was still creased in pain, but she looked a lot better than when they'd first come into the room.

When the doctor came, Molly and Mary retired to the kitchen while he examined the patient, and stayed there until he called them in.

'I'm going back to the surgery to call for an ambulance. Can someone wait with Miss Clegg until it comes?' He was a man in his sixties, with thinning white hair, kind eyes and a gentle smile.

'I'll wait,' Molly said, following him to the door. 'Is it bad, Doctor?'

'I think she's broken her ankle, but because of the swelling it's hard to say for sure. If it wasn't for her age I'd leave it until tomorrow to see how it goes, but a fall at her age can be very dangerous and I'd rather she was in hospital. A shock like she's had can bring on a stroke or a heart attack, and the best place for her is hospital.'

Molly slipped home to make sure the dinner was ready to serve up, and after telling Jill briefly what was happening, asked her to make sure her dad's meal was put on the table for him. Then she went back to sit with Miss Clegg while Mary nipped home to see to her family.

Molly sat at the side of the couch holding the old lady's hand. 'Yer know, we've been neighbours all these years an' I don't even know yer first name.'

'Victoria.'

'Ooh, er, aren't we posh!' Molly grinned. 'I've never known a Victoria before, only the old Queen.'

'I was named after her.' Miss Clegg turned her head

15

on the pillow and smiled. 'My mother was a school teacher at Saint Clement's in Toxteth before I was born, and Victoria was on the throne then. I had good parents, Molly, and a very happy childhood.' The old lady turned her head away, but not before Molly had seen her eyes fill with tears. 'I never thought I'd come to this.'

'Now don't be worryin' that lovely little head of yours, sunshine, 'cos when yer get to 'ospital they'll soon 'ave yer up an' about, you'll see. Won't keep yer any longer than they 'ave to. An' don't worry about the 'ouse, I'll take the key and pop in now an' again to make sure everything's all right an' keep it aired, ready for when yer come 'ome.'

'I'm frightened of hospitals.' The voice was a whisper. 'Always have been.'

'Yer'll be fine!' When the knock on the door came, Molly patted the old lady's hand and kissed her cheek. 'Mark my words, yer'll be as right as rain in no time.'

The two ambulance men were pleasant and gentle, but the fear on Miss Clegg's face pierced Molly's heart. She tried to keep a smile on her face, but when the ambulance men lifted the stretcher she knew if she let the old lady go in the ambulance on her own she'd never forgive herself. Someone had to show they cared what happened to her.

'Hang on a minute till I get me coat.' The family could see to themselves for once, Molly told herself, it wouldn't hurt them. Patting the old lady's hand and throwing a smile to the ambulance men, she hurried from the room, calling, 'I'm comin' with yer.'

Chapter Two

Jack Bennett folded the *Echo* and pushed it down the side of the chair when Molly walked through the door. 'Where the heck 'ave yer been? I've been worried sick about yer.'

'I stayed until Miss Clegg was settled in the ward.' Molly slipped out of her coat and threw it on the couch. 'She hasn't broken her ankle, but they're worried about her, she's very poorly.' Molly banged her clenched fist down on the table. 'Fine bloody neighbours we are! An old lady's lyin' in her house for three days, not able to move, an' nobody missed her! We deserve to be hung, drawn and ruddy quartered!'

'What did they 'ave to say at the hospital?' asked Jack, a worried expression on his face as he leaned forward.

'Oh, yer know what they're like, don't tell yer nothin'. An' when they do yer can't understand the words they use. From what I could make out, they're concerned about any effect the shock of the fall might have, an' 'er not 'avin' anythin' to drink or eat for three days hasn't helped.'

Molly fell heavily on to the couch and kicked her shoes

off. 'It's been one hell of a day, I know that much. What with Miss Bond, an' then Miss Clegg, I'll be glad when I'm in bed an' the day's over.'

'What did Miss Bond want yer for?'

'It was about our Jill.' Molly's head was splitting and she pressed her fingers to her temple. 'She said Jill is very clever and she wants her to go to high school.'

Jack was quiet for a while, then he asked, 'What did you say?'

'That it was out of the question, that's what!' Molly shivered, her teeth clenched. 'And don't start, Jack, 'cos I feel bad enough about it as it is. I cried me eyes out all the way 'ome, so don't go on about it.'

'It's a bloody shame, though, isn't it? The rich get richer an' the poor get poorer. It's always been the same. Kids like our Jill don't stand a snowball's chance in hell.' Jack's face was flushed with anger. 'If I'd had a better education I'd be earnin' a decent wage now, instead of the pittance I get each week.'

Molly stood up, a weary droop to her shoulders. 'I'd better get yer socks darned or yer'll 'ave none to wear tomorrow.' She opened the drawer of the sideboard and took out her box of sewing materials. 'I'll 'ave a word with our Jill in the mornin', she'll understand.'

Jack stretched out his legs and clasped his hands behind his head. He was a fine-looking man, six foot tall with a shock of dark curly hair, deep brown eyes and a set of strong white teeth. 'I'm not 'alf proud of her, she's a credit to us.'

Molly licked the end of a piece of wool and narrowed her eyes as she threaded it through the eye of the darning needle. 'I'd be proud of 'er even if she was as thick as two short planks, 'cos she's as pretty as a picture and she's got a lovely nature.' Her head bent over her darning, she added softly, 'I'm proud of all my kids.'

Jack had never seen his wife go so long without a smile on her face, so now he tried to coax one. 'Our Jill gets more like you every day, yer know, love. I can remember when you wore yer blonde hair down to yer waist, just like she does. She's as slim as you were, got the same bright blue eyes, an' a smile that would charm the birds off the trees.'

'I'm glad yer've got a good memory, Jack Bennett, 'cos things 'ave changed a bit over the years.' Molly lifted a lock of fine hair. 'See all the grey strands? And,' she patted her tummy, 'in case yer hadn't noticed, me eighteen-inch waist disappeared years ago.'

'You're still a fine-lookin' woman, Molly. I wouldn't swap yer for any of these film stars. Not even Jean Harlow, an' she's me favourite.'

'Don't be tryin' to soft soap me, Jack Bennett.' Molly's lips curved upwards in the beginning of a smile. 'Yer like all men, think we women 'ave got nothin' between our ears. D'yer think we don't notice every time the young one in number sixteen comes out to clean 'er windows that half the men in the street appear from nowhere to 'old the flamin' ladder for 'er?'

Keeping his face straight, Jack tapped a finger against his cheek. 'Number sixteen? Now who the heck lives there?'

Molly threw the finished sock and hit him in the face. 'Come off it, Jack, yer as bad as the rest. Yer eyes come out on sticks every time yer see 'er.'

Jack threw back his head and let out a hearty chuckle. 'There's no law against lookin', lass! But I wouldn't swap you for her, she's too skinny for my liking. I like my woman to 'ave a bit of meat on her, someone soft an' cuddly. Someone to keep me warm in bed.'

'Don't be gettin' any ideas, sunshine.' Molly reached for the poker from the brass companion set. She slid it between the bars on the grate and poked at the dying embers, hoping to coax a flame, but the fire was past resurrection. 'It's not worth puttin' more coal on, we'll be goin' to bed soon.' She rubbed the back of her hands across her eyes, tired from the strain of darning black on black by gas light. If it hadn't been for going to the school, she'd have done her mending in the afternoon while it was still daylight.

Jack reached in his pocket for his tin of tobacco, his face thoughtful as he rolled himself a cigarette. He ran his tongue along the edge of the rice paper before saying, softly, 'Even if I could get some more overtime in, it still wouldn't be enough to pay for our Jill, would it?'

Molly clicked her tongue against her teeth. 'Jack, if yer worked any more hours, yer may as well take yer ruddy bed to work with yer! An' it's not just what it would cost to send 'er to high school, it's what we'd be losin' with her not bringin' any money in. I've been lookin' forward to her startin' work 'cos I'm fed up tryin' to make ends meet every week. Fed up robbin' Peter to pay Paul. I feel sad for our Jill, an' if there was anythin' I could do I'd move heaven an' earth to do it. But I can't, so let's forget about it, eh? Our Jill's got to pull 'er weight, just like the others will when they're fourteen.'

Molly moved to sit on the arm of the couch, her hand ruffling his hair. 'How long is it since you or me had anythin' new, Jack? The kids are wearin' second hand clothes from Paddy's market, an' the only pleasure they get is the Saturday matinee with a ha'penny to spend on sweets.' She gave a deep sigh. 'Yer've no idea how I've 'ad to scrimp an' scrape, Jack, or yer'd understand how I've been waitin' for our Jill to start work so I could buy some of the things we haven't been able to afford for years.' Her hand swept around the living room of the small two-up-two-down terraced house.

'Everythin' in this room is sixteen years old. The springs 'ave gone on the couch, the lino's torn, the curtains are practically in shreds an' I've forgotten what the pattern on the wallpaper was, it's been up that long. An' it's the same upstairs, everythin' wants renewing.'

'Not much of a husband, am I, Molly? It's a poor man who can't support his family.'

'Don't talk so daft!' She was quick to defend him. 'I wasn't moanin', I was just stating facts. I'm lucky compared to some women round 'ere whose husbands are out of work. I don't know how some of the poor buggers manage. At least you've got a job an' I'm sure of yer wages every week.'

'But that doesn't help our Jill, does it? She's got the brains to make somethin' of herself an' I'm holdin' her back. How d'yer think that makes me feel? About two foot tall, that's what!'

'Listen to me for a minute, Jack, an' see if I can knock

21

some sense into that head of yours. We've got four kids, not one. An' I'll not make fish of one an' fowl of the others. Our Doreen leaves school next year, God willing, an' Tommy eighteen months later. Don't yer think they'd be jealous if they were goin' to work and turnin' their money up, while our Jill was goin' to a posh school?'

'That's different,' he said. 'They haven't got her brains.'

'Don't yer ever let me hear yer say that in front of the others.' Molly jumped up and wagged a finger in his face. ''Cos if yer do, I'll break yer flamin' neck. There'll be no favourites in this 'ouse, d'yer hear?'

'I'm sorry, love. I shouldn't have said that. You're right, of course you are.'

Molly was standing in front of him, her hands on her hips and an angry glint in her eyes. 'So we'll hear no more about it, eh?'

Jack reached for her hand. 'Yer haven't half got a temper, Molly Bennett.'

Molly tried to keep her face straight, but she could never hold out against him for long. 'Yer'd give anyone a temper you would, with yer pie-in-the-sky ideas. Can't say no to anyone, that's your trouble. Honest, if a tramp knocked on the door now, yer'd give 'im the shoes off yer feet, wouldn't yer?'

Jack looked down at his shoes. 'Molly, even a tramp would turn his nose up at these.' He lifted his foot to reveal a hole, an inch round, in the sole of his shoe. 'It's only faith, hope and charity holdin' them together.'

'Oh, dear God.' A wave of tenderness swept over

Molly. It wasn't fair that a man who worked as hard as Jack should have to walk around like that. 'I only owe me club woman a couple of pounds, I'll ask 'er for a ten bob cheque when she calls next week an' yer can get yerself a new pair.'

'Nah, I'm all right for a while. See to yourself and the kids first.'

'What do I need anythin' for? I never go anywhere. An' the kids can hang on for a while. There's only our Tommy. The arse is nearly out of 'is kecks as usual, but I can patch them up an' he'll get a few more weeks out of them.' Molly folded her arms, grinning. 'Why the hell do I worry about a big strappin' feller like you?'

''Cos yer love me, that's why.'

Molly smiled. She couldn't argue with that. She loved every bone in his body and every hair on his head.

Molly pulled Miss Clegg's door shut and dropped the key in her apron pocket. The old lady was coming out of hospital tomorrow and Molly had lit the fire to warm the house up.

As she crossed the street, she glanced over to where Ruthie and Bella were tugging at the ends of a piece of clothes line she'd given Ruthie to use as a skipping rope. She heard her daughter shout, 'Gerroff! It's my rope, so let go.'

Bella's lips were clamped together as she glared at Ruthie. 'I let yer play with me top an' whip.' She stamped her foot in temper, her pale face set as she hung on to the rope like grim death. 'I'm goin' to tell me mam on yer.'

Molly shook her head and sighed. 'Less of that, d'yer hear?' she bawled. 'Any more of it, an' I'll take the rope off yez.'

'Havin' trouble, Molly?'

She grinned when she saw Nellie McDonough standing on her step a few doors up. 'The size of them, an' at each other's throats over a flamin' skippin' rope! That one of mine 'as a right little temper.'

'I've been killin' meself laughin' at the antics of them,' Nellie laughed. 'They can't get the hang of jumpin' when the rope's in the air, an' not on its way down. Just look at your Ruthie now, she's goin' to end up arse over elbow if she's not careful.'

Molly grinned at the expression on her daughter's face. Ruthie's forehead was creased in determination, her tongue hanging out of the side of her mouth. But still she couldn't master it. She was finding skipping and doing crossovers wasn't as easy as it looked when the big girls were doing it.

'Roll on next year when she starts school,' Molly said. 'It can't come quick enough for me.'

Nellie walked towards her, a grin creasing her chubby face. She was a big woman, was Nellie, with a mountainous bust and half a dozen chins. But she had a pretty face, nice rosy complexion, clear blue eyes, dimples in her cheeks and a sunny smile. She and her husband George had moved into the street the same week as Molly and Jack, both couples newly weds. Nellie had been the first to start a family, followed a year later by Molly. The same thing had happened the following year, and the year after, causing Molly to joke that Nellie's disease was contagious. Many's the laugh they'd had over the day Molly told Nellie that, after a spell of six years, she was expecting again. Nellie had stared hard, shaken her head and said, 'Not for me this time, kid, I'll sit this one out if yer don't mind.'

'Your Jill leaves school today, doesn't she?' When Molly nodded, Nellie went on, 'By rights, our Lily should be leavin' today as well, but because she's five weeks short of fourteen, they say she's got to stay on till Christmas.'

Nellie's chins moved in the opposite direction to her shaking head. 'Fancy, just for five ruddy weeks, some silly sod said she's got to stay on for another six months! Barmy, that's what they are.'

'Our Jill starts at Allerton's bakery on Monday.' There was pride in Molly's voice. 'She'll be servin' behind the counter.'

'So our Steve told us. Since he started work last year, 'e doesn't half throw 'is weight about. Bosses the other two around somethin' shockin'.'

'He's a nice lad, is your Steve.' Molly pushed her hair back out of her eyes. 'Nellie, I'll 'ave to get crackin' on the dinner. I'll see yer later, ta-ra.'

'Is that you, Jill?' Molly was rolling out pastry to make a crust for the meat pie they were having for their tea while Ruthie stood watching, her eyes taking in every move her mother made. 'I'm in the kitchen.'

'It's me, Mam.' Tommy stood inside the kitchen door. 'The rag man's in the street, 'ave yer got anythin' for him?'

'The only old clothes I've got are the ones I'm standin' up in.' When Molly looked up there was a grin on her face. 'If yer'd like to go to school tomorrow with a bare backside, give 'im yer kecks.'

Tommy grinned back. 'If I blackleaded me bottom, nobody would be any the wiser.'

'I could do with blackleadin' yer face, so no one would know yer belonged to me.' Molly ran the back of her hand across her forehead, leaving a streak of flour in its wake. 'Just look at the state of yer. Toes kicked out of yer shoes, socks around yer ankles, a flippin' big hole in yer jersey an' knees as black as the hobs of hell. If I didn't know better, I'd think yer hadn't seen soap an' water for months.' She sprinkled some flour on to the rolling pin. 'Anyway, it's the tin bath in front of the fire for you tonight, me lad, so don't be tellin' yer mates yer'll see them after tea.'

'Ah, ray, Mam! I can wash meself in the kitchen sink!' Tommy was a big lad for his age, and the spitting image of his dad. 'I'm too big for that tin bath.'

Molly felt Ruthie pulling on her pinny. 'What is it, sunshine?'

Ruthie pursed her rosebud mouth. 'Can I 'ave an ha'penny, Mam?'

Molly looked down into her daughter's pixie-like face which was framed by straight fair hair cut on a level with her ears, the thick fringe hanging to her eyebrows. 'I don't know, yer'll 'ave me in the workhouse.'

Molly sighed as she reached for the penny she'd put on the shelf, ready in case the gas went when her pie was in the oven. 'Take 'er to the corner shop, son, an' get a ha'porth of dolly mixtures. Yer can 'ave the other ha'penny for yerself.'

'She's a blinkin' nuisance.' Tommy's face wore a look of disgust. 'Me mates all call me a cissie 'cos I 'ave to drag her everywhere with me.'

'That's just too bad,' Molly said. 'Now, scoot, the pair of yez.'

'Tell our Tommy not to 'it me, Mam.' Ruthie was glaring at her brother. 'He's always pinchin' and cloutin' me.'

'I've been generous with me money, an' I'll be generous with me 'ands if yez don't get out of me sight.' Molly's tone was enough to send the pair flying, Tommy dragging Ruthie behind him. 'I'll be glad when they're all workin' an' off me hands,' Molly muttered aloud as she carefully picked up the pastry and placed it over the earthen basin. With quick movements she cut around the edge of the dish with a knife, letting the overlapping pastry fall on to the table. She would make a jam tart with it when the pie was in the oven. Her nimble fingers moved around the dish squeezing the pastry between two fingers to make a pattern before cutting some slits in the top and sliding it on to the top shelf in the oven.

'Where's our Tommy off to?' Jill leaned against the door. 'He was pulling Ruthie along as though the devil was after 'im.'

'The devil wouldn't worry our Tommy,' Molly said dryly. 'He's a mate of his.' She turned the knob on the stove to lower the gas. 'How did yer last day go, love?'

'All the girls were crying.' Jill lowered her head, her long blonde hair swinging to cover her face. 'Mam, d'yer think I could go to night school? Miss Bond said I could take a course in shorthand an' typing.'

Molly's brow furrowed in concentration, then a smile spread across her face. Now why hadn't she and Jack thought of that? Good old Miss Bond! 'Of course yer can, sunshine, if that's what yer want.'

'Oh, I do, Mam!' Jill flung her arms around Molly's neck. Although she hadn't shown it, she'd been very disappointed when her mother had told her she could have gone to high school if they could have afforded it. She understood how the family were placed, and bore no grudge, but it didn't stop her crying herself to sleep at nights, thinking about what might have been. 'Miss Bond said it's only a couple of bob a term, so I can pay for it meself, out of me pocket money.'

'Me an' yer dad will see yer right, don't worry.'

'Thanks, Mam! I do love you.'

'An' I love you, too.' Molly sniffed, rubbing the back of her hand across her nose. 'Now do us a favour, there's a good girl. Take a jug an' get half a pint of milk from the dairy. Yer know 'ow yer dad hates conny-onny in his tea.'

The following Monday Molly gave the children their tea early, sent Doreen and Tommy out to play and gave Ruthie a colouring book and some crayons to keep her quiet. Like a cat on hot bricks she kept going to the front door, eager for a sight of Jill to find out how her first day at work had gone. And when she saw her daughter turn into the street, she rushed through to the kitchen where Jill's dinner was being kept warm on top of a pan of boiling water.

'Well, how did it go, love?' Molly sat facing her daughter across the table. 'I've been that nervous, worryin' how yer were doin', I've been to the lavvy so many times I've worn a groove in the yard.'

'Great, Mam, honest! The girls told me the names of the different loaves an' cakes, an' they showed me how to put the cakes in a box and tie it up.' Her mouth full, Jill began to giggle. 'I 'ad a job with the string at first, breaking off too much or too little, but they said I'll soon get the hang of it.' She swallowed hard before reaching down for her old school satchel which she'd taken to work with her carry-out in. 'I've got a pressie for yer, Mam. The boss's son, Mr John, gave us all a few cakes that were too squashed to sell.'

Jill took a paper bag from the satchel and with a look of pride and pleasure, passed it to Molly. 'There's six cakes in there, one each.'

'Well, I never!' Molly tore at the bag then sat back gazing at the assortment of cakes. The chocolate eclair was squashed, with the cream oozing out of the sides, but it was enough to make Molly's mouth water. 'It's bloody years since I 'ad a chocolate eclair. An' look at that cream slice, it's as good as new.'

Jill roared with laughter. 'It is new, Mam! It was only baked this morning! You wouldn't 'ave got it if a loaf hadn't fallen on it.'

'Well, God bless the loaf,' Molly said. 'Let's hope another one falls tomorrow.'

'You have the eclair, Mam, before the others come in. Yer know what a seven bellies our Tommy is.'

'I was goin' to say I wouldn't be selfish,' Molly laughed, 'but I think I'll eat the cake first, then say I was selfish.'

'What about me?' Ruthie was eyeing the cakes, then having decided, pointed to the iced bun. 'Can I 'ave that one?'

''Course yer can, sunshine.' Molly handed the bun over before biting into the eclair. 'Mmmm!' Her tongue darted out to lick the cream from her lips. 'Bloody lovely!' In seconds the cake had disappeared and Molly sucked on her fingers, her eyes wide with the pleasure of such a luxury. She gave a deep sigh of satisfaction. 'I'm beginning to like your Mr John. He sounds like a man after me own heart.'

'I don't have to take carry-out, either! Mr John gives all the staff a hot meat pie at dinner time.'

'Now I know I'm goin' to like 'im.' Molly put the cream slice and jam doughnut on a plate and carried it through to the kitchen. 'I'll hide these before Big Chief Sittin' Bull an' Maid Marion come in. You an' yer dad can 'ave them for yer supper.'

With a feeling that all was well with her world, Molly grinned. 'With a bit of luck, half a dozen loaves will fall tomorrow.' Her eyes rolled to the ceiling. 'I was only kiddin', God, so don't hold that against me. Mr John seems a nice bloke, an' I don't wish 'im no harm.'

'Mam,' Jill called through to the kitchen, 'they take evening classes in that school in Rice Lane. I'll go along on Wednesday, me half day, and make some enquiries.'

'Okay, love.' As Molly walked through to the living room there was the loud crash of glass breaking. 'Oh, dear God, that's someone's window gone for a burton. Please don't let it be our Tommy.'

Molly dashed into the street to find Tommy standing in front of the Clarkes' house next door, while legging it up the street hell for leather was his mate Ginger Moran, with a ball tucked under his arm.

'I didn't do it, Mam!' Tommy's eyes were wide with fright as he surveyed the broken window. 'It was Ginger!'

'You little flamer! How many times 'ave I got . . .'

Molly's words petered out as her neighbours' door opened and Nobby Clarke came out, roaring like a bull. Pushing Molly aside, he grabbed Tommy by the neck of his shirt. 'Yer little bleeder! I'll break yer bloody neck for yer!' He shook the terrified boy like a rag doll, until Molly moved into action.

'Ay, yer can cut that out, Nobby Clarke, it wasn't our Tommy.' She put her hand on the arm of the angry man. 'An' if there's any tellin' off to do, I'll do it.'

But Nobby wouldn't release his grip. 'Tell 'im off! It's a bloody good hidin' he wants, an' I'll give it to 'im.'

Jill entered the fray. 'Take your hands off my brother, he hasn't done anything.'

'You stay out of it,' Nobby growled, 'unless yer fancy a go along.'

Tommy was howling in fear. 'I didn't do it, honest I didn't.'

Molly, fearful for her son, beat Nobby about the arms and shoulders. 'Let go of 'im.'

But Nobby wasn't in the mood to listen. He'd been in a bad temper since the horse he'd put his last shilling on,

31

which was supposed to be a dead cert, had trailed in last, and now he had no money to do his nightly round of the pubs that stood on the corner of every street crossing Walton Road. And Tommy was the perfect outlet for his temper.

Molly was worried, wishing Jack wasn't working overtime. She was well able to stick up for herself, but was no match for Nobby Clarke when he was in this violent mood. She whispered to Jill, 'Go an' get Nellie.'

But Nellie was already on the scene, together with several other neighbours. 'That's enough, Nobby, leave the lad alone.'

'You keep yer nose out of it an' get back where yer belong.' As he spoke, he was tightening his grip on the neck of Tommy's shirt and the boy's face was turning blue. 'He wants teachin' a lesson.'

'Yer big bully!' Mary Watson shouted from the step of the house opposite. 'Pick on someone yer own size.'

Nellie whispered a few hurried words in Molly's ear, then, when her friend was standing behind Nobby, mouthed, 'Ready?'

Molly nodded, then put her arm around Nobby's neck, across his Adam's apple, and pressed as hard as she could.

At the same time Nellie flexed her arms before bringing them up, full force, under the arms holding Tommy prisoner. The sudden two-pronged attack took Nobby by surprise, and when his grip relaxed Tommy took advantage and fled, rubbing his neck as tears streamed down his face. Molly released her hold and stepped back. She watched without sympathy as Nobby staggered a few steps before falling to the ground. Then she stood over him.

'I'll see Ginger's mam an' make sure yer window's fixed tomorrow. An' if it makes yer feel any better, I'll make sure our Tommy gets a clip round the ear off 'is dad. But they're only kids after all, an' they didn't do it on purpose.'

She shook her head as she looked down on him with disgust. 'You're pathetic, Nobby Clarke, d'yer know that? Yer want to take a good look at yerself sometime. It's a nightmare livin' next to you, havin' to listen to yer constant bawlin' and shoutin', an' yer filthy language. Sometimes we can't hear ourselves think because of the racket yer make when yer come 'ome from the pub with yer belly full of ale.'

Nobby scrambled to his feet, conscious of the growing number of neighbours brought out of their houses by the commotion. Blustering, he said, 'Yer better 'ad get the window fixed, or there'll be trouble. An' what goes on in my 'ouse is none of your business.'

'It is when it interrupts the peace of my 'ouse,' said Molly. 'Next time yer take off, I'll have the law around.' She started to walk away, then turned back. 'It's a poor excuse for a man yer are, Nobby Clarke. An' I'll tell yer this – if yer ever lay a finger on any of my kids again, it's Jack yer'll 'ave to answer to. Bear that in mind.'

Chapter Three

'For two pins I'd 'ave it out with him, yer know,' Jack said when Molly came downstairs after putting Ruthie to bed. 'I'm not havin' him pushing my wife around, or nearly stranglin' one of me kids. Who the hell does he think he is?'

'Leave well alone, Jack, it's no use causin' more trouble. He came off worse in the end . . . sprawled on the ground with all the neighbours lookin' on. That put a dent in 'is pride, I can tell yer.' Molly sighed as she leaned on the sideboard. 'I was feelin' on top of the world when our Jill came 'ome from work, made up 'cos she likes her job. Then the queer feller 'ad to go an' spoil it, the bad-tempered bugger!'

'Don't let him get yer down, love,' Jack said, 'he's not worth it.'

'Yer right, he's not worth wasting me breath over.' Molly straightened up. 'I think I'll walk round to me ma's for a bit of fresh air. Yer'll see to the kids for me, won't yer?' She was already on her way to the hall for her coat. 'Give them a shout when it's time for bed, an' don't stand any messing from them either.' She slipped her arms into her coat. 'Make sure they get a wash before they go to bed. This mornin' our Tommy had a tide mark round 'is neck bigger than any I've seen on the shore at New Brighton. He was goin' out the door like that, too, until I collared 'im. God knows what sort of a house 'is teacher thinks he comes from.'

Jack lifted his cigarette and sent a smoke ring floating up to the ceiling. There was a grin on his face as he watched it disappear. 'If yer keep talkin' much longer, love, it'll be time to come back before yer get there.'

'I'm goin', I'm goin'!' Molly dropped the front door key into her pocket and tutted when it fell right through. 'One of these fine days I'll sew this pocket up.'

'If yer've got tuppence to spare, will yer get me five Woodies from the corner shop on yer way past?' Jack asked. 'Or if yer haven't got tuppence, a penny for two loosies?'

'Oh dear, oh dear.' Molly clicked her tongue. 'What an extravagant 'usband I've got. Yer'll 'ave me in the workhouse with yer gamblin', drinkin' and smokin'.'

She was halfway down the hall when she heard, 'Yer forgot to mention me womanising.'

'I'm the only woman you're likely to get, Jack Bennett! I'll put up with yer gamblin' and drinkin', but other women . . . never!'

Jack heard the front door open and shouted, 'Get me the Woodies an' when we go to bed I'll prove that I'm more than satisfied with the woman I've got.'

'Sod off, Jack Bennett! Yer get more like a dirty old man every day.'

With that parting shot, she banged the door behind

her, her body shaking with laughter. And the smile stayed on her face as she walked the three streets to the little terraced house where her parents lived.

'Hello, lass.' Bob Jackson opened the door. 'We were hoping yer'd come round to let us know how Jill got on.'

Molly could hear the music before she even stepped into the hall. 'John McCormick, is it, Da?'

Bob nodded. 'There's not much on the wireless so we got some of the old records out.'

Molly, light on her feet, waltzed into the centre of the living room and struck up a pose. Both hands on her chest, her head thrown back, she sang at the top of her voice. 'The Rose of Tral . . . ee . . . ee.'

'Oh, it's yourself, is it?' Bridie Jackson had lived in Liverpool for forty years, but she'd never lost that lovely lilting Irish accent. She'd been sixteen years of age when, in 1895, she'd set sail from her home and family in County Wicklow to seek work in Liverpool. 'Will yer not sit yourself down and let the best singer in the world finish his song?'

'Now, sure, that's what I'll be doin'.' Molly had the accent off to perfection. Hadn't she been hearing it all her life? While Bridie sat with her eyes closed, lost in the richness of John McCormick's voice, Molly gazed at the face that had never lost its beauty. It might have dimmed a little since the young Bridie Malone had set foot on English soil, but it had never disappeared. At fifty-six, Bridie was still a fine-looking woman, and Molly loved the bones of her.

She turned her eyes to her father, and smiled to see that he too was watching his wife's face. He was a good

37

man, her da, the best father a girl could have. He was sixty now, and still working as hard as he ever had. Never had a day off sick in his life.

The record screeched to an end. It had been played so many times over the years, the hole in the middle had grown too big for a perfect sound. But to Bridie it was a reminder of the home she'd left those many years ago. She'd always promised herself to go back and see her family, but there was never enough money for the fare. Now her parents were dead and a sister was the only living relative left.

'D'yer want the other side on, Ma?' Molly asked. 'It's yer favourite, "I'll Take You Home Again Kathleen", isn't it?'

'Sure, now, I'd like that fine, as long as yourself doesn't mind?'

Bob had already turned the record and was busy winding the handle on the gramophone. 'It only takes five minutes, lass, then I'll put the kettle on for a cuppa an' yer can tell us about Jill's big day.'

Molly didn't listen to the words of the song, they always made her feel so sad. Instead her thoughts dwelt on her ma and da. When she was little she'd never asked to be told a fairy story, because the story of her mother's life was better than any fairy tale.

If I was clever enough to write a book, she thought now, I'd write one about me ma and da. What a lovely romantic story it would make! Her mother had arrived in Liverpool tired, hungry and frightened after being tossed and turned as the boat ploughed its way across the rough Irish Sea, the passengers herded together like animals.

Bridie had felt so alone in Liverpool, a strange, noisy city, so different from the tiny village she'd come from. All her worldly possessions were packed into the cardboard box she carried by its string. Clutched in her hand was a piece of paper with the name and address of an Irish family she was to stay with until she found work.

Four weeks later she got herself a job in service with a family in Princes Avenue, down Toxteth way. The family were very rich, the husband something big in shipping. Bridie found herself a maid of all work, rising to start at six in the mornings, and fetching and carrying until ten at night. Her only time off was one evening a week, and a full day off once a month. For that she was paid the princely sum of four shillings a month and her keep. It was on one of her days off that she met the man who was to become her husband. It was a Sunday, and she had walked down to the Pier Head with a bag of stale bread the cook had given her to feed to the birds. She always did this on her day off because she had no family or friends in Liverpool and had nowhere else to go. And looking across the Irish Sea made her feel nearer her homeland.

Fate had taken a hand that Sunday in the shape of a gust of wind that blew Bridie's hat off and sent it flying through the air to land at Bob's feet. He had picked up the hat, seen Bridie and walked towards her. It had been love at first sight. They married six months later and were as much in love now as they were that day.

Feeling emotional, Molly gulped to try and clear the lump in her throat. She glanced across at her da, and when she saw him reach for his snuff box, was transported back in time. In her mind's eye, she could see her mother, plain as anything, handing her a halfpenny and saying, 'Remember, now, me darlin', it's a ha'porth of S.P. Golden Virginia snuff . . . it's the only kind your father likes.' And he used the same brand to this day.

Molly rested her head on the chair as her mind went back even further in time, to when she was very young. Every night when her ma tucked her up in bed, Molly would beg to be told a story before she went to sleep. 'Tell me about the big house, Ma,' she would say, then listen wide-eyed as Bridie told her of the years she'd spent as maid of all work in the home of the rich family.

Life was hard for those who worked downstairs in that big house. On the go all the time, never a moment to themselves. Bridie, the lowest in rank, was assigned all the rough work. She was up on the stroke of six every morning, an hour before Rose, the parlour maid, and Mrs Beecham, the cook, put in an appearance. With a large wrap-around apron covering her long black dress, and a mob-cap on her head, her first task was to rake out the grates in the drawing room and dining room, then relight the fires so the rooms would be warm when the family came down to breakfast. Then the rooms, hallways and stairs had to be dusted, and heaven help her if the mistress's eagle eye spotted a speck of dust anywhere.

When she was finished, it was down to the kitchen to prepare breakfast for Mrs Beecham and Rose. If the cook was in a good mood, Bridie would be invited to sit at the large wooden table and have a drink of tea and a slice of toast. But if the heavily built woman hadn't slept well, then Bridie would be told to start preparing the potatoes and vegetables, and it would be ten o'clock before a drink or bite of food passed her lips.

It wasn't that Mrs Beecham was an unkind woman, Bridie told Molly, but she was a hard task master and never let anyone forget their place. At eight o'clock the kitchen would become a hive of activity as the bells on the wall started to ring. Mrs Beecham would glance at the line of bells, then hand a tray to the waiting Rose. 'That's the master bedroom, take this up quickly.'

A man was also employed by the family, but he didn't sleep in. His name was Mr Edmonds and he helped around the house when he wasn't driving the master to work in his horse drawn carriage. He was a real snob was Mr Edmonds, thought himself a cut above everybody else. Bridie was glad she didn't have much to do with him and kept out of his way as much as possible.

Although the hours she worked were long and the work hard, Bridie wasn't unhappy. She loved polishing the beautiful furniture, the likes of which she'd never seen before. The feel of the shining mahogany beneath her fingers was a pure delight, as were the rich drapes hanging at the windows. She didn't envy the family their rich life-style, but she appreciated the beauty of their possessions.

The master was a kindly man, more friendly and approachable than his wife, who was inclined to look down her nose at those she considered beneath her. But because she spent most of her time downstairs, Bridie wasn't often at the wrong end of the mistress's sharp tongue. And she loved the two children, Nigel who was

41

ten, and Sophie, a happy eight year old.

The best times for Bridie were when the mistress was entertaining. She would stand on a stool at the basement window and wait for the guests to arrive. She couldn't see the road, but she could hear the clip-clop of the horses' hooves as they pulled carriages along Princes Avenue and her heart would be pumping as the vehicles drew up outside the house. She only had seconds to take in the finery of the women with their fancy hair styles, the velvet bands around their foreheads, the furs and the feathers. These were the times she envied Rose her status as first parlour maid. Dressed in a long black dress, with a starched white frilly apron and lace headdress, Rose would open the door to the guests and relieve them of their coats. Then when she had a minute to spare, she would rush downstairs to babble excitedly about the beautiful clothes the women were wearing.

But hearing about it second hand wasn't good enough for Bridie. She wanted to see the fashions, the lovely colours and the jewellery for herself. So one night when the family were having a dinner party, she told Mrs Beecham she'd left a duster in the hall and asked if she could go and get it while the guests were in the dining room.

'It wasn't a lie,' Bridie hastened to tell the enthralled Molly. 'I had left a duster, but sure, hadn't I done it deliberately?'

Anyway, she had crept up the basement stairs and hidden behind the door at the top. It had been an uncomfortable, worrying fifteen minutes. Any second

Bridie was expecting Mrs Beecham to come looking for her. But when the guests, all laughing and chattering, came out of the dining room and crossed the hall to the drawing room, the sights she saw were well worth being dragged downstairs by the ears for. Such finery she could never have imagined in her wildest dreams. The rich satins and silks in every colour of the rainbow, the feather boas, the perfumes, the long cigarette holders between the slim fingers of the elegant women . . . Bridie had never seen anything like it in her life and probably never would again.

But as she'd crept down the stairs, back to the basement where she belonged, she told herself she'd not change places with any of them. 'Sure, who'd want to wear a dress that had no top to it, was cut so low you could see the woman's breasts? It wasn't decent, so it wasn't. And to see a woman smoking, sure what's the world coming to?'

The record finished but Bridie still sat with her eyes closed, and Molly knew her mother's mind was back in the lush, green fields of her homeland. Impulsively, she got up and crossed to kiss Bridie's cheek. 'Tell yer what, Ma. When Doreen an' Tommy start work, an' we've got a few bob comin' in, we'll all go to Ireland for a holiday. What d'yer say to that, eh?'

'Sure now, wouldn't chance be a fine thing?' A wistful smile crossed Bridie's finely chiselled face. The one regret she had in life was that she only had the one child. She had given birth to two children after Molly, but both had been stillborn. And the doctor told her she would never have another. It had been a bitter blow to her and

Bob, but as she said, it was God's will, and He knew best.

'I mean it!' Molly said. 'As soon as we've got enough money we'll be on that flippin' boat to Dublin, an' yer can show us this beautiful place yer always talkin' about.'

'We'll see, lass, we'll see. If God wants me to go back, then go back we will.' Bridie shook her head to rid herself of the memories. 'Now, will yer not be telling us how me first grandchild got on today?'

There wasn't much to tell because Jill hadn't had time to go into details, but Molly made the most of what she knew. After all, didn't her parents' life revolve around her and her family? 'She's goin' to see about night classes on Wednesday, so I'll let yez know how she gets on.'

'Sure, education is a powerful thing,' Bridie said. 'And wouldn't we all be better off if we'd had one?'

'In our day, sweetheart, there was no such thing as education for the working class.' Bob sipped on a cup of tea so strong you could stand the spoon up in it. 'But times are changing, an' one day the working man will stand up to be counted.' He smiled that special smile he kept for the woman he adored. 'Anyway, we've got all we want in life . . . we've got each other.'

Molly saw the love shining in his eyes and vowed she'd break Jack's neck when she got home. Why doesn't he look at me like that? He's got no romance in him, has that husband of mine, she thought.

'Our Tommy got 'imself into trouble today,' she said, her head nodding. 'Mind you, that's nothin' new, he's never out of trouble. But I've got to say he outshone 'imself today. First he came 'ome from school with the backside out of his kecks. Sliding down the railway embankment he said, bold as brass, as though new kecks were ten a penny. I was flamin', I can tell yez. I made 'im go up to his bedroom as a punishment, an' said he 'ad to stay in for the rest of the day. But he made such a commotion upstairs, it was me bein' punished, not him. In the end, to get a bit of peace I said he could go out to play as long as he stayed in the street.' Molly looked from one intent face to the other. 'Guess what 'appened then?'

Bob was trying to keep a straight face. Hadn't he been the same at Tommy's age? Always in trouble, in school and out. 'Got into a fight, did he?'

'Our Tommy never gets into a fight, Pa, he's never out of one! No, nothin' as tame as that. He put a ball through next door's window.'

Bridie gasped. 'Glory be to God, he never did!'

'Well,' Molly said, 'to be fair to 'im, he didn't actually kick the ball, that was Ginger Moran. But Tommy was playin' with him so he's as much to blame. An' yez know what a temper Nobby Clarke's got. He flew into a rage an' wouldn't listen. Honest to God, I thought he was goin' to kill our Tommy. If Nellie McDonough hadn't been there I think he would 'ave, 'cos I couldn't 'ave stopped 'im on me own. But we both set on 'im an' he had to let our Tommy go. Between the two of us, he ended up on the ground.'

Bridie looked shocked. 'May the saints preserve us! Molly, 'tis a terrible sight to see a woman fightin' in the street like a common fish wife. 'Tis ashamed of yerself yer should be.'

'Ma, with Jack not bein' there I 'ad to do something, otherwise he'd 'ave throttled our Tommy! I'll give 'im a hiding meself for bein' naughty, but I'll not 'ave anyone else lay a finger on 'im.'

Bob was biting on the inside of his mouth to stop himself from laughing as he imagined the scene. Nellie McDonough was a big woman, and his daughter could handle herself, too! It would take a brave man to cross the pair of them. 'He wouldn't like it, two women getting the better of 'im. I bet he was as mad as hell.'

Molly could see the humour in her da's eyes, and winked. 'The neighbours all enjoyed it. Passed an hour away for them.'

Bridie put a hand to her mouth, a look of horror on her face. 'You mean all the neighbours were out? Oh, what is the world coming to? I never thought I'd live to see the day when a daughter of mine would be brawling in the street like a navvy.'

Molly burst out laughing. 'Ma, if yer could only see yer face, it's a picture no artist could paint.'

Bridie looked from husband to daughter, her eyes suspicious. 'Sure, yer'd not be pulling me leg, would you, now?'

''Course I am, yer daft ha'porth. Yer'd fall for the cat, you would, Ma.' Molly stood up, wrapping her edge-to-edge coat more closely around her body. 'I'd better get back before the kids 'ave Jack tearing 'is hair out.' She blew her mother a kiss. 'See yer tomorrow, Ma. Goodnight and God bless.'

'Goodnight and God bless, lass.'

Molly turned at the door, a wicked glint of mischief in

her eyes. 'By the way, Ma, yer haven't got a tanner to lend us to get a pane of glass for next door's window, 'ave yer?' Without waiting for an answer, she swayed down the hall laughing her head off.

By this time, Bob didn't know what to believe. Opening the door for Molly, he whispered, 'Were you winding us up, or did next door's window get broken?'

'Oh, yeah, it got broken all right. But it was Ginger not our Tommy what did it. Don't tell me ma, though, she worries too much.'

As she turned the corner, Molly could see by the light from the street lamp Jill standing by the front door talking to Steve McDonough. 'Oh, aye, what's goin' on here?' Molly smiled at Steve. He was a nice lad and she was very fond of him. 'For a few minutes I thought yez were a courtin' couple.'

Jill's head went down, but not before Molly had seen the blush that crept up from her neck to cover her face. Oh dear, she thought, I've put me big foot in it again. 'Was yer mate in, Jill?'

'I'll tell you later.' Her head still down, Jill pushed the front door open. 'Ta-ra, Steve.'

'What's up with her? Somethin' must have rubbed 'er up the wrong way.' Molly pulled a face. 'Anyway, how's life treatin' yer, Steve? Job goin' all right, is it?'

'The job's all right, but the money's lousy. Me dad said I'll be glad in the end, 'cos I'll get a good job, being skilled, like. But that's donkey's years off yet.'

Molly looked up at him. Only fifteen and he must be nearly six foot. He was certainly a fine-looking lad: nice thick dark hair, warm brown eyes and deep dimples in his cheeks. And as nice inside as he was out.

'Time passes quick enough, Steve, so don't be wishin' yer life away.' The corners of her mouth turned upwards into a smile. 'Did yer hear what happened tonight, with His Nibs next door?'

'Yeah, me mam told me.' Steve stretched to his full height. 'I wish I'd been here, I'd 'ave sorted him out quick enough. I'd 'ave knocked him into the middle of next week.'

'Yer know, son, I believe yer would 'ave.' Molly squeezed his arm. 'I'd better get in or my feller will be thinkin' I've run off with the coalman. I'll see yer, Steve. Look after yerself.'

'You too, Mrs Bennett. Ta-ra.'

Chapter Four

Jill came home from night school looking the picture of dejection. 'It was awful, Mam! I don't think I'll ever learn. It's all squiggles and curves, and I'll never get the hang of it.'

Molly, sitting across the table from her daughter, patted her hand. 'Come on, cheer up! It's not like you to give in so easily. Yer can't expect too much in just one night. Everyone must feel the same when they first start.'

'But I was the only raw beginner there! For some of them it was their second term, and others had been studying from books. I was the only one who didn't 'ave a clue an' I felt stupid.'

'Eh, eh, now, none of that! Yer not stupid an' yer know it. If it's books yer need, then books yer'll get. An' in a couple of weeks yer'll be knockin' spots off all of them, wonderin' what yer were ever worried about.'

'Mam's right, love,' said Jack. 'Nothin' comes easy for any of us, we all have to learn.'

'I wouldn't mind if I could do some homework, like the others do, but I've nothing to learn from! When I go back on Wednesday I'll be as wise as I am now.'

'Tell me what book yer need an' I'll get it.' Molly had never seen her daughter so despondent and her heart went out to her. 'D'yer know what it's called?'

Jill nodded. 'I asked the girl sittin' next to me, and she said she bought hers from a second-hand shop in Walton Road. It only cost her threepence.'

Molly nodded. 'I've seen the shop when I've been passin' on the tram. Write down exactly what it is yer want, an' I'll get it for yer.' She peered into Jill's face. 'Now, can me an' yer dad 'ave a smile, please? We're not used to seein' yer with a miserable gob on yer, an' yer don't suit it.'

The shop in Walton Road didn't have the book Jill wanted, so Molly had to pay one and twopence for a new one. But it turned out to be well worth the money. Jill spent every spare minute with her head buried in the book and a notepad by her side to practise on. Over the next few weeks the squiggles and curves began to make sense, and she never came home from night school without a smile of satisfaction on her pretty face.

'There yer go, Mrs Birchall.' Jill placed two paper bags on the glass-topped counter and held out her hand. 'That'll be sixpence ha'penny, please.'

'In the name of God, yer can't see what yer gettin' for yer money these days.' The old lady rummaged in a well-worn purse and took out a shilling. 'I'll have to stop eating, there's nowt else for it.'

'Well, now.' The smile on Jill's pretty face widened.

'You'll have to resist the temptation of iced buns in future.'

'Aye.' Mrs Birchall was carefully putting the bags in her shopping basket. 'They're the only little luxury I get in life, an' that's only every Preston Guild. Next time I 'ave me needle and thread out, I'll sew me flippin' mouth up an' stop eatin' altogether.'

'How's your husband these days?' Jill had been working at the shop for just over a year now, and knew all the customers by name, and their families. And when the shop was slack, as it was now, she'd spend a little time talking to them. She was very popular, always had a smile on her face and a kind word for everyone. 'Is he still working at Bibby's?'

'Yeah. I don't know what 'e earns 'cos 'e never lets me see 'is wage packet, but accordin' to him, 'e gets paid in buttons.' The lined face smiled back at Jill. 'When yer get married, love, start off as yer mean to go on. Make sure yer 'usband hands 'is money over.'

'Oh, that won't be for a long time yet. I'm only fifteen – too young to be thinking about things like that.'

'Aye, well, take yer time about it. Don't be a bloody fool like me. Married at seventeen I was, an' I've regretted it ever since. Sweet as honey 'e was, my Bill, when we were courtin'. Swept me off me feet with all 'is sweet talk.' Her basket cradled in the crook of her arm, Mrs Birchall gripped the brim of her faded blue hat with both hands and pulled it down over her ears.

'As soon as I 'ad the ring on me finger, 'e changed just like that.' She snapped a finger for emphasis, then shook her head. 'On the Saturday I was 'is lovely blushing

51

bride, but by the Monday I was a maid of all work, with a mob-cap on me 'ead, a pinny on, an' a mop an' bucket in me hand. And it's been the same ever since.' She wagged a thin finger at Jill. 'Yer know the old sayin': Marry in haste, repent at leisure? Well, there's never been a truer one. I've been regrettin' it for over forty years now.'

Jill smiled. 'I'll remember that, Mrs Birchall.' She watched the old lady pass the window, then turned to Mr John who had been listening with amusement. 'Poor woman. It's a shame, isn't it?'

'Don't let her put you off, Jill, she just happened to marry a waster. Not all men are like Bill Birchall.'

'Yeah,' she said. 'I know by me dad and me granda.'

Mr John began to put the leftover loaves on to a wooden tray. 'It's been a busy day, there's not much of anything left.' He lowered his head as he turned to carry the tray through to the back. 'Don't look now, but your young man has been hanging around outside for the last ten minutes.'

'He's not my young man, Mr John,' Jill said hotly, colour flooding her face. 'He's just a neighbour, lives a few doors from us. I've known him all my life.'

'Whatever he is, he's getting impatient. You just empty the glass cases and get on your way. Mavis and Doris will help me clean up.'

'No, I'll do the cases, like I always do, and clean the glass. Then I'll mop the floor. Whatever Steve wants, he'll have to wait.'

'It's Saturday night, Jill, and young people should be out enjoying themselves. Just do as I say and empty the cases. When you've done that I'll have a few things ready for you to take home.' He walked through to the bakery at the back, shouting over his shoulder, 'You'd better get a move on, your neighbour seems to be getting impatient.'

Steve grinned self-consciously, his hands clasped behind his back, his eyes looking somewhere over Jill's shoulder. 'I was passing, so I'd thought I'd wait an' go home with yer.'

'You just happened to be passing last Saturday, too!' Jill walked quickly ahead, leaving Steve to chase after her. 'Mr John saw you, and he made me leave before the cleaning up was done. I felt terrible leaving Doris mopping the floor when it's supposed to be my job.'

Steve stopped automatically when they reached the tram stop, but Jill charged ahead. 'I'm walking home.'

'But it's five stops!' He grabbed her arm. 'I didn't know Mr John had seen me, I didn't intend 'im to. So don't fall out with me over it. And it's daft to walk all that way just because yer've got a cob on with me.'

Jill began to relent. She didn't mind Steve meeting her, it was just that she'd felt so embarrassed stepping over the wet floor as Doris was mopping. 'I haven't got a cob on with you, but don't do it again or you'll get me into trouble. And I'm walking home to save the tram fare.'

'Blimey, it's only a penny!' Steve pulled her to a standstill. 'Anyway, yer don't think I'd let yer pay yer own fare, do yer? It's only right an' proper for a man to pay for a girl.'

'Steve, I want to walk home.' Jill pulled her arm free and continued walking, with a reluctant Steve beside

53

her. 'I know it's only a penny, but I've walked home every day this week, so that's sixpence I've saved.'

Steve glanced sideways at the girl he thought the prettiest he'd ever seen. She wasn't loud like other girls her age, she was real ladylike, always had been. He'd felt protective towards her since they were little and played in the street together. No one had ever dared shout at Jill, or bully her, when he was around. Many's the scrap he'd got into over one of the lads pulling her plaits and making her cry. 'What yer savin' up for, Jill?'

'A typewriter.' She turned to look at him now, her eyes glowing with excitement. 'I can get a second-hand one for about five shillings, so I'm saving every penny I can. It'll take me till after Christmas to save up enough, but I'm determined to get one. Then I'll be able to practise at home instead of the few minutes I get every week at night school. I'll never get my speed up the way I'm going on.'

They covered the ground quickly, too quickly for Steve who couldn't bring himself to say the words he'd been rehearsing all day. It had been easy talking to himself in the mirror in his bedroom, but he was now finding the deed a lot harder than the practice. But when they turned the corner into their street he knew it was now or never. 'D'yer feel like comin' to the pictures with me? Tarzan's on at the Walton Vale.'

Jill's heartbeat quickened. She'd never been out on her own with a boy before and she felt a thrill of pleasure. It was the first time she'd been asked out, and she was glad it was Steve because she felt comfortable with him. And she wasn't blind to the fact that his attitude towards her had changed over the last few months – there was a difference in the way he looked at her now. 'I don't think me mam would let me go.' Jill kept on walking but her steps slowed. 'She'll say I'm too young to be going out with a boy on me own.'

'Nah! Yer mam won't mind yer comin' out with me!' Steve's heart felt lighter. 'It's only to the pictures.'

'I don't like asking 'er,' Jill said. 'She'll bite me head off.'

'I'll ask 'er, if that's all yer worryin' about. I don't think she'll mind 'cos she's knows I'll look after yer.'

Jill came to an abrupt halt, her face flushed with embarrassment. 'She's standing at the door talkin' to your mam. Don't ask now for heaven's sake, not in front of your mother.' Without another word she dashed ahead, flashing a brief smile at Molly and Nellie before darting into the house.

'What the 'ell's up with her?' Molly asked as Steve joined them. 'Someone put 'er nose out of joint?'

'I asked 'er if she'd like to come to the pictures with me.' In for a penny, in for a pound, thought Steve. All it needed was a bit more courage. The worst part had been asking Jill, and now he'd got that over he may as well be hung for a sheep as a lamb. He looked up at Molly, who was standing on the top step, the dimples in his cheeks deepening when he grinned. 'She said you wouldn't let 'er, 'cos she's too young.'

'Is that all?' Molly laughed. 'Silly faggot, gettin' herself all het up over that. I don't mind 'er goin' to the pictures with yer. If it was someone I didn't know then I might think twice, but not with you.'

Nellie's rumbling laugh rang out. 'He's got his eye on your Jill, Molly, so watch 'im.'

'Aw, cut it out, Mam, will yer!' Steve shot his mother a dirty look. After going through all this, surely she wasn't going to put a spoke in his wheel?

'Go 'ome, Nellie, an' leave the lad alone, yer only embarrassin' 'im.' Molly stepped back into the hallway. 'Come in, Steve, an' we'll see what Jill's got to say.'

Steve held Jill's elbow as she boarded the tram and his heart nearly burst with pride when he saw the conductor looking at her with an appreciative eye. She was certainly a girl to be proud of, with her slim figure, blonde hair falling around her shoulders and a face like an angel. The only blot on his horizon was the amount of money in his pocket. He sat silent as the tram trundled on its way, trying to work out what he could afford. The tram fare was twopence each return, so if he took her in the fourpenny seats, he'd just about have enough left for a small slab of chocolate. It meant he'd be stony broke all week, but it would be worth it.

In the darkness of the cinema Steve tried to steer Jill to the back row, but she was following the beam from the usherette's torch and they ended up in two seats near the front. Jill sat up stiffly in her seat, her eyes glued to the screen. But when Buster Keaton came on, she lost her reserve and roared with laughter. Steve laughed too, but it wasn't Buster who made him laugh, it was the happiness he felt at having Jill by his side.

By the time Tarzan came on, Jill was relaxed and talkative. 'Isn't Maureen O'Sullivan lovely? Ah, look at

Cheetah, isn't he clever?' But when Johnny Weismuller was fighting a crocodile she screwed her eyes up tight. 'Ooh, I can't look!' The best moment for Steve was when a tiger leapt from a tree on to Tarzan's back. Jill screamed and turned her head from the screen, grabbing Steve's arm. 'Tell me when it's over.'

Feeling all grown up and ten foot tall, Steve took her hand in his. 'Don't be daft, it's only a picture.'

Jill was all starry-eyed when they came out of the picture house. Tarzan had triumphed once again, killing everything that crossed his path, and Jill was filled with admiration for his bravery. As they made their way to the tram stop she couldn't stop talking about the film and Steve began to get jealous. There were no lions or tigers lurking in the doorways of the shops on Walton Vale, so he couldn't prove he was just as brave as the great Johnny Weismuller. But there was one thing Tarzan did that he could do. He pulled Jill round to face him, and prodded a finger in his chest. 'Me Tarzan. You Jane.'

Jill doubled up in a fit of the giggles, and the laughter lasted all the way home, two young people happy in each other's company. But when they stood outside the Bennetts' house, shyness took over. Jill hugged her handbag to her chest, gazing at her feet. 'Thanks, Steve. I really enjoyed meself.'

'Will yer come out with me again next Saturday?' he asked, wondering if it was right to kiss a girl on their first date. He wanted to, but decided he'd better not. It might frighten her off.

'I'd like to, if yer can afford it.' Jill looked into his

eyes. 'I know you don't earn much, so I could pay for meself.'

'Yer will not! I'm askin' yer to come, so I'll pay.'

'Okay.' Jill smiled. 'I'll probably see you before, but if not I'll be ready at half-seven next Saturday.'

Steve waited until the door closed on Jill, then he jumped up, his feet clicking together like Charlie Chaplin. His fist punched the air as he skipped the few yards to his own doorway. He knew a lot of the lads in the neighbourhood fancied Jill, he'd heard them talking. But they never got near her because she wasn't the type to hang around street corners with the rest of the youngsters who were too young to be treated like adults, and too old for games like hopscotch or kick the can.

Steve slipped the key in the lock. Jill Bennett was his girl now, and woe betide anyone who thought otherwise.

Jill could feel her face redden when she walked through the door and saw the smile on her mother's face. 'I thought you'd be in bed.'

'What! Go to bed when I'm dyin' of curiosity, wantin' to know how me daughter got on on her first date! Not likely!' Molly pressed her back against the couch. 'Come on, sit down an' tell us all about it. Did yer 'ave a nice time?'

Tossing her head, Jill tried to make her words sound casual. 'It was fine, I really enjoyed the picture.'

Jack was sending warning glances at Molly but she pretended not to see them. What was the good of having a daughter if you weren't going to share the big moments in her life? She moved to sit on a chair by the table, and rested her chin on her cupped hands. 'Tell me all about it. What seats did yer sit in, and what was the picture about? Did Steve 'old yer hand? An' did 'e give yer a goodnight kiss?'

'Molly!' Jack threw his cigarette end into the fire. 'Don't be so nosy!'

'It's all right, Dad.' Jill could see the interest in her mother's eyes and the desire to share her daughter's life. And she loved her so much she wanted to make her happy, wanted to share everything with her. 'We sat in the fourpenny seats and the film was called *Tarzan Meets Jane*. Steve bought me a slab of Fry's cream, which he ate most of himself. He didn't hold me hand and he didn't give me a goodnight kiss. I'd 'ave slapped his face if he'd tried. Now, are yer satisfied?'

'My God, this shorthand's a good thing, isn't it?' Molly snorted. 'Yer can say everythin' yer want in a few words.'

Jack chortled. 'Yer could do with learnin' it yerself.'

'Watch it, Jack Bennett, or I'll knock yer into the middle of next week. Anyway, if yer were any sort of a father yer'd be interested in yer daughter's first date. Want to make sure everythin' was above board.'

'I don't think I need to worry about Jill goin' out with Steve. If it 'ad been a stranger, I'd 'ave been sittin' behind them in the picture 'ouse, watchin' every move.'

'Pity someone wasn't watchin' your every move when we were courtin'.' Molly grinned. 'Right Romeo, you were.' She turned her gaze to her daughter. 'Your dad's right, though, sunshine. Steve's a nice lad an' yer'll come to no harm with him.'

'I'm going out with him again next Saturday.' May as well get it over with now, she thought. 'He's takin' me to the pictures again.'

'Good for him! Yer spend far too much time on those blasted books of yours.' Molly saw Jack's head jerk up, and quickly added, 'Oh, I know yer like what yer doin', love, an' I know it'll be worth it in the end. But yer only young once so try an' get a little 'appiness out of life as well.'

'I will, Mam, don't worry.'

'Well,' Molly pushed her chair back, 'now me curiosity's been satisfied, I'll put the kettle on. Next Saturday, bring Steve in for a cup of tea. Yer dad would appreciate havin' a man to talk to, wouldn't yer, love?'

'What yer mam means, love, is that she might get more out of Steve than she will from you.' Jack grinned. 'Isn't that the truth, Mrs Woman?'

'Someone's goin' to get their ears boxed if they're not careful,' Molly warned. 'The best of it is, he's just as nosy as I am! If he's said once, "I wonder how our Jill's gettin' on", he's said it a hundred times.'

Jack roared with laughter. 'Trust you to let the cat out of the bag.' He winked at Jill. 'I wasn't worried about yer, not with Steve, I just hoped yer were havin' a nice time.'

Molly walked to the kitchen muttering under her breath, 'He'd talk 'is way out of anythin', that man.'

Chapter Five

The creaking springs of the bed brought Jack out of a deep sleep. His mind not quite alert, he tried to remember what day it was. He squinted at the illuminated hands of the alarm clock on a small table at the side of the bed. Half-past eight! He sat up quickly in panic, thinking they'd overslept, then remembered it was Sunday. Molly was sitting on the side of the bed, stretching her arms and yawning. 'What are you getting up so early for, love? Get back into bed and have a lie in while yer can.'

'I've been lying awake for ages, so I might as well get up.' She turned to smile at him. 'You get yer 'ead down again.'

Jack stretched over and put his arms around her waist. 'Come back for half an hour an' give us a cuddle.'

'Oh, aye, feelin' frisky, are yer?' Molly spoke softly. The walls of the bedroom were thin and she didn't want to wake the children. 'I know what your cuddles lead to.'

While she was talking, Jack was running his hand up and down her back and Molly shivered with pleasure. 'Oh, you certainly know 'ow to get round a woman.'

Jack nuzzled her neck. 'Come on, half an hour.'

Molly swivelled round and slipped her legs between the sheets. Snuggling up to him, she whispered, 'Can't beat a little cuddle, can yer?'

Jack ran his hand over her hips and tummy. Molly was a warm, passionate woman, and his caresses were sending ripples of pleasure through her body. 'Mmm, that feels good.'

Before he knew what was happening, Jack had been pulled across to lie on top of the warm, soft body. He sighed with pleasure. 'I love you, Molly Bennett.'

'An' I love you, Jack Bennett.' Molly wrapped her arms around his waist, pulling him close. 'Loads and loads.'

'Take it easy,' he warned, 'or I won't be able to help meself.'

'Let's enjoy ourselves.' Then Molly's mind cleared briefly. 'But for God's sake, be careful.'

Lost in the warm softness of her, his passion and need at its height, Jack asked himself how he could do both.

When Miss Clegg came out of hospital, the neighbours had agreed to take turns making sure she had a hot dinner every day. And Sunday was Molly's turn. With a tea towel covering the plate, she let herself in with the spare key she'd insisted Miss Clegg gave her in case of emergency. 'Cooeee!' called Molly as she walked down the hall. ' "It's only me from over the sea," said Barnacle Bill the sailor.'

'Hello, Molly.' Miss Clegg was looking her age now, the fall had certainly taken it out of her. But she was always cheerful and very grateful for the help she was given. 'It's a nuisance you having to come over on a Sunday when you've the family to see to. You must be cursing me.'

'We've had our dinner, so don't be worryin'.' Molly set the plate on the table. 'It's mutton chop today, with carrots and roast potatoes. And I want to see the plate as clean as a whistle when I come back. You eat every bit, d'yer hear?'

Victoria Clegg grinned. 'Yes, madam.'

'Come an' sit yerself down at the table then, and tuck in.' Molly dropped a kiss on the snow white head. 'I'll be back later.'

As she was crossing the road Molly was surprised to see her mother and father walking down the street, arm in arm. 'Well, where are you two off to all dressed up?'

'We thought we'd take a little trip, get some fresh air.' Bob gripped his wife's hand. 'Need to blow the cobwebs away, don't we, sweetheart?' But they agreed to come in for a few minutes.

'Look who's here.' Molly moved some papers off the couch for her parents to sit down. 'Walkin' down the street like two lovebirds, they were.'

Jack lowered the Sunday paper. 'Well, this is a surprise! But it's always nice to see you.'

'Doreen, put the kettle on an' make a drink for Nanna an' Granda,' Molly said. 'An' put plenty of tea in the pot. Yer know Granda likes his tea strong.'

Bridie lifted her hand. 'No thanks, lass, we'll not be staying long.'

Molly narrowed her eyes. 'Where yez off to, all dolled up to the nines?'

'Shall we tell her?' There was love in the look exchanged between Bridie and her husband. 'Sure she'll probably say it's crazy we are.'

Bob Jackson ran his fingers around the brim of the trilby hat he was holding between his knees. He was looking very smart in his navy suit, white shirt and blue tie. 'We're going down to the Pier Head.'

'The Pier Head!' Molly's eyes widened in surprise. 'On a day like this, yer'll get blown off yer feet!'

'We've a reason for going today.' Bob reminded Molly of an eager young boy. 'It's exactly thirty-nine years to the day since I met yer mam at the Pier Head, an' we thought we'd like to go back, for old times' sake.'

'Ooh, can I come with yez, Granda?' Tommy asked excitedly. 'Let me come, please?'

'And me!' Doreen pushed her chair back. 'I want to come, too!'

'Oh, my God, there's never a show without Punch!' Molly rolled her eyes. 'Yer nanna and granda don't want to be draggin' you two with them.'

Bridie and Bob exchanged glances, then Bridie said, 'Now why wouldn't we want our grandchildren with us? We'd like it just fine. And afterwards they can come home with us an' have a bite to eat.'

'Yippee!' Tommy was on his way to get his coat when his mother pulled him up short.

'Ay, buggerlugs! It's school tomorrow, so it's early to bed for yez.'

'Ah, ray, Mam!' Doreen's face looked mutinous. 'We

never go anywhere! I've only been to the Pier Head twice in me life!'

'For someone who's fourteen an' leavin' school at Christmas, you should 'ave more sense. If yer put as much energy into yer learnin' as yer do into playin' out, yer'd be a damn sight better off.'

'Ay, Nan, d'yer know our Jill's got a boyfriend?' Tommy stood in front of Bridie, a twinkle in his eyes. 'She's goin' out with Steve McDonough.'

'Well, now, isn't that just fine!' Bridie looked across to where Jill was sitting with her eyes down, her fingers making patterns in the plush of the deep maroon chenille tablecloth. 'He's a broth of a boy, is Steve.'

Sensing her daughter's embarrassment, Molly changed the subject. 'Tommy's tryin' to get round yer, Ma, can't yer see?'

'Blind I'm not, me darlin'.' Bridie never, ever raised her voice. 'An' I'll not be twisted round anyone's finger. But I've been thinkin' you could do with a bit of a break, with all the running around you do. So why don't me and yer da take the children to the Pier Head and then take them home with us for the night? They can sleep in ours an' go straight to school in the morning.'

Molly felt two pairs of eyes begging her to say yes and her resolve weakened. Doreen was right, they didn't get many treats. 'Okay, yer twisted me arm. Go an' change into yer clean school clothes an' yer'll be ready in the morning.'

Elbowing each other aside, Doreen and Tommy raced for the stairs. 'Don't forget that neck of yours, Tommy

Bennett,' Molly shouted after them, 'an' make sure yer ears are clean.'

'Is there somethin' special about today, Ma?' Jack asked. 'I've never known you do this before.'

Bob stood up to put his trilby on in front of the mirror. When it was set at the rakish angle he found agreeable, he turned to Jack. 'It only comes now and again that the date falls on a Sunday, son. Only every so many years.'

When Bridie stood up, Molly exclaimed, 'My, my, Ma, yer do look posh! Like one of them fashion models yer see in the windows of them fancy shops down Bold Street.'

Bridie was wearing a grey coat which nearly reached her ankles, and a matching grey felt hat with an ostrich feather curling from the side of the brim to cover the crown. With her slim figure and ramrod straight back, she could pass for a woman twenty years younger. 'Would yer be wantin' me to walk round like a tramp? Sure I only make the most of what the good Lord gave me.'

'I'm goin' to have a word with Him when I go to church,' Molly said. 'Ask Him why He gave you all the good parts.'

Bridie stroked Molly's hair. 'Is it not thanks yer should be giving Him for all the good things He's given you? Hasn't He given you the biggest heart in the whole world, and the strong shoulders to carry everyone's troubles as well as your own. And given you a good husband and four lovely children. You've a lot to be grateful for, Molly Bennett.'

There was a mad scramble down the stairs as Doreen

and Tommy fought to be first at the kitchen sink to swill their faces. After passing an inspection from their mother, they were ready for the off. 'Is it the number twenty-two tram we get to the Pier Head?' Bob asked, as Molly followed them down the hall.

'Yeah, that'll take yez right there.' As Molly waved them off she heard Tommy asking, 'Granda, can we look at your train books when we get home?'

Bob was a train enthusiast and he'd got Tommy as bad as himself. The two of them liked nothing better than to spend a few hours at Lime Street or Exchange station, train spotting. Tommy had a notebook full of numbers and heaven help anyone who so much as laid a finger on it.

'Honest to God, I'll swear they're as much in love as they were when they got married.' Molly stood with her back to the fire, her skirt lifted so the warmth could travel upwards. 'Fancy anyone remembering the exact place, time and day they first met.'

'I remember the first girl I fell in love with,' Jack said softly, a shy smile on his face. 'It was September the sixteenth, a Wednesday night, an' I was at the Grafton. There was this girl there with a lovely hourglass figure and long blonde hair down to her waist. She was wearing a blue skirt and a white blouse, an' all the boys were around her like flies. I had to queue up to dance with her.'

Molly's mouth gaped. 'Well, I never!' She made a grab for him and hugged him in a bear-like grip, raining kisses on his face. 'Jack Bennett, you've remembered that all this time! Oh, no wonder I love the bones of yer, an' every hair on yer head.'

67

Jill was looking on with a smile on her face. Fancy her dad remembering all that! And fancy all the men wanting to dance with her mam! She hoped when she got married, her husband would be as nice.

There was a play on the wireless at eight o'clock so Molly had the tea over and the dishes washed in time to sit down and listen in comfort. 'Ay, isn't this the gear! No kids, only peace, perfect peace.'

Jill was sitting at the table brushing up on her homework, Jack was in his favourite fireside chair, his long legs stretched out to feel the warmth from the fire, and Molly was sewing a tear in a pair of Tommy's trousers. Then over the sound of the voice coming from the wireless came a loud, angry roar. Molly looked up from her sewing and gave a deep sigh. 'Oh, he's not goin' to start again tonight, surely to God?'

The shouting coming through the wall from next door grew louder and angrier, until they could no longer hear the wireless clearly. 'This is bloody ridiculous!' Molly put her sewing down beside her. 'What the hell we ever did to deserve a neighbour like Nobby Clarke, I'll never know.'

'How would yer like to be married to a man like 'im?' Jack asked. 'I don't know how Ellen puts up with it.'

'Jack love, I wouldn't be married to a man like 'im. I'd 'ave throttled 'im years ago.'

'It's the kids I feel sorry for,' Jill said, her pencil tapping on her strong white teeth. 'They must be terrified listenin' to that.'

There were loud bangs now accompanying the angry

voice, and Molly's nostrils flared with anger. 'What the bloody 'ell's he doin'? It sounds like he's tearin' the place to pieces.' She wriggled to the edge of the couch and levered herself up. 'I'm not puttin' up with that, he's goin' to get a piece of me mind.'

'Now, Molly!' Jack warned. 'Keep out of it.'

'If yer think I'm goin' to let a bad-tempered devil spoil me night for me, yer've got another think comin', Jack Bennett. This is our home an' I'm not puttin' up with 'is roarin' and bawlin'.'

Jack got up and switched off the wireless. 'No point in havin' it on, we can't hear it.' He pushed Molly back down onto the couch. 'I'll go an' 'ave a word with 'im.'

She was up like a shot. 'Oh, no yer don't! He's an evil man is Nobby Clarke. Evil an' violent. If you go, it'll end up in a fight and then we'll 'ave the whole street out. But he wouldn't have the nerve to fight with a woman.'

'Mam,' Jill said quietly, 'if you go, won't it make it worse for Mrs Clarke? He'd probably take it out on her.'

'He's takin' it out on 'er now, from the sound of things, so I can't make it any worse. She's terrified of him, the big bully. Haven't yer noticed, in all the years they've lived 'ere, she hasn't made a friend in the street? Too scared to, if yer ask me. She walks down the street with 'er head down, frightened of 'er own flamin' shadow.'

Molly untied the knot at the back of her pinny and threw it on the couch. 'Don't worry, there won't be any trouble. I'll just tell them to lower the noise so we can 'ear the wireless.'

'Don't go, Molly!'

'Jack, if yer worried about 'im havin' a go at me, come and stand at the door an' I'll give yer a shout if 'e takes off.'

With Jack keeping an anxious eye on her, Molly knocked on the Clarkes' front door. After a few heavy bangs, the door opened slowly. But Molly couldn't see anyone. She looked at Jack and shrugged her shoulders. 'Is anyone there?'

'Me dad said to go away.'

Molly's eyes travelled down to where the sound of the voice had come from. All she could see was a little face, filthy dirty, with a runny nose and two round, wide eyes.

'Is that you, Gordon?' Molly pushed the door further open to reveal the youngest of the Clarkes' four children. 'What are you doin' up this time of night? Yer should be in bed at your age.' Gordon was five but very undersized for his age. He was so thin he looked half starved. As he peered up at Molly, he ran the back of his hand across his runny nose then wiped it down the front of his dirty jersey.

When Gordon didn't answer, Molly said, 'Tell yer dad I want 'im, there's a good boy.'

'Me dad's fightin' with me mam, an' 'e told me to tell whoever was at the door to go away.'

'What they fightin' about?'

'Dunno.'

'What did yer mam say?'

The big eyes looked surprised. 'She didn't say nuthin'.'

Oh dear, what do I do now? Molly wondered. The child looked terrified enough without her making it

70

worse. She could hear the shouting and the banging still going on inside the house, but it was what was going on inside the young boy's head that worried her. No child should have to live in a house where there was constant fighting. And the bad language she could hear wasn't fit for a docker's ears, never mind a child's. Poor little bugger, he wasn't the size of sixpennorth of copper and as thin as a rake.

Molly leaned forward. 'Tell yer dad it . . .' Her words ended in a scream of fear as two arms encircled her waist and she was lifted off her feet.

'Molly, me darlin', you're as pretty as ever.'

She let out her breath. There was only one person that bellow could come from. 'Corker, yer frightened the life out of me!' Her feet once more on the ground, Molly turned to face Jimmy Corkhill. 'I haven't see you for ages.'

Jimmy was a merchant sailor, a colourful, larger than life character known to every adult in the neighbourhood as Corker, and to the children who followed him around as Sinbad the Sailor. He was six foot five in height and built like an ox. His weatherbeaten face was covered by a thick beard and moustache, the same colour as the hair showing beneath his peaked navy blue cap. 'I've been away for six months, Molly me darlin', sailing the seven seas.'

Corker lived with his widowed mother at the top of the street. He'd never married, and to anyone who asked why, he'd say he was married to the sea. 'But you'll be glad to know I'm home for a few weeks now.' He let out a hearty chuckle as he gathered her in his arms and

71

swung her around. 'I can tell by your face you've missed me.'

'Stop actin' the goat, Corker.' But Molly was smiling. Even looking at this mountain of a man was enough to cheer her up. 'Put me down.'

Releasing Molly, Corker tilted his head towards the Clarkes' open door. 'What's going on in there?'

'That's Nobby in one of his tempers,' she said. 'I came to ask them to put a sock in it because we can't listen to the wireless in peace.' She nodded at Gordon who was looking with wide eyes at Corker. 'But this little one's been sent to tell me to go away.'

Without a word, Corker picked the boy up and set him down next to Molly on the pavement. Then, clenching his fist, he pounded the door, sending it crashing back against the wall. 'Is this a private fight,' he roared, 'or can anyone join in?'

There was complete silence. Not even a whisper came from within the house.

'Well, it looks as though they've settled their differences.' Corker picked Gordon up and set him down in the hall. Patting the boy's head, he said in a gentle voice, 'Tell your dad it was Corker, an' if he wants me I'll be with me friends next door.' He jingled some coins in his pocket and brought out a threepenny bit. 'Here y'are, sonny, buy some sweeties tomorrow. Now go in and tell your mother that it's time little boys were in bed, before the bogey-man gets them.'

They waited till the door closed, then walked towards Jack, still standing on the step. 'Long time no see, Corker.' He held out his hand and winced as the big man gripped it firmly. 'Take it easy, I need that hand for me work tomorrow.'

Corker roared with laughter. 'Don't know me own strength, Jack.'

'Don't be standin' at the door, come on in.' Molly gave the big man a push. 'Tell us about some of the exotic places yer've been to an' cheer us up.'

Corker's massive frame filled the doorway. His twinkling eyes rested on Jill and he clicked his tongue. 'My, my! You've grown into a beautiful princess while I've been away. If I was twenty years younger, Jill, I'd be knockin' on your door.'

Jill smiled with affection as she remembered the times her Uncle Corker had swung her over his head to straddle his shoulders, and the smiles of the people they passed on their way to the swings in the park. She surprised herself and her parents when she answered, 'If you were twenty years younger, Uncle Corker, I'd be waiting for your knock.'

Molly grinned. It was funny how Corker drew everyone to him. He gave out the feeling that he was a man you could trust with your life. 'Yer've shut next door up, anyway,' she said. 'Pity yer not here all the time to keep Nobby in his place.'

'Is he always like that?' Corker held his packet of Players Extra Strong out to Jack, then struck a match and lit both their cigarettes. 'Sounded like a madman.'

'That's just what he is,' Molly said angrily. 'He's got a wicked temper. Ellen 'as a hell of a life with 'im.'

'You didn't know Ellen when she was a young woman, did you?' Corker inhaled deeply. 'She was quite a

73

beauty. Nice slim figure, always well dressed and made up, and a smashing dancer. Could 'ave had her pick of the lads, and that's no exaggeration. God alone knows why she settled for Nobby Clarke, he's never been any good.'

'I've never known 'er any different than she is now.' Molly looked surprised. 'She always looks so plain and dowdy.'

'Aye, well, you see what marriage can do to yer!' Corker's laugh ricocheted around the room. 'With the sea yer have the best of both worlds. The beauty without the nagging.'

'How long are yer home for?' Jack asked. 'Short leave, is it?'

Corker shook his head. 'No, I've signed off the ship I was on 'cos it keeps me away from home for too long. Me ma's not getting any younger, an' I think it's about time I spent more time with her. I haven't been much of a son to her, away all the time, and it was brought home to me when I saw her this time. She's gone to look real old. So I'll take a few weeks off now, then sign on for a short trip so I'll be 'ome to spend Christmas with her.'

'Oh, she'll be over the moon,' Molly said. 'She never complains when I see 'er, but she must get lonely.' Then she chuckled. 'She's always praising yer, thinks the sun shines out of yer backside.'

'Yeah, she still treats me like a young boy, askin' if I get enough to eat.' Stroking his beard, Corker turned to Jack. 'Fancy a pint, me old mate?'

Jack's face coloured. He had fourpence in his pocket, just enough to get him to work the next day. 'I don't think so, Corker, not tonight.'

'Oh, come on, man!' Corker didn't need to be told Jack was skint. He didn't need to be told a man had his pride either. 'Keep me company, let me buy yer a pint. I'm home for a couple of weeks, so you can mug me next time.'

'Go on, love, it'll do you good.' Molly's eyes sent a message to say she could spare enough for a pint. It would do Jack good to go out, he didn't get much out of life. 'But don't yer bring 'im rollin' home, Corker, or I'll flatten yer.'

The next morning Molly got through her work quickly. She had something on her mind and the sooner she got it over with the better. Her washing was put in to steep, the living room dusted and the beds made. Then she dressed Ruthie and took her across to Mary Watson's to ask her neighbour to keep an eye on her for half an hour.

The next stop was a knock on the Clarkes' door.

Ellen Clarke opened the door an inch in answer to Molly's knock. 'Who is it?'

'Who the 'ell d'yer think it is, Ellen, the bloody bailiffs?' Molly breathed out hard, her patience ebbing. 'Open the flippin' door.'

'I'm busy.'

'Yez were busy last night an' all, weren't yez? So flippin' busy we couldn't hear ourselves think in our 'ouse.' Molly put her foot to the bottom of the door and pushed. 'What the . . .?' Her words petered out when she saw the red and blue bruises on her neighbour's cheek. 'Oh, God, Ellen, what's 'e done to yer?' Her anger evaporating, Molly stepped inside the dark hall. 'Why the 'ell d'yer put up with it?'

'What else can I do?' Ellen put a hand to her tender cheek. 'When 'e gets in a mood there's nothin' will stop 'im.'

'Oh, yes there is!' Molly snorted. 'There's the bloody rollin' pin! Give 'im a crack over the 'ead with that an' he'll soon come to 'is senses.'

'You don't know 'im like I do, Molly. I daren't even answer 'im back 'cos it makes him worse.'

'So yer just stand there like a flippin' lemon an' let 'im knock yer about, is that it? And 'is flippin' language is choice, too! I can do me share of swearin', but I draw the line at the language 'e uses. Some of the things he came out with last night was enough to make yer hair curl!'

Molly pushed a hand into the pocket of her pinny, thinking of the things she'd do with her fist if Nobby Clarke was her husband. 'Yer want yer bumps feelin', Ellen. I'm blowed if I'd let a man knock me about. If yer ask me, he's not all there on top . . . got a slate loose or somethin'.'

'It doesn't take much to start 'im off.' Ellen folded her arms across her thin chest. Everything about her was thin. Her body, face, nose and mousy hair. Her eyes were small, always darting around as though she was frightened of someone coming up behind her. 'Last night he took off because I didn't 'ave anythin' to put on the bread for our tea.' Ellen sat down and pointed to a chair, inviting Molly to sit. She'd never told anybody before what her life was like, but seeing the compassion in Molly's eyes, she began to open up.

'He doesn't worry that 'e doesn't give me enough money to live on. I didn't 'ave a penny to me name yesterday to buy anything for 'is tea, but Nobby won't even listen.'

'Yer mean yer get yer wages on a Saturday, an' are skint by the next day? What the 'ell d'yer do with yer money?'

'By the time I pay me rent, coal, and money for the gas meter, there's not much left out of the thirty-five shillings 'e gives me. I live on tick from the corner shop all week, an' by the time I pay that back, there's nothin' left.'

Molly's tongue darted out to wet her lips as she gazed around the cold, cheerless room and her nose wrinkled at the smell of damp pervading the air. No fire burned in the grate, the old sideboard was falling to pieces with two of its doors hanging open, the hinges broken. Every surface was devoid of ornaments or photographs, except for a chipped saucer standing on the hob with a half-used candle stuck in thick wax. And the oilcloth on the wobbly table that stood in the middle of the room was covered in stains and cigarette burns.

Molly shivered. This was a room that had never known laughter, happiness or love. Her gaze rested on Ellen. 'Thirty-five shillin's a week? Is that all he turns up to keep six of yez? Bloody 'ell, girl, he must earn more than that!'

'I don't know what 'e earns, but that's all I get. The bookie gets the rest. He 'as a bet on the gee-gees every day, his few pints every night an' his ciggies.'

Molly snorted in disgust. 'The miserable bugger!' She

shook her head, lost for words. 'What did the kids 'ave for their breakfast . . . fresh air?'

'Bread and marge.' Ellen was pinching the flesh on her thin arms, her eyes moist, her voice choked with emotion. 'I'll 'ave to wait for them to come 'ome from school to go to the corner shop for me. I can't go out with me face like this.'

'I've got to go meself, so I'll get some things for yer.' Molly stood up, looking with pity at the pathetic figure. 'Yer've no need to tell me what yer want, I'll use me nous. Anythin' I forget, yer can send the kids for.'

'Ta, Molly.' Ellen followed her to the door. 'Yer won't say anythin' to the neighbours, will yer? It's bad enough 'aving to live with it, I don't want everyone lookin' at me with pity.'

'The neighbours are not goin' to keep yer, Ellen, so I wouldn't be worryin' what they think.' Molly rubbed her arms briskly. 'Ooh, that wind's cold, cuts yer right through to the marrow. I'll get me coat then go up to the shop. I'll see yer later. Ta-ra for now.'

Chapter Six

'Mornin', Maisie!' Molly held her tummy in while she squeezed through the shop door. It was a double door, but one side was always kept locked. 'Only a flippin' ghost could get through this door. I wish yer'd open it up proper.'

'You'll have to put up with it, I'm afraid, Molly, 'cos when both doors are open it's like a blinkin' gale blowing behind this counter. Red flannel drawers is what I need, with the wind whistling up me skirt.' Maisie Porter grinned. 'Where's Ruthie?'

'Playin' in Bella Watson's.' There were no customers in the shop so Molly leaned her elbows on the counter, ready for a good natter. It was a friendly shop, open seven days a week, and sold everything under the sun from small bags of coal to babies' dummies. It was the smell Molly liked: paraffin, newly chopped bundles of firewood and the freshly baked bread delivered every morning.

'What can I do yer for, Molly?'

'I'm gettin' a few things for Ellen Clarke, she's not feelin' too good today. So I'll get her shoppin' first, then nip back for me own.' Molly cupped her face in her hands, her expression thoughtful. 'I was goin' to ask yer what she usually buys, but I think I'll take a chance and use me own judgement. Now then, let's see, I'll 'ave two large tin loaves, half of marge, pound of sugar, two ounces of tea, and six ounces of brawn.'

Maisie placed the two loaves on the counter. She was a small, wiry woman with auburn hair showing traces of grey and laughing brown eyes. 'She usually only gets a quarter of brawn.'

'Well, it's 'er lucky day then, isn't it? I'll 'ave five pound of spuds and a large tin of peas, as well.'

'Are you sure?' There was doubt on Maisie's face. 'She never buys that much. Usually it's two pound of spuds, small tin of peas, and never more than two ounces of marge.'

'Who's doin' the shoppin' here, you or me?' Molly laughed. 'It's a wonder yer make any money the way yer try to put people off buyin'.'

'It's Mrs Clarke I'm thinking about, she has to count every penny.'

Alec Porter came through from the back of the shop carrying a side of bacon over his shoulder. 'Mornin', Molly!' He heaved the bacon up and hooked it on to the rail hanging from the ceiling. 'How's my favourite customer today?'

'Ooh, ay, Maisie, I've got a click!' Molly stuck her nose in the air, rolled her eyes and patted her hair. 'Yer 'usband fancies me.'

'That's one thing I don't have to worry about.' Maisie opened her mouth wide and winked. 'He's too busy for a fancy woman. And too tired, too! He wouldn't have the energy.'

'Did I hear right, Molly, you're shopping for Mrs Clarke?' Alec wiped his hands down the front of his navy and white striped apron. 'Funny little woman, that. Never a word to say for herself, and I don't think I've ever seen her smile.'

Molly didn't answer right away. She spent a few seconds turning things over in her mind. When she spoke her tone was serious. 'If I tell yez somethin', yer won't let it go any further, will yez? I feel a bit mean tellin' yer her business, but I think yer might be able to help 'er out now an' again. You know, any bits yer might 'ave over.' Molly quickly related all that had happened while Maisie and Alec listened intently.

When she'd finished, Alec said, 'I can't abide a man who hits a woman.' He pursed his lips. 'Worst sort of coward in my book.'

'The poor soul,' Maisie said. 'Now I know why her kids are the only ones around here who never come in to buy sweets with their pocket money. They probably don't get any.'

Molly was gazing at the row of biscuit tins by the window. They were tilted and she could see ginger snaps, custard creams, arrowroot and Marie. The last tin contained an assortment of broken biscuits, and it was to this she pointed. 'Put half a pound of them with 'er things an' stick them on my bill.'

Maisie pulled at the lobe of her ear. 'Okay, you pay for the biscuits an' I'll only charge 'er for two ounces of brawn.'

Molly straightened and dipped into her pocket for her purse. 'Put a tin of corned beef and half a pound of onions with that lot.' She passed Maisie half a crown. 'Take the money for the corned beef an' onions out of that. I want me bumps feelin', 'cos even with our Jill's money comin' in every week it's still a struggle to make ends meet. But I've never been as hard up as Ellen. Her an' the kids look half starved, poor buggers.'

While Maisie was getting the order together, Molly eyed a poster stuck in the window. 'Eh, Maisie. See that Carter's Little Liver Pills sign? Does it mean the pills are little, or that they're only good for people with little livers?'

Maisie roared. 'That's more like it, Molly Bennett! D'yer know, I thought for a while that this was goin' to be the only day you've ever been in this shop and not made me laugh?'

'Maisie, if I ever lose me sense of humour I'll throw meself off the Seacombe ferry into the River Mersey.' Molly put her basket on the counter and watched as Maisie started to fill it. 'Keep the change out of the half crown and take it off Ellen's bill at the end of the week. And here's a tanner to put off me Christmas club. It'll be 'ere before we know it.'

'I can't afford all that!' Ellen Clarke viewed with mounting horror the groceries spread out on her table. 'Yer've bought far too much of everythin'.'

'Oh, for 'eaven's sake, stop yer moanin'! Apart from bread, yer've got enough there to last yer two days. Maisie isn't chargin' yer for the brawn 'cos it was cut yesterday.' Molly crossed her fingers behind her back and asked God to forgive her for telling lies. But He wouldn't mind, not when it was to help someone. 'An' the biscuits are from me for the kids.'

'You're very good, Molly. I'm sorry yer have to listen to all the rows, but there's nothin' I can do about it.'

'I'll watch out for Nobby passin' on his way 'ome from work, an' I'll tell him to keep 'is voice down in future. If it doesn't work, I'll ask Jack to 'ave a word with him.'

'Yer won't tell 'im about this, will yer?' Ellen nodded her head towards the things on the table. 'He'd kill me if he knew I'd told anyone.'

''Course not, I'm not that thick.' Molly bustled towards the door. 'I'd better go, the coalman was down the street when I came in. I don't want to miss 'im 'cos I've only got enough to light the fire tonight.'

He was knocking on Molly's door when she stepped into the street. 'There y'are, Molly, I was beginnin' to think yer were out flying yer kite.'

'I've 'ad me eyes peeled for yer, Tucker, we're right down. Put us a bag in, will yer?'

Tucker Dunne patted his horse's rear to move him nearer the side entry. He didn't need to lead him, the horse had been doing the same round for years and knew every stop. 'It's gone up to one and six a bag, Molly.'

'Bloody hell! The way things are goin', we'll 'ave to go to bed after tea to keep warm.' Molly looked into the blackened face before her. Tucker had been her coalman for years, but if he ever washed his face she wouldn't know him if she fell over him. It wasn't only his face that was black either! His donkey jacket, trousers, and the cap pulled low over his eyes were, as Molly put it, as black as the hobs of hell.

'How does yer wife manage with yer clothes, Tucker? I wouldn't know where to start on that lot.'

White teeth flashed in the dark face. 'I'm not allowed near the house with this lot on. We've got a little wash house in the yard, thank God, an' I have to strip out there every night. Then she makes me walk to the house in me bare feet, an' wash from top to bottom in the kitchen sink before I'm allowed in the livin' room.'

Tucker owned his own business, passed down from father to son, and the coal yard was next to the house. There was a stable there for the horse, too, and Tucker rubbed him down every night and made sure the stable was kept warm and the straw changed regularly. 'Me wife doesn't like the job I do, but she doesn't refuse the money at the end of the week.'

'Aye, well, they say where there's muck there's money,' Molly grunted. 'I wouldn't mind a bit of dirt comin' my way if there was money with it.'

His white teeth gleamed from a black face, and chuckling heartily, Tucker smacked his trousers, sending out a cloud of coal dust. 'Yer see, me wife does have a point.'

'Yer not kiddin'!' Molly backed away, coughing and spluttering. 'I'll go an' open the yard door for yer.'

Still laughing, Tucker walked to the cart. He raised his hands over his shoulders and pulled a bag of coal on to the leather square he wore across his back. He didn't mind the dirt. Never had, even when he was a kid and his dad used to take him out with him on his rounds. It was better than working in a factory any day. He was his own boss and answerable to no man.

While Molly waited for change of her two bob piece, she glanced up the street and saw her mother hurrying towards her. 'Looks like I've got a visitor.'

'Hello, Mrs Jackson.' Tucker smiled. 'I'll be round your way in the morning.'

Bridie nodded. 'See you tomorrow, Tucker.'

Molly sensed this wasn't just an ordinary visit, her mother was all keyed up about something. 'What's brought you round, Ma?' Molly closed the door and followed Bridie into the living room. 'Is me da all right?'

'Sure he's just fine.' Bridie was moving from one foot to the other, her hands clasping and unclasping. 'Yer'll never guess what's happening, Molly, not in a million years will yer guess.'

'Park yer carcass, Ma, an' take the weight off yer feet.' Molly pushed her mother down gently on to one of the wooden chairs round the table. 'Now, what's up?'

'We're all being electrocuted.' The words poured from Bridie's mouth. 'They're goin' to electrocute the whole street.'

Molly screwed up her face, biting on the inside of her mouth to keep the laughter back. 'Ma, they electrocute murderers.'

'What's that yer saying?' Bridie's finely arched eyebrows drew together. 'Why would you be talkin' about murderers?'

'Just take it easy, Ma, and tell me what's happening.'

Bridie tutted with impatience. What was the matter with her daughter, hadn't she just told her what was going to happen? 'We've had letters from the landlord. Everyone in the street. And why you're looking so stupid, I don't know. D'yer not understand plain English?'

The light dawned, and Molly began to shake with laughter. 'Yer mean yer getting electricity laid on to your 'ouse?'

'Isn't that just what I've told yer?'

Molly opened her mouth to say that getting electrocuted was something very different, but changed her mind. 'Have yer brought the letter with yer?'

Bridie shook her head. 'Wasn't I that excited I dashed out an' left it on the table? Sure, I couldn't get round here quick enough to tell yer. And I can't wait to see yer da's face when he comes in from work.'

'Let 'im read the letter for 'imself, Ma, don't you tell him. Otherwise he'll think he's in for a nasty shock.'

Bridie was so overjoyed she didn't hear the humour in her daughter's voice. 'Won't it be grand, now? Just a flick of a switch on the wall and we'll have light. There's some very clever people in the world, that's for sure. Whatever will they be thinkin' of next?'

'I wish they'd get round to givin' us electric.' Molly was rummaging in the sideboard cupboard for a saucer that matched the china cup she had in her hand. There wasn't a cup in the kitchen that didn't have a crack or a broken handle, and although her mother would never say anything Molly knew she didn't enjoy drinking from them. 'Just think, no more flamin' gas mantles.'

'I was talking to Mrs Shenstone from next door, an' she was after telling me the landlord told her that the whole district will have electric within a year,' Bridie said. 'Now won't that be a fine thing?'

'Oh, God, I hope so,' Molly said. 'I'd be over the moon.' She took hold of her mother's hand and imitated the lovely, lilting Irish brogue. 'To be sure now, Bridie Malone, isn't it good news yerself has brought?'

A wistful smile came to Bridie's face at the use of her maiden name. Sure didn't it bring back some fond memories?

'Mam, where d'yer think I should try for a job when I leave school?' Doreen dipped a chip in the mound of tomato sauce on her plate and popped it in her mouth. 'I don't know whether I'd like to work in a shop or a factory.'

'It's not so easy to get a job that yer can pick an' choose,' Molly answered. 'If yer get one, just count yerself lucky no matter what it is.'

'I think shop work is best,' Jill said. 'You get to meet people and you can have a laugh and joke with them.'

'Don't get much wages though, do yer?' Doreen was very like her sister in appearance, but her face had a harder look to it, and she didn't have Jill's gentle nature. 'I think yer get more money in a factory.'

'I don't do so bad,' Jill answered. 'I've had a shilling rise off Mr John, and I've only been there sixteen months.'

'And the food yer bring 'ome with yer is worth a few bob, don't forget,' Molly said, her head nodding knowingly. 'It all counts.'

Doreen picked up her empty plate to take through to

the kitchen. 'If I get a job in a jeweller's, d'yer think they'll let me bring some diamonds 'ome with me?'

'Ay, wouldn't that be the gear?' Molly chuckled. 'There'd be no flies on me! I could wear me tiara while I'm eatin' the chocolate eclairs I get off Mr John.'

Jill pushed her chair back. 'Is it all right if I go for a walk with Steve, Mam? Only for half an hour.'

'As long as yer in for ten o'clock, no later. An' don't bang the front door on yer way out or yer'll wake Ruthie.'

The kids were in bed and Jack was enjoying his last cigarette before they damped the fire down, put the guard in front with clothes on to air off, and climbed the stairs. 'I wonder what's goin' on with the King and this woman they say he's in love with? The papers seem to think it's serious.'

'Me an' Nellie were only talkin' about that today. I don't know what he's thinkin' about! His father's only been dead a matter of months, an' here he is knockin' around with this Wallis Simpson, who's been married and divorced twice! An' on top of that, she's American!' Molly snorted. 'The old King would turn in 'is grave if he knew.'

'If yer can believe all the papers say, the Government is up in arms about it,' Jack said. 'By all accounts they want him to give her up, but he's refusing.'

'I'm surprised his mother, Queen Mary, hasn't put 'er foot down with 'im. He's only been King for a few months, an' carryin' on like this, it's not right.'

'He hasn't been crowned yet, love, his coronation's

not till next summer. Anythin' can happen before then.'

'Aye, he might come to 'is senses.' Molly stretched her arms over her head and yawned. 'It's been a funny old day, with one thing and another. Listenin' to Ellen Clarke's troubles, bein' told coal's gone up twopence a bag, me ma rushin' round to say they're bein' electrocuted, and to round off the day, our King's got himself a fancy woman.'

Molly stood up, pressing her hands into the small of her aching back. She put the fireguard in front of the fire, and as she hung a pair of Doreen's knickers over it, she tilted her head to look at her husband.

'D'yer know, Jack, if I 'ad a hankie, I wouldn't know whether to laugh or cry into it.'

Chapter Seven

Two weeks before Christmas, on the eleventh of December, King Edward was due to address the nation on the wireless. And like every other family in the land, the Bennetts were gathered around their sets anxious to hear what the King had to say. Rumours had been rife for months, but apart from what they read in the papers, nobody really knew what was going on.

'Put it up a bit, love,' Jack said, lighting up a cigarette.

Molly turned the knob on the set before sitting on the couch next to Jill. 'I bet yer he tells us there's nothin goin' on between him and this Wallis Simpson.' She tapped her fingers on the arm of the couch. 'He's bound to put his country before her.'

'Sshh!' Jack leaned forward. 'He's starting now.'

There was complete silence in the room as the King started to speak. His voice was low, and he sounded nervous as he told his subjects that he could not live without the woman he loved by his side.

'Oh, my God, I would never 'ave believed it if I hadn't heard it with me own ears,' Molly gasped, white faced.

Jack was silent as he listened to the King saying he was

abdicating and that his brother, George, would be sworn in as their King.

After a long silence, Jack said quietly, 'I always liked 'im, thought he was a man of the people, never dreamed he'd let the country down like this.'

'All I can say is, he must love 'er very much to give up a crown for 'er.' Molly wiped a tear away. 'Only time will tell if he'll live to regret it.'

'He will, you mark my words.' Jack felt let down, and it made him sound angry. 'He's a fool.'

Molly sighed as she pushed herself up from the couch. 'Well, he's made 'is bed so let him lie on it. It won't make any difference to our lives. An' I for one am not goin' to let it spoil my Christmas.' She managed a smile. 'As Corker would say, there's worse things happen at sea.'

'Good lord, 'ave yer bought the shops up?' Jack rushed forward to relieve Molly of a couple of bags. 'How on earth 'ave yer managed to carry this lot on yer own?'

'Sheer bloody willpower, that's 'ow!' Molly flexed her fingers, white where the string handles on the heavy bags had stopped the flow of blood. 'I caught sight of meself in a shop window an' nearly died of fright. I looked like a big gorilla, with arms reachin' to me knees.'

Jack put the bags on the floor by the sideboard. 'Have yer got all yer Christmas shoppin' in now?'

Out of the corner of her eye Molly saw Ruthie scramble off her chair and make towards the bags, followed closely by Doreen and Tommy. Standing with her feet apart, hands on her hips, Molly barred their way. 'Oh, no, yez don't! Just keep yer thievin' hands off.'

'Ah, ray, Mam!' Tommy's voice was in the process of changing and it ranged in tone from a high squeak to a low growl. 'Let's see what yer've got.'

'Come on, Mam,' Doreen coaxed. 'Just a quick dekko.'

'Not on yer nellie, sunshine! Christmas mornin' is when yer'll see them, an' not before. Now sit down before I clock yez one.'

Doreen tutted, bringing a warning glance from her father. But as she sat down, he heard her whisper to Tommy, 'Yer'd think we were babies.'

'Act like babies, an' yer'll be treated like babies.'

Molly slipped her coat off and fell heavily on to the couch, pulling off the too tight shoes from her swollen feet. 'Ooh, that's a relief. Me feet 'ave been givin' me gyp.'

'Couldn't you 'ave left some of the shoppin' till Monday? There was no need to do it all at once.' Jack knelt in front of her and took a foot in his hands. Rubbing gently, he said over his shoulder, 'Make yer mam a cup of tea, Doreen.'

'I didn't intend gettin' so much, but once I'd started I thought I may as well go the whole hog. It's off me mind now, an' I can spend the next few days givin' the house a good goin' over.' Molly closed her eyes as the gentle rubbing began to ease the pain. 'Mm, yer can keep that up all night, it's lovely. Just what the doctor ordered.'

'Why didn't yer take Doreen along to give yer a hand?' Jack lifted the other foot from the floor. 'She could have carried some of the bags.'

'I 'ad to leave Ruthie with her, an' anyway, she'd 'ave seen what everyone was gettin' for Christmas! An' I can get around better on me own. I got off the tram at London Road first, and went into TJ's. Then I walked to Blacklers and Woolies.'

Ruthie leaned her elbows on Molly's knees, her face cupped in her hands. 'Did yer see Father Christmas, Mam?'

'No, sunshine, I didn't.' Molly ruffled her hair. 'He doesn't see grown-ups, only children.'

'Here's yer tea, Mam.' Doreen gazed longingly at the bags. 'What did yer get me? Go on, tell us.'

'I'm not tellin' yer, nose fever! It's supposed to be a surprise on Christmas mornin'.' Molly grimaced as she lifted the cup. 'Blimey, there's more tea in the flamin' saucer than there is in the cup! Yer a dirty faggot, our Doreen.'

'I tripped over the edge of the lino, I couldn't 'elp it.' There was a sullen look on Doreen's face. 'Just tell me if I can wear it or eat it?'

Remembering how she'd been just as inquisitive when she was Doreen's age, Molly smiled at her daughter. 'Yer won't be disappointed, sunshine, I promise yer.'

'I 'ope yer got me a book on trains,' Tommy grunted. 'It wouldn't be fair if yer didn't. It's all I've asked for.'

'An' I asked Father Christmas for a dolly,' Ruthie said, her tiny brow furrowed. 'I should get it, 'cos I've been a good girl.'

'Only a few more days, then yer'll all know whether I'm the best mam in the world or a mean old thing.'

'Are we 'aving a tree, Mam?' Doreen twirled the end of her hair around her fingers. 'A big one, like last year.'

'Depends what they've got left at the market on Christmas Eve.' Molly patted Jack's arm. 'That'll do, love. Yer'll get cramps in yer fingers if yer not careful!' She rested the saucer on the arm of the couch. 'Yer can come to the market with me, Doreen, help me carry the shoppin'. I'll ask Ma to mind Ruthie.'

Jack stood up, rubbing his knees to get the circulation back. 'You stay there, love, an' I'll see to the tea.'

'No, I'll do it.' Her hands clenched into fists, Molly pushed herself up. 'Our Jill should be 'ome any minute and she'll be hungry. It's egg, chips and peas tonight.'

Molly was dividing the chips into equal portions on the six plates when Jill came through to the kitchen, her eyes sending out sparks of excitement. 'Where's our Doreen?'

'She's just gone to the lavvy, why?'

'I'll tell you when she comes in.' Jill opened the kitchen door and shouted down the yard, 'Hurry up, Doreen, I've got somethin' to tell you.'

'What is it?' The bottom of Doreen's gymslip had caught in the elastic of her knickers and she was tugging it out as she came through the door. 'What's the big hurry?'

'Mr John said you can come and work in the shop the two days before Christmas.' The words tumbled from Jill's mouth. 'He said we'll be very busy, and if yer like, you can come in and keep the shelves and window filled up.'

'Ooh, er!' Doreen clapped a hand to her mouth. 'Will I be able to do it?'

'Of course you will! All you've got to do is bring in cakes and bread from the back and make sure the stands and shelves are full. It'll be a doddle.'

Doreen's eyes narrowed. 'Will I get paid?'

Jill nodded. 'Three shillings for the two days. Mind you, you'll be on the go all the time, and we'll be working very late on Christmas Eve.'

'Three shillings!' Doreen's eyes and mouth were wide open. 'Ooh, ay, Mam, did yer hear that?'

'I did, an' I think it's marvellous.' Molly put her arms round her daughter's shoulders and squeezed. 'Yer first wages, sunshine. Isn't Mr John kind to think of yer? Yer mustn't forget to thank 'im.'

Filled with excitement and delight, Doreen ran through to the living room. 'Did yer hear that, Dad?'

Jack nodded. 'Like yer mam said, it's a marvellous opportunity. Give yer a taste of what it's like goin' to work. But I'm a bit worried about leaving yer mam to do all the shoppin' on her own.'

'Oh, don't worry about me.' Molly came in carrying two plates in each hand. 'She can't miss a chance like that. With three bob in her pocket, she won't call the King her uncle.' She set the plates down before giving Tommy a nudge. 'That leaves you an' me, sunshine! D'yer fancy yer chances gettin' a Christmas tree on the tram?'

Tommy grinned. 'Will I get paid?'

'Yeah, when Donelly docks, an' he hasn't got a ship yet!' Molly winked at Jack over Tommy's head. 'If we ask yer dad nicely, 'e might mug us to a cup of tea in Reece's. How does that sound?'

'Great!' Tommy speared a chip with his fork. 'An' a jam doughnut with sugar on.'

Molly closed the door after seeing the two girls off to work, and coming back down the hall she laughed to herself. 'That Doreen's a hard clock if ever there was one. One day workin' in the shop an' yer'd think she owned the place.' The house was quiet as Molly stood in the middle of the room wondering what to do first. It was Christmas Eve and she had so much on her mind it was reeling.

'Dishes first,' Molly spoke to the empty room, 'then clean the grate out an' set the fire. After that, a quick flick round with the duster before I get Tommy and Ruthie up.'

Tommy was fast asleep when Molly went into the room that was so small there was only space for a bed, a chest of drawers and a chair. When Tommy was small he'd slept in with the girls, but when Ruthie came along Jack had built a partition across a third of the room so their only son could have some privacy.

Molly looked down at the sleeping figure, a smile on her face. He was well away, and it seemed a shame to wake him. But there was so much to do she couldn't afford to let him stay in bed any longer. 'Come on, sleepy head.' Molly shook his shoulder. 'Christmas Eve, sunshine, so wakey-wakey.'

Tommy turned over, grunting, 'What time is it?'

'Time to get a move on. Look sharp now, Tommy, there's a good boy. I'm goin' to get Ruthie up.'

★ ★ ★

'What time we goin' to town?' Tommy asked, munching on a piece of toast. 'An' what's happenin' to her?' He jerked his head at Ruthie. 'She's not comin' with us, is she?'

'Mary Watson's mindin' her for me.' Molly was rummaging through a drawer in the sideboard. 'Where the 'eck did I put me club card? I could 'ave sworn I put it in 'ere.' She pulled out a pink card and held it aloft triumphantly. 'Got it! Now you keep yer eye on yer sister while I nip up to Maisie's an' get me Christmas club out.'

As she closed the front door behind her, Molly said a little prayer that Tommy wouldn't ransack the place looking for where she'd hidden the presents. Not that he'd find them, mind, 'cos they were all in Nellie's. But he didn't know that and could wreck the place in his search.

Molly's step slowed as she reached the Clarkes'. She hadn't spoken to Ellen much since the incident over the noise. In fact she thought Ellen was sorry she'd confided in her and had been avoiding her ever since. I wonder what sort of a Christmas they're going to have, Molly asked herself. Then, with a determined shake of the head, she walked quickly on. She had enough on her own plate without worrying about anyone else. Then she stopped in her tracks. Wasn't Christmas supposed to be a time of goodwill towards all men? You'll regret it, Molly told herself as she retraced her steps and knocked on her neighbour's door.

'What d'yer want?' Peter, six years of age, had the

wizened face of an old man. A face that had never known a smile, and eyes devoid of emotion.

'Tell yer mam I want to see 'er a minute.' Molly smiled to show she meant no harm, she'd come as a friend. Then a movement in the boy's hair brought a look of horror to her face. My God! The child's hair was alive with fleas!

'What is it?' Ellen came up behind her son. 'Oh, it's you.'

Molly bit back the quick retort that sprang to her lips. Remember, goodwill towards all men, she told herself. 'I just called to see if there was anythin' yer needed that I could get for yer?'

Ellen's thin chest heaved. 'Thanks, but no. The kids can get me any shoppin' I need.'

'Peter, you go inside while I talk to yer mam, private like.' Molly watched the boy glance at his mother before turning and walking back along the hall. 'Step outside a minute, Ellen.'

She pulled the door to before stepping into the street. 'What is it?'

Molly kept her distance, having no wish for one of the jumping fleas to land on her. She'd had enough of that when her children were younger. It had taken her months to get their heads clean and she had no desire to go through that again. 'Are yer all right for presents for the kids?'

Ellen's laugh was hollow. 'Presents! Yer must be jokin', Molly! Tomorrow will be no different to any other day in this 'ouse.'

Molly tutted, her face sad. 'It's a bloody shame, yer

know, Ellen. The poor kids didn't ask to be born, an' they don't deserve a father like Nobby.'

'Tell me somethin' I don't know, Molly! D'yer think I don't know what it's like for them? If miracles happened an' wishes came true, my kids would 'ave the best of everythin'. But miracles don't happen in real life, so I'll just 'ave to get on with it.' Ellen's chin dropped to her chest. 'I do love me kids, Molly, even if yer don't think I do. I'd give my right arm for them to wake up tomorrow mornin' an' find Santa had been an' left them presents an' a Christmas stockin' full of goodies.'

Why didn't I just keep on walking? Molly was asking herself. How can I enjoy Christmas, knowing that in the house next door there are kids without even a proper dinner, never mind presents? 'Can't yer get something on tick, until after the holiday?'

Ellen's head was shaking, her lips forming a straight line. 'I'm up to me neck in debt at the corner shop as it is, I wouldn't 'ave the nerve to ask for more.' She looked Molly straight in the eye. 'I've tried to get a job. I'll scrub floors, anythin', but there's nothin' doing.'

Molly let out a deep sigh. 'I wish I could help, Ellen, but I'm not that flush meself. I will try, though. I'll see if me an' Maisie can do somethin' between us. It won't be much, but even that'll be better than nothin'.'

Ellen screwed up her eyes tight. 'I should tell yer not to worry about us, but pride is somethin' I can't afford. Not where my kids are concerned anyway. If yer can do somethin', Molly, I'll be ever so grateful. An' I'd pay yer back, somehow.'

'I could strangle that 'usband of yours,' Molly said.

'Yer'd be better off without 'im, living off the parish.'

'It doesn't work like that.' Ellen sounded bitter. 'I've been told that a wife's place is with 'er husband.'

'I bet he's got enough in 'is pockets to go out celebratin' tonight, though, hasn't he?' Molly was so angry, if Nobby Clarke had walked up the street at that moment she'd have gone for him. 'Laughin' an jokin' with all 'is mates, all hail fellow, well met. I wonder what they'd say if they knew what he was really like?'

Molly wrapped her coat closer to her. 'I'll see what I can scrounge off Maisie an' give yer a knock later.' She walked away a few steps, then turned. 'I've got a bottle of sassafras oil in our 'ouse, left over from when my kids had dirty heads. I'll pass it in when I've been to the shop.'

'Maisie, I'm on the cadge again.' The shop was full of customers using up their club money so Molly's explanation was told in brief bursts each time Maisie passed, getting a customer's order together. 'Can I 'ave two bob worth of sweets on tick? I wouldn't ask, but I've still got a lot of shoppin' to do for meself an' I'm running a bit short.'

'You're a sucker for a hard luck story, Molly.' Maisie weighed out half a pound of margarine before patting it into an oblong shape with two flat wooden spoons. 'Was it a quarter of tea, Mrs Milcraine?' Her eyes on the scale as she weighed the tea, Maisie whispered, 'Tell yer what, Molly, I'll fill two stockings, you fill the other two. Okay?'

'Maisie, yer an angel.' Molly's smile was wide. 'Yer'll get paid back in heaven.' A loud guffaw brought all eyes to her. 'Mind you, I won't be there to see it. I think I'm destined for that place down below, where they've always got the fire stoked up.'

St John's market was so crowded you could hardly move. Tommy had never been before, and the crowds and the noise frightened him. 'Looks like everyone's had the same idea as meself,' Molly shouted in his ear. 'Just grab hold of the back of me coat and hang on like grim death.'

With her elbows bent, Molly bulldozed her way through the mass of heaving bodies. This was no time to act like a lady, and anyone who stood in her way was pushed aside. When he'd got used to the noise, Tommy began to look around and was soon caught up in the hectic atmosphere. He was fascinated by the smells all around him, fruit, bread, flowers and the pine Christmas trees. The loud voices of the stall-holders had him spell-bound. At six o'clock on a Christmas Eve they were eager to clear their stalls and they vied with each other to attract customers.

'Here y'are, folks!' A chicken in one hand and a turkey in the other, one market trader caught Molly's eye. 'Come on, missus, yer won't get cheaper anywhere in Liverpool. Two bob the chicken, three bob the turkey. Or yer can 'ave a goose for three bob. Practically givin' them away, I am. But I was always soft hearted, that's me one an' only fault.'

'Then yer wife's a lucky woman.' Molly grinned. 'I'll be back in a minute, I want to look at the trees first.'

'There's a nice one, Mam.' Tommy pointed to a tree leaning against the stall, his eyes eager. 'It's a belter.'

Molly looked sideways, her eyes on a level with Tommy's mouth. 'What height are yer, son?'

'I dunno!' Of all the silly questions, he thought. 'What yer want to know for?'

'I'd say yer were about five foot six.' Molly sized him up. 'Yeah, easily. But that tree is well over six foot.'

'So what?' Tommy stood up straight. 'I bet yer I can carry it.'

'All the way home?'

'We're gettin' a tram, aren't we?'

'An' yer think the conductor would let yer on with a tree that size? No chance!' Molly saw the disappointment on her son's face. 'Yer'd never get it on the tram, son, it's too big. What about that one over there? It's got nice thick branches, an' it would fit under the stairs on the tram.' Molly bargained the trader down with a hard luck story and got the tree for a shilling. Feeling pleased with herself, she asked if she could leave it there while she got the rest of her shopping in. She'd bought her potatoes and veg the day before at Waterworth's so only needed fruit and a turkey.

The next half hour was an eye opener for Tommy as he listened to his mother bargain with the stall-holders. She ended up with a bag full of apples, tangerines, bananas, dates and nuts, all for a shilling. Then she bought a spray of holly for twopence, and got a piece of mistletoe thrown in for nothing. It was when they came to buying a bird that Tommy's admiration for his mother reached its peak. She asked the prices at one stall, turned, and walked to a stall immediately opposite. Then she stood back while the two butchers battled it out for her custom.

'Mam, yer were brilliant!' Tommy leaned the tree against the tram stop, his face beaming. 'A chicken and a turkey, all for four shillings!'

'It's the way yer hold yer mouth, son.' Molly laughed. 'Talk about act daft an' I'll buy yer a coal yard, isn't in it! I'm dead pleased with meself, though, even if I 'ave only got enough money left to get us 'ome.'

Molly was hanging the holly up when they heard the strains of 'Silent Night' coming from the street. 'Oh, not more carol singers, they must think we're made of money.'

'I've got an odd ha'penny, that'll have to do.' Jack handed the coin to Tommy. 'Here y'are, son, take it out to them.'

When Tommy came back he was followed by Jill and Doreen. 'You two are late, I was beginnin' to think yer'd left 'ome.' Molly stood back to admire her handiwork. 'Been rushed off yer feet, have yez?'

'It's been mad busy all day.' Jill was carrying a cake box which she handed to Molly with a smile. 'A present for you from Mr John.'

Molly wrapped a piece of tinsel around her neck and dived for the box. 'Ooh, er!' Nestling on a bed of tissue paper was a Christmas cake. It had white icing on top, with a tree and a red robin standing either side of a silver sign which read 'Happy Christmas'.

'He's a good man, that Mr John,' Molly said. 'Generous and thoughtful.'

'He doesn't half make yer work hard, though,' Doreen grumbled. 'Flippin' slave-driver, he is.'

'Jack, get off yer backside an' make them somethin' to eat, will yer? I want to get the tree finished.' Molly picked up one of the silver balls that had decorated every tree they'd had over the years. 'I've got the turkey to clean yet, ready to put in the oven before we go to midnight Mass.'

'The tree looks nice, Mam,' Jill said. 'I wish we had some fairy lights for it.'

'Next year, sunshine, next year. There'll be three of yez workin' then, please God, so we'll be able to break eggs with a big stick.'

While the girls were eating their supper, being amused by Tommy's account of his first venture into Reeces and St John's market, Molly beckoned Jack into the kitchen. 'Do us a favour, will yer, love? Take these four stockings next door. Nobby won't be there, he'll be in the pub as per usual. I've wrapped them in newspaper so the kids can't see them, but make sure yer give them to Ellen so she can hide them till the mornin'.'

'Yer a cracker, yer know that, love?' Jack nuzzled Molly's neck. 'Yer've got a heart as big as a week.'

'Aye, an' a purse as flat as a pancake.' Molly gave him a push. 'Go on with yer, yer daft ha'porth, an' let me wrestle with this flamin' turkey.' Jack had just reached the door when she grabbed his arm. 'I forgot to tell yer, I've asked Maisie an' Alec down for a drink tomorrow night. Shame they've got no kids, it must be a bit miserable for them bein' on their own over Christmas. Me ma an' da will be here, so we can 'ave a bit of a sing-song.'

Jack was only away for a few minutes. 'God, yer can smell the sassafras oil a mile away! She must have doused the poor kids in it!'

'Go way!' Molly feigned surprise. 'Must be havin' the same trouble we 'ad when our kids were little.'

Chapter Eight

The first snow flakes started to fall as they stepped out of the front door and Molly laughed with delight. 'Lovely! If it sticks, it'll look real Christmassy tomorrow.'

Jill spread out her hands to catch the falling flakes. 'Don't they look pretty . . . just like feathers.'

Jack turned his head and smiled when he saw the pleasure on the faces of his two daughters. It was the first time Doreen had accompanied them to midnight Mass and she was walking tall, feeling very grown up. Tommy, after a few moans, had agreed to listen for Ruthie. 'Have yer got money for the collection plate?'

Both girls nodded, Doreen patting her coat pocket. 'In here.'

The church was filling up rapidly, so when Molly spotted an empty pew near the front she pushed the girls towards it. She knelt to say a short prayer then sat back and looked around, hoping to spot her ma and da. When her eyes lit on them, she smiled and waved, mouthing, 'See you later.'

Molly gazed along the pew and her heart swelled with pride. She was so lucky to have such a lovely family. A mother and father she adored, the best husband in the world, bar none, and wonderful children. She certainly had a lot to be thankful for.

She was brought back from her thoughts by the people in the pew in front standing to let a man pass to the empty seat in front of Molly. He sat down, coughing as he turned his head, and Molly wrinkled her nose as the smell of beer wafted up her nostrils. Fancy coming to church straight from the pub! Probably only came to Mass once a year, hoping it was enough to save his soul. Another Nobby Clarke by the looks of his red nose and big beer belly. An angel on the outside, a devil on the inside.

Molly mentally chastised herself. Christmas is no time to be thinking ill of anyone, so while I'm thanking God for all the good things I've got, I'll add a little prayer for the sinners.

The alarm clock had barely finished its first shrill ring before Molly's hand shot from beneath the bedclothes and banged her palm on the off button. It was freezing in the bedroom and she pulled the blankets up to her chin, promising herself just ten more minutes. But the more she thought of all the things she had to do, the more those extra minutes became a penance rather than a luxury.

'Jack!' Molly's elbow came into contact with her husband's ribs. 'Time to get up, love.'

'What time is it?'

'Seven o'clock.' Molly swung her legs over the side of the bed. 'Put a move on.'

Jack sat up, rubbing his eyes. 'Do we 'ave to get up so early? I feel as though I've only been in bed five minutes.'

'I want to set everything out nice for the kids.' Molly rubbed her arms briskly before reaching for her old blue fleecy dressing gown. 'While I'm doin' that, you can get the fire started.'

'No rest for the wicked.' Jack was pulling his trousers on. 'They were so late gettin' to bed, they might sleep till about ten.'

'Aye, an' pigs might fly.' Molly pulled the belt of the gown tight. 'Don't make a sound when yer comin' down, d'yer 'ear?'

'Okay, boss, I'll be as quiet as a mouse.'

While Jack raked the ashes from the grate and carried them out to the bin, Molly laid four old lisle stockings on the table. Into each of them she dropped a tangerine, apple, banana, packet of sherbet dab, peanuts in their shells and a bag of sweets. Then on the top she placed the presents her ma and da had sent round for the children. Tangee lipsticks for Jill and Doreen, a mouth-organ for Tommy and a knitted doll's outfit for Ruthie. Then she hung them from the mantelpiece, securing them with ornaments and well away from the fire which was now beginning to show some life.

'It's freezing out there, the snow's thick.' Jack shivered, rubbing his hands up and down his arms. 'I'll wash me hands, then put the kettle on.'

'Uh, uh!' Molly shook her head. 'Yer've got to get the presents from Nellie's. Take a dekko, an' if their light's on, give a knock.'

While Jack was away, Molly put the finishing touches to the tree; two chocolate Father Christmases, chocolate animals wrapped in silver paper, sugar mice and two net bags of chocolate money. 'There, it's beginnin' to look like Christmas now.'

The door burst open and Jack staggered in carrying a heavy typewriter. 'This thing weighs a ton.' He plonked it on the table, panting for breath. 'Can I 'ave a cup of tea now?'

'Oh, for cryin' out loud, will yer stop yer moanin' an' get back for the rest of the stuff? The kids will be down before I've got everythin' ready.'

'Slave driver,' Jack muttered. He tilted his head to one side. 'The tree looks nice, love.'

'I 'ad to leave it till the last minute to put the chocolate things on, 'cos our Ruthie an' Tommy would have pinched them.' Molly stood back to admire her handiwork, then turned and jerked her head at Jack. 'Move yerself, love, please! I'll make the tea while yer out.'

'It's like a madhouse down there,' he said, coming through the door for a second time and dropping an armful of parcels on the couch. 'Yer can't hear yerself talk for the noise.'

Molly got busy sorting the presents out. On one chair she carefully placed Doreen's new skirt and blouse, plus her first pair of long stockings. On the next chair went Tommy's new short grey trousers, a shirt and a book on trains.

'Shove up a bit an' make room for the new addition to the family.' Molly laid Ruthie's doll on the couch, tracing a finger over its rosebud mouth and long blonde

110

curls. 'She'll be over the moon with this.' Covering the doll with the blanket embroidered by Bridie, Molly gave a deep chuckle. 'She's a proper little bossy boots, our Ruthie, so God help the poor doll.'

'It's a wonder the kids aren't awake by now.' Molly opened the door of the cupboard set in a recess of the wall by the fireplace and took out a pillowslip. 'I'm coverin' the typewriter with this so I can see our Jill's face when I take it off.'

'Come an' drink your tea before it gets cold.' Jack was standing with his hand behind his back, and when Molly went to pass he grabbed her arm and lifted a spray of mistletoe over her head. 'How about me Christmas kiss, Mrs Bennett?'

Molly walked into his arms and he held her close. 'Mmm, yer lovely and warm. Let's go back to bed.'

She slapped his hand playfully. 'Behave yerself, Jack Bennett, an' give the kids a shout.'

Jack stood at the bottom of the stairs. 'Wakey, wakey!'

Tommy must have been standing on the landing, ready and waiting, for no sooner were the words out of Jack's mouth than he was being pushed aside by his son. Afterwards, Jack swore that Tommy had come from the top of the stairs to the bottom without his feet once touching the ground.

'Hey, hold yer 'orses.' Molly grabbed hold of Tommy's arm. 'Wait till yer sisters come down an' yer can all open yer presents together.'

'Ah, ray, Mam!' he wailed. 'They won't be down for ages!'

But the three girls had been lying in bed waiting, and within minutes they were downstairs and the house became alive with shrieks of delight and laughter.

For the next hour the noise was deafening. Paper, orange peel and nut shells littered the floor, but Molly was so happy to see the pleasure on her children's faces, she didn't see the mess around her. All her scrimping and saving had been worth it for this moment. She hadn't paid the rent this week, and she owed the corner shop a few pounds, but she'd make it up over the next few weeks. Right now, she thought, I might be skint, but I'm happy.

Jill had ripped a page from her homework book and was practising on the typewriter, Tommy was blowing into the mouth-organ and turning the pages of his new book at the same time, while Doreen stood on tip-toe, humming to herself as she peered into the mirror, her mouth puckered as she made her first attempt at drawing a Cupid's bow on her top lip with the Tangee lipstick.

Ruthie, her eyes wide with excitement, was sitting on Jack's knee, her new doll cradled in her arms. 'What shall we call her, Dad?'

'Well, now, let me see.' Jack held his head in his hands. 'How about Shirley, after Shirley Temple?'

A wide smile creased the little girl's face. 'Mam, did yer hear that? Me dolly's name is Shirley!' She shook her mother's arm. 'She's got curly hair like Shirley Temple, too!'

Molly smiled. 'Yer mustn't forget to thank yer grandma for knittin' those lovely clothes for her.' She lifted the doll's pink dress. 'Look, she's even got knickers on.'

'Oh, I will, Mam,' Ruthie said, her small face serious. 'I'll give Grandma and Granda a big hug an' kiss.'

Molly put her hands over her ears to muffle the sound of the mouth-organ. There was no tune, just a loud noise. But then Tommy had always been tone deaf, same as he had two left feet. 'I'll kill me ma for givin' 'im that.' Molly rolled her eyes. 'Remember when she bought 'im a drum? We all 'ad splittin' headaches for weeks.'

'These are me favourite present.' Doreen lifted the long rayon stockings from the chair, handling them as though they were made of gold dust. 'I'm not puttin' them on yet, in case I ladder them.'

'Now the kids are sorted out, would you like your present, love?' Jack asked.

'Oh, yes, please.'

Jack sat Ruthie down and went out to the hallstand. He came back with his hands hidden behind him. 'Which hand d'yer want?'

'Stop actin' the goat, Jack Bennett, an' give it here.'

As Jack handed the box over, Molly gave him a parcel. 'Open yours first.'

Jack was delighted with the thick navy blue jersey. 'Just the thing to keep the life in me old bones.' And the gloves Molly handed him from Bridie and Bob were equally welcome. 'I've done very well for meself, haven't I?' Jack laid his presents aside and pointed to the box on Molly's knee. 'Are yer goin' to open it?'

Molly's shoulders were moving up and down in antici-pation as she lifted the lid from the box. Her gasp of pleasure brought the children to crowd around, and all eyes rested on the brooch nestling on a bed of cotton wool. It was square shaped, made up of clear glass stones that changed colour as Molly moved her hand. 'It's beautiful, Jack.' She was overcome with emotion. She knew it wasn't an expensive brooch 'cos Jack didn't have much money to himself, but she'd never had anything so pretty bought for her before. 'Look at the colours when I move me hand.'

Jack sighed with relief. He didn't know what women liked, but the girl in the shop had assured him his wife would like it, and from the look on Molly's face, she was right. 'I'm glad yer like it, love.'

'Like it! I love it! I'll wear it tonight on me navy dress an' look like a million dollars.'

Molly glanced up to see the children nudging each other. 'What are you lot up to?'

'Nothing, Mam,' said Doreen. 'We're waiting to see what me gran bought yer.'

Molly knew what her present was, she could feel by the shape, but not for the world would she let them see. And her look of surprise when she held the slippers aloft would have fooled anyone. 'Lovely warm fleecy slippers, with a red pom-pom on. Just the job for keepin' me feet warm when I'm sittin' on me throne down the yard.'

'Dad, can I get behind that cushion, please?' Jill waited for Jack to lean forward, then slipped a hand down the back of him. 'These are from the four of us.'

Molly's mouth gaped as she held her hand out for the bag. She hadn't expected this. It must be Jill's doing, 'cos the others didn't have any money. How like her to say it was from all of them. 'Oh, my God, Jack, will yer look at this!' Molly draped the pale blue voile scarf across her palms. 'Isn't it gorgeous!'

'You can wear it round your neck tonight.' Jill had been reluctant to spend the money she'd been saving to buy a typewriter, but she couldn't let Christmas pass without buying her parents a present. And she'd wanted some new clothes for herself, to wear when she went out with Steve. She was glad she had, now, 'cos her mother's face was a joy to behold. And, Jill stole a glance at the Olivetti typewriter, she'd got what she wanted as well. 'It'll look nice with yer navy dress.'

'Yeah, it's the gear, Mam.' Tommy was enjoying this. He was glad their Jill had said it was from the four of them. He'd pay her back when he started work. It wouldn't be that long now, only eighteen months.

'Hey, hold on a minute.' Jack was holding up a maroon tie, his face glowing with pleasure. 'Yer mam won't be the only swank at the party tonight. When I get all dolled up, she won't be in the meg specks.'

The children preened themselves with pride. For the first time in their young lives, they'd found that there was more pleasure in giving than there was in receiving.

'Yer know, Jack, God's been good to us.' Molly was peeling potatoes by the sink, while Jack was topping and tailing the carrots. 'We've got each other, four lovely healthy children, an' me ma an' da.' She threw a peeled potato into a pan of water. 'We're very lucky.'

Jack rested his hand on the colander. He'd been an only child, and when his parents had died just after he

115

got married, he was left without kith or kin. But he had adopted Molly's parents as his own, and loved them dearly. 'We've got a damn' sight more than that to be thankful for, love. We've got coal for the fire, enough food for our bellies, and a house full of love and warmth.' He went back to his carrots. 'Aye, love, as yer said, God's been good to us.'

Molly gripped the edge of the heavy wooden table. 'Ready, Jack? Then heave!'

They carried the table to the space they'd made for it under the window. 'That's better.' Molly stood with her palms flat on the table, her chest heaving. 'At least we'd be able to swing a cat around now. That's if we 'ad a cat, like.'

'Where yer goin' to sit them all, love?' Jack scratched his head. 'We 'aven't got enough chairs.'

'With the ones out of the bedrooms we will.' Molly wiped her hand across her forehead. 'I'm sweatin' cobs.'

'Yer should 'ave let our Tommy help me, I told yer it was too heavy for you.'

'He's got 'is nose stuck in that flamin' book and nothin' will shift 'im, bar an earthquake.'

Jill leaned on the brush she'd been sweeping the lino with. 'Shall I fetch the chair down out of our room, Mam?'

'Yeah, there's a good girl.' Molly looked at her daughter and wondered how she'd managed to produce such a beautiful girl. Jill looked lovely, in a blue skirt and white broderie anglaise blouse. With her clear blue eyes, fanned by long black lashes, and her hair brushed till it shone like burnished gold, she looked as pretty as a picture. 'Oh, I forgot to tell yer, I've asked Nellie and George down tonight, an' told them Steve can come if 'e wants.'

Jill fled without answering, feeling embarrassed but very pleased at the news.

'I'm a bit worried, love.' Jack's forehead was puckered in a frown. 'We've only got a bottle of port in, an' that won't go very far.'

'Stop yer worryin', for 'eaven's sake. Me da's bringin' a bottle of sherry an' Maisie's bringin' somethin'. Anyway, who needs drink to 'ave a good time? I don't!'

When the first knock came, Tommy flew to open the door. 'Granda, wait till yer see what I've got!' He was waving his precious book under Bob's nose as his granda stood on the step scraping the snow off his shoes. 'It's full of pictures of trains from all over the world.'

'Is it now?' Bob raised his eyes in mock surprise. Not for the world would he say he'd been the one who'd told Molly the name of the book and where she could buy it.

'For cryin' out loud, will yer let them take their coats off and get a warm! And put that ruddy book away.' Molly rolled her eyes to the ceiling. 'God give me strength.'

'Why not bring it round to our house tomorrow?' Bridie asked, seeing the look of disappointment on Tommy's face. 'Sure, you an' yer grandad can while away the whole day just looking at the wonder of it.'

'Ay, Jack Bennett, just take a gander at yer daughter.' Molly folded her arms, a look of pride on her face as she

117

sized Doreen up and down. 'Quite the little lady, all dressed up an' nowhere to go.'

Wearing her new skirt and blouse and long stockings, Doreen stood inside the door looking sheepish. 'Do I look all right?'

'You look fine, love,' Jack said. 'Yer mam was right, a proper little lady yer look.'

'Are me seams straight?' Doreen turned for their inspection. 'It's not half 'ard trying to get them in a straight line.'

''Tis grand yer look, Doreen,' Bridie said. 'Real pretty.'

A knock on the door announced the arrival of Maisie and Alec, followed within minutes by Nellie, George and Steve.

'Take all the coats upstairs an' lay them on the bed, there's a good girl. An' tell Jill to come down. She's been on that flippin' typewriter all day.'

'Is she pleased with it, then?' Bridie asked.

'I'll say she is!' Molly laughed. 'I 'ad to drag 'er downstairs for her dinner, she was busy typing away, as happy as a pig in you know what.'

Ruthie settled herself on her granda's knee, her dolly resting in her arms. She'd never been allowed to stay up so late, and heeding her mother's warning to behave herself, stayed as quiet as a mouse.

Jack poured out drinks while Molly and her daughters handed round plates of sandwiches and mince pies. There was lots of talking and laughter, and Molly felt on top of the world. What more could you ask out of life than to have all your family and friends around you?

'I think someone's ready for beddy-byes,' Bridie said

softly, bending to kiss Ruthie's brow. 'She can't keep 'er eyes open.'

'Yes, I'll take her up.' Jack lifted his daughter gently. 'It's been a long day for 'er, she must be dead beat.'

Molly waited till Jack came down to say Ruthie was fast asleep in the land of nod. Then, a glass in one hand and a plate balancing on her lap, she winked at her mother. 'Give us a song, Ma.'

''Tis yerself that should be entertainin' us,' Bridie said. 'You'll not be wantin' to hear an old woman like me.'

'Go on, missus, yer know I've got a voice like a fog horn. You start, an' we'll all join in.'

Bridie put her hand to her mouth and cleared her throat. Then she began to sing 'Danny Boy' in such a clear, sweet voice, she held her audience spellbound. The silence was so deep, you could have heard a pin drop. And the only movement was from Molly as she wiped away a tear.

There was much clapping when the song ended, and shouts of 'Encore', but Bridie shook her head. 'Later, perhaps. Sure yer want a song to liven yourselves up, not one to be bringin' the tears to yer eyes.'

No one was prepared to follow a voice like Bridie's, not until they'd had a few more drinks down them anyway, so Alec began to make them laugh with tales of the tricks his customers got up to. Like the woman who brought some corned beef back, complaining it was underweight. Alec had weighed it and, sure enough, it was only three ounces instead of four. But Maisie, who had served the woman's son with the meat, insisted it had been the right weight when it left the shop. After much shouting and swearing, the woman stormed out to return minutes later, pulling her son along by his ears. 'Tell Mr Porter what yer did, yer thievin' little bugger!' The boy was scared stiff. How was he to know his mam would miss the slice he'd eaten on the way home?

There weren't enough chairs to go round, so Jill was sitting on the second stair while Steve lounged against the door. 'I believe yer got a typewriter?'

She nodded. 'It's second hand, but it's in good nick. I've been practising all day, an' now I'm used to it I can't half go fast.' She smiled up at Steve. 'What did you get?'

'The usual, shirt, socks and hankies.' Steve was glad it was dark in the hall and she couldn't see his face. 'I've got you a little present.'

Taking a deep breath, he gave her a quick peck on the cheek before handing her a small bag, saying gruffly, 'It's not much.'

Jill stared at the bag. 'You shouldn't have bought me anything! I feel awful now, 'cos I haven't got a present for you.'

'Don't be daft.' Steve moved from the door to lean against the wall. 'I wanted to buy yer something.'

Jill put her hand in the bag and brought out a bottle of perfume. 'Thank you, Steve.'

'It's Californian Poppy, d'yer like it?'

'I've never had a bottle of scent before, but I've heard the girls in work say this is the best.' Jill unscrewed the black top and pulled out the little rubber stopper. 'I'll put a bit on, behind me ears.'

'Jill, if I ask yer somethin', will yer promise not to laugh?'

'How can I promise when I don't know what it is? If

it's funny, then I won't be able to stop meself laughing.'

'Will you be my girl?'

This time it was Jill who was glad of the darkness. Her face was flaming and her heart thumping like mad. 'I'm only fifteen, me mam would say I'm too young to be courting.'

'Yer'll be sixteen in a few months, an' I'll be seventeen. We're not that young.' Steve moved from the wall and bent towards her. 'Are yer only sayin' that 'cos yer don't want to be my girl?'

'No!' The word came out involuntarily. 'I do want to be your girl. But don't let on, or I'll get me leg pulled.'

Steve felt ten foot tall. If he had his way he'd tell everyone, but if that was the way Jill wanted it, he didn't really care. As long as he knew she was his girl, that was enough for him.

There was a lull in the conversation as Jack filled their glasses, and through the silence came the sound of shouting from next door. Then came a roar, followed by a crash that sounded like a chair being thrown against the wall.

'In the name of God!' Bridie clutched a hand to her heart. 'What was that?'

'That, Ma, was our neighbour,' Molly said, her nostrils white with anger. 'We often get that, when he's in one of 'is fightin' moods. But if 'e starts tonight an' spoils me party, I'll go round an' stiffen 'im.'

'Now why would he be in a bad temper, today of all days?'

'Nobby Clarke doesn't need an excuse for throwin' 'is weight around, bashin' the kids an' Ellen. They're easy targets, can't 'it him back.'

'We live a few doors away an' we can hear 'im sometimes,' Nellie said. 'It's the kids I feel sorry for, poor blighters.'

'Sshh!' Molly had her ear cocked. 'It's gone quiet, let's hope it stays like that.'

A splutter from the gas light suspended from the ceiling brought a grunt of disgust from Molly. She looked up and saw a flame flickering through a hole in the fine gauze of the mantle. 'That's all I need!' She threw her hands in the air. 'Bloody Nobby Clarke, an' now me gas mantle's gone for a burton an' I 'aven't got a spare one.' She slapped herself across the cheek. 'Serves me right for bein' so bloody big-headed. I've been pattin' meself on the back thinkin' I'd remembered to get everythin' in, an' lo and behold, I've forgotten a little thing like a ruddy gas mantle.'

'I'll get a couple of candles, love,' Jack said. 'That light's goin' to go out any minute.'

'I'll nip up to the shop and get you a mantle.' Alec stood up and shook his trouser legs until the creases were hanging straight. 'It'll only take five minutes.'

'I'm sorry, Alec,' she said. 'It's a hell of a night to ask yer to go out. The snow's comin' down pretty heavy.'

'He won't shrink.' Maisie laughed. 'An' if he runs fast, he can dodge the snow flakes.'

'I'll 'ave a hot toddy ready to warm yer up.' Jack grinned as he added, 'Aren't I generous, offerin' yer a drink of yer own whisky?'

Alec donned his coat and wrapped a woollen muffler round his neck. 'I'll be back in five minutes.'

Chapter Nine

'I wonder what's keepin' him?' Maisie glanced at the clock for the umpteenth time. 'Five minutes he said, an' he's been gone twenty.' The gas mantle had disintegrated completely since Alec left, and they were sitting in the glow from the fire and the flickering light given out by the candle standing in a saucer on the sideboard. 'I'm beginning to think he's got a woman on the side an' he's taken advantage of the situation to nip round an' see her.'

Molly chuckled. 'Don't be puttin' ideas into my feller's 'ead, Maisie, or he'll think he's missin' out on something.'

'One woman's enough for me, thanks.' Jack laughed. 'I've got me hands full with you.' He cocked his head. 'This'll be him at the door now.'

The smile slid from Jack's face when he opened the door to see Alec standing behind Ellen Clarke and her two eldest children: Phoebe, who was nine, and Dorothy, seven.

'I found them walking the streets,' he explained. 'I couldn't leave them, it's not fit weather for man nor beast.'

Jack recovered quickly when he saw the shivering trio. 'Come in an' get a warm.'

The girls didn't need asking twice, but Ellen hesitated. 'Yer've got visitors.'

Alec gave her a gentle push. 'In you get! The snow's about six inches deep an' your shoes look as though they're made of cardboard.'

Molly's expression when they all trooped in was comical. What the hell was going on? 'What yer doin' out on a night like this, Ellen?'

Ellen's narrow eyes darted round the room, taking in the curiosity and surprise on the faces awaiting her reply. She couldn't think of an excuse, so she told them the truth. 'Yer might know, Nobby's up to 'is antics again. Like a raving lunatic he is, so I brought the girls out before he murdered the lot of us.'

'Where's the young 'uns?' Molly asked, her face anxious. 'Don't tell me yer've left them on their own with 'im, surely to God?'

'They're in bed. I've brought the key with me, so I'll go back when he's 'ad time to cool down.'

Bridie looked at the two shivering girls and her heart went out to them. They were standing with their heads down, but she noticed their eyes kept swivelling to the tree and paper decorations. 'Come and sit yerselves down by the fire and get a warm.' She squashed into the side of her chair and beckoned to Dorothy. 'Auntie Molly will make a cup of tea that'll warm the cockles of yer hearts.'

Maisie slid along the couch, motioning to Phoebe. 'Come on, sweetheart, sit by me.' She took the girl's thin

hands in hers and began to rub some life into them.
'You're like ice.'

Molly's eyes widened in horror as she watched Bridie
press Dorothy's head into her shoulder and begin to
stroke the dull, mousy hair. Oh, God, the fleas! Her eyes
began to flash warnings, but her mother was too busy
crooning words of comfort to the young girl. Molly
closed her eyes, her imagination running riot as she
pictured the fleas jumping from one head to another.
'Jill, put the kettle on, love.' Molly was in despair, but
what could she do? 'Jack, be an angel and put the new
mantle on, will yer, so we can see what we're saying.'

'Stand up, George, an' let Ellen near the fire.' Nellie
patted the chair vacated by her husband. 'Come on,
Ellen.'

Molly walked into the kitchen, muttering under her
breath, 'The whole ruddy street will be walkin' tomorrow.'

But as she was carrying two cups of steaming hot tea
through, she hovered by the door, her eyes taking in the
scene. The two girls were so thin their shabby coats hung
on them, and below their legs were like match sticks. On
each of their pinched faces was a look of bewilderment,
as though they'd never known such warmth and kindness
in their young lives. They looked so pathetic, Molly felt
ashamed of herself and sent a prayer winging its way to
heaven to ask God to forgive her for her uncharitable
thoughts.

Nobby Clarke roared with rage when he saw Ellen
march the two girls out. And when he heard the door

bang, he punched his fist into the wall with such force the plaster beneath the wallpaper caved in. How dare she walk out on him! She'd pay for this when she came home, he'd knock the living daylights out of her.

Nobby staggered to the window, his mind hazy from the half bottle of whisky he'd drunk. He saw Ellen trudging through the snow, her arms around the shoulders of his daughters. She wouldn't stay out long, not in this weather, and she had nowhere else to go. She'd soon come crawling back, and when she did he'd show her what for. He'd teach her who was boss!

Leaning on the window sill, Nobby saw Alec come out of the house next door and this increased his anger. Bloody neighbours, never even passed him the time of day. Thought themselves too good for him. But he didn't need them, he had plenty of good mates down at the pub.

When he heard voices outside, Nobby lifted the net curtain. This would be them, he knew they wouldn't stay out long. His lip curled in a sneer. Just wait till he got hold of her, she wouldn't know what hit her. He'd make sure she never walked out on him again.

Nobby dropped the curtain when he saw Ellen and the girls weren't alone. What the hell was the bloke from the corner shop doing with them? In his fuddled mind, he saw this as an added reason for teaching his wife a lesson.

The group passed the window and Nobby waited for the click of the key in the door, his fist clenched ready for action. But there was no sound until he heard a banging on the Bennetts' door. Pressing his face against the window pane, he watched as the group disappeared from view.

Well, of all the . . .! The bitch! He'd show her, and anybody else who got in his way. Who the hell did they think they were, taking his wife and kids in? In his rage, Nobby wrenched the living room door open and staggered into the hall. Too drunk for coherent thought, it was pure instinct that brought his hand away from the door latch. He wasn't frightened of them, he told himself, Nobby Clarke was frightened of no one. He'd take the whole bloody lot on, all at once if need be, and make mincemeat out of them.

But even in drink, Nobby was cunning enough to find excuses for not getting involved in a fight. 'It's not worth it,' he said aloud, his voice thick, his words slurred. 'I'll just wait for Ellen to come back and deal with 'er in the privacy of me own 'ome. That way I won't be fillin' people's mouths.

'Yeah, that's the best thing.' He held on to the door to steady himself before reaching for the arm of the chair. Then he fell down heavily, saliva running from the corners of his mouth. 'I'm in no hurry, I've got all the time in the world.'

Molly and Jack stood on their step seeing their visitors off. 'God, it's cold enough to freeze the you know whats off a brass monkey!' Molly shivered. 'Thank heaven we can 'ave a lie in in the mornin'.'

'All in all, it's been quite a night,' Jack said, watching the group stop outside Nellie's where Ellen was staying the night. Phoebe was to sleep at Maisie's, and Bridie and Bob were taking Dorothy home with them. Ellen hadn't liked the idea at first, terrified of the consequences. But the men had arranged that Jack and Alec would see her home tomorrow, and if Nobby was reasonable, the girls could follow. If not, they'd take it from there.

Molly made a bee-line for the fire, holding up her dress to feel the warmth while Jack collected glasses and emptied overflowing ashtrays.

'Let's 'ave a quiet cuppa before we go to bed.' She lifted the kettle from the hob and set it on the fire. 'This won't take long to boil.' They sat in companionable silence for a while, each lost in their own thoughts. Molly, her hands curled around the hot cup, broke the silence. 'I could kill Nobby Clarke for spoilin' me night. The first time I've ever 'ad a party, an' he 'as to go and ruin it.'

'I don't know, love, I think everyone enjoyed themselves. The kids from next door certainly did.' Jack flicked the ash from his cigarette into the grate. 'If yer ever think yer hard done by, Molly, just think of Ellen. Life's no bed of roses for her or her kids.'

'I know, I'm a selfish nit.' Molly took a sip of tea then spluttered it out as she shook with laughter. 'One thing yer can say about Ellen, she's not selfish. She gave everyone in this room a present tonight.' The tea was threatening to spill over as Molly's whole frame shook, and she set the cup down on the floor by her feet. 'Mind you, it'll be a few days before any of us know quite how generous she's been.'

'What are you on about, missus?' Jack gazed at the rosy

cheeks creased in a smile, and without knowing why, started to chuckle. 'Come on, Tilly Mint, out with it.'

'Oh, yer'll find out for yerself soon enough.' The springs on the couch creaked as Molly doubled up with laughter. 'Honest to God, I've never known anythin' so funny in me life.' She wiped at the tears with the back of her hand. 'The fleas must 'ave thought it was their birthday, hoppin' from one head to another.' Another spasm of laughter had her gasping for breath. 'Yer not the only one sittin' in that chair, Jack Bennett, yer've got company.'

His eyes rolled from one arm of the chair to the other. 'They've got fleas?'

'Got them! They're alive with the bloody things.' Between guffaws and gulps, Molly told how he'd come to smell sassafras oil when he'd taken the stockings around. 'I gave Ellen the oil 'cos their heads were crawlin' with the ruddy things.'

'Oh, my God!' Jack looked horrified. He never had an itchy head, but right now he could swear he felt something move. 'Yer ma will do her nut.'

'I know! An' don't forget Nellie an' Maisie! An' there's us as well, unless the fleas are fussy.'

'Yer should have said something, Molly.'

She took a deep breath. 'What could I 'ave done, Jack? Thrown them all out in the snow? I wanted to say somethin', but when I looked at the poor things, half starved and terrified, I couldn't bring meself to make a show of them in front of everyone. I couldn't humiliate them, love, now could I? You wouldn't 'ave wanted me to do that, would yer?'

'No, love, I wouldn't.' He reached for the poker and rattled it between the bars on the grate. 'Yer'll have to tell Ma, though, an' the others. It wouldn't be fair not to.'

'First thing in the mornin', I promise.' Molly took one of his hands in hers and held it tight. 'I know I've got a queer sense of humour, love, but when I'd got over the shock, an' realised there was nowt I could do about it, I started to see the funny side. If yer can't laugh things off, yer may as well be dead.'

There was a tender look in Jack's eyes. 'I'll say this for yer, Molly Bennett, my life would be very dull an' empty without yer.'

Ellen Clarke paced the floor of Nellie's living room. All night she'd tossed and turned on the couch, unable to sleep. 'I'd better go 'ome, Nellie. The longer I stay out the worse it'll be.'

'Yer not goin' anywhere till the men come.' Nellie's arms were folded beneath her huge bosom. 'Jack an' Alec said they'd be here for ten, an' it's only just nine o'clock. So park yer carcass an' get that toast down yer.'

'I couldn't eat a thing, Nellie, me tummy's too upset.' Ellen kept on pacing, her hands clasping and unclasping. 'I'd rather go 'ome, face the music an' get it over with.'

Nellie put her two hands on Ellen's shoulders and pushed her down, none too gently, on a chair by the table. 'Over my dead body yer leave this 'ouse, Ellen Clarke, so shut yer cake-hole an' get that toast down yer.'

One look at Nellie's determined face told Ellen it was

no use arguing. She picked up a slice of toast and nibbled at the corner. 'He'll kill me when he gets 'is hands on me. You don't know what he's like, Nellie.'

'Maybe I don't know what he's like, but there's one thing I *do* know.' Nellie stood over the frightened woman. 'If he so much as lays a finger on you or the kids, I'll swing for 'im.'

'Oh, he won't touch me in front of anyone, he's too crafty for that.' Ellen's laugh was hollow. 'He'll be as nice as pie, as though butter wouldn't melt in 'is mouth. Until he's got me on me own, then all hell will break loose.'

Nellie pulled a chair out and sat facing her. 'I think Jack an' Alec will put the fear of God into 'im, so don't be worryin'. Jack Bennett's no shrinking violet, he's a big feller, an' I don't think Nobby will want to cross swords with 'im in a hurry.'

Ellen sighed as she flicked a crumb from her lips. 'I don't mind so much for meself, it's the kids I worry about.'

Nellie scraped back her chair. 'I'd better make meself presentable before the gang arrive.' She smiled down into the pale, pinched face. 'Can't let the men see me in me dinky curlers, might put them off.'

'There's time to eat yer breakfast,' Molly said. 'Ten o'clock yer said yer'd be there.'

Jack stood in front of the mirror adjusting his tie. 'I just hope I can keep me temper. Right now I feel like choking the bastard.' His face was red with anger when he turned to face Molly. 'Every time I think of those

131

poor kids walkin' the streets on Christmas Day, me blood boils.'

There was a rap on the knocker and Molly groaned. 'Who the hell can this be?' She looked down at her old dressing gown. 'Just look at the state of me, I look like Orphan Annie.'

'I'll go,' Jack said. 'It's probably Bob or Alec, bringing the girls.'

'But they're supposed to meet at Nellie's.' Molly ran a hand over her tousled hair. 'Don't let anyone in, Jack.'

'Don't act the goat,' he said, making his way down the hall. 'I can't keep anyone on the step in this weather.'

Molly stood near the living room door, her ear cocked. When she heard Corker's booming voice she looked around for a way of escape. But there was none, unless she went down the yard to the lavvy. And a fat lot of good that would do her 'cos she'd have to come out sooner or later.

'Molly, me darling, compliments of the season to yer.' Corker lifted her off her feet and planted a kiss on her cheek. 'I went to eight o'clock Mass with me ma, had a bite to eat, then left her peeling the spuds while I came to share a Christmas drink with me old mates and wish them the compliments of the season.'

Her feet back on the floor, Molly looked up at the giant of a man who was grinning down at her. 'Corker, it's only ten in the mornin'! An' just look at the state of me . . . I'm hardly dressed for a party.'

He reached in his pocket and pulled out a bottle of port wine. 'You look beautiful to me, Molly me darlin'. A sight for sore eyes is what you are.'

'Away with yer blarney, Jimmy Corkhill.' In spite of her embarrassment Molly couldn't help but smile. 'Save that for the girls yer've got in every port.'

'Sit down, Corker,' Jack said, struggling into his jacket. 'I've got to go out for a few minutes, but I'll be back before Molly's got the glasses on the table.'

Corker took his peaked cap off and threw it on the couch before lowering himself on to a chair. 'If you're going far, you'll need more than that jacket on. It's bitter cold.'

'I'm not goin' far.' Jack looked across at Molly, his eyes asking if they should tell Corker. When she nodded, Jack sat on the arm of the couch and quickly related the events of the previous night. 'Me an' Alec are taking them home. An' Nobby's going to get a piece of my mind, I can tell yer. The way I feel now, I could cheerfully clock 'im one.'

Corker stood up, his face red with anger. 'And I'll be right alongside yer,' he roared. 'It's about time someone took Nobby Clarke down a peg or two.' He picked up his cap, then stretched to his full height. 'It'll give me the greatest of pleasure to be the one to do it.'

'Perhaps yer should stay out of it, Corker,' Molly said, but her words were half-hearted. In her mind she was seeing Nobby's face when he opened the door and saw this giant standing there. Oh, what wouldn't she give to see the fear in his eyes! The same sort of fear she'd seen in Ellen's so many times.

'Molly's right,' Jack said. 'There's no need for you to get involved. Me an' Alec will sort 'im out.'

'I'm comin' with yer,' Corker boomed, 'so don't be

wasting yer breath trying to talk me out of it.'

'Yer'd better be makin' tracks, then,' Molly said. 'Ellen will be on pins. An' go out the back way, so Nobby won't see yer passin'.' She stood by the kitchen door as the two men walked down the yard. 'Don't forget it's Boxing Day. No fightin', d'yer hear?'

'No, don't come,' Ellen cried, 'there'll only be trouble.'

'There'll be no trouble unless Nobby starts it,' Corker said, looking down at the two girls. They stood shivering, looking so frightened he could feel his blood begin to boil. No children should be as afraid of their father as these two were. And no wife should look as terrified as Ellen did this minute. Just let Nobby Clarke say one word out of place, Corker thought, and I'll throttle him.

'There's no need for you to come, Alec,' said Jack. 'Me an' Corker will sort it out.' He took the two girls by the hand. 'Come on.'

Nobby's face drained of colour when he saw the two men with his wife and daughters. His eyes blinking rapidly, he ran a hand through his uncombed hair. 'I wasn't expectin' company.'

'We came to see if yer'd sobered up, Nobby,' Jack said. 'Make sure it was safe for your family to come home.'

Nobby smirked. 'Aw, yer know 'ow it is, Jack, I 'ad a few drinks too many, that's all.' He threw a dirty look at Ellen. 'The trouble with the missus is, she can't take a joke.'

'Oh, a joke, was it?' Corker bellowed. His gaze started at Nobby's feet and travelled slowly upwards until he met his eyes. 'I must be like your wife, no sense of humour, 'cos I don't think it's funny, either.'

'Aw, I got a bit drunk, that was all.' Nobby was quickly weighing up the situation. There was no way he was going to take on Corker. The big man would flatten him with one blow. The only thing he could do was swallow his pride and talk himself out of it.

'Storm in a teacup it was.' Nobby's attempt at a smile made him look even more sinister. 'I went out lookin' for the wife an' kids, but they were nowhere to be seen.'

Afraid as she was, Ellen couldn't prevent the gasp that left her lips. The flaming liar! God, but he was evil, her husband. He was too much of a coward to stand up to Corker or Jack. Hitting someone who couldn't hit back was more in his line.

'Come on in.' Nobby was wrestling with his anger as he jerked his head at Ellen. 'I'll make yez a cup of tea to warm yez up.'

She put a hand on each of the girls' shoulders, and as she pushed them forward turned her head to gaze into Corker's face. She felt so ashamed that the man she used to dance with at the Rialto and the Grafton should see her reduced to this.

Corker wasn't happy with the situation, and he moved forward to have another go at Nobby. But the shame and fear he saw in Ellen's eyes pulled him up short. He understood she was pleading with him to let things be, not to start any trouble. So he stood back and watched her follow the girls into the house.

But while Corker was watching Ellen, Jack's eyes were on Nobby. He could see the anger his neighbour could barely hold in check, and knew that once the door was closed, and Nobby thought he was safe, Ellen and the children would be in for it.

'There's not goin' to be a repetition of last night, I hope, Nobby.' Jack kept his voice low. 'I'm not one to interfere, but nor will I stand by an' see a woman ill-treated.'

Nobby put his hand on the door latch and half closed the door. With his family safe inside, he began to feel cocky. He'd say what he had to say then close the door quickly before they had time to retaliate. 'No one asked yer to interfere, an' if yer hadn't then none of this would 'ave happened.'

That was enough for Corker. He lifted his foot and kicked the door so hard it crashed back against the wall, trapping Nobby's hand. 'Tellin' us to mind our own business, are yer, yer jumped up little pip-squeak?' he thundered. 'Tellin' us we should just stand by while yer batter yer wife and children?'

Nobby winced with the pain from his squashed hand. It felt as though every one of his fingers were broken. But he was too terrified even to bat an eye, never mind move his hand. 'No, no, Corker,' he blustered, 'yer've got me wrong. I didn't mean that at all.'

'Oh, I haven't got you wrong, Nobby Clarke,' Corker said. 'I've got your number right enough. But a word of warning. I'm goin' next door now to have a drink with me friends. If I hear one sound from this house I'll be round like a shot, and believe me, by the time I've finished with yer yer won't know what hit yer.' He glared at Nobby for a second to make sure he'd got the

136

message. Then, with a look of disgust on his face, he turned to Jack. 'Let's move. There's a bad smell around here.'

Ellen was standing in the middle of the room when Nobby came in, the girls either side of her. She could feel her husband's anger and steeled herself for the blows she was sure would come. But Nobby was too busy nursing his injured hand which was throbbing like hell. He jerked his head at Phoebe. 'Go an' put the kettle on, the two of yez.'

The girls glanced at their mother, and when she nodded they walked with their heads bowed into the kitchen. But they made no attempt to put the kettle on. Instead they stood behind the door and peeped through the crack. The saw their father prowling the room, noises like a wild animal coming from his mouth. And when he stopped in front of their mother and raised a clenched fist to her face, they clung together in fear.

'So, yer've been cryin' to the neighbours, 'ave yer?' Nobby was seething. It was all her fault, and by God she'd pay for it. 'Makin' a fool of me, eh?' His nose was within an inch of Ellen's face. 'Well, yer know what yer'll get for doin' that, don't yer? A bloody good hidin' is what yer'll get.'

Phoebe and Dorothy dashed into the room. 'If yer 'it me mam I'm goin' to tell next door.' Phoebe stood in front of Ellen. Although she was shaking with fear, she was determined that this time she wasn't going to stand by and see her mother take a beating.

'Get upstairs, the pair of yez,' Nobby snarled, 'before I take me strap to yez.'

'No!' Phoebe's thin face was white with fear, but she wasn't going to give in. Not this time. 'You 'it me mam an' I'll run for Mr Bennett.'

'An' I'll scream,' Dorothy nodded, her thin lips clamped together. 'I'll scream the 'ouse down an' Sinbad will come an' fight yer.'

Nobby was speechless. He looked first at Ellen, then from one daughter to the other. Their faces told him that while they were frightened, they would carry out their threat. They'd never done this before . . . not one of his kids had ever dared answer him back. 'Why you little . . .' Nobby was so angry he rested his sore hand on his chest while going for his belt with the other. He was undoing the buckle when a picture of Corker flashed before his eyes. He was in no doubt that the big man would think nothing of booting the door in, and he also knew that if he was at the receiving end of a blow from one of those massive hands, he'd end up with a broken nose.

Nobby let his hands fall to his sides. There was no point in asking for trouble. He'd bide his time, then woe betide these three. 'Go an' get yer brothers out of bed,' he growled. 'They'd 'ave been up hours ago if yer mother wasn't so bloody stupid.'

A nod from their mother sent the girls scrambling up the stairs, their shoes clattering on the bare boards. They were too young to understand that in defying their father for the first time they were rebelling against the life of misery he forced them to lead. Last night, for just a few hours, they'd seen what it was like to be part of a loving family. They'd felt the warmth and kindness, and they'd heard the laughter of happy people. They'd never questioned their life before because it was all they had ever known. They were used to being laughed at by the kids in school because their clothes were torn and shabby, used to hearing their bellies rumbling with hunger as they huddled together for warmth in the cold, cheerless house. And from an early age they'd learned to keep out of their father's way. One innocent word or titter could earn them a lashing from his belt.

This was the life they had always known and accepted. But last night their young eyes and minds had been opened to a different life, one they envied. As they grew older, would they be strong enough to tame Nobby? Or would he wear them down, like he had their mother? Strip them of pride and self-respect?

Ellen was asking herself this as she stood in the kitchen waiting for her heartbeat to slow down. Please God, she prayed, give them a better life than I've got. Don't let them suffer for my weakness and stupidity. She could hear Nobby mumbling to himself as he paced the living room floor. She knew he wouldn't be content until he got his hands on her. Her punishment hadn't been cancelled, only postponed.

Chapter Ten

Doreen rubbed her elbow over the window of the tram, clearing a circle in the condensation caused by dampness rising from the clothes of the passengers who were stamping feet and rubbing hands, their noses ranging in colour from bright red to blue. Although it had stopped snowing there was an icy cold wind blowing that could penetrate the thickest of clothes.

Doreen recognised the Metropole Theatre on Stanley Road. Only three more stops now. The shiver that ran through her body was more from apprehension than the cold. She was on her way to her first interview for a job and the prospect terrified her. In the handbag she'd borrowed from Jill was the card she'd been given when she'd gone to sign on at the Labour Exchange yesterday, and her school report.

Her mam and dad had been over the moon, and she'd been feeling very pleased with herself when she went to bed. But lying in the darkness, the house silent, sleep eluded her as doubts set in. What happened when you went for an interview? Did you get a written test, or did they just ask you questions? She hoped they didn't give her any sums to do because she wasn't any good at arithmetic. She was hopeless at spelling, too!

Doreen peered out of the tram window. This was where she got off. She let out a deep sigh as she made her way down the aisle to the platform. Holding on to the rail, she could see they were passing the North Park. How often she'd gone there to play when she was younger. With a bottle of water, a ha'porth of lemonade powder and a few jam butties, she and her mates often used to spend the day there.

The tram was shuddering to a halt when Doreen jumped to the pavement outside the large building that was Johnson's Dye Works. She stood in front of the main entrance long enough to smooth down the front of her old school coat, which still looked shabby even though her mam had sponged and pressed it. Then, straightening her shoulders, she pushed the door open and stepped inside. As she did so, a group of girls about the same age as herself turned to stare at her. 'Are yez all here for an interview?' Doreen asked the girl nearest to her.

'Yeah.' The girl had a round, pale face and long black hair. She had her coat wrapped around her body and looked as frightened as Doreen felt. 'We've been told to wait 'ere till someone comes for us.'

Another girl detached herself from the group and came to stand next to Doreen. 'Is this yer first job, or have yer worked before?'

'I only left school at Christmas.' Doreen was busy counting the girls. There were nine of them, ten including herself. 'I wonder 'ow many jobs are goin'?'

'Dunno!' The girl was small and slim, with a round smiling face framed by thick, black hair cut in a short bob, and laughing brown eyes. 'I've only just left school, too. My name's Maureen, what's yours?'

Doreen didn't answer, her eyes were on the middle-aged, officious-looking woman walking briskly down the corridor towards them. 'Good morning.' She held her hand out. 'Can I have the cards from the Labour Exchange, and your school reports, please?'

After a brief glance at each card, the woman said, 'Come this way.' She led them to a door halfway down the corridor. 'Wait in here until your name is called.'

Maureen linked her arm through Doreen's and pulled her towards the chairs set around the room. 'Let's stay together. I'm shakin' like a leaf.'

'Me too!' Doreen managed a shaky smile. 'It's worse than waitin' to get the cane.'

'I hope we both get taken on,' Maureen said. 'If you go in first, will yer wait outside for me to let me know 'ow yer got on?'

'Yeah!' Doreen was thinking she'd like to work with this girl, 'cos she seemed so friendly. 'An' you do the same if you go first.'

'D'yer live round here?' Maureen asked. 'I live down Scottie Road.'

'I'm not far away, in Walton! If we get taken on, we could catch the same tram in the mornings.'

'Wouldn't it be the gear?' Maureen's infectious laugh rang out. 'We could be friends.'

The door opened and a voice from outside called, 'Miss Shepherd.'

143

'That's me!' Maureen jumped up. 'I'll see yer later, kid.'

Doreen was the fourth to be called, and by that time she was in a nervous sweat and her legs felt like jelly as she crossed the room. The same officious-looking woman was waiting for her. 'Follow me. In here.' The woman opened a door on the opposite side of the corridor. 'Miss Doreen Bennett,' she called, pushing Doreen gently over the threshold.

Doreen managed a half smile, and remembering her mam's warning to watch her manners, croaked, 'Thank you.'

The first thing her eyes focused on was the highly polished desk and the small woman sitting behind it. Not knowing what to do, she stood by the door waiting.

'Sit down.' Hazel eyes peered over the top of the pince-nez glasses perched on a small, upturned nose. 'Your name is Doreen Bennett?'

Doreen licked her dry lips. 'Yes, miss.'

'My name is Miss Jones, and you have no need to be afraid, I'm just going to ask you some questions.'

Doreen swallowed hard to rid herself of the lump in her throat. The woman was old, older than her mam, and she didn't half look stern. She reminded Doreen of the history teacher at school.

When the first questions were fired at her, Doreen told herself she didn't stand an earthly chance of being taken on. She could see her school report on the desk in front of Miss Jones so there was no point in telling lies. No, there was no particular subject she was good at, she admitted, and yes, she was always near the bottom of the class. By this time Doreen had given up hope of getting a job. So when asked, she agreed she was a bit of a tomboy and often used to get the cane for playing pranks.

Miss Jones had her head bent whilst asking the questions, the twinkle of amusement in her eyes hidden from Doreen. It was rare to have someone be so honest. According to most of the girls she interviewed they were all angels, wouldn't say 'boo' to a goose.

'Tell me about your family.'

Surprised by the question, but thinking she had nothing to lose, Doreen's outgoing nature surfaced. Her smile flashed, her tongue loosened and without realising it, she talked herself into a job.

'Right, Doreen! You will report back tomorrow morning for a medical, and providing you pass that, you can start work on Monday morning.'

Doreen gaped. It took seconds for the good news to sink in, then she took a deep breath and said softly, 'Thank you, Miss Jones.'

'Give this card to Miss Howard and she'll explain everything to you. Hours, wages, and which department you'll be starting in.' Miss Jones took off her pince-nez glasses and with two fingers rubbed the bridge of her nose. 'Ask her to send the next girl in, please.'

Doreen stepped into the cold air and the warmth of Maureen's smile. 'How did yer get on?'

'I'm to come for a medical tomorrow.' Doreen giggled. 'I can't believe it! I've got a job!'

'Yer not the only one, so don't be swankin'.' Maureen put her arm through Doreen's and squeezed. 'I'm comin' back tomorrow for a medical as well.'

145

'Ooh, I hope they put us together. Wouldn't it be the gear?'

'Yeah.'

Maureen's white teeth flashed. 'We can be friends, can't we?'

Her hands one on top of the other, Molly rested them on the round top of the dolly peg. It was hard work plunging it up and down on the dirty clothes in the wash tub. Her muscles hurt and her palms were red and sore. 'Anyone would think I was doin' the flippin' washin' for an army,' she complained. Gazing out of the kitchen window at the heavy sky, she tutted: 'The flamin' weather's enough to give anyone the willies. If I'm any judge, we're in for another fall of snow, so that puts paid to gettin' me clothes out on the line.'

Molly plunged the dolly peg into the tub a few more times then gave up. 'That's it! They can steep for half an hour before I mangle them.' She walked through to the living room where Ruthie was sitting at the table, head bent over a colouring book. Drying her hands on the corner of her pinny, Molly smiled. Poor kid, she'd been stuck in the house since before Christmas because of the bad weather. 'How about a cuppa, sunshine, an' a custard cream?'

Ruthie looked up, smiling. 'Ooh, yes, please, Mam.' She'd been licking the ends of the coloured crayons and her lips were covered in red and blue streaks. 'See what I've done, Mam? Aren't I clever?'

As Molly gazed at the country scene on the page, she had a job to keep the smile from her face. Ruthie had painted the grass red, the trees blue and the sheep green. 'That's very good, sunshine. Wait till yer dad sees 'ow clever yer are. When yer start school in a few weeks I'll bet yer the cleverest girl in the class.' She ran a finger down the silken cheek. 'I'll put the kettle on and we'll 'ave a little party all on our own.'

There was a look of tenderness on her face as she walked to the kitchen, leaving Ruthie painting the sky brown and singing, 'Polly put the kettle on, Polly put the kettle on, Polly put the kettle on, we'll all have tea.'

'Kids can be a ruddy nuisance sometimes,' Molly said, striking a match under the kettle. 'But I wouldn't swap them for all the tea in China.'

'Where's our Doreen gone, Mam?' Ruthie's two hands were curled around her enamel mug. 'Yer said she wouldn't be long an' she's been gone ages. I want to show 'er me paintings.'

'I don't know where she's got to, sunshine. I expected her back ages ago.' The rat-tat of the front knocker brought Molly to her feet. 'Speak of the devil and she's bound to appear. This'll be her now.'

She stood aside to let Doreen pass. 'I'd just about given yer up! Where the 'ell 'ave yer been?' She followed her daughter down the hall. 'How did yer get on?'

Doreen threw her coat over a chair and made for the fire. Fanning her hands out towards the warmth, she grinned. 'I got the job.'

'Oh, great!' Molly sat down and rested her elbows on the table. 'Good on yer, kid, I'm proud of yer.'

Doreen rubbed her hands together. 'I had to wait ages

for a tram, an' I'm freezing.'

'The tea in the pot's still hot, I'll pour yer a cuppa.' Molly was smiling like a Cheshire cat. 'Then yer can tell me all about it.'

Ruthie was dying to show Doreen her colouring book, but a sixth sense told her this wasn't the right time. So she spread her arms on the table, rested her chin on her hands and waited to hear what all the excitement was about. Just wait till I see Bella Watson, she was thinking as she studied her sister's face. She hasn't got any big sisters who go out to work and give her a penny pocket money every week.

'Get that down yer.' Molly put the cup of steaming tea in front of Doreen. 'Then start talkin'.'

'If I pass the medical, I start work on Monday mornin' at eight o'clock.' Doreen pulled a face. 'The wages are lousy, though, only twelve and six a week.'

'That's not to be sneezed at!' Molly said, folding her arms. 'It's better than a kick up the backside.'

'It's not as much as our Jill got when she started work.' Doreen's eyes narrowed as she put her cup down. 'If I've got to give you ten bob a week, like Jill does, I'll 'ave nothin' left after I've paid me fares to work.'

Ooh, old crafty boots, Molly thought. I bet she's got it all figured out. Still, she had to admit her daughter had a point. 'I'll 'ave a word with yer dad, see what he says. I'm sure he'll say the same as me. We can't expect yer to cough up as much as Jill.'

Doreen's frown cleared. On the way home, she'd been thinking that if she only had to give her mother eight shillings a week, she'd be left with enough to go to the pictures once a week and save up to buy herself some decent, grown-up clothes. Like the dress she'd seen in a shop window the other week. She'd stood for ages with her nose pressed against the glass, imagining herself wearing the pale blue dress with its sweetheart neck, tight waist and ragamuffin sleeves. It was nine and eleven, a lot of money for one dress, but if she saved hard for a few weeks she could buy it.

Molly sat patiently waiting for her daughter to speak. In the end she leaned forward and tapped her on the arm. 'Do I 'ave to drag it out of yer?'

With a picture of the blue dress still in her mind, Doreen smiled. 'The woman who interviewed me was called Miss Jones. She was very prim an' proper, dead old-fashioned, but nice. The one who gave me all the details was Miss Howard. She said I'll be startin' in the sewin' room, then when I've been there a while and know the job inside out, I'll be moved to another room.'

Molly looked surprised. 'I thought Johnson's was a dye works?'

'It is, but they do lots more besides. In the sewing room they repair things like curtains, turning the collars on shirts, beddin' and lots of other things.' Doreen's face was animated now. 'They've got a glove room where they dye or repair gloves, a hat room where they clean and re-model hats, and lots of other departments. I can't remember everything Miss Howard told me, but all the girls are trained to work in any of the departments.'

'Well, I'll be blowed,' Molly said. 'All the times I've passed that place an' I thought it was only a dye works.'

Doreen shook her head. 'No, they do all sorts. Eiderdowns, evening dresses . . . you name it, they do it.'

'They're noted for not payin' good wages,' Molly said, 'but I believe they're very good to their employees. It looks as though yer've landed on yer feet, love. If they teach yer 'ow to use a sewing machine, yer'll be able to make yer own clothes.'

'I've already thought of that,' Doreen answered, her gaze on the tea leaf floating on the top of her tea. 'The only thing is, we haven't got a sewing machine.'

'Now, yer never know yer luck in a big city!' Molly laughed. 'Our Jill didn't 'ave a typewriter, did she? But she 'as now! There's plenty of second-hand shops around, or even pawn shops! Yer'd be surprised the things people pawn when they're skint. An' most of the time the poor buggers can't afford to redeem their pledges so the shop sells them.'

'Will yer make me a dress, our Doreen?' Ruthie asked, coaxingly. 'A blue one with a sticky-out skirt?'

'Ah, ray, give us a chance! I don't know one end of a sewin' machine from the other!'

'Yer'll soon learn.' Molly nodded her head knowingly. 'Yer grandma used to be able to use a machine. That's years ago, of course, but sewin' is like most things – once yer learn yer never forget.'

Doreen leaned forward, her long hair falling over her face. 'I didn't know that!'

'Yeah, well, it was before your time. She used to 'ave a little hand machine an' she was a dab hand at makin' dresses for me.' Molly smiled at the memories. 'She never used a pattern, did Ma, but she 'ad a knack for it.

Nothin' ever got thrown away when I was little. Ma could make me a dress or coat out of anythin'. She bought the machine second hand, an' it was on its last legs then. But she got her money's worth out of it all right. Her pride an' joy it was, an' she broke her heart when it conked out an' couldn't be repaired.'

'I'll go round there tonight an' tell me nan and granda about me job.' Doreen pushed her chair back and carried her cup through to the kitchen. 'Oh, and I've made a new friend!' Her head appeared round the door. 'Her name's Maureen Shepherd an' she starts on Monday as well.'

Ruthie screwed her eyes up. Was this the right time to ask if Doreen was going to give her a penny a week pocket money, like their Jill did? No, perhaps not, caution told her. I'll wait till she's in a good mood. 'Come and see me colourin' book, our Doreen. Aren't I clever?'

Steve's heart was in his mouth when he knocked on the Bennetts' door. He had seen Jill just once since Christmas Day, and then only to exchange a few words in the street, and he'd missed her so much he'd taken his courage in both hands tonight. Please let her open the door, he prayed as he heard footsteps in the hall. If it's anyone else, what am I going to say?

'Hello, Mrs Bennett.' Steve blushed to the roots of his hair. 'I wondered if Jill felt like comin' to the Carlton?'

'Only one way to find out, son, an' that's to ask her.' Molly held the door wide. 'Weather put a halt to yer courtin', has it?'

Steve hung his head to hide his embarrassment. 'They

reckon it's good weather for ducks. Trouble is, I'm not a flippin' duck!'

'Look who's here.' Molly entered the room ahead of Steve, a gleam in her eye. 'Romeo calling for Juliet.'

Jill's eyes widened in surprise. 'Hi, Steve!'

'D'yer feel like comin' to the Carlton?' he asked gruffly, conscious of all eyes on him. 'William Powell an' Myrna Loy are on in *The Thin Man*.'

Why didn't I answer the door? Jill asked herself. Fancy having to talk in front of the whole family. 'I've got no shoes to wear.' She pointed to the fireplace. 'Mine got soaking on the way home and they're by the fire, drying out for work tomorrow.'

Doreen had been standing in front of the mirror combing her hair. Now she crossed the room and stood in front of Steve. 'I start work on Monday.'

Steve tore his eyes away from Jill. 'Oh, smashin'! I'm made up for yer.'

Doreen preened herself. 'In the sewing room at Johnson's.' She tossed her long hair back. 'When I've learned to sew, I'll be able to make me own clothes.'

'Oh, I'm sure Steve is very interested to hear that!' Molly said dryly. 'He can put in an order for a suit.'

Jack saw a hot retort forming on Doreen's lips and decided it was time to intervene. 'Why don't you stay, Steve, an' we can have a game of cards? No money, of course, we'll play for matches.'

Steve gave him a grateful look. 'Yeah, I'd like that. Thanks, Mr Bennett.'

'Can we play rummy?' Doreen asked. 'It's the only game I know.'

'You've changed yer mind quick,' Molly said. 'Five minutes ago yer were goin' round to yer nan's.'

'It's too cold,' Doreen answered loftily. 'I'll call tomorrow on me way home from Johnson's.'

Molly's brow puckered as she rummaged in the sideboard drawer for the pack of cards. If I had a bad mind, I'd say she was staying in 'cos Steve is here, she thought. She glanced at Doreen as she threw the cards on the table. My God, I don't need to have a bad mind to see she's giving him the glad eye! Fourteen years of age and flirting! With her sister's boyfriend at that! Not that it would do her any good, 'cos even if she was older and looked like Constance Bennett, Steve wouldn't even see her. There was only one girl for him, and that was Jill. You only had to see the way he looked at her and you could tell he was crazy about her.

While Jack dealt the cards, Molly told herself she was imagining things. Fourteen was too young to be interested in boys. But noting Doreen's fluttering eyelashes, the toss of her head which sent her hair swirling round her face, and her inane smile, Molly told herself it hadn't taken her daughter long to discover the opposite sex.

They were picking up their cards when they heard the back door open.

'Oh, my God, will yez look at the state of him!' Molly was staring horror-stricken at the sight of Tommy standing in the kitchen doorway. He was absolutely soaked. Small pools were gathering on the lino as the water dripped off his coat. 'What the hell 'ave you been doin'?' Molly scraped her chair back. 'Don't you dare set foot in this room.'

153

'Ah, ray, Mam! I've only been playin' snowballs.' Tommy's cheeks were red and shining. 'Can't I go upstairs?'

'Can you hell's like! Get those clothes 'off while I go an' get yer somethin' to put on.' Molly dashed up to his bedroom to get his pyjamas before remembering she'd washed the only pair he possessed.

Muttering angrily that she'd like to break his flaming neck, she grabbed her old dressing gown and ran down the stairs. 'Here, put this on.'

'Ah, ray, Mam!'

Tommy's horrified expression was so comical, Molly had to bite on the inside of her cheek to stop herself from laughing. 'I'll "Ah, ray, Mam" yer! Get those clothes off so I can hang them up to dry, otherwise there'll be no school for yer tomorrow an' then the School Board will be after yer.'

'Do as you're told, son.' Jack spoke softly, feeling more than a little sorry for him. What could you expect kids to do when there was snow around? 'Take yer clothes off an' give yerself a good rub down with the towel.'

They all sat straight-faced as Tommy banged around in the kitchen, and nobody batted an eye as he shot through the living room wearing Molly's dressing gown. They gave him a few minutes to get upstairs, then the laughter erupted.

'Oh, I needed a good belly laugh.' Molly wiped the back of her hand across her eyes. 'That was as good as a tonic.'

'It put me in mind of all the snow fights I used to

have,' Jack chuckled. 'Poor blighter, I felt sorry for him.'

Steve was holding his stomach, his shoulders shaking. 'I came home like that once, an' me mam gave me a clip around the ears.'

'Tommy's gettin' too big for me to do that,' Molly said. 'I'd 'ave to stand on a stool to reach 'im.'

'He'll never hear the last of it.' Doreen was grinning. 'Wait till I see 'im tomorrow.'

'When you see him tomorrow, Doreen, you'll keep this closed.' Jack put a finger to his mouth. 'We've 'ad a good laugh at his expense and that's the end of it. D'yer hear?'

'Come on.' Molly picked up her hand of cards. 'It'll be bedtime before we get a game in.'

At ten o'clock, Molly sent a mutinous Doreen off to bed. 'Yer goin' for a medical tomorrow, so yer'll have to be up early. It's the tin bath in front of the fire as soon as yer dad and Jill 'ave left for work.' She jerked her thumb towards the door. 'Now, hop it.'

'I think I'll be makin' tracks, too,' Steve said. 'You'll all be wantin' to go to bed.'

'Aye, we're not night birds.' Molly shuffled the cards into a neat pack. 'You see Steve out, Jill.'

'Will yer come to the pictures with me tomorrow night?' Steve was holding Jill around the waist. 'We haven't been on our own for ages.'

'The weather hasn't been fit! I've only got the one pair of shoes, and by the time I get home they're soaked.'

Steve twisted a strand of her long blonde hair around his finger and pulled her face towards his. 'How about if

I meet you outside the shop and we go straight to the flicks?'

Jill didn't need much persuading. She'd missed Steve, and every night in bed had prayed the weather would pick up so they could go out together again. 'Yeah, that would be great. And you could meet me outside night school on Wednesday, if you like?'

'You know I'd like,' Steve whispered in her ear. 'D'yer know what else I'd like?' When Jill shook her head, he said, softly, 'A kiss.'

She struggled in his arms. 'Ooh, what if me mam comes out?'

Steve chuckled. 'Then I'll kiss yer mam, instead.'

'Oh, yer daft thing, go on with yer!'

'I'm taking that as permission to kiss you.' Before Jill could protest, Steve's lips came down on hers. Up till now, because of Jill's shyness and their lack of privacy, their embraces had only been light, more like pecks than kisses. But Steve was feeling brave tonight as he held her close in the darkness and kissed her eyes and cheeks before searching for and finding her mouth. 'Put your arms around me,' he begged, 'just for a minute.'

Jill slipped her arms around his neck, held him briefly as she returned his kiss, then gently broke away. 'I'm frightened of me mam seeing us.'

'Your mam knows I'd never do anythin' to hurt you.' Steve was glad of the darkness. Jill was the only girl he'd ever been out with, the only one he'd ever wanted to go out with, but he was too inexperienced to put into words what he felt for her. So he contented himself with the thought that she was his girl, and they had the whole future ahead of them. Time enough to tell her how much he loved her.

In the living room, Molly was asking Jack, 'Did yer see the way our Doreen was flirting with Steve? She's a right little minx, that one! Fourteen and actin' like twenty-four!'

'I'd have to be blind not to 'ave seen!' Jack chuckled. 'She had poor Steve wriggling in his chair, his face the colour of beetroot.'

Molly was pulling Tommy's sodden trousers into shape before hanging them over the fireguard. 'If I'd been our Jill, I'd have scratched Doreen's eyes out.'

'Then it's a good job our Jill hasn't got your temper, love.' Jack lit his last cigarette of the night and leaned forward to throw the spent match into the grate. 'I don't think our Doreen realised what she was doing. She's at an awkward stage, too old for dolls and too young for boys.'

Jill popped her head around the door. 'I'm off to bed. Goodnight and God bless, Mam. God bless, Dad.'

'Goodnight and God bless, sunshine.'

'Oh, I nearly forgot.' Jill's head re-appeared. 'Steve's meeting me outside work tomorrow, we're going to the pictures.'

'Okay, love.' Molly waited until she heard Jill's tread on the stairs. 'Gettin' back to our Doreen, I think I'm goin' to have to put me foot down with her. She can be real impudent at times, a right little madam.'

'When she starts work she'll soon have that knocked out of her. Let's give her the benefit of the doubt. Put it down to childishness and hope she'll grow out of it.' Jack drew deeply on his cigarette before flicking it into the fire. He stood up, yawned, and stretched his arms above his head. 'We'll keep an eye on her, an' if she steps out of line she'll have me to answer to.'

Molly sidled up to him and put her arms around his waist. 'Mmm! That's my man! I love the strong silent type.'

Jack held her tight. 'And I love the noisy, loud-mouthed, humorous type. Someone who keeps me on me toes, so I never know what's going to happen next. Someone with a heart as big as her mouth.' He held her from him and winked. 'In fact, someone just like you. You'll do for me, Molly Bennett.'

Chapter Eleven

'Sit down and make yerselves at 'ome.' Molly fussed, pulling chairs out for her guests. 'I thought we'd be better off all sittin' at the table where we can see each other.' Just in time she spotted Nellie McDonough about to sit down on a chair she'd had to bring down from the bedroom to make the number up, and quickly grabbed her friend's arm. 'Eh, up, Nellie! That chair's on its last legs, it won't stand yer weight. Here, sit on this one.'

When they were all seated, Molly's beaming smile travelled round the table, welcoming each of her five neighbours. These were the women who had agreed, after a lot of coaxing, to make up a committee to arrange the street party they were having on the twelfth of May to celebrate the coronation of King George VI.

There was Ada McClusky, Lizzie Furlong and Vera Parker from the bottom end of the street, and Nellie, Mary Watson and herself from the top end. 'I know we've got six weeks, but it's not that long when yer come to think about it,' Molly said. 'If everyone in the street is goin' to contribute towards it, I thought it would be a good idea to start collectin' a few coppers off them each week. It's no good leavin' it till the last minute or we'll have no money to play around with.'

Ada McClusky nodded, her chin touching her chest. 'Good idea! I couldn't pay it all out in one go, but I wouldn't miss a few coppers each week.' There were grunts of approval from the others. They were all feeling very important, never having been on a committee before. 'We could do so many houses each.' The small chair that Nellie was sitting on was completely hidden by her huge bulk, and to all appearances she was sitting on air. 'Mind you, there's bound to be some miserable buggers who don't want to give anything.'

'Yer can say that again!' Lizzie Furlong huffed. 'They'll come to the party but won't want to pay for it.'

'We'll worry about that when we see 'ow it goes,' Molly said. 'I don't begrudge payin' for them that can't afford it, like Tessie Saunders. Her feller's out of work. But I'm blowed if I'm forkin' out for some of the misery guts I could mention. Tight-fisted so-an'-sos.'

'I've brought a pad with me,' said Mary Watson, the youngest of the group. 'What d'yer think about dividing the street into six, an' we all have our own numbers to collect from?'

'That's fine by me.' Vera Porter saw all the heads nod in unison. 'You give us a list each an' we'll have a go on Saturday mornin', before anyone's got a chance to spend all their wages.'

'While you're doin' that, I'll pour the tea out.' Molly put her hands on the table and pushed herself up. 'Yer know, I haven't half put on weight since our Ruthie started school. I don't know I'm born with not havin' to run around after her all day, but I'm piling the pounds on. If I keep this up, I'll be as big as a flamin' house!'

'Yer've got a long way to go to catch up with me.' Nellie's whole body shook when she started to laugh, and the chair beneath her groaned ominously. 'Once around me, twice around the gas works!'

'You suit it,' Molly called from the kitchen. 'I couldn't imagine yer any different.'

Nellie was studying the list Mary had passed to her. 'What about Ellen Clarke next door?'

'Leave Ellen to me.' Molly came through carrying a wooden tray with the cups of tea on. 'She can't afford to give anythin' so it's no good embarrassing her. I'll throw an extra copper in every week to make up for 'er.'

'Who's goin' to take charge of the money each week?' Lizzie Furlong was pulling at the long white hairs that grew from the wart on her chin. She was no oil painting, was Lizzie, but God had made up for her homely looks by giving her a generous, caring nature and a dry sense of humour. 'Don't leave it with me, or I'll be dippin' into it when I'm skint.'

Molly chuckled. 'That's every day, isn't it, Lizzie?'

'Not every day,' she laughed back. 'The one day I never borrow is on a Sunday. It's bad luck.'

Mary passed the rest of the lists out before saying, 'We could start spending some of it. If we're goin' to decorate the whole street, we'll need loads of that crinkly paper in red, white an' blue. We could get that in, an' start cutting it into strips.'

'Yeah!' Molly rubbed her hands in glee. 'We'll 'ave the best street party in Liverpool.'

Nellie put her cup down on the tray. 'Shall we 'ave a meeting next week and see 'ow we got on with the collectin'? We could start writing down all the things we'll need in the way of food and drinks.'

'An' don't forget to write down 'ow much yer get from each house as yer get it,' Molly reminded them. 'Yer know what bad minds some of them 'ave got, they'll think we're on the fiddle.'

'We can meet in our 'ouse, if yez like,' Nellie said. 'Save Molly havin' to put up with us every week.'

'It's no bother,' Molly told her. 'In fact I like havin' visitors. Now I haven't got Ruthie under me feet all day, me time's me own.'

'That's settled then.' Lizzie folded her list and put it in her pocket. 'If anyone needs a handcart to carry all the money they collect, give us a shout an' I'll borrow the window cleaner's.'

'Huh, that's a laugh!' Ada McClusky tittered. 'We'll probably get all the doors shut in our faces.'

'No, you won't!' Molly said. 'I've told nearly everyone in the street, so they'll be expectin' yez.'

'If yer believe that, yer've got more faith in human nature than I 'ave.' When Nellie shook her head, her chins swayed in different directions. 'If they're expectin' us, I'll bet yez any money the kids will be sent to open the door with instructions to say "Me mam's out".'

'Everyone knows their own tricks best, Nellie,' Molly laughed. 'But I'll 'ave yer a bet on it. I'll bet yer a pound to a pinch of snuff that most of them will pay up.'

'Nah!' When Nellie grinned her eyes disappeared in the folds of flesh. 'I couldn't win an argument! Unless it's with my feller, of course. An' he only lets me win 'cos I'm bigger than 'im.'

Vera Porter pushed her chair back. 'I'd better be makin' a move. If I don't get to the shops before they close at one o'clock, it'll be too late to make a pan of scouse for dinner.'

'Yeah, I'll have to put me skates on, too! I want to go round to me ma's before I start on our dinner.' Molly picked the tray up. 'Will yez see yerselves out? An' good luck on Saturday! If a man opens the door, use yer charm on 'im. Yer never know, yer just might get a penny extra.'

'My God, she'll be tartin' us all up an' sendin' us down Lime Street next!' Nellie pressed her open palms on the table and heaved herself up. 'Yer wouldn't get much for me, Molly, I'd 'ave to pay the men.'

Molly kept her face straight. 'Now why didn't I think of that? That's one way of makin' money. All yer'd 'ave to do would be lie back an' think of England! Good idea, Nellie, we'll bear it in mind.'

'Wipe your feet, love, I don't want yer traipsing dirt all through the house.' Bridie closed the door and sighed as she followed her daughter down the hall. 'I no sooner finish cleaning than I've got to start all over again, otherwise the whole house would be caked in dust.'

'I'm not surprised.' Molly gave her mother a quick peck on the cheek. 'I didn't realise they'd have to dig all the flagstones up to lay the electric cables. The street's in a right mess.'

'I keep tellin' meself it'll be worth it in the end, but it's been weeks now and it's getting me down.' Bridie looked worn out. She'd filled old stockings with rags and put them under the doors in an effort to keep the dirt out, but to no avail. Half an hour after she'd polished and mopped there would be a film of dust over everything. Even in her hair and up her nose.

'It'll be worth it, Ma!' Molly leaned forward and smiled into her mother's face. 'Remember what yer said when yer first heard yer were bein' "electrocuted"? Just a flick of a switch, yer said, an' the room will be filled with light. Well, it won't be long now.'

'Just wait till yourself has all this to put up with, my girl, an' yer'll soon change yer tune.'

'Aye, well, a bit of dirt won't worry me too much,' Molly laughed. 'I'm not as fussy as you.' She followed her mother through to the kitchen and watched her fill the kettle. 'Will they be finished before the coronation? Yer couldn't 'ave a street party the way it is.'

'That's the last thing on me mind, sure it is.' Bridie spooned some tea from the caddy into the pot. 'I'll just be glad to get me house back to normal.'

'You an' Pa can come round to us. Yer can't let the coronation pass without celebratin'. It's the only way the people 'ave of showin' they care, and wishing 'im well. After all, the poor bugger probably doesn't want to be King, an' he wouldn't 'ave been only for that brother of his.'

'I wish you'd watch yer language, Molly! It's not respectful to refer to the King as a "poor bugger".' Bridie poured the boiling water into the pot. 'Years ago yer'd have been sent to the Tower of London, so yer would.'

Molly chuckled as she reached for two cups from the shelf. 'They don't behead people any more, Ma! Yer'll not get rid of me that easy.'

'Tut-tut.' Bridie clicked her tongue. 'Behave yerself and carry the cups through. I don't know who you take after, and that's a fact. You never heard bad language from me or yer pa.'

'I must be a throwback, then.' There was a twinkle in Molly's eyes as she poured milk into the cups. 'Yer weren't friendly with the milkman by any chance?'

'Oh, away with yer!' Bridie pulled a chair out and sat down. ''Tis the death of me yer'll be, one of these days.'

'Not for a long time, Ma, not for a very long time.' Molly sat facing her and wagged a finger in her mother's face. 'You are not to die until yer a hundred, and that's an order. Understand?'

'Understanding an order and being able to obey it are two different things, me darlin'. Only the good Lord will know when my time is up.'

'Oh, this is a very cheerful conversation, I don't think! I come round for a cup of tea and a natter, an' end up with the heebie-jeebies! Can't we find somethin' nice to talk about?'

Bridie smiled. 'I've never known you be short of a few hundred words, so I haven't.'

Glad to see the smile back on her mother's face, Molly racked her brains for something of interest that had happened in the two days since she'd last been round. 'I'll start at the top, shall I? Jack's fine, he got some overtime in last night and he's working late again tonight. Our Jill's still courtin' strong. She went to the flicks with Steve last night, and he'll be meetin' her after night school tonight, as per usual. She's a smashin' kid, is our Jill. Lovely nature, quiet, well spoken, and never a cross word out of her.' Molly tapped her fingers on the table as her eyes rolled upwards. 'I wish I could say the same about our Doreen. She's a right little madam, that one! Gives me all the old buck of the day, she does, except when her dad's there. Then yer'd think butter wouldn't melt in 'er mouth.'

'Jill's a lovely girl, so she is, an' don't I love every hair of her head?' There was a trace of a smile on Bridie's face as her eyes held Molly's. 'But, sure, it wouldn't do for us all to be alike. Doreen's more outgoing, got a different nature altogether. She's quick-tempered, says things before she thinks, and is sure she knows it all.' Bridie's smile widened. 'A long time ago, I knew a girl just like Doreen, an' sure isn't she sitting just a few feet away from me right this minute?'

Molly was silent for a few seconds, then her head went back and a hearty laugh rang out. 'Was I that bad, Mam?'

"'T'was a merry dance yer led Pa and me, and you needn't be sittin' there looking all innocent like, as though you can't remember. You had so many different boyfriends, Pa and me lost count. Off out yer'd go every night, with yer face made up like a clown and tottering on heels so high it's a wonder yer didn't fall off.' Bridie pushed a strand of hair out of her eyes. 'We blessed the day Jack Bennett came along an' we knew our worries were over . . . you'd finally grown up.'

Molly held up her hands in mock surrender. 'Okay, Ma, you win! I was a right little upstart, there's no gettin' away from that! But I think yer only rememberin' the things yer want to! What yer forgettin' is that when I left school an' started work I was still wearin' short socks an' navy blue, fleecy-lined school knickers! An' I had to be in by nine o'clock, or Pa would be out lookin' for me . . . remember? I was sixteen before I was allowed to stay out till ten o'clock, or go to the pictures or dances with me mates.' Molly smiled at the memory. 'Ruled me with a rod of iron, you an' Pa did.'

'And didn't yourself need it? Weren't yer just as determined and stubborn as Doreen is now? Sure, yer don't have to look far to see who she takes after.'

'Ma, Doreen wants to do at fourteen what I wasn't allowed to do until I was sixteen.'

'I understand all that, an' I agree with yerself that she needs to be kept in check. But don't be too hard on the girl . . . this bold front she puts on is only a show. Doreen's going to surprise you one of these days and yer'll be proud of her.'

'I hope yer right, Ma.' Molly glanced at the Westminster chiming clock on the sideboard, her mother's pride and joy. 'I'll 'ave to be making tracks soon, it's my turn to pick Ruthie an' Bella up from school. So I'll quickly finish off what I started before we got sidetracked with our Doreen. Me son an' heir, Tommy, is still as mad as a hatter. But I can never stay angry with 'im for long 'cos he won't let me. I can be in the middle of givin' him a right roasting, and what does he do? Comes an' puts his arms around me an' tells me he loves me when I'm mad! An' I'm daft enough to let 'im get around me . . . fool that I am.'

'There's not much wrong with young Tommy, take it from me,' Bridie said firmly. 'He's as good as gold when he's round here. Talks for hours with Pa, all about trains. Did yerself know he wants to be a train driver when he's older?'

'Yeah, he's set 'is mind on it. I hope it keeps fine for 'im, 'cos it's all he ever talks about.' Once again Molly turned to the clock. 'Five minutes and then I'll 'ave to be off. I want to put the dinner in the oven before I go to pick the kids up.'

'Ruthie still liking school is she?'

'Loves it! She sits next to her mate Bella and they're both comin' on like a house on fire. Next time yer see her, ask her to show yer how she can write 'er name. She's that proud of 'erself, she's walkin' ten feet tall.' Molly pushed her chair back. 'If I don't put a move on I'll be late at the school.' She ran a hand over her mother's hair. 'Don't let the mess get yer down, Ma, it'll soon be over an' yer'll 'ave yer house like a little palace again.'

'If Pa's not too tired, we might walk round to yours tonight.' Bridie followed her daughter to the front door. 'I'll be glad to get some fresh air in me lungs.'

Molly pulled a face as she glanced up and down the street. 'To think I'll 'ave this to go through soon. Still, it's worth it to have leccy light, I suppose.' She stepped carefully over the bricks and rubble. 'See yez tonight, then, Ma. Ta-ra.'

★ ★ ★

Jill's face lit up when she saw Steve's tall figure waiting outside the gates of the school. Saying a quick goodnight to the girls who were in the same class, she ran towards him. 'We're taking our exams next week.' Her face was aglow as she linked her arm through his. 'The teacher said I should do well.'

'Don't I even get a hello?' Steve grinned down at her. 'Are the exams more important than me?'

'Of course not, don't be daft! But I want to pass, otherwise I've wasted the last two years!' Jill gazed up at him, blue eyes meeting brown. 'You want me to pass, don't you?'

Steve squeezed her arm. 'I want anythin' that makes you happy.' But deep down he knew that wasn't the truth. He was happy with her working at Allerton's because he knew who she was with every day, and there was no one there to steal her affections. But if she went to work in an office somewhere, who knew who she'd be mixing with? He was terrified of her meeting someone who would take her away from him. 'When will yer know the results of the exams?'

'In a couple of weeks. The term finishes at the end of June, and if I pass that's my lot! No more night school.'

'I'll be glad of that.' Steve's arm went around her waist. 'I'll be able to see yer every night.'

'Here's a tram, let's run for it.' Jill took his hand and pulled him forward. 'Let's sit upstairs.'

On the back seat of the top deck, Steve put his arm around her shoulders. 'You'll be sixteen in June, an' I'll be seventeen. There's only a few days between our birthdays, so 'ow about goin' into town for a meal to celebrate?'

'We couldn't afford it!' But Jill's eyes were shining. 'It would be lovely, though, wouldn't it? I've never been out for a meal before.'

'Me neither!' There was an ache in Steve's heart as he gazed at her lovely face. If only they were a bit older, he thought, they could get engaged. Then he'd know she belonged to him. 'As my birthday present to yer, I'll take yer out for a meal.' It would mean walking to work every day to save enough money, but if it would make Jill happy he'd willingly walk to the ends of the earth. 'How about that?'

'We'll go halfy-halfy,' she giggled. 'And that will be my birthday present to you.'

'We'll see.' Steve pulled her close. 'Me mam's always sayin' yer shouldn't wish yer life away, but I can't help wishing the next few years away. I'd be out of me time then, earning enough money to buy yer an engagement ring an' save up to get married.'

'Our time will come, Steve, let's enjoy what we have now.' Jill peered out of the window, then tapped his knee. 'This is where we get off.'

Steve was quiet as they walked, hand in hand, towards their street. As they turned the corner, he pulled her to a halt. 'You are my girl, aren't yer? I mean, we are goin' to get married when we're old enough?' Holding his breath, waiting for her answer, he told himself he shouldn't be pushing her, but he needed to know for his own peace of mind. She was all he thought about, night and day, and he needed to know she felt the same.

'Of course I'm your girl.' She pushed him playfully. 'You don't see any other boys around, do you?'

'That's not what I meant, Jill.' Steve's face, in the light from the streetlamp, was serious. 'I know yer my girlfriend now, but d'yer think yer'll ever be me wife?'

'I'm not sixteen yet, Steve.' Jill looked up into his handsome face. She was too shy and inexperienced to put her feelings into words, but she thought too much of Steve to leave him looking so unhappy. 'But if I was eighteen, seventeen even, I'd be saying to you, "Let's go into town in me dinner hour on Saturday, Steve, and choose an engagement ring." '

He let out a cry of happiness as he held her close to him. He rocked her to and fro, his warm breath on her cheek. For the first time, he whispered, 'I love you, Jill.'

Bridie and Bob stepped from Molly's hall into the street. 'You've cheered yer ma up, anyway,' Bob said as he pulled his cap over his eyes. 'She's been as miserable as sin for the last few weeks.'

'Away with yer now!' Bridie said indignantly. 'It's not yerself that has to be dustin' the house every five minutes.' She turned her head and saw Jill and Steve standing under the streetlamp at the end of the street. 'Is that Jill, or are me old eyes deceiving me?'

Molly popped her head out. 'That's her all right, and Steve! Love's young dream isn't in it.'

'Ah, well,' Bridie said. 'Weren't yer young once yerself?'

'It's that long ago, Ma, I've forgotten.'

'Thanks very much!' Jack laughed. 'Was me first kiss

that exciting yer can't remember?'

'Kiss me in bed tonight, an' see if me memory returns.' Molly poked him in the ribs, bringing a grimace to his face. 'Yer'd better make it good, 'cos me memory's terrible these days.'

'I feel sorry for yer, lad,' Bob said, taking his wife's arm. 'Yer've got yer hands full with this daughter of ours.'

'I'm saying nothing.' Jack winked. 'I know which side me bread's buttered.'

Jill was the first to see her grandparents walking towards them and quickly stepped from the shelter of Steve's arms. Blushing and feeling guilty, she croaked, 'Hello, Nan, Granda!'

'Hello, me darlin'.' Bridie smiled. 'Good evening, Steve, how's the world treating you?'

'Fine, Mrs Jackson!' Feeling brave, Steve put an arm around Jill's shoulders. 'Couldn't be better.'

''Tis glad I am to hear it.' Bridie turned to Bob with a twinkle in her eye. 'D'yer not think they make a handsome couple, Bob?'

'That they do.' He gave his wife a gentle push, hinting that they should be on their way. 'Almost as handsome as we are.'

Bridie took the hint. 'It's way past our bedtime, so it is. We'll be on our way and wish you goodnight an' God bless.'

There was a tender look on Jill's face as she watched her grandparents walk up the street, arm in arm. 'They look like Darby and Joan, don't they? I love me nan and me granda. They're so kind and gentle, never raise their voices to each other.'

Steve took her hand and turned her towards home. 'We'll be like them. Never fight or argue.'

'Better not,' Jill said, as they stopped outside her door. 'Start shouting at me and you won't see me for steam . . . I'll be off!'

Steve glimpsed a figure out of the corner of his eye. 'Here's Mrs Clarke,' he whispered before stepping back.

'You're out late, Mrs Clarke,' Jill said. 'Is something wrong?'

'No more than usual.' Ellen Clarke moved the front of her coat to reveal the jug she was hiding from prying eyes. She was fed up making excuses, telling lies to cover up. What was the use? 'My feller was workin' late an' he fell asleep after 'is tea. He wasn't very happy when he woke up an' found it was nearly time for the pubs to close.' She let out a deep, weary sigh as she closed her coat. 'Of course I got the blame, as usual. I should've known he'd want to go for a drink and woken 'im up, he said. So because I didn't, and to teach me a lesson, he made me go to the pub on the corner for a jug of ale.'

Jill could think of nothing to say except, 'I'm sorry, Mrs Clarke.'

'I'll come in with yer,' Steve moved to Ellen's side, 'in case he takes off.'

'No, thanks, lad.' Ellen shook her head. 'I'll be all right, I'm used to it.' With a droop of her shoulders she walked away.

Jill and Steve watched in silence as Ellen rapped on the knocker, the sound echoing in the empty street. Then they heard the door open and a loud roar followed by a sound that sent shivers down Jill's spine. It was the sound of a heavy blow, followed by a whimper.

Steve rushed forward, but Jill grabbed his arm and held on tight. 'No, Steve! Mrs Clarke wouldn't thank you for interfering. She's the one that would suffer after you'd gone.'

Steve banged a clenched fist into his palm. 'One of these days someone is goin' to give Nobby Clarke what he deserves, an' I hope that someone is me.'

'Forget it, Steve, please?' Jill took his hand and held it between hers. 'God will pay him back.'

Steve closed his eyes and gulped in the fresh air. When his heartbeat had slowed, he gazed into Jill's anxious face. 'I swear to God I'll never lay a finger on you.' He cupped her face in his hands and kissed her lightly on the lips. 'You an' me, we'll never be like the Clarkes.'

'I know. We'll be like me mam and dad, or Nanna and Granda.'

Steve searched her face. 'Yer did it mean it when yer said yer'd marry me when we're older, didn't yer? You're the only girl for me, always 'ave been. If I can't have you, I'll never marry anyone else.'

'Steve, you're my boyfriend. There is no one else. We love each other, so let's be happy.'

When his face split into a wide grin, his dimples deepened. 'I'm the happiest feller in the whole of Liverpool.' He kissed her briefly before turning her towards the door. 'Time for you to go in before yer mam comes after me with the rollin' pin.'

Chapter Twelve

'Jack, will yer be careful, for heaven's sake? This ladder's rocking like mad!' Molly, her two hands gripping the sides of the ladder, looked up to where her husband was perched on the second rung from the top. 'Me hands are red raw, tryin' to hold it steady!'

'Molly, how the heck can I hammer nails in without moving? Stop moanin', will yer, and let me get on with the job.' Jack, hammer in hand, gazed down at the worried expression on his wife's face. 'Look, love, I've nearly finished, just two more nails.'

With its being a national holiday for the coronation, all the men were off work. They would have been happy having an extra lie-in, but their wives had other ideas. From eight o'clock the street had been a hive of activity, and while she hung on to the ladder like grim death, Molly felt a glow of pride at the result. Everywhere was a mass of red, white and blue. Bunting was stretched across the street from house to house, and even wound around the lamp posts. Union Jacks, their poles securely jammed by the window frames, swayed gently in the slight breeze that was blowing, and coloured balloons had been tied to the door knockers. In most windows there were pictures of the King and Queen and the two Princesses, Elizabeth and Margaret.

'That's it!' Jack stepped carefully down each rung of the ladder. He grinned into Molly's face. 'How about a cuppa for the workman?'

'You can make it,' she said. 'I've got too much to do.' A frown creased her forehead. 'I hope they've all done what they said they would, otherwise we'll be in queer street.'

'Molly, will yer stop being such a fuss pot? Everythin' will run like clockwork, just wait an' see.'

'Huh! It's all right for you, Jack Bennett, you wouldn't care if yer backside was on fire! There's about two hundred people in this street, countin' the kids, an' that's a lot of mouths to feed.'

'You've had parties before, for Empire Day, an' they've turned out all right. Everyone enjoyed themselves.'

'They were hit an' miss ones, where everyone brought what they wanted . . . a few cakes or sarnies. This one is different,' Molly said. 'We've been savin' up for weeks for it, an' it better be good or a few of us are goin' to have to leave town.' Her imagination took over and she could see herself running down the street, with Nellie, Mary, Vera, Lizzie and Ada hot on her heels, and their neighbours chasing them with mops and brushes.

Jack saw the amusement in Molly's eyes. 'What's the joke?'

'I'll tell yer some other time.' She scratched her head. 'What shall I do first? I know, I'll slip up to Nellie's and see where we go from here.' She walked away a few steps, then turned her head. 'Take my advice, Jack, and sit an' have yer cup of tea in peace. 'Cos in about an hour, our house is goin' to be like Casey's court.'

'Tommy, walk our Ruthie round to me ma's for us, get her from under me feet.' Molly saw rebellion on her son's face and quickly added, 'The corner shop's open, I'll give yez a penny each for sweets.'

'I'm comin' back for the party, aren't I?' Ruthie's mouth quivered. 'Me an Bella want to sit together.'

'Now, as though we'd 'ave a party without you! Of course yer comin' back! Tommy will bring yer home at two o'clock. That's when the fun starts.'

Molly watched him dragging his sister along by the hand, and could hear him threatening, 'Make a show of me, an' I'll clock yer one.'

'Tut! He'll batter 'er as soon as they turn the corner, but there's nowt I can do about it, I've got too much on me mind.'

'What d'yer want me to do?' Jack asked.

'Help me get the table into the street.' Molly whisked the oilcloth off and folded it. 'Let's turn it on its side, it's easier to get through the door.'

'Molly, I've done it before, don't forget. I'm not exactly stupid!'

'I'm sorry, love, me nerves are shattered.' She glanced at Jack and grinned. 'I'll make it up to yer later.'

'If I've got the energy,' he growled as he lowered the table on to its side. 'Yer've got me worn out.'

Molly took hold of two of the table legs, a smile on her

177

face. She had been a bit rough on him, had him running around like a blue arsed fly. But, like she said, she'd make it up to him. If she had the energy! It was no easy task getting the big, heavy table through the living room door, down the hall and into the street. Both were breathing heavily as they set it down on the pavement.

'Blimey, they've been quick!' Dozens of tables, all shapes and sizes, were standing outside, waiting to be placed in a row down the middle of the street. 'Heave ho, Jack, let's get cracking.'

As soon as the Bennetts' table was set down, all the neighbours followed, adding on to the line, regardless of whether they matched for width. Then the men disappeared. They'd done their bit, now it was down to the ladies.

Molly beckoned to the committee members and they formed a small circle. 'Now, if we all do what we said we would, our own little jobs, the tables should be well ready for two o'clock. Are we all organised?'

'Our end is,' Ada McClusky said. 'Three other women are goin' to give us a hand so we've plenty of help.'

'An' I'm so organised I'm ahead of meself.' Nellie shook with laughter. 'My feller's threatened to leave 'ome three times 'cos I haven't let him park 'is backside since he got up.'

'What about the drink?' Vera Porter asked. 'Who's seein' to that?'

'We've got the lemonade for the kids, that's in Mary's house,' Molly said. 'An' Nellie's got the barrel of ale in her yard. The men can carry it out when the kids 'ave eaten.'

'Another thing,' Vera asked, 'what about music? It's not goin' to be much of a party without music.'

Molly started to rub the side of her nose. It was a habit she'd had from when she was a kid. When she'd had her dummy taken off her, where most children suck their thumbs, Molly had taken to rubbing her nose, and the habit had stayed with her. 'We thought Corker would be home, and he'd be playin' his concertina. He said he would be, but so far there's been no sign of him.' She changed hands to rub the other side of her nose. 'We'll have to ask Tommy Wilson if he'll have a go with his mouth-organ, or get someone to bring their gramophone out. Somethin' will turn up. We'll worry about it when the time comes.'

'Yer've done well, Molly, the tables look grand.' Jack put his arm around her shoulders and squeezed. 'It was worth puttin' up with yer fussin' and yer temper.'

'Jack, I didn't do it all on me own,' she said, a happy smile on her face. 'The others did as much as me.'

But even Molly hadn't expected things to turn out so well. True, the neighbours had all coughed their money up each week without complaint, which was a surprise. But a bigger surprise was the amount of food they'd brought out today, to add to what they'd already paid for. The tables were groaning under the weight of dishes of trifle decorated with hundreds and thousands, cake stands full of jelly creams, plates piled high with fairy cakes, iced buns, and wet nellies. There were plates of brawn, egg, paste and sardine sandwiches, and sausage rolls cut in half. The children,

179

wide-eyed with amazement at the sight of so many goodies, were so overcome they made no effort to touch anything until Nellie McDonough bawled, 'Get stuck in, kids!' Then squeals of delight filled the air as the children grabbed for whatever took their fancy. The exceptions were the Clarke children. They sat like outcasts, with their heads down and hands clasped between their legs.

Molly had been keeping her eye on them. She'd had a job persuading Ellen to let them come, so she was determined they would enjoy themselves. God knows, they got little enough in life. Their dad was probably propping a bar up somewhere, spending money that should have been putting food in their bellies. She stood between two of them and said quietly, 'Come on, kids, eat as much as yez can before it all goes.' She waited until they'd got over their shyness then moved to stand behind Ruthie's chair. It was then she spotted Miss Clegg standing at her door. 'Come on, Victoria, sit down an' join the party.'

Miss Clegg shook her head. 'Let the children enjoy themselves.'

'Don't be so daft! Yer only a slip of a girl yerself, aren't yer?' Molly would have had to walk to the bottom of the street to get around the tables, so she shouted to Mary, 'Make room for Miss Clegg next to Corker's mam, she'll have someone to talk to.'

Mary didn't need asking twice. She was very fond of her neighbour, a real lady she was. And she'd insisted on contributing as much to the party collection each week as those with big families.

Victoria Clegg allowed herself to be led to a seat, even though the noise of the children was deafening. It was nice to be included, made to feel wanted. Heaven knows, she spent enough time on her own. Hers was a lonely life, especially since that fall she'd had. It had left her unsteady on her feet, and the furthest she walked was to the corner shop. The neighbours were good, though, she didn't know how she'd manage without them. Every day one of them called, without fail, to see what shopping she needed.

'Molly!'

Molly turned her head to see Nellie doing a little jig as she pointed down the street. And when she saw the cause of her friend's excitement, Molly let out a shout of delight. Strolling up the street, a huge grin on his face, his seaman's bag slung casually over his shoulder, was Corker.

'Boy, am I glad to see you!' Suddenly the weight of worrying whether everyone enjoyed the party was lifted from Molly's shoulders. With Corker there, playing his concertina and singing sea shanties, it couldn't fail to be a success.

Molly didn't know how right she was about Nobby Clarke. When the Black Horse pub by Walton Church opened its doors, Nobby was leaning against the wall waiting to be let in. To hell with their stupid street parties, he thought, I'll celebrate in my own way. He had it all planned out. Start at the Black Horse, then a pint in as many pubs as he could get to before they put the towels on. Then home for a bite to eat and a few hours'

181

kip until it was opening time again and he could meet up with his cronies down at the local.

There were a lot of pubs on the stretch of road Nobby had chosen, and even with his capacity for ale, that was a lot of pints. His eyes were becoming blurred, his steps unsteady. Several angry remarks were shouted after him by people he barged into without a backward glance or an apology. But he was so drunk he was incapable of thinking straight. It was pure instinct that took him staggering into a small pub on County Road, where the barman took just one look before giving the aye-aye to the manager who was standing at the far end of the bar talking to two of his regular customers.

'Leave it to me, Ted,' the manager said, 'I'll deal with him.'

Nobby was holding on to the bar for support, his head lolling, spittle running from the corners of his mouth. His glazed eyes tried to focus on the man behind the bar. 'P-p-pint – bither.'

'I'm sorry, sir, I can't serve you. You've had enough, and I think you should go home.'

Nobby's chin fell on to the counter. He tried to speak but the sounds that came from his mouth were unintelligible, like those of an animal. The manager shrugged his shoulders. 'Give us a hand to get him outside, Ted, otherwise he's either going to conk out or be sick all over the place. And I'm not having him do either, not in here.'

Taking an arm each, the men lifted Nobby's feet from the floor and carried him out of the pub to prop him up against the wall outside.

'Wait till his wife gets a load of him,' Ted laughed, 'she'll flay him alive. I know my missus would.'

The manager wiped his hands down his trouser legs, a look of disgust on his face. 'Why do some men never know when they've had enough?'

Jimmy Pearson was driving his Green Goddess tram down County Road. It was his usual number twenty-two route, from Fazakerley terminus to the Pier Head. He liked his job, did Jimmy, but today he was feeling hard done by. All the factories and shops were shut down for the national holiday, but a skeleton bus and tram service was running, and it was just his luck to have been one of the drivers told to turn in. He could see everyone enjoying themselves at the street parties taking place in all the little side streets, dancing and singing away to beat the band, and here he was, driving a flaming tram! Still, he knocked off at five, there'd still be enough time to join in the fun.

Jimmy could see a stop coming up and turned the handle on the brake. Two passengers got on, and Jimmy waited for the conductor to press the bell before setting the tram in motion. A new King, eh? he was thinking. Wonder what he's like? Not that it would make much difference to the ordinary people in the street, they weren't likely to ever set eyes on him.

'Be glad to get to the depot for a cuppa, me mouth's as dry as emery paper.'

Jimmy's eyes swivelled to the platform where the conductor, Johnny, was standing. 'Aye, I could do with a drink meself. An' I don't mean tea, either!'

'Never mind, we'll get a few jars in when we get home.' Johnny laughed as he nodded to the street they were passing where a noisy party was in full swing. 'This lot 'ave got a head start on us, though.' He turned his head just in time to see a man stagger into the middle of the road, right in front of the tram. 'Look out, Jimmy!'

But Jimmy had already seen the man and was turning the brake handle as quick as he could. 'Bloody fool! Walked right into us!'

The tables had been cleared away, all except one which was left for the barrel of beer to stand on, next to bottles of port and sherry. A sturdy stool had been found for Corker to sit on, and with his huge hands through the leather straps at each end of his concertina, he started the party in earnest. The children sat at his feet, drawn to him like a magnet. He wasn't like anyone else they knew. With his ruddy complexion, twinkling blue eyes, bushy beard and moustache, his sailor's hat perched on the back of his head, and the size of a giant, to the children he was larger than life, just like the Sinbad in their story books. A chair had been placed near Corker for Miss Clegg, and she was clearly enjoying herself. With a glass of port in her hand, she hummed along to the tunes of 'Rose of Tralee', 'When Irish Eyes Are Smiling', and 'Old-Fashioned Mother Of Mine'.

'Someone's enjoying herself.' Molly was standing with Nellie and Mary, while their husbands acted as barmen. 'It'll do 'er the world of good.'

'Another couple of drinks, then I'll start to enjoy

meself.' Nellie took Molly's empty glass. 'I'll fill us up. What about you, Mary?'

'No, I'll wait till our Bella's in bed, then I can really let meself go. I'll give her another half hour, then it's be-bye-beddy-byes for her.'

'Yeah, that goes for our Ruthie, too.' Molly glanced across to where Ellen Clarke was standing near her door with her four children. 'It's lousy for those kids, yer know. They don't even know 'ow to enjoy themselves.'

'I know, I've been watchin' them,' Nellie said. 'Scared of their own shadow, they are.'

'Tell yer what, Nellie, bring a drink back for Ellen. I'll get 'er an' the kids over here.'

'Aye, aye, boss!' Nellie said, performing a very nifty twirl for someone her size. 'Anythin' yer say, boss!'

'She's two sheets to the wind, that one,' Molly laughed, 'but I think the world of 'er.' She patted Mary's arm. 'I won't be a tick.'

Molly stood in front of Ellen. 'Come an' have a drink with us, Ellen, an' let the kids sit an' listen to Corker.'

She drew back. 'We're all right 'ere, honest.'

'Speak for yerself, Ellen! The kids would love to watch Sinbad, wouldn't yer, kids?'

Four pairs of eyes turned to their mother. 'Can we, Mam?' Phoebe asked. Ellen saw Molly put her hands on her hips, and knew her neighbour was ready to do battle if she refused. 'Okay, but behave yerselves.'

'Right, that's them sorted out. Now for you.' Molly linked arms with Ellen and practically dragged her towards where Mary and Nellie were standing. 'Nellie, did yer get a drink for Ellen?'

'Sure did, kiddo!' Nellie handed the glass over. 'Here's mud in yer eye, Ellen!'

When Jack came over to say he'd take Ruthie in and put her to bed, Ellen said she'd take her two youngest in. After two glasses of sherry she was much more relaxed and talkative, and when Molly told her to come back when she'd got the kids to bed, she agreed.

'Your Jill and our Steve are enjoyin' themselves,' Nellie said. 'Neither of them can dance, but they're havin' a go.'

'That's one thing our Doreen's better at than Jill,' Molly said. 'Look at the state of 'er an' that boy from down the street, they look as though they were born dancin'.'

'Yeah, she's got rhythm all right, your Doreen.' Nellie ran a podgy finger round the rim of her glass, watching Molly under lowered lids. 'How d'yer feel about bein' our Steve's ma-in-law, kid, 'cos I think that's the way it's goin'?'

'Nellie, I'd be over the moon! If I had to choose someone for 'er, your Steve would be me first choice. I think he's a cracker.' Molly's chest heaved as she let out an exaggerated sigh. 'Of course it would mean 'aving you in the family, but there's always a sting in the tail, isn't there?'

'Yer cheeky sod! I'll have you know your daughter would be marrying into a well-to-do family.' Nellie stuck her nose in the air and struck up a haughty pose that she thought matched her posh accent. 'We're not your plain common or garden riff-raff, you know.' Her nose went even higher. 'In fact, if my son marries your daughter,

I'll expect her to come with a dowry.'

'Oh, rest assured my daughter won't come empty-handed.' Molly matched the accent. 'We've got an heirloom been in the family for years, that will be her dowry.' Molly burst out laughing. 'It's that aspidistra plant I've got on me sideboard.'

Just then Corker started on 'My Old Man, Said Follow the Van', and Molly grabbed Nellie's hand. 'Come on, let's join in the fun.'

Corker's weatherbeaten face broke into a huge grin when he saw Molly and Nellie, their arms around each other's waists, kicking their legs in the air and singing at the top of their voices. He went straight into 'Maybe It's Because I'm a Londoner', and by this time everyone was doing their own version of a jig.

Jack stood on the edge of the crowd, next to Nellie's husband, George. 'Just look at the state of them! It's surprising what a few drinks can do, isn't it?'

'My one's showing everythin' she's got.' George doubled up with laughter. 'One leg of her drawers is hangin' down.'

'I don't think that'll bother her,' Jack said. 'She's enjoyin' herself too much.'

'Ooh, I've had it!' Molly stopped, gasping for breath. 'I'm gettin' too old for this lark.'

'Go on, yer can't take it!' Nellie danced on, her hands on her wide hips, her mountainous bosom floating up and down. One by one the neighbours dropped out and formed a circle around her, clapping and egging her on. But Corker noted Nellie's red face, and the rivulets of sweat running from her forehead down her cheeks and neck into the valley between her breasts. She's had enough, he thought, but won't give in. I'll let her keep her pride and pack in meself.

'Right, that's yer lot!' As he laid his concertina down at the side of the stool he heard rumblings of disappointment. 'Oh, I'll be back after I've 'ad a pint, don't worry. Give yez time to get yer second wind back.'

Corker downed the pint without taking the glass from his lips, and Jack shook his head in amazement. He'd never seen that before, even from Corker. As the big man ran his tongue over his lips and moustache, he let out a sigh of satisfaction. 'I needed that, me throat's sore with all that singing.'

'I'll get yer another one.' Jack took the empty glass and turned to the table where the now almost empty barrel stood. He turned the small tap on and looked around as he waited for the glass to fill. It was then he saw the policeman walking up the street. 'There's a bobby comin', Corker, I think he's come to complain about the noise.' Jack was laughing as he turned the tap off. 'It must be your voice . . . like a foghorn, it is.'

Molly watched the policeman's approach with interest. It wasn't often they saw a bobby in their street. She saw him stop by Lizzie Furlong, then Lizzie pointing to the group standing near Corker.

'Mrs Clarke?' The young, fresh-faced policeman looked at Molly.

'No, she's just gone in the house, taken her children in.' Molly's brows lifted in apprehension. What on earth did he want Ellen for?

'Which house is it?'

'Two doors up.' Molly had the feeling that the serious expression on the constable's face meant he was the bringer of bad news. 'Is something wrong?'

The bobby hesitated. 'Do you know Mrs Clarke well?'

''Course I do! We've been neighbours for years!'

'What is it, lad?' Corker asked. 'Is it trouble?'

'I'm afraid so. Her husband's been in an accident.'

Molly gasped. 'Oh, my God! Is he hurt bad?'

'Look, I think I'd better talk to Mrs Clarke.' The constable adjusted the helmet strap under his chin. 'Perhaps you'd come in with me? She might be glad of someone she knows being there.'

'I'll come.' Corker handed his glass to Jack. 'I've known her all me life.'

'No!' Molly said quickly. 'Me an' Nellie will go. Better for Ellen to 'ave a woman there.'

By now the news had trickled through the crowd and there was complete silence as the trio walked through the open door of the Clarkes' house.

Ten minutes later Molly appeared, white-faced. 'Nobby's in 'ospital. He was run over by a tram.'

'How bad is he?' It was Corker who asked.

'It's serious from what the policeman said. Ellen's got to go to the 'ossie right away. Me an' Nellie are goin' with her, so will yer see to everythin' for us, Jack? I don't know 'ow long we'll be away.'

'Didn't the policeman say how it happened?' Corker asked. 'It seems strange to be run over by a tram.'

Molly gazed at the faces of those standing near. 'Will yez come inside while I get me coat?'

In private Molly told Jack, George and Corker all she knew. 'He was blind drunk from all accounts. Walked straight in front of the tram. The driver had no chance. Apparently the poor bugger's in hospital 'imself, suffering from shock. It happened hours ago, but nobody knew who Nobby was! All he 'ad on him was a wage packet, an' the police had trouble gettin' in touch with the firm to find out where he lived.' She paused for breath. 'Nobby's in a bad way. The tram went over 'is legs.'

'How's Ellen takin' it?' Jack asked.

'I wouldn't know! She's sittin' like a statue, not sayin' a word! Me an' Nellie had to ask all the questions.'

'She's in shock,' Corker said. 'It affects yer like that.'

Jill came bursting into the room, followed by Steve. 'What's up, Mam?'

Molly told her daughter just as much as she thought she should know. 'Would you go in an' sit with the two girls, love? God alone knows 'ow long Ellen will be away.'

'We'll stay with them, won't we, Steve?'

'Yeah, all night if need be.' He put his arm around Jill's waist. 'Tell Mrs Clarke not to worry about them, we'll make sure they're all right.'

'I'd better get back.' Molly tutted as she looked at her reflection in the mirror. 'I look a mess, but I'll 'ave to do. This is no time to be worryin' about me appearance.'

Corker put a ten shilling note in her hand. 'Give this to Ellen in case she needs it. Tell her to get a taxi home.'

'Ta very much, Corker.' Molly slipped her arms into her coat. 'I'll see yez as soon as we can get away. Depends on what we find when we get to the 'ossie. Me an' Nellie will stay for as long as Ellen needs us.'

Chapter Thirteen

Molly pulled Ellen to a halt outside a door at the end of the long hospital corridor. 'The Almoner's office, where the feller said yer should come.' She looked over Ellen's head at Nellie, who was holding on to Ellen's other arm. 'D'yer think they'll let us go in with 'er?'

'Don't ask me, I 'aven't got a clue!' Nellie's eyes rolled upwards. This silence of Ellen's was getting her down, it wasn't natural. She hadn't spoken one word on the way down, shown no emotion whatsoever. With her face set, her eyes blank, and her tongue silent, it was as though she'd been turned into a zombie. 'Perhaps Ellen would rather go in on 'er own?'

'No! I want yez to come with me.' Ellen still didn't turn her head. 'If they'll let yez.'

'Only one way to find out.' Molly rapped with her knuckles, waited for a voice to answer, then turned the knob and poked her head around the door. 'Mrs Clarke's 'ere. Her 'usband was in an accident.'

The Almoner looked up from the papers on her desk. 'Ask her to come in, please.'

'Is it all right for me an' another neighbour to come in

191

with 'er? She's in a bad state, yer see.'

When the Almoner nodded, Molly opened the door wide and pushed Ellen through. 'Sit down, Mrs Clarke.' A hand holding a pen pointed to a chair on the opposite side of the desk. When Ellen didn't move, Molly gently put an arm around her waist and led her forward. 'Sit down, Ellen, me an' Nellie will be right behind yer.'

Beatrice Pritchard had been Almoner at Walton Hospital for more years than she cared to remember. She was a spinster, still living with her parents in their comfortable home in Wavertree, but her single status was not due to lack of admirers. She was a fine-looking woman, was Beatrice, and many men had pursued her with marriage in mind, only to find she was wedded to her job. She rested her elbows on the desk and faced Ellen.

'You've been told what happened, Mrs Clarke?'

Ellen gave a curt nod, her eyes fixed on a notice on the wall.

'Your husband was very seriously injured and I'm afraid the doctor holds out little hope of his recovering.' Beatrice waited for some sign that her words had registered. When none came, she turned her hazel eyes to Molly and Nellie. 'Has Mrs Clarke any family?'

'She's got four children,' Molly told her, 'but as for other family, yer know, like parents or sisters and brothers, I honestly couldn't tell yer 'cos she's never mentioned any.'

The Almoner's gaze went back to Ellen, sitting stony-faced, her hands clasped tightly in her lap. 'Mr Clarke is in the operating theatre now, and I really don't know how long it will be before you're allowed to see him. You might have a long wait.'

'I've got to get 'ome to me children.' Ellen suddenly came alive. 'I can't leave them, they're too young.'

'Can't one of the neighbours see to them? I think you should stay, your husband's condition is critical.'

'We'll see to the kids, Ellen,' Nellie said, as Molly nodded her head vigorously in agreement. 'They'll come to no 'arm.'

'No, I'm goin' 'ome!' Ellen's lips formed a straight, determined line. 'I can't do nothin' here, an' I want to be with me children.'

Years of experience and observation had given Beatrice the ability to size people up, see things other people didn't. Like the shabbily dressed, undernourished, pathetic creature sitting across the desk from her now. A typical downtrodden wife, if she'd ever seen one. All her spirit and pride knocked out of her by a bullying, drunken husband. She hadn't seen Mr Clarke but the police officer had passed on all the details of the incident. According to eye witnesses, the man was so drunk he was staggering all over the road. And the manager of a nearby pub, brought out by the commotion, told how he'd refused to serve the man because in his opinion he had had far too much to drink.

'Are you on the phone?' Even as the words left her mouth, Beatrice was cursing herself for asking such a stupid question. It was obvious the woman didn't have two ha'pennies to rub together, never mind the luxury of a telephone. Her tone gentle now, she said, 'If your husband's condition deteriorates, we will need to contact you.'

'Our corner shop 'as a telephone,' Molly said. 'Maisie wouldn't mind yer ringin' there. I can give yer 'er number.'

The Almoner wrote the number down, then excused herself. 'Mr Clarke had a few things in his pockets, I'll get them for you.' She touched Ellen's arm briefly before hurrying from the room.

'I think yer should stay, Ellen,' Molly said. 'Me an' Nellie would see to the kids for yer.'

'No!' she spat. 'The sooner I get out of this place the better.'

Molly pulled a face at Nellie, then sat in silence until the Almoner returned. 'There wasn't much, I'm afraid. His clothes had to be cut from him.' Beatrice put some loose change on the desk, and an empty wage packet. 'If you don't hear anything tonight, I suggest you come back first thing in the morning.'

Ellen scooped the change up and put it in her pocket. Then she reached for the wage packet. After a quick glance, that too was pushed into her pocket. Then she stood up. 'Thank you, miss, I'll be goin' now.'

'My name's Miss Pritchard, Mrs Clarke, and if you need any help you know where to find me. I do hope there's better news for you tomorrow.'

'Ay, you, yer cheated!' Phoebe glared across the table at her sister. They were playing snakes and ladders with Jill and Steve, and Dorothy, who had rolled the dice to four, had moved her counter five places so she could go up a ladder.

'I didn't cheat!' Dorothy shouted, her face flushed

with guilt. 'Yer a fibber, our Phoebe!'

'I'm not a fibber.' Phoebe looked across at Steve. 'You saw 'er, didn't yer?'

Steve scratched behind his ear, a smile hovering on his lips. He hadn't been watching when Dorothy made her move, his eyes had been on Jill. 'I wasn't counting.'

'Me neither,' Jill said, then noting Phoebe's rebellious face, added, 'Tell you what, you have a free roll, Phoebe, in case Dorothy did make a mistake.'

With a smug smile of satisfaction, Phoebe picked up the egg-cup used for throwing the dice. She gave it a good shake, then stayed her hand. Her head tilted to one side, she asked, 'Are you two goin' out together?'

'Yes,' Steve said proudly, reaching for Jill's hand. 'She's me girlfriend, aren't yer, Jill?'

The game forgotten, Dorothy put her hands on the table and rested her chin on them. She thought Jill looked like a fairy princess with her long blonde hair and pretty face. 'Are yez gettin' married?'

'Not for a long time,' Jill laughed. 'I'm not sixteen yet.'

'Yer will be in a few weeks,' Steve reminded. 'And I'll be seventeen.'

'Can I come to yer weddin'?' Phoebe asked, her eyes round. 'I've never been to a wedding.'

'It's a long way off,' Jill laughed. Then, gazing at the two thin faces watching her hopefully, she added, 'Of course you can come to our wedding, can't they, Steve?'

His heart was nearly bursting with happiness. He felt like hugging Phoebe for bringing the subject up. Every night in bed he dreamed of the day he and Jill would marry, but there was no one he could talk to about it. 'Yer can both come as our invited guests.'

Their differences forgotten, Phoebe and Dorothy faced each other, eyes shining, their laughter filling the room. 'Ooh, the gear!' Phoebe's face was transformed. Fancy that now, being invited as a guest! Then her brow puckered. 'Can me mam come, as well?'

How different she looks when she smiles, Jill was thinking. She's really quite pretty. 'There's a long way to go yet, but yes, your mam can come as well.'

'Yippee!' Dorothy punched the air. 'Just wait till we tell 'er.'

'In the meanwhile,' Steve said, 'can we get on with the game? It shouldn't take too long, I've only got two matchsticks left.'

'That's because our Dorothy's been cheatin'.' But there was no animosity in Phoebe's voice, she was feeling happier than she'd ever felt. To be able to play games and talk without being shouted at, or getting a clip around the ear, was new to her. She would treasure the memory of this night, she thought as she tossed the dice. And when it rolled to a six, her cup of happiness was overflowing.

'Have they behaved themselves?' was the first thing Ellen asked when she walked into the room, followed by Molly and Nellie.

'Yeah, we've 'ad a smashin' time,' Steve said. 'Haven't we, kids?'

'I won nearly all the games, Mam,' Dorothy said, a grin covering her face. 'Look 'ow many matchsticks I've got.'

'Yer'd better get home, Jill, an' you, Steve.' The look on Molly's face told her daughter not to ask any questions. 'It's work tomorrow, don't forget.'

'Ah, ray, can't we finish the game?' Phoebe begged. 'It won't take long.'

It didn't go unnoticed by Molly or Nellie that neither of the girls asked about their father. It's a funny how-d'yer-do, Molly thought as she saw Jill and Steve out. 'I won't be long, but tell yer dad to go to bed if he's tired.'

'How is Mr Clarke?' Steve asked.

Molly pulled a face. 'Ask yer mam, she'll tell yer. Now, poppy off an' get some sleep.'

Steve cupped Jill's elbow. 'I'll see Jill home.'

'Blimey, it's only next door! Oh, go on then,' Molly laughed as she stepped back into Ellen's hall, 'but make it snappy, she needs her beauty sleep.'

As she was closing the door, Molly saw Steve put his arms around Jill and heard him say, 'She doesn't, yer know. She couldn't be more beautiful than she is now.'

'What it is to be young,' Molly muttered softly as she made her way down the dingy hall with its peeling paper and scuffed brown paintwork. 'He's a cracker, though, an' I love the bones of him.'

When Ellen took the girls up to bed, Molly and Nellie went into the kitchen to make a cup of tea. 'We'll stay and 'ave a drink with 'er,' Molly said as she filled the battered kettle. 'I don't like the way she's actin', it just ain't natural.'

'It's a rum do, if yer ask me,' Nellie huffed as she opened cupboard doors. 'They've got me fair flummoxed, an' that's a fact. The girls didn't even ask after Nobby.'

'Aye, well, perhaps if we 'ad to live with 'im, we'd understand. God forgive me for sayin' so, but he's a right bastard, is Nobby. No one knows what his family 'as to go through.'

'There's no sugar.' Nellie closed a cupboard door. 'An' there's no fresh milk, only conny-onny.'

'Beggars can't be choosers, Nellie! Just grin an' bear it, like Ellen 'as to every day of 'er life.'

Ellen's face was drawn when she came down, but at least she was talking. 'We won't forget the King's coronation in a hurry, will we? Nobby certainly knows 'ow to pick his time.'

'Sit down and 'ave a drink.' Molly pulled out a chair facing Ellen. 'Now there's only me an' Nellie, yer can relax, tell us 'ow yer feel.'

'I don't feel anythin', an' that's the truth,' Ellen said. 'I'm just numb.'

Molly's tummy balked when she picked up the cup. It was minus a handle and there were dozens of brown-stained chips around the rim. But she forced herself to take a sip of the sickly sweet tea. 'Me an' Nellie are worried stiff about yer. It's not natural, the way yer behavin'. Why don't yer let yerself go an' have a good cry?'

'What for?' Ellen delved into her pocket and placed the wage packet in front of Molly. 'Take a look at that, an' then yer'll know why I've no tears to shed for Nobby Clarke.'

Puzzled, Molly picked up the packet. 'Three pounds, twelve an' six, it says here.'

Ellen's laugh was bitter. 'He gives me one pound

fifteen shillings to keep the six of us, an' keeps more than that in 'is pocket every week to pay for 'is gee-gees, beer and ciggies.'

Nellie gasped. 'That's not all 'e gives yer, surely?'

'No, I'm tellin' lies, it's not all he gives me.' Again the bitter laugh. 'He gives me a belt every time 'e passes me, just for the fun of it.'

'Tut, tut.' Nellie's finger was pushing dents in the fat on her elbows. 'He should be ashamed of 'imself.'

'So don't expect me to cry for Nobby, I've shed enough tears over 'im.' Ellen banged her cup down, her face flushed with anger. 'I couldn't afford to pay anythin' towards the party today 'cos I'm always skint, but Nobby's been out every night this week, comin' home drunk. And he got so plastered today, he walked in front of a flamin' tram! Must 'ave cost 'im a pretty penny to do that 'cos he can certainly hold 'is ale. So while he's been livin' the life of Riley, me neighbours 'ave 'ad to pay towards givin' his kids a bit of pleasure.'

It was shame that finally broke Ellen. Her head dropped and sobs racked her body. Molly and Nellie were round the table in a trice.

'There now,' Nellie said, 'it'll do yer good to 'ave a cry.'

'Yes,' Molly agreed. 'Get it all out of yer system.'

Ellen raised her tear-stained face. 'These tears aren't for Nobby, I'm not such a hypocrite. They're for all the years I've had to put up with 'is violence. Havin' me pride beaten out of me, an' havin' to live in a muck midden like this 'cos I can't afford any better on the pittance he gives me. Seein' me kids being knocked around if they look sideways at him, an' sendin' them out to school in the mornings with their bellies empty.' She gulped to clear her throat. 'I know yez'll think I'm terrible, and may God forgive me for sayin' it, but I 'ope he doesn't get better.'

Molly knelt down by the side of the chair and gathered the broken woman to her breast. Rocking her like a baby, she stroked the lank hair. 'My heart goes out to yer, Ellen, you an' the kids.'

Nellie was standing near, tears running down her face. 'Don't you worry about God forgivin' yer, girl. He's not soft. He knows everythin' that goes on. It's Nobby what should be worryin'.'

'Look, Ellen, pull yerself together, go to bed and try to get some sleep.' Molly lumbered to her feet. 'Me an' Nellie will nip up to Maisie's and let 'er know, just in case the 'ospital rings.'

'Okay.' Ellen pushed her chair back. 'An' ta, both of yez. I don't know what I'd 'ave done without yez.'

'If yer want me in the night, just knock,' Molly said. 'If not, I'll be here first thing, just as soon as I've seen to Ruthie.'

'Don't bother comin' to the door with us, we'll see ourselves out.'

Nellie patted Ellen's thin arm. 'You take care of yerself, girl. Goodnight, an' God bless.'

After taking Ruthie over to Mary Watson's the next morning, Molly flicked a duster around the furniture and rinsed the dishes. Speaking to the empty room, she said, 'I'll give meself a quick cat's lick an' a promise, then go an' see Ellen.' But as she was running a comb through her hair, the knocker sounded. 'Oh, God, she must 'ave heard from the 'ospital.' Her tummy doing somersaults, Molly dashed along the hall. 'Corker! Am I glad to see you!'

Gabbling fifteen to the dozen, she related all that had happened. Then, after a slight pause to catch her breath, she said, 'I'm just goin' to see Ellen now.'

'I'll come with you.' Corker stroked his beard as he watched Molly slip into her coat. 'Doesn't 'ave much of a life, does she?'

'Yer can say that again! It's not a life, it's a bloody existence!'

When Ellen saw Corker her face flushed. She would have kept them standing on the step but Molly brushed her aside. 'Not heard anythin' then, Ellen?'

She shook her head. 'I'm just gettin' ready to go to the 'ospital. I couldn't go earlier, 'cos I had the kids to see to.'

'I'm comin' with yer,' Molly told her. 'I've got the dinner ready for puttin' on.'

'No, I'll go,' Corker said quietly. 'May as well make meself useful, seein' as I'm home for a week.'

'I'll be all right on me own!' Ellen cried. Her hands were shaking and she tried to control them by folding her arms. 'I can manage. No one 'as to come with me.'

'I know I don't have to, Ellen, but I want to.' Corker pushed his cap to the back of his head. 'After all, what are friends for?'

Molly gave her a push in the back. 'Get crackin', Ellen!' But when she didn't move, Molly tutted in exasperation as she went into the hall. 'Here's yer coat. Now, for cryin' out loud, will yer move!'

Ellen's whole body started to shake. 'I'm frightened.'

'Get us a glass or a cup.' Corker jerked his head at Molly. When she came back he reached into his inside pocket, brought out a small bottle of whisky and poured a fair measure into the cup. 'Get that down yer, girl, it'll steady yer nerves.'

Ellen screwed up her face as the fiery liquid slid down her throat. She coughed and spluttered, but with Molly standing over her she knew she had no option but to empty the cup.

'There now, yer'll soon feel better.' Corker put the cork back in the bottle and placed it on the table. 'That's for when we come back. Now, are yer ready?'

Ellen's lips quivered. 'What will the neighbours think?'

'Sod the bloody neighbours!' Corker put a hand to his mouth. 'Excuse my language, ladies, it slipped out. But honestly, Ellen, the way yer behavin' would make a saint swear.'

Molly was standing outside her door watching them walk down the street when Nellie came up behind her. 'No news yet, kid?'

'Not a dickie bird! I was goin' with Ellen, but Corker insisted.' The corners of Molly's mouth curved upwards into a smile. 'They look a scream, don't they? She's so small, not a pick on her, an' Corker's the size of a flippin' house!'

'Aye, I'd want 'im on my side in a fight,' Nellie said. Then a look of concern crossed her face. 'I wonder what they'll find when they get to the 'ossie?'

'I dunno!' Molly sighed. 'Come an' have a cuppa with me, Nellie, I'm feelin' down in the dumps. See if yer can think of somethin' funny to cheer me up.'

'Well,' said Nellie, following Molly down the hall, ''ave yer heard the one about the Englishman, the Irishman and the Scotsman . . .'

An hour later Molly was seeing Nellie out when a taxi drew up outside and Ellen and Corker stepped out. 'My God, yer've been quick!'

'We managed to flag the taxi down outside the hospital,' Corker said, 'an' it only took five minutes to get us home.'

'Are yez comin' in for a drink?' Molly asked. 'The kettle's on the hob.'

Ellen shook her head, wrapping her faded coat closely around her thin body. 'Not me, I've got a lot of washin' to do.'

Molly's mouth dropped. 'Aren't yer even goin' to tell us 'ow Nobby is?'

Corker chipped in, 'That's all right, Ellen, you go 'ome. I'll let them know how things are.'

A vision flashed through Nellie's mind of the dirty clothes piled up on the kitchen floor waiting to be washed, but she quickly dismissed it. Half an hour wasn't going to make much difference, and she was eager to know how Nobby was.

'He's in a bad way.' Corker took his cap off and sat down. 'They had to amputate both his legs.'

'Oh, dear God!' Molly gasped, her face the colour of chalk. 'Poor Ellen.'

203

'That's why I told her to go home. I didn't want her to 'ave to go through it all again.' Corker took a packet of Capstan from his pocket and struck a match. He inhaled deeply before meeting the eyes of Molly and Nellie. 'He's in a hell of a state, I can't see him pullin' through.'

'Oh, no!' Molly's breath caught in her throat. 'I'm not goin' to pretend I like Nobby, but I wouldn't wish that on me worst enemy.'

'Me neither,' Nellie said, biting on her bottom lip. 'It must 'ave been terrible for Ellen, seein' him like that.'

'We were only allowed in with him for a couple of minutes, an' there's so much paraphernalia around the bed, we couldn't get near. He's unconscious, didn't know we were there.' Corker drew on his cigarette. 'I had a word with one of the doctors an' he doesn't hold out much hope. In fact, although I don't want yer to tell Ellen this, the doctor said it would be a blessin' if he died without regaining consciousness. He'll have no life if he does pull through, won't be able to do a thing for 'imself.'

'Is Ellen goin' in tonight?' Molly asked. 'Me an' Nellie will go with 'er, won't we, Nellie? I'll ask Jill an' Steve to sit with 'er kids.'

'She can go in any time, 'cos Nobby's on the critical list. I've told her there's no point in goin' in until somethin' happens, one way or the other, but I think she feels she should go.' Corker looked from Molly to Nellie. 'Whatever happens, Ellen's goin' to need friends.' A smile lit up his ruddy face. 'I'm glad that with you two around she won't have far to look for them.'

204

'Jill, will yer do us a favour, sunshine?' The family were seated around the table having their evening meal, and all eyes turned to Molly. 'Will you an' Steve sit with Ellen's kids again? She'll put the young ones to bed, so it's only Phoebe and Dorothy. Yez don't mind, do yez?'

'No, of course not.' Jill lowered her head to hide a smile, but she wasn't quick enough for her mother.

Blimey, Molly thought, I'm not asking her a favour, I'm giving her one! Still, they don't get much time on their own, only when they go to the flicks. If we had a parlour house now, they'd have somewhere to do their courting.

'Can I go next door, Mam?' Ruthie put on her innocent face. 'I'd be good.'

'Can yer heckers like! By the time I go out, you'll be fast asleep in the land of nod.'

Jack leaned across and smiled into his daughter's disappointed face. 'I'll put you to bed, eh? And I'll read yer one of yer fairy stories.'

That did the trick. Ruthie beamed. 'Will yer read me *Jack and the Beanstalk*, Dad?'

'Anythin' for a quiet life, sunshine.' Jack held a bone from the sheet of spare ribs between his fingers and inspected it, hoping to find a piece of meat he'd missed. But it was as clean as a whistle. 'As I say, anythin' for a quiet life.'

'Are you goin' out, Doreen?' Molly called from the kitchen.

'I'm meetin' Maureen, we're goin' for a walk to see all the street decorations.'

'In by ten o'clock, mind!' Molly came through and

started to clear the table. 'None of this half past ten lark, like it was on Monday, d'yer hear?'

'All right, Mam, keep yer hair on! I'm not deaf!'

'None of yer lip, young lady, or yer'll be feelin' the back of me hand.' Molly wagged a warning finger at her daughter before ruffling Tommy's hair. 'And you, young feller-me-lad, be in this 'ouse by nine o'clock or else there'll be trouble.'

'Aye, aye, sir!' Tommy gave a smart salute, a cheeky grin on his face. 'Yer'd make a good sergeant-major, Mam!'

'Perhaps I should join the army, then!' Molly chuckled. 'You lot wouldn't know what had hit yez! No dinner on the table, no beds made . . . oh, yer'd love that.'

'I wouldn't be here to see it, love,' Jack said. 'You join the army, I join the army.'

'We all would,' Doreen said. 'Where you go, we all go.'

Molly hummed a little tune as she carried the plates through to the kitchen and slid them into the soapy water in the sink. It was nice to get a compliment now and again, even if it was a back-handed one. She was lucky where her family were concerned. There was many a woman in Liverpool who'd swap places with her, given the chance.

Molly took her hand out of the water to rub the side of her nose. 'No, I've got nothing to complain about. True, I lose me rag with them sometimes, which is only natural 'cos they're not angels, but I'm not so daft I don't know when I'm well off.'

'Did yer say something, love?' Jack called.

Molly shook the water from her hands before sticking her head round the door. She gave her husband a broad wink before saying, 'I'm havin' a private conversation with the only sensible person in the house . . . meself!'

Chapter Fourteen

'Mam!' Jill burst into the room, her face radiant. 'I passed me exams!'

'Ooh, the gear!' Molly dropped the blouse she was sewing to run to her daughter. Her arms clasped tightly around the slim waist, she jumped up and down, raining noisy kisses on Jill's happy face. 'That's marvellous, sunshine, I'm so pleased for yer.'

Jack was standing behind his wife, a smile of pride and satisfaction lighting up his handsome face. 'I'm delighted, love.' He cupped her face in his hands. 'Mind you, I knew yer would, never had any doubts.'

'Full marks I got, for me typing and shorthand.' Jill took an envelope from her bag. 'And I've got a certificate to prove it.'

Steve had followed Jill into the room and stood looking on, a grin on his face. 'Isn't she clever, Mrs Bennett?'

'Yer can say that again!' Molly reached once more for her daughter and held her in a bear hug.

'Mam, you're strangling me, I can't breathe!' Jill was grinning from ear to ear as she disentangled herself from her mother's arms. 'No more night school.'

Molly winked at Steve. 'I wonder who she takes after? Not me, that's for sure.'

'No, she takes after her father's side,' Jack said, then ducked when Molly threw a cushion at him. 'All my family were brainy.'

'Oh, aye, clever clogs!' Molly's mind was working hard to find the right reply. 'If yer so clever, 'ow d'yer spell encyclopaedia?'

'You think I can't, don't yer?' Jack let out a hearty chuckle. 'Tell yer what, you write it down an' I'll tell yer if yer right.'

'Ha, ha, very funny! Why don't yer admit yer as thick as two short planks, like me?' There was pride and love in the gaze Molly turned on her daughter. 'What yer goin' to do now, sunshine, look for an office job?'

'I don't know what to do.' Jill pulled a face. 'I love working at Allerton's, I'd be sad to leave. And Mr John's been so good to me, I'd feel mean.'

'He's one in a million, yer'll go a long way to get a boss like 'im,' Molly agreed. 'But he'd understand if yer were leavin' to better yerself.'

'No use wasting what yer've worked two years for,' Jack said. 'Get yerself a decent job and do somethin' with yer life.'

Molly glanced at Steve out of the corner of her eye. Jack's remark had taken the smile off his face. He's probably worried, Molly thought, in case Jill goes up in the world and thinks she's too good for him. But my daughter's not like that. She thinks the world of him, and nothing will change that.

'Steve wants me to go up to his, to tell his mam and dad.' Jill smiled at him. 'Shall we go?'

Outside, Jill linked her arm through Steve's. 'I hope your mam doesn't think I'm swanking.'

'Nah!' He moved his arm to put it around her waist. 'She'll be tickled pink.'

Jill stopped and turned to gaze into his face. 'You're happy for me, aren't you, Steve?'

'I'm a bit jealous.' Steve put a hand under her chin. 'Jealous of anythin' that might take you away from me.'

'Don't be daft! How can getting another job make any difference? I'm not going to work at the other end of the world!'

'If I 'ad my way, I'd lock yer up until the day we get married.' Steve's dimples showed when he grinned. 'Take no notice of me and give me a kiss.'

Jill looked up and down the street. 'Just a quick one, then we'll go and see your mam and dad.'

Back in the Bennetts' house, Jack lit up a cigarette. 'Yer know, love, I feel as happy as if I'd come up on the pools. I hope she gets herself a decent job, one with prospects.'

'She deserves it after stickin' at night school for two years.' Molly picked up the blouse she'd discarded. 'I'd better get on with this, our Doreen wants it for work tomorrow.'

'I don't know why she can't do 'er own sewing,' Jack said. 'There's no excuse, seein' as she's sewing all day in work.'

''Cos she can't be bothered, that's why! She's off out

211

every night, flyin' her kite! God only knows where she gets to.'

'It's yer own fault for being so soft with her. Yer want to put yer foot down, make her see to her own clothes.'

Molly chuckled. 'If I put me foot down with our Doreen, she'd stand on it.' She measured a length of cotton from the reel and broke it off between her teeth. 'I'm puttin' a few coppers away every week to buy a second hand sewin' machine. That'll keep her in. She's mad about clothes an' has big ideas about makin' her own. But there's method in me madness wantin' a machine, 'cos if she's half as handy with one as she brags, she can make me an' our Ruthie some dresses. God knows we could do with some.'

'Oh, aye,' Jack laughed. 'Who d'yer want to get all dolled up for?'

'Well, there's this feller in the Maypole. The spittin' image of Clark Gable, he is.' There was a twinkle in Molly's eyes as she rested her hand on her lap. 'But it's not 'im I want to get dolled up for. There's another bloke I've got me eye on, much more handsome. I think yer know him – his name's Jack Bennett!'

'Still no change?'

Ellen shook her head. 'Not really. He opened 'is eyes for a few seconds this mornin', but he didn't seem to see anythin'.'

Molly pointed to a chair. 'Park yer carcass, Ellen, yer look absolutely worn out.'

'I don't only look it, Molly, I feel it.' Ellen sat on the edge of the chair, hopelessness and despair written all

212

over her. 'I feel like goin' to bed an' never gettin' up again.'

Nobby had been in hospital two weeks now, and against all the odds he was still clinging to life. Every day Ellen made the long trek to the hospital, just to sit beside his bed for a short while. She hadn't told anyone, but she walked there and back because she couldn't afford the tram fare, and was physically and mentally worn out.

'What do the doctors say?' Just looking at Ellen made Molly want to cry, she looked so pathetic. 'Don't they tell yer anythin'?'

'I don't see a doctor, only the sister on the ward.' Ellen let out a deep sigh. 'Nobody expected Nobby to last this long, so they're not goin' to commit themselves one way or the other. All they'll say is that he's still critically ill.'

It was Molly's turn to sigh. 'Something's got to happen soon, one way or another, he can't go on like this for ever.'

'You're right about one thing. Somethin' 'as got to happen soon.' Ellen was picking nervously at a loose strand of cotton on the sleeve of her coat. 'I've got to find meself a job, or we'll be out on the street, me an' the kids.'

'That bad, is it?'

Ellen nodded. 'I haven't paid the rent this week, an' I owe the corner shop for the stuff I got on tick last week. All the money I've had in the last two weeks is the money Nobby had comin' from work, the loose change he 'ad in his pocket, and the ten bob you gave me from

213

Corker. If I don't get a job soon to pay me ways, we'll be out on the street.'

'There must be somewhere yer can go for help! Have yer asked Miss Pritchard at the 'ospital?'

'Yeah, she gave me an address to go to for Public Assistance and a bloke came to see me yesterday. Yer should 'ave heard the questions he asked, I felt terrible! After lookin' all over the 'ouse to see if I 'ad anythin' to sell, he wanted to know every ha'penny I've 'ad since Nobby went in 'ospital.'

'It's called the means test,' Molly told her. 'There's a few families in the street on the parish, an' they had the same thing.'

'After goin' through all that, d'yer know what I'll be gettin' from next week? Fifteen shillings a week to keep the five of us! That'll just pay me rent, gas an' half a bag of coal. Nothin' over for food or clothes. So it's a case of gettin' meself a job or puttin' me head in the gas oven.'

'Yer can cut that sort of talk out, Ellen Clarke, it doesn't get yer anywhere.' Molly dragged her chair nearer. She slapped Ellen's hand, tutting, 'If yer don't stop pullin' at that cotton, yer'll have no coat on yer back! Now, let's put our heads together an' see what we can come up with. What sort of work can yer do?'

'I'm only fit for cleanin', but I tried that once before an' there were no jobs goin'.'

Molly gazed at the thin pale face, the straight dull hair and shabby clothes. If Ellen went after a job looking like something the cat had dragged in, no one would give her a second glance, never mind a job.

'Look, Ellen, yer might not like what I've got to say,

214

but I'm goin' to say it anyway. So hear me out, 'cos it's for yer own good.' Molly took a deep breath. Why do I get meself involved? she wondered. Then she looked at Ellen's face and found her answer. Someone had to get involved.

'Before yer go after a job, yer'll have to do somethin' about yerself.' When Ellen's mouth opened to protest, Molly waved an impatient hand. 'No, I've started now, and if it kills me, I'm goin' to finish. After yer've heard what I've got to say, yer can walk out of that door an' never speak to me again, that's up to you. But at least I'll know I've done me best.

'I may be tellin' tales out of school, but right now I couldn't care less, so here we go.' Molly leaned her elbows on the table and cupped her face in her hands. 'Corker told me he knew yer years ago, an' that yer were nice-lookin', always dressed up to the nines, a smashin' dancer and full of fun. We know Nobby dragged yer down, but he's not here now! Yer don't have to be lookin' over yer shoulder all the time, waitin' for the next go-along!' Molly paused for breath. 'Yer've touched rock bottom now, so the only way to go is up. Make somethin' of yerself, and yer life. For the kids' sake, as well as yer own.'

'Oh, aye?' The sarcasm was thick in Ellen's voice. 'Shall I get the tram into town and visit the shops? A dress from Lewis's perhaps, a coat from Blackler's, and some make-up from Owen Owen? Is that what yer mean? Well, you're the one with the big ideas, tell me 'ow I can do all that with only tuppence between me an' the workhouse?'

215

'By gettin' rid of that chip on yer shoulder for a kick off!' Molly closed her eyes. I want me bumps feeling, she thought, sitting here trying to help someone who doesn't want to be helped! Then she saw the funny side of the situation, and when she opened her eyes she was grinning. 'Well, I haven't put a smile on yer gob, but I've put yer in a right temper. At least that's somethin'.'

Ellen lowered her head. 'I'm sorry, Molly, but me nerves are shattered. I'm at me wits' end and don't know where to turn.'

'Then don't bite the hand that's tryin' to feed yer! I want to help yer, but how can I, when yer won't let me?'

Ellen sat up straight. 'Tell me what to do.'

'That's better!' Molly was thoughtful for a while, sorting things out in her mind. 'Look, I can't do it all on me own, I'll need to ask some of me friends. But don't worry, I'm not goin' to blab to the neighbours.' She saw the doubt on Ellen's face and hastened to reassure her. 'Ellen, yer need help and yer not in a position to pick an' choose who gives it! But I promise yer troubles will go no further than two of me best mates. So go 'ome and leave things with me. I'll see yer later.'

'Good afternoon, Mr Reynolds, an' how's the world treating you this fine day?'

'Oh, lord, here they come, the terrible twins!' Tony Reynolds slapped an open palm to his forehead, knocking his straw hat to the side of his head. 'I knew me luck wouldn't last.' His ruddy cheeks widened into a smile. 'Hi, ya, Molly, Nellie! Come to buy me shop up, have yez?'

Molly was looking at the selection of meat on display in the window. 'I'd like that leg of mutton, but I won't 'ave it for two reasons. First, I can't afford it, and second, there's two flamin' big blue-bottles walkin' all over it. So instead I'll 'ave a pound an' a half of mince.'

Tony reached into the window for the tray of mince-meat. 'How's the family, Molly? I know yer ma's all right, she was in this morning.'

'Still talkin' about the wonder of electricity, is she?' Molly laughed. 'She's like a child with a new toy. Every time I go she switches the light on, just to show off.'

'I can't wait to get "electrocuted" meself.' Nellie's body shook with laughter. 'I thought that was the funniest thing I'd heard in years! Still, Bridie's got the last laugh, sittin' pretty with her lovely bright light while we're groping around in ruddy doom and gloom.' She saw Tony about to put the tray back in the window. 'Hang on, I'll have the same as Molly.'

Molly handed a two bob piece over, and as she waited for her change asked, as casually as she could, 'Who helps yer with the cleanin', Tony?'

'In the shop, yer mean?'

'Yeah! Do it yerself, do yer?'

'Yes, worse luck. All the trays, knives, counters and chopping blocks have to be scrubbed every night. And twice a week the inside of the window. By the time I get home, it's time for bed. The missus goes mad, swears I've got a fancy woman on the side.'

'Ever thought of gettin' a cleanin' woman?' Molly asked. 'Yer'd get home earlier every night if yer 'ad one.'

'I've tried a few, but they don't last.' Tony wiped his hands down the front of his blood-stained apron. 'The time's awkward for most women, they need to be home to see to their family.'

'If yer could get a woman, would yer take 'er on? Someone local?'

'For heaven's sake, we'll be 'ere all day at this rate!' Nellie clicked her tongue. 'Tony, we know someone who's desperate, on 'er uppers, are yer interested?'

'Depends if she's reliable, and doesn't want payin' too much.' Tony began to see the attraction of finishing early every night, and his interest grew. 'Do I know her?'

'No, she's one of our neighbours,' Molly told him. 'Her 'usband's in hospital, she's got four kids an' is in dire straits.'

Tony's eyebrows nearly touched his hairline. 'Four kids! Oh, no, she wouldn't be reliable! It's no good takin' someone on who'll turn up in fits and starts.'

'She wouldn't let yer down, Tony, I promise.' Molly's heart was saying a prayer. 'Two of the kids are old enough to look after the house, an' me and Nellie are goin' to help, aren't we, kid?'

'Yer've got nowt to lose, Tony. If she's no good, then sack her!' Nellie's huge bosom heaved. 'But go 'ed, at least give the woman a chance.'

Tony looked from one to the other. 'Oh, all right, yer've twisted me arm an' I know when I'm licked. Tell 'er to come an' see me in the morning, an' if she suits, she can start on Monday.'

'Ooh, I love yer, Tony!' Molly beamed. 'But if she suits, why can't she start right away? Just think 'ow nice it'll be to get 'ome earlier, 'ave more time with yer missus.'

'Go 'ed, pile it on!' But Tony was laughing. These two would get blood out of a stone. 'Tell 'er it's five days a week, no Wednesday 'cos it's half day closing. An hour and a half, from five o'clock. And I'll pay her five bob a week. Explain all that to her, an' if she still wants to come tell her to see me in the morning. Now, are yer both satisfied?'

'Tony, yer a real gent,' Molly said, making her way to the door. 'Her name's Ellen Clarke, an' she'll be 'ere at nine in the morning.'

'Thanks, Tony.' Nellie edged sideways through the door. 'Ta-ra for now.'

The two friends stood on the pavement looking very pleased with themselves. 'Not bad goin', eh, kid?' Nellie anchored the handle of her shopping basket in the crook of her arm. 'Ellen will be made up.'

Molly was running her eyes along the blocks of shops either side of the road. 'Now, where else can we try?'

'Ah, ray, Molly!'

'Oh, stop yer moanin', Nellie! If we can get 'er fixed up with another little job at five bob a week, that'll really help her out. And it'll give 'er a bit of confidence to ask around herself.' Molly weighed the shops up. 'I was pullin' Jack's leg last night about the feller in the Maypole, said he looked like Clark Gable. I think I'll try me charms on 'im, see if there's anything goin' there.' She grabbed hold of Nellie's arm. 'Come on, me old cock sparrer, I need yer to back me up.'

'I dunno,' Nellie grunted as she allowed herself to be

219

led across the road, weaving in and out of the traffic. 'The things I let you talk me in to! I need me brains testin'!'

Molly sat drumming her fingers on the table as she watched Doreen's reflection in the mirror. She hadn't mentioned the events of the day to Jack, waiting until Doreen and Tommy went out. If they got word of what was going on, it would be all over the street in no time. Sometimes Molly thought the neighbours knew more about her than she did herself. Tommy was out playing with his mates, so it was only Doreen now. 'How long are yer goin' to be titivating yerself up?'

Sliding the comb through her long hair, Doreen's eyes met her mother's in the mirror. 'What's the hurry?'

'I'm not in any hurry,' Molly lied. 'It's just that yer get on me nerves, preening yerself like a flamin' peacock.'

Doreen gathered the loose hairs from the comb and threw them in the grate. She'd blossomed since she left school, had grown into an attractive girl. She knew it, too, and never went out until she was satisfied she was looking her best. 'I'm goin' now, I'm meetin' Maureen off the bus.'

'Ten o'clock, mind!' Jack looked up from the *Echo*. 'No later.'

'Okay, okay!' Doreen glanced in the mirror once more, then, happy with what she saw, she waved good-bye. 'See yez!'

Jill was sewing a button on her overall and Ruthie's head was bent over a colouring book. It didn't matter about Jill, she would never repeat anything, but Ruthie had as big a mouth as the other two.

Molly leaned forward and tapped Jack on the leg. 'D'yer feel like goin' for a pint with George?'

Jack's eyes appeared over the paper. 'No, I don't feel like goin' out. I'm glad to sit down and relax after a day's work.' He looked at her suspiciously. 'What brought this on? You know I never go out through the week.'

Molly glanced at Ruthie. 'Will yer run up to the corner shop for me, sunshine? I need a small tin loaf for our breakfast. It's still light, so yer'll come to no harm. An' yer can 'ave a ha'penny for sweeties.'

Ruthie scrambled off the chair. 'Can I 'ave a penny to buy a yo-yo?'

Molly reached for her handbag. 'Five years of age an' already she's a ruddy blackmailer.' She put a shilling into the eager hand. 'Keep tight hold of me change an' come straight back.'

Jack folded the paper. 'Out with it. What 'ave yer got up yer sleeve now?'

As Molly got into the story, Jill put the needle down and sat back to listen. With so much to tell, and so little time to tell it in, Molly didn't even pause for breath. 'Mary's comin' over when she's got Bella to bed, an' she's goin' to wash and cut Ellen's hair so she'll look tidy tomorrow. She's got a coat she can 'ave, too. It's not new, but it's a damn sight better than the thing Ellen's wearing.'

'Mam, she can have that navy skirt of mine,' Jill said. 'There's nothing wrong with it, it's just that I've had it over a year and I've had me money's worth out of it.'

'Ooh, thanks, love!' Molly was delighted. 'Yer a bit

221

fatter than Ellen, she hasn't got a pick on 'er, but we can move the waist button.'

Jack was shaking his head. What would this wife of his get up to next? Still, he told himself, everything she did was to help someone. 'Does George know he's goin' for a pint, or is he gettin' his marching orders, like me?'

Molly grinned. 'He's goin' to volunteer, like you just did.'

'I can't get over you two!' Mary Watson was winding Ellen's hair into dinky curlers. She'd washed it three times with carbolic soap, then trimmed it. It was as straight as a die, no perm in it, so it was probably a waste of time putting curlers in. Still, if they could just get a kink in it, it would be worth it. 'Fancy goin' in two shops an' asking if there were any jobs going! I wouldn't 'ave had the nerve.'

'It wasn't nerve we 'ad, it was cheek!' Molly and Nellie looked at each other and giggled. 'Tony Reynolds was a push-over, wasn't he, Nellie? It was like leadin' a lamb to the slaughter.'

'Yer should 'ave heard her with the feller from the Maypole,' Nellie gurgled. 'I nearly wet meself when she told 'im he looked like Clark Gable. He grew ten inches before me very eyes.'

'That's until I asked 'im if there were any jobs goin',' Molly laughed. 'He shrank down to size then.'

'What did he say?' Mary thought the whole thing was hilarious, like something out of a Keystone Cops film.

'They didn't need anybody.' Molly doubled up with laughter. 'And he really thought they didn't until me an' Nellie 'ad a go at him. Then he decided that perhaps they could do with someone to make the orders up. And with a bit more persuadin' we convinced 'im it would be handy if the bags of loose tea and sugar were weighed out, save them a lot of time when the shop was busy.'

'Was he glad to see the back of us!' Nellie's eyes disappeared in the folds of flesh as she rocked with laughter. 'Saw us to the door before we took his own job off him.'

'I don't know about 'im being glad to see the back of us,' Molly said, 'I was glad to get out before he changed 'is mind.'

'Not bad goin', eh, Ellen?' Mary bent to look into Ellen's face. 'Two interviews tomorrow, that can't be bad.'

Ellen didn't answer. She was gobsmacked, stunned into silence by the speed of events. She'd never sleep tonight, she was so nervous and worried about the interviews tomorrow. Please God, let me get the jobs, she prayed silently. I need the money badly, but I also need me pride back.

'There, that does it.' Mary patted Ellen's head. 'I'll come over in the mornin', and if the curlers haven't done the trick, I'll have a go with me curling tongs.'

'Our Jill's left yer a skirt an' blouse, Ellen, so with them an' Mary's coat, yer'll be done up like a dog's dinner.'

'Try them on,' Nellie coaxed. 'Let's see what yer look like.'

Ellen's eyes widened in fear. She couldn't get

223

undressed in front of them, her underclothes were in rags! 'They'll be all right.'

Molly had seen the look and understood. 'Yer've got nothing we haven't got, Ellen, but if yer embarrassed go in the kitchen and get changed.'

When Ellen came through the kitchen door the three women were pleasantly surprised. The coat was a loose swagger, so it didn't look out of place on the thin frame, and the blouse and skirt showed up well beneath it. 'Yer look a different woman, Ellen,' Molly said, to accompanying nods from the other two. 'Wait till . . .' Her words petered out when Jill's navy skirt parted company from Ellen's hips and fell in a heap around her ankles. She looked so comical, Molly turned her head away so her neighbour couldn't see the laughter in her eyes. Not for the world would she want Ellen to think she was making fun of her.

Molly felt Nellie's grip on her arm just as a strange, high-pitched laugh rang out. She turned to see a sight she never thought she'd ever witness. Ellen was standing with her head thrown back, laughter gurgling from her throat and tears streaming down her face.

'Oh, my God, she's gone hysterical!' Molly rushed to Ellen's side. 'It's all right, Ellen, just calm down, there's a good girl.'

Ellen shook her head, wiping at the tears with the back of her hand. 'I'm all right, Molly, honest! It's just that it's ages since I 'ad anythin' to laugh about.' Again that shrill sound rang out. 'I haven't been to the pictures for years, but listenin' to you an' Nellie, imaginin' the pair of yez with that feller from the Maypole – well, it reminded me of Laurel an' Hardy.' She pointed to the skirt around her ankles and doubled up in a fit of giggles. 'This was the last straw . . . I must look a scream.'

'Well, I never!' Molly was flabbergasted. 'D'yer know, it's the first time I've heard yer laugh, or seen a proper smile on yer face?' She turned to Nellie, her hands on her hips. 'I'm beginning to see what Corker meant! She looks a different woman with a smile on 'er gob.'

'Wait till her hair's done in the morning.' Mary was happy and sad at the same time. 'Yer won't know her.'

'An' I'll be here with me powder, rouge and lippy.' Nellie wasn't going to be left out. Ellen's plight had touched her, and she'd made up her mind to do all she could to help. 'She'll look like a million dollars when she goes out of this 'ouse temorrer.'

'Get the skirt off.' Molly's voice was gruff with emotion. 'I'll put a tuck in it.'

Nellie and Mary sat at Molly's table making desultory conversation while every few seconds their eyes strayed to the clock on the mantelpiece. 'I thought she'd be back by now,' Molly said gruffly. 'Me nerves are on edge.'

'She didn't half look smart when she walked down the street this mornin'.' Nellie's arm was red where she'd been pinching at the fat. 'I wish she'd hurry up an' put us out of our misery.'

'In bed last night, I was thinkin' she wouldn't be a bad lookin' woman if she paid some attention to herself.' Mary's finger was making patterns in the chenille table-cloth. 'A bit more flesh on her bones, a perm and some make-up would work wonders.'

225

'All that takes money, somethin' that's been in very short supply in Ellen's life,' Molly said. 'In fact everything's been in short supply as far as I can see. I wonder 'ow long it is since someone held her close, gave 'er a kiss and told 'er they loved her?'

'If yer don't shut up, yer'll 'ave me in tears.' Nellie transferred her pinching to her other arm. 'I hope she gets the jobs, that'll cheer us up.'

When the knock came, Molly had the door open in two seconds flat. 'About time!' She pulled Ellen along the hall, asking, 'How did yer get on?'

'I got both jobs.' Ellen was all smiles. 'Five bob a week each.'

There were sighs of relief and pleasure. 'Thank God for that!' Molly said. 'But what took yer so long?'

'I called at the 'ospital. I can't go tonight 'cos I'm startin' at the butcher's. I'll 'ave to try an' fit me visits in when I can.'

'How is Nobby?' Nellie asked.

'Still the same. He opened 'is eyes when I sat down, but he looked through me, as though I wasn't there.'

Molly put her arm around the thin shoulders. 'Yer've done well today, kid, an' we're all proud of yer. Now it's up to you to get the best out of life that yer can for yerself an' the kids.' She smiled across the table at Nellie and Mary. 'If she ever gets stuck, needs a bit of help like, she can always come to us, can't she? After all, what are mates for?'

Chapter Fifteen

The postman sauntered up the street at his usual pace, whistling softly as he deposited letters through the appropriate letter-boxes. His peaked cap pushed to the back of his head, his bag of mail slung over his shoulder, he was thinking that this was the kind of morning when his job was a pleasure. The sky was a lovely clear blue, with white fluffy clouds floating like balloons. It's going to be a real scorcher, Tommy Maher thought, slipping a letter under a door that had no letter-box, I should have left me vest off.

Molly was standing on her front step watching Tommy's progress with impatience. 'Get a move on, slow coach!' she called. 'Yer late this mornin', where the hell 'ave yer been?'

'I'm not late, I'm dead on time!' Tommy was proud of his timekeeping. Never late, and never a day off since he'd started work. 'Anyway, what's the hurry, Molly, expectin' somethin' important, are yer?' He pulled a wodge of mail from his bag and began rifling through. 'Nothin' for yer today, I'm afraid.'

'Oh, come off it, Tommy Maher, of course there is! I

posted four meself, yesterday.'

Tommy burst out laughing as he handed a batch of envelopes over. 'Only pullin' yer leg, Molly.'

'Aye, well, pull the other one, it's got bells on.' She flicked through the envelopes, counting. 'Ten cards. Not bad, eh?'

'How old is Jill today?'

'Sweet sixteen and never been kissed,' Molly laughed. 'At least not in my presence.'

'Smashin'-looking girl, your Jill,' he said, moving off. 'If I was a bit younger I'd be chasing her.'

'Yer'd be too late, she's spoken for.' Molly waved goodbye and as she stepped into the hall saw Jill halfway down the stairs, yawning and rubbing the sleep from her eyes. 'Happy birthday, sunshine!' She waited till Jill was on the bottom stair then handed the envelopes over. 'Sixteen today, eh, love?' Molly gave her a hug. 'I hope yer 'ave a lovely birthday.'

'Thanks, Mam.' Jill put the cards by her plate on the table. 'I'll swill me face and clean me teeth first, wake meself up.'

'Yer toast is ready so don't be too long. I'm dyin' to see who the cards are from.'

When Jill came back from the kitchen, washed, dressed and wide awake, Molly brought a plate of toast in and placed a jar of jam near to hand. 'Now hurry up an' open yer cards, I'm dyin' of curiosity.'

Jill took a bite of toast then reached for the top envelope. She was alert now and beginning to feel excited. Being sixteen was a big step in a girl's life, she was a young woman now. 'It's from Mrs Watson and family.' She read the verse in the card before passing it to her mother. 'Read the verse, Mam, it's lovely.'

Ruthie's card had a fluffy kitten on the front, and Jill was delighted when she saw her sister's childish scrawl. 'Ah, bless her, she's written it herself.'

'First card she's ever sent,' Molly said proudly. 'Yer'd 'ave died laughing if yer'd seen her writin' it. Her tongue was hangin' out of the side of her mouth, and the concentration on her face . . . well, yer'd 'ave thought she was makin' her last will and testament.'

Tommy's card brought loud guffaws from both of them. It was covered in dirty finger marks and ink stains. 'Don't know why he bothered to sign it,' Molly said. 'It couldn't be from anyone else. Still, the thought was there.'

Jill picked up the next card, saw the handwriting and put it to one side. 'You're not seeing that, it's from Steve.'

'Spoil sport,' Molly laughed. 'It would 'ave brightened me day.'

'I'll have to read the others on the tram,' Jill said after glancing at the clock. 'Otherwise I'll be late for work.'

'Yer lucky it's half day closing.' Molly was flicking through the remaining envelopes. She picked out two and handed them to Jill. 'Open these, it'll only take a minute.'

When a ten shilling note dropped out of the first card, Molly was rewarded by the look of surprise and pleasure on her daughter's face. 'You can't afford this.' Jill handed the note over. 'It's too much!'

'Me an' yer dad didn't know what to buy yer, so we

thought it best to give yer the money so yer can get what yer want. And don't worry, I've not left meself skint.' Molly moved across to the fireplace and took down a parcel from the mantelpiece. 'That card in yer 'and is from Doreen, an' she left yer this, as well.'

'Isn't it exciting!' Jill tore at the paper wrapping. 'I wouldn't mind having a birthday every day.' She let out a squeal. 'Oh, Mam, look, a blue velvet hair band! Isn't it gorgeous? I'll wear it when I go out with Steve tonight.'

'Yer'll suit it, love, it's the same colour as yer eyes.'

'I'll have to scarper, or I'll never get to work on time.' Jill put her arms around her mother and kissed her. 'I've got the best family in the whole world and I love all of you.'

'Away with yer,' Molly sniffed. 'Get off to work while I go an' wake Tommy an' Ruthie. Can't 'ave them being late for school.'

'I'll be home about two,' Jill said, happily picking up her cards to show the girls in work. 'I'll see you later, Mam, ta-ra.'

Molly slapped her bottom playfully. 'Ta-ra, sunshine.'

'Have yer got a minute, Molly?' Ellen was looking much better these days. Her face had filled out a little, there was colour in her cheeks and she had more confidence. She walked with her head held high, and even had a word for the neighbours, something she'd never done when Nobby was home. 'I won't keep yer a minute.'

'I'm not stuck for time,' Molly told her. 'I've done all me work, the washing's on the line and the dinner only needs a match under it.' She pointed to a chair. 'Just finished work, 'ave yer?'

'If yer can call it work! It's a dead cushy number at the Maypole.' Ellen sat down and folded her arms. 'As yer know, I usually go straight from there to the 'ospital, but I couldn't bring meself to go today, somehow.'

When Ellen started to pick at her nails, Molly knew there was something bothering her. 'What's up? Nobby's still improving, isn't he?'

'So they tell me, but I can't make 'im out. If yer saw him, yer'd think he was gettin' better. The sister says he's eating all right, he's propped up in bed an' his eyes are open all the time now. But he frightens the life out of me. He looks me up and down with a sneer on his face. Never says one word, but if looks could kill, I'd be dead.'

'Ellen, yer expecting too much! He's not goin' to be full of the joys of spring, not after what he's been through.'

'I keep tellin' meself that, but I still can't help feelin' there's something not quite right. I mean, why doesn't he ask after the kids, or ask me to bring things in for 'im? The old Nobby would be screamin' and shoutin', blaming everyone but 'imself for what's happened! But he's never said one word to me, I may as well not be there!' Ellen shook her head. 'I'm not clever, not even good at explainin' what I mean, but I've lived with 'im long enough to know him inside out, an' I'll swear the man in that bed is not the Nobby I knew.'

'And he's not, is he!? The Nobby you knew 'ad two legs, this one hasn't! How d'yer think we'd feel if we'd 'ad our legs cut off, eh? The poor man must be out of 'is mind.'

'Yer've hit the nail on the head, Molly, 'cos that's just what I think. He is out of 'is mind.'

'Ye gods and little fishes, Ellen, what's the matter with yer? The man's in 'ospital. If there was anythin' wrong, don't yer think the doctors would know?' Molly clicked her tongue on the roof of her mouth. 'I think yer expecting too much too soon, an' yer letting yer imagination run away with yer.'

Ellen leaned forward, her eyes pleading. 'I know I'm always askin' favours of yer, Molly, but can I ask yer just one more? Come to the 'ospital with me an' see what you think. See if I am imaginin' things.'

'I can't come today! Our Jill's home at two, an' I want to be with her 'cos it's her birthday. I've iced a sandwich cake, an' I've got a jelly setting in a bowl of cold water. It's not much, we're not havin' a party or anythin', but I can't let her birthday go without putting a little spread on.' Molly sighed inwardly when she looked at Ellen. Oh, dear, here I go again, a sucker for punishment. 'I'll come with yer tomorrow.'

'Oh, thanks, Molly, yer a real pal.'

A ruddy fool more like, Molly told herself when Ellen had gone. She's got this cockeyed idea in her head, and I'm dafter than she is for going along with it. They say there's a fool born every minute and I must be the biggest fool of all. I'd fall for the flaming cat, I would!

Jill slipped her hand through Steve's arm. 'Thanks for your card, Steve, it's lovely.' She tilted her head to smile into his face. 'I'm glad I didn't let me mam see it, not with all those kisses on. She'd have pulled me leg soft.'

'Sixteen kisses for sixteen years.' Steve pressed her hand. 'When yer sixty, there'll be sixty kisses on yer card.'

'I've had a lovely day,' she told him. 'The girls in work bought me handkerchieves and stockings, I got a lovely silk scarf off Mr John and a pretty blouse off me nanna and grandpa.'

'The day isn't over yet. We're goin' somewhere nice, an' that's my present to yer.'

Jill could see a tram rumbling its way towards the stop and pulled on Steve's hand. 'Let's sit upstairs.'

'Where would you like to go?' he asked, thinking he'd never seen her looking lovelier. It was a warm summer evening and she was dressed in a pretty floral dress with a sweetheart neck, nipped in waist and full skirt. Her long blonde hair, brushed till it shone, was set off by the band Doreen had given her. 'D'yer want to go to the flicks?'

'It's up to you.' Jill's vivid blue eyes met his. 'I'll go wherever you want.'

Steve shook his head. 'It's your birthday, you choose.'

'It's such a nice night, can't we go down to the Pier Head? We could watch the ferry boats come in.'

'Why watch when we can go on one? We could sail to Seacombe and walk to New Brighton.' Steve covered her hand with his. 'The sea air will do us good.'

They were travelling along Scotland Road and Jill pointed out of the window. 'I love to see the Mary-Ellens in their long black skirts and the black knitted shawls around their shoulders. But they must be roasting in them in this weather.'

'They dress like that in any weather,' Steve said. 'Scottie Road wouldn't be the same without the Mary-Ellens.'

The fine weather had brought many people down to the Pier Head. There was nothing nicer, on a pleasant, warm evening, than to sail on a ferry across the Mersey. For twopence you could dream you were boarding one of the big liners about to set sail for some faraway shore.

Steve was smiling happily when he came back from buying the tickets.

'Come on, there's a ferry in.' The queue at the landing stage moved forward quickly, and soon Steve and Jill were standing looking over the rails of the ferry.

'I don't ever remember being on a boat before,' she said. 'Me mam said she used to take me to New Brighton when I was a baby, but I can't remember. Then when the others came along, she couldn't afford to take us.'

The ferry shuddered, then began its slow turn to head in the direction of Seacombe. When it gathered speed, Steve hung over the rail to watch the white foam made by the boat ploughing its way through the water. 'Come and have a look-see, Jill.'

Jill leaned over, then quickly stepped back. 'Be careful, you might fall in.'

Hearing the anxiety in her voice, Steve moved from the rail. 'Let's walk along the deck.' With an arm around her waist, he pointed back to the Liverpool water-front. 'See those Liver Birds? I bet they could tell a few tales. They can see everythin' from up there.'

'What about these birds?' Jill was looking up at the seagulls, swooping low over their heads, then soaring away, high in the sky. 'I love watching birds, they're so graceful.'

'Well, I wouldn't stand there with yer mouth open!' Steve grinned.

The journey was over too soon for Jill. With the light breeze blowing across the Mersey, the seagulls flying overhead and Steve's arm around her waist, she could have stayed on the boat all night. But she comforted herself with the thought of the journey back.

They strolled lazily in the direction of New Brighton, stopping first to buy a quarter pound box of Cadbury's which Steve presented to Jill with a flourish, then an ice-cream from a Wall's stop-me-and-buy-one cart.

'This is the life,' Jill sighed dreamily, her tongue streaking out to lick the ice-cream. 'I could go a bundle on this.'

'Wait till I'm out of me time an' on decent money,' Steve said. 'We can do this every weekend.'

'Sounds heavenly.' Jill started when Steve bent down quickly to pick something from the ground. 'Did you drop something?'

Steve held his hand out to reveal a brass curtain ring. 'I thought at first it was a gold ring.' He gazed at the ring, then into Jill's face. 'Let's pretend it is a proper ring. Hold yer hand out.'

Jill started to laugh, then saw that Steve was serious. 'I can't wear that! Me finger would go all green.'

'It's only pretend,' Steve said. 'Go on, just to please me.'

235

Jill held out her left hand and watched as Steve slipped the rusty brass curtain ring on her third finger. 'You're as daft as a brush, Steve McDonough.'

'Now we're engaged.' His face was a picture of happiness. 'Wear it for tonight, then keep it in yer purse until I can buy yer a proper ring.' He tucked Jill's hand into his arm. 'Every time yer open yer purse, yer'll think of me.'

'I don't need anything to remind me of you,' Jill told him, in a rare show of emotion. 'I think about you all the time.'

Steve's heart doing somersaults, they strolled on in comfortable silence. He kept glancing sideways, wanting to pinch himself to make sure he wasn't dreaming, that this beautiful girl walking beside him really did belong to him. He must be the luckiest bloke in the whole world. When they reached New Brighton they noticed many young people hurrying in the same direction. Most of the girls were wearing silver dance shoes and pretty dresses, while the men wore suits, with shiny patent leather shoes tucked under their arms.

'I wonder where they're all going?' Jill was making a mental note of the fashionable dresses. Doreen had promised to make her one when their mam bought a sewing machine. 'They're all dressed up, there must be something big on.'

'They're goin' dancing, to the Tower Ballroom,' Steve said knowingly. 'Some of the fellers in work come over here a couple of times a week.'

'Don't the girls look lovely?' Jill looked down at the dress she'd thought was nice until now. These girls certainly didn't get their dresses for four and eleven from TJ's. 'They're really glamorous.'

'Jill, sweetheart, they couldn't hold a candle to you,' Steve said. 'You knock spots off all of them.'

'Thanks, Steve.' She smiled. 'They say love is blind.'

'I've got a good pair of eyes in me head, Jill, an' I bet if yer went in the dance, just as you are, the fellers would be fallin' all over themselves to dance with yer.' Steve pulled her to him and held her close, ignoring the stares of people passing. 'Just take a good look in the mirror an' yer'll see I'm right.'

Jill pulled away, embarrassed by the public show of affection. 'Come on, it's time to turn back. Me mam doesn't like me to be out late.'

They walked back, arm in arm, Jill's head resting on Steve's shoulder. She broke the silence, speaking more to herself than to him. 'When I get a decent job, I'm going to buy meself nice clothes.'

'Yer'll do for me, just as yer are.' Steve dropped a kiss on her head. 'Isn't there a song that says, "just the way you look, tonight"? Well, that song says it all. I love you just the way yer are.'

There was a ferry waiting at the landing stage, they caught a tram right away, and all too soon were standing outside Jill's front door. 'Are you coming in?'

Steve shook his head. 'I'd rather have yer to meself for a few minutes. Did yer enjoy yerself?'

'Oh, yes, Steve, it's been lovely. I'll never forget me sixteenth birthday as long as I live. The whole day's been perfect, but tonight was the best.' Jill's head moved to see if the coast was clear, then she planted a quick kiss on his mouth. 'Thank you, Steve.'

She couldn't see the twinkle in Steve's eyes, but the deepening dimples in his cheeks told her something was amusing him. 'What are you laughing at?'

'Haven't you forgotten somethin'?'

Jill frowned. 'Like what?'

'Like a certain brass curtain ring, on a certain finger?'

'Oh, flippin' heck, I'd forgotten!' Her face crimson, Jill tugged at the ring. 'It's a good job yer reminded me. Me mam would have had a duck egg if she'd seen it.'

'Don't forget to keep it in yer purse until I can buy yer a real one.'

Steve saw one of their neighbours turn the corner, and kissed Jill quickly before the man came too close. Ted Johnson was noted for being talkative when he'd had a few pints and Steve didn't want the evening spoilt by having to listen to the ramblings of a drunken man. 'I'll call for yer tomorrow night, eh? We can go for a walk.'

Jill kissed her fingertips and placed them briefly over Steve's mouth. 'Okay. Sleep well and dream of me.'

They stopped outside the ward doors and Ellen took a deep breath. 'Now for it.'

Molly's grip on the paper bag tightened. She thought it would look mean if she didn't bring something in, so she'd bought an apple, an orange and a banana. Now she was wishing she hadn't come. Ellen's nervousness had rubbed off on her and she was feeling very apprehensive. 'Let's get it over with,' she said, gruffly. 'I 'ate 'ospitals. The sooner I'm out, the better I'll like it.'

As they approached the bed, Molly saw the arched

structure under the bedding, covering the bottom half of Nobby's body. 'What's that?' she whispered.

'Sister said it's to keep the clothes off 'is wounds,' Ellen whispered back. 'You know, where they 'ad to cut 'is legs off.'

Nobby, propped up on three pillows, was staring straight ahead at the wall opposite. He didn't turn as they neared the bed, nor did he acknowledge Ellen's greeting. She shrugged her shoulders at Molly in a gesture that said, 'I told you so'.

I'm not coming all this way for nothing, Molly told herself as she pushed past Ellen. God loves a trier, and I'm going to try. 'Hello, Nobby! How are yer? It's about time I came to see yer, isn't it?'

Molly gave a gasp as she backed away in horror, banging her hip on the sharp corner of the locker at the side of the bed. But she didn't even feel the pain as her mind reeled. Never in all her life had she seen such hatred or venom as there was in the eyes boring in to hers. And Nobby's stare didn't waver. With his nostrils flared, his top lip raised in a cruel snarl, he reminded Molly of the devil.

Ellen put her hand on Molly's arm. 'Shall I get yer a chair, Molly, an' yer can sit down?'

She shook her head. 'No, ta, Ellen, I don't want to sit.' She was having difficulty breathing. What had she ever done to Nobby Clarke that he should hate her so much? Then she tried to think rationally, remembering what she'd told Ellen, that anyone would be the same if they'd gone through what he had. Knowing he was never going to walk again was enough to send him off his rocker.

239

While Molly waited for her heartbeat to slow down, she told herself to show compassion and sympathy. Perhaps that was what Nobby needed, a little understanding of the torment he must be going through. And what he'd have to go through for the rest of his life. Taking a deep breath, she turned and put the paper bag on the side of the bed. 'I've brought yer a bit of fruit, Nobby . . .' Her words trailed off when she looked up, straight into the unblinking eyes that had been watching her every move. It was still there, the hatred, cruelty and venom. And in her mind, Molly added another word . . . murder.

Molly's hand was shaking as she picked up the bag of fruit and put it on the locker. 'I'll be goin' now, Ellen.'

'I'm comin' with yer.'

'Come on, then, girl.' She cupped her hand under Ellen's elbow. No wonder the poor thing looks terrified, she thought, I'd be the same if I had to come here every day and put up with that.

'I told yer, didn't I?' They were out of the ward and walking down the corridor when Ellen spoke. 'He's not in 'is right mind, is he?'

'I don't know what to think,' Molly admitted. 'But we'll ask someone who should know.'

The matron was small in stature but not lacking in efficiency. She didn't waste time or try to fob them off. 'Yes, Mrs Clarke, we are experiencing some difficulty with your husband. He is very bad-tempered and abusive. The staff are finding him a difficult patient as he refuses to co-operate.' She looked at the small watch pinned to her uniform. 'The doctor is due to do his round

240

soon, I'll mention your concern.' Her eyes were questioning. 'Before the, er, accident, what sort of a disposition did your husband have? Pleasant, happy, bad-tempered?'

'He's always 'ad a terrible temper,' Ellen said, thinking honesty was the best policy. 'Least thing would set 'im off, an' he was violent, too!'

'I rather gathered that. But it is the doctor's opinion that he will improve mentally when he comes to terms with his disability, so we'll just have to wait and see. It's early days yet.' She rose from behind the desk, signifying the interview was at an end, and looked kindly at Ellen. 'It must be hard for you, coming in every day and having a family to look after. Why not cut the visits down to once or twice a week? We can always contact you if necessary.'

Walking down the long hospital path, Ellen said, 'I'm out of me mind worryin' what's goin' to happen. I couldn't cope with havin' Nobby home the way he is, he'd have me in an early grave.'

'I don't envy yer, Ellen,' Molly grunted. She prayed God would forgive her for her thoughts but the man was evil and there was no getting away from it. And after today she didn't ever want to set eyes on him again.

'Our Jill's late, she's usually in before you.' Molly put Jack's dinner down in front of him. 'I 'ope nothing's wrong.'

'Mother hen worrying about her chicks, eh?' Jack speared a carrot on the end of his fork. 'What will yer do when they all fly the coop?'

'Jack, I'll worry about me kids until me dying day.' Molly sat opposite, her face downcast. 'And I'm not in the mood for jokes, I've 'ad a terrible day.'

'Why?' Jack stopped chewing. 'Not sick, are yer?'

Molly shook her head, then told him in detail about her hospital visit. When she'd finished, Jack asked, 'Why d'yer have to take everyone's troubles on board? Haven't yer got enough with yer own family?' He gazed at Molly's pale face and troubled eyes, and his temper rose. 'Nobby Clarke's not worth makin' yerself ill for! You are not to get involved, d'yer hear? I don't often interfere with what yer do, but I am this time! I want to come home from work to see me wife with a smile on her face, not sittin' worryin' about other people.'

Molly held her hand up. 'Okay, boss! But yer've no need to get all het up about it, I wouldn't go to see Nobby Clarke again for a big clock. Put the fear of God into me, he did.'

Jack jerked his head. 'Here's our Jill now.'

Jill leaned her weight on the table, gasping for breath. 'Mam, never in a month of Sundays will you guess what's happened.'

'Yer've got a rise?' Molly asked.

'No, better than that!' Jill straightened up, her face aglow. 'I've got an interview for a job as a shorthand typist.' Satisfied with the surprise on her parents' faces, she hurried on. 'Mr John got it for me. He had to go and see his solicitor today, on some business, and when his solicitor happened to mention they'd put an advert in the *Echo* for a junior typist, Mr John put a word in for me. Isn't that marvellous!?'

'Oh, love, I'm made up for yer.' Molly reached for her daughter's hand. 'That's just the sort of news I needed to cheer me up, after the lousy day I've had.'

'Why, what's wrong?'

'Not a thing, sunshine, just a storm in a teacup.' Molly wasn't going to say anything that would take that look of happiness away. 'When d'yer go for the interview?'

'Tomorrow afternoon, Mr John's giving me a couple of hours off.' Jill gave a little twirl. 'Ooh, Mam, I'm excited and terrified at the same time.'

'There's no need to be frightened, love,' Jack said, 'they can't eat you.' His brows drew together in thought. 'Are there any other girls being interviewed?'

'Yes, a couple, Mr John said.' Jill pulled a face. 'I keep telling meself not to build me hopes up because the chances are I won't get the job.'

'And why not!' Molly demanded indignantly. 'Yer as good as the next, any day.'

'Never mind as good as, she's better than! You walk in there tomorrow with yer head held high, love, and yer'll bowl 'em over.' Jack's face split into a grin. 'Mind you, I'm biased, but they need their eyes an' brains testing if they don't hand yer the job on a silver platter.'

'Dad's right, sunshine, it'll be a cake walk.' There was more confidence in Molly's voice than she felt. Not that she didn't think her daughter was good enough, but she'd probably be up against competition from girls who'd been to high school and that would be a big plus in their favour. An extra prayer tonight wouldn't go amiss, Molly told herself as she scraped her chair back. Three Hail Marys, three Our Fathers and a prayer to Saint

243

Anthony. 'I'll get yer dinner, it's keepin' warm on top of a pan.'

Jill pulled on her arm. 'Leave it for five minutes, Mam, I want to go up to Steve's. I'm supposed to be going out with him tonight, but I want to wash me hair and iron me blouse and skirt. I need to look me best tomorrow, make a good impression.'

'Don't forget to take the certificate yer got from night school,' Jack said. 'They'll want to see it.'

'I won't.' Jill was already halfway down the hall. 'Mr John's giving me a reference to take as well.'

'Keep yer fingers crossed, love,' Jack said, before turning his attention back to his now cold dinner.

'I'll keep everythin' I've got crossed! Me fingers, me legs and me eyes.'

Molly giggled and the sound warmed her husband's heart. 'An' if yer dare call me Buster Keaton, I'll clock yer one.'

Chapter Sixteen

'I feel a right idiot, sittin' talkin' to meself.' Bridie swung a wooden chair from the table and set it in the doorway of the kitchen. 'There, that's better.' She smoothed down the front of her dress over her knees. 'As I was sayin', not a wink of sleep did I get last night. I've offered more prayers in the last twenty-four hours than I have in the whole year.'

'You an' me both, Ma.' Molly had her hands full trying to wash Ruthie. The little girl was perched on the draining board, naked except for her knickers, her face all screwed up as her mother rubbed the soapy flannel in every nook and cranny. 'Will yer keep still, for heaven's sake, yer like a flamin' worm!'

'Well, yer 'urting me, an' yer've rubbed soap in me eyes.' Ruthie was willing herself to cry in a bid for sympathy, but to her disgust she couldn't summon up even one tear-drop. 'Have yer finished?'

'I haven't started yet! Just look at yer knees, they're as black as the hobs of hell.' Molly pulled a face at Bridie. 'Her an' our Tommy are a fine pair, they both hate the sight of water.'

'Talk of the devil an' he's bound to appear.' Bridie smiled as Tommy came to stand beside her. 'Wasn't yer mother just after singin' yer praises?'

Tommy's two hands were cupped together, and he winked at his grandmother before opening them wide enough for the head of a white mouse to poke through.

Bridie scrambled from her chair, making the sign of the cross and screaming. 'Keep that thing away from me!'

Molly spun round, the flannel dripping water on to the brown-tiled floor. 'What's he up to now?'

'It's only a mouse, Mam!' Tommy held his hands out. 'Ginger gave it to me, look 'ow tame it is.'

'If yer think for one minute that I'm 'aving a flamin' rat in the 'ouse, then yer've got another think comin', me laddo! Now out with it!'

'Ah, ray, Mam! Can't I keep it?'

'Never mind "Ah, ray, Mam"! Just get that thing out of 'ere . . . give it back to Ginger, let his mam 'ave the pleasure of it.'

Tommy hung his head. 'His mam won't let 'im have it. She chased 'im with it.'

'No, she's not soft!' Molly huffed. 'Just take it out, Tommy, before I belt yer one.'

Tommy looked towards his nan, but the sympathy he was hoping for wasn't forthcoming. Bridie was pressed against the wall, a grimace on her face.

'What can I do with it?' Tommy asked. 'I can't give it back to Ginger.'

'For all I care, yer can stick it where Paddy stuck 'is nuts,' Molly said. 'Just get it out of here, pronto, before I lose me temper.'

Ruthie's brow was puckered as Molly washed her back. 'Mam, where did Paddy stick 'is nuts?'

Molly let out a peal of laughter. Get out of that one if yer can, Molly Bennett! 'Paddy stuck 'is nuts somewhere where the sun don't shine, sweetheart.'

'Where was that?' asked the inquisitive child.

Molly was thoughtful for moment. 'Well, that's where the mystery comes in, 'cos nobody knows. Paddy kept it a secret.'

Ruthie's eyes swivelled from side to side as her brain ticked over. 'If it's somewhere where the sun don't shine, an' nobody ever saw it, 'ow d'yer know Paddy wasn't tellin' fibs?'

''Cos Paddy never told lies, that's why.' Molly was giggling inwardly. Paddy mightn't have told lies, but here's me lying me head off! Still, it's only to keep the child happy. Like a fairy story, really. And it was making life easier for her, 'cos Ruthie wasn't struggling any more. 'Yer've heard nanna talk about the leprechauns, haven't yer, sunshine? The little fairies that live at the bottom of people's gardens in Ireland? Well, the story is that they were a friend of Paddy's, an' they were the only ones who knew where he stuck his nuts.'

Bridie moved from the wall to lean against the door jamb. 'Molly, me darlin', yer'd talk yer way out of anything, so yer would. If I didn't know yer'd never set foot in Ireland, I'd be willing to swear yer'd not only kissed the Blarney Stone, yer'd swallowed the thing whole.'

Molly lifted Ruthie down from the draining board. 'It did the trick, Ma, kept a certain someone nice an' quiet.'

She gave her daughter a slap on the bottom. 'Run upstairs an' get yer nightdress, sunshine, there's a good girl, while I make Nanna a cup of tea.'

'What about seeing to the dinner?' Bridie was gazing at the stove. 'No pans, no smell of cooking.'

'We're not 'aving a hot meal, the weather's too nice.' Molly put a light under the kettle then followed her mother into the living room. 'Jack said he felt like some tripe and onions, and the rest of us are 'aving brawn with lettuce an' tomatoes.'

Molly took two china cups and saucers from the sideboard cupboard. They only saw daylight when her mother came. 'What about me da's dinner? I've never known yer be out when he comes in from work. I think yer slippin', Ma!'

'He's calling here straight from work to see how Jill got on,' Bridie said, huffily. 'We decided we'd like fish cakes an' scallops for a change, so we'll call in at the chippy on the way home.'

A knock on the door coincided with the whistling of the kettle. 'Ma, be an angel and answer the door, will yer, while I see to the tea?'

Molly was pouring the boiling water into the pot when she heard Corker's booming voice, and a smile lit up her face. 'Get another of me best cups out, Ma!'

Corker had to bend his head to get through the door. 'Molly, me darlin', yer a sight for sore eyes.' He put his huge hands around her waist and lifted her high. His eyes twinkling with humour, he grinned into her face. 'It's good to see yer, Molly.'

'An' it's always a treat to see you, Corker.' Molly's

dress was riding high, exposing too much leg for her liking. 'Will yer put me down, so I can make meself decent?'

Corker's laugh boomed out. 'I've no objection to seeing a bonny pair of legs, Molly. Not after being at sea for six weeks.'

'If it's legs yer want to see, Corker, the legs on our table 'ave got more shape to them than mine.'

'Such talk,' Bridie tutted, in mock disapproval. 'Come and pour some tea for your visitor.'

The china cup lost from sight in his huge hand, and Ruthie settled on his knee, Corker asked, 'How's the family, Molly?'

She brought him up-to-date, finishing with Jill's interview and Tommy's attempt at making a mouse an addition to the family.

'And next door – Ellen an' Nobby?'

Molly glanced from her mother to Ruthie, and when her eyes met Corker's they sent a message that she wasn't able to tell him all there was to tell. 'Nobby's holdin' his own, that's all I can tell yer about him. But Ellen seems fine. She's got two part-time jobs, and although she only took them 'cos she needed the money desperately, they've done her the world of good. Brought 'er out of herself, given her some confidence.'

Bridie's little finger curved as she raised her cup. 'Will yer not be telling Corker how she got the jobs?' When she shook her head at Corker, Bridie kept her face straight. But her eyes gave her away. She couldn't disguise the love and admiration she felt for her daughter. 'When her and Nellie McDonough get together, sure

249

yer never know what they'll get up to. Bold as brass, the pair of them.'

Molly had Corker in stitches as she recalled the events of that afternoon, both in words and actions. By the time she was finished he was wiping tears from his eyes. 'Only you and Nellie would 'ave got away with a stunt like that, Molly, but I take me hat off to yez. Ellen's lucky she's got such good friends.'

Molly stopped in mid-sentence when Jill walked in unexpectedly. She stood inside the door, her face expressionless. For seconds the only sound in the room was the ticking of the clock. In the end it was Molly who couldn't stand the suspense any longer. 'Well, out with it, sunshine, how did it go?'

Jill spread her hands out, disappointment in the gesture. 'They're going to write to me.'

'Well, the miserable buggers!' Molly exploded. 'Why couldn't they tell yer there an' then whether yer'd got the job or not?'

Jill put her handbag on the sideboard. 'It wasn't only me, there were two other girls and they were told the same thing.'

'Don't look so down-hearted, darlin',' Corker said. 'That's how they do things. It doesn't mean you haven't got the job.'

'Of course it doesn't, sweetheart!' Bridie put her cup on the table and gave her granddaughter a hug. 'You stand as much chance as the other two, so yer do.'

'How did the interview go?' Molly wanted to go to her daughter but was afraid that if she did she'd burst out crying. 'D'yer think yer did well?'

'Yes, but so do the other two!' Jill managed a weak smile. 'There's three solicitors, Pearson, Sedgewick and Brown, and I got Mr Sedgewick. He was very nice, friendly like, and I wasn't a bit nervous with him. I showed him my school report, the certificate from night school and the letter from Mr John. Then he dictated a letter to me, and I was made up because I could keep up with him. And when I'd typed the letter out, he read it and seemed pleased that I hadn't made any mistakes.'

Molly felt calm enough now to go to her daughter. She took her in her arms and hugged her. 'Good for you, sunshine, I'm proud of yer.' She held Jill at arm's length and smiled into her face. 'I bet yer a pound to a pinch of snuff yer get the job.'

'Ooh, I hope you're right, Mam, I really do. But it'll be next week now before I hear anything.'

Molly turned to Bridie and grinned. 'A few more sleepless nights, Ma, and a lot more prayers. I think I'll add Saint Theresa to me list for good measure.'

Molly opened the door to Corker about eight o'clock. 'You again, Corker! Yer'll 'ave the neighbours talking.'

He declined when Molly stood aside to let him pass. 'I won't come in, Molly, thanks. I've been next door since I left, an Ellen's told me about yer goin' to the hospital with her yesterday. Didn't get a very good reception, did yer?'

'Sshh!' Molly put a finger to her lips. 'It's a sore point with Jack. He did 'is nut yesterday, 'cos I was so upset. But whatever Ellen 'as told yer, then take it from me she's tellin' yer the truth.'

Corker stroked his beard. 'I might take it upon meself to go an' see Nobby tomorrow. In the meantime, I'm trying to coax Ellen to come for a drink with me.'

'Ye gods, Corker!' Molly laughed. 'Yer determined to give the neighbours somethin' to talk about, aren't yer? Yer'll be the talk of the wash-house.'

'Yer know my feelings on that score, Molly, the neighbours can take a running jump as far as I'm concerned. It's Ellen I'm thinkin' about. She gets no pleasure out of life at all, an' it's not right.' Corker stared hard into Molly's eyes. 'You haven't got a bad mind, Molly, yer wouldn't see any harm in me taking Ellen for a drink, would yer?'

'I wouldn't, no! But we've got some nosy beggars in this street, an' Ellen has to live here.' Molly pressed her lips together, a look of determination on her face. 'But she's got a few good friends, too, an' we'll look after her.' She chuckled. 'I'll set Nellie on anyone who even looks sideways at her.'

'Thanks, Molly.' Corker looked relieved. 'Now another reason for me visit. Is Jill around?'

'Yeah, she's inside playin' cards with Jack an' Steve. Why?'

'If I can talk Ellen into coming for a drink, would Jill sit with the two girls? The boys are in bed already.'

'I think she'd jump at the chance. It would mean her an' Steve havin' some time on their own. But yer'd better ask her yerself.'

Half an hour later Molly was standing by the front window, peeping through the net curtain. 'Here they come. Ellen looks like a scared rabbit, as though every

252

eye in the street is watching.'

'If everyone is like you, they will be.' Jack rustled the *Echo*. 'I don't know whether I approve of this, yer know.'

'Oh, grow up, for heaven's sake!' Molly let the curtain fall back into place. 'Where's the harm in it? God knows, Ellen could do with a bit of pleasure in 'er life. She never goes over the flamin' door, only to work an' back. Some life that is!'

'I understand all that,' Jack said patiently. 'I don't begrudge Ellen gettin' some fun out of life, but yer know as well as I do that the neighbours will 'ave a field day . . . nice juicy bit of gossip, they'll lap it up.'

'Let them!' Molly straightened the chenille cloth on the table, then stood back to make sure the overhang was even. 'Pity they've got nothin' better to do.'

'I couldn't give a damn about the neighbours,' Jack said, his voice angry as he folded the paper and threw it on the couch. 'But I do give a damn about you an' Jill getting involved. I just wish yer'd stay out of it.'

'Oh, aye, Jack, stay in me own backyard, eh? Don't help anyone, just look after number one, is that it? Be selfish, an' to hell with everyone?'

As Jack closed his eyes, pictures of Nobby flashed through his mind. Nobby with his face contorted with anger, evil written all over it. Then Ellen appeared. A sad, pathetic creature, worn down by years of abuse and brutality. And the children. No flesh on their bones, rags on their backs, empty bellies and haunted eyes.

Jack sighed, rubbing a hand across his forehead. 'I'm sorry, love, you're right as usual. I'm a selfish bastard,

253

all cosy and content in me own little world, without a thought for anyone else. Never even gettin' off me backside or liftin' a finger to help. And that's wrong. I can't just take what I want from life without putting somethin' back.'

Molly sat on his knee and put her arms around his neck. Holding him close, she whispered, 'I love the bones of yer, Jack Bennett.'

He chuckled. 'What about the rest of me?'

'Oh, yer'd pass in a crowd.' Molly ruffled his hair before standing up, a wicked twinkle in her eye. 'A very big crowd.'

There was no letter for Jill on Monday or Tuesday, but on the third day when Tommy Maher turned into the street and saw Molly at the door, he dropped his heavy post bag and broke into a trot. Waving the letter over his head, he called, 'It's come, Molly!'

Her hands trembling, Molly took the letter. 'Thanks, Tommy, yer a pal.'

'I hope she's got the job.' He kept his eyes on the post bag, there were some dishonest people about. 'Let's know tomorrow, won't yer?'

Molly nodded before closing the door. She looked at the typed name and address on the envelope, as though concentrating on it would reveal its contents. She put the letter by Jill's plate, paced the floor a few times then picked it up again. 'Oh, blow it, I can't stand it any longer, she'll 'ave to get up.'

'Jill!' Molly gently shook the sleeping form. 'Come on, sunshine.'

She rolled on her back, rubbing her eyes. 'What time is it?'

'It's early yet, but I thought yer'd like to know, the letter's come.'

Jill was out of bed and down the stairs like greased lightning. Molly wasn't so sure-footed in the darkness of the hall, and by the time she got downstairs Jill was already reading the letter. 'I've got it, Mam! I've got the job!' She was hopping up and down with excitement. 'I start two weeks next Monday.'

Molly held her hand out for the letter, but the words were all running into one. Taking it to the window, she held the paper closer to her face, muttering, 'I'll get meself a pair of glasses one of these fine days.'

Her prayers had been answered. Oh, thank you, God, thank you!

Jill came up behind her mother, put her arms around her waist and together they did a little jig. 'Wait till yer dad comes home, he'll be over the moon.'

'And me nanna and grandpa.' Then the tears of happiness and relief started, and Jill sat at the table and sobbed her heart out while Molly made her breakfast.

'Come on, sunshine, yer've got to eat. Can't go out on an empty stomach.'

Jill wasn't hungry, but she nibbled on a piece of toast to please her mother. 'I didn't tell yer before, Mam,' she sniffed, ''cos I didn't think I'd get the job, but the wages are ten bob a week more than I'm getting now.'

Molly's mouth gaped. 'Oh, love, that's marvellous! Fancy that, now! But it couldn't happen to a nicer person. Your Mr Sedgewick knew a good thing when he saw one.'

'I'll be sad to leave the shop, though,' Jill said. 'They've all been so good to me, especially Mr John.'

'It's him yer've got to thank for this job.' Molly nodded knowingly. 'A reference from him must 'ave gone a long way.'

'I won't be working on a Saturday, so I'll be able to go down and see them all,' Jill consoled herself. 'I won't half miss them.'

'Yer've got the chance of a lifetime,' Molly said, her mind going back to Miss Bond. 'Grasp it with both hands.'

When Tommy came home from school that day, Molly sent him to tell her mother the good news. And as she knew they would, her ma and da hot-footed it around as soon as they'd had their tea. With a warm glow of happiness in her heart, and a grin on her face stretching from ear to ear, Molly sat back and watched the different reactions to Jill's good fortune. Jack was so happy you'd think he'd won the pools, and Bridie and Bob were full of admiration, praise and pride. But Doreen now – well, although she professed to be pleased, Molly thought she detected a note of envy in her voice. But that's only natural, she defended Doreen in her mind. She's only a kid, and seeing Jill getting all the attention is probably making her feel a bit left out.

Tommy's response made Molly chuckle. Although he didn't say it, you could see he was asking himself what all the fuss was about. 'I leave school at Christmas, so I'll be workin' meself soon.'

Ruthie though, crafty and with an eye to business, was only interested in one thing. 'Will I get an extra penny pocket money now, our Jill?'

Molly was walking back from the corner shop when she saw Corker ahead of her, his seaman's bag slung over his back. She hurried to catch up with him. 'Back to a life on the ocean wave, eh, Corker?'

'Aye, the ship sails with the afternoon tide, Molly.' He swung the bag from his shoulder and set it on the ground. 'If it weren't for the money, I wouldn't bother.' He stroked his beard and grinned. 'Terrible thing, money, isn't it, Molly? The root of all evil.'

'Aye, yer right there, Corker, but we'd be lost without it.' She swapped the heavy basket to her other arm. 'How long are yer away this time?'

'Six weeks. I won't be doin' any long hauls again, not with me ma the way she is. I feel bad leaving her, but what can I do? The sea's me life, it's all I know.'

'I'll keep an eye on yer mother, Corker, like I did last time. Me an' Nellie will take turns, make sure she's all right. We do the same with Miss Clegg. It keeps us out of mischief.'

'And Ellen?' Corker raised his bushy eyebrows. 'She's been tellin' me about what you, Nellie and Mary Watson have done for 'er. Without you, she said she'd be in the work-house.'

'I can take a hint, Corker,' Molly laughed. 'I'll make sure Ellen comes to no harm.' She squinted up at him. 'Yer know, I'm surprised no one has said a word about you an' Ellen! Twice yer've taken her for a drink, and there's not been a dickie-bird said. Either yer good at dodgin' people, or they're not as bad-minded as I thought.'

'Yer know my feelings on what people think, Molly, I really couldn't care less.'

'I don't suppose yer've been in to see Nobby again?'

'No chance! That once was enough for me.' He gave a low whistle. 'I think Ellen's right, the man is out of 'is mind. He never opened 'is mouth to me, just kept on staring. But I'll tell yer this, Molly, and I'm serious, if he'd had a knife he'd 'ave plunged it into me, and laughed while he was doing it.'

'I don't know what's to become of any of them,' Molly said. 'I feel so sorry for Ellen an' the kids, but what can I do?'

'You're doin' enough, Molly, and I'm grateful to you. Pass my thanks on to Nellie as well, will yer?' Corker picked up the ropes tying the top of his bag, lifted it from the ground and swung it over his shoulder. With a smile on his ruddy face, he bent and gave Molly a peck on the cheek. 'There, that should give the neighbours somethin' to talk about.'

'See yer soon, Corker.' Molly watched him walk away. 'Take care, now!'

'You too, girl! Ta-ra!'

Jill stepped off the tram in Dale Street, trembling and feeling sick inside. Steve was right, she should have stayed at Allerton's. She'd been happy there, surrounded by warmth and friendliness.

'It's too late now,' she told herself as she turned the

corner into Castle Street. 'As me mam said, I can't put the clock back.'

Jill gazed at the first-floor windows of the buildings she passed until she came to the one she wanted. Printed on the glass in gold lettering were the names Pearson, Sedgewick and Brown. Solicitors. Taking a deep breath and pushing her hair behind her ears, she mounted the stairs.

'Good morning, Miss Bennett. I'm Joan Sutton, Mr Sedgewick's secretary.'

'Good morning.' Jill shook the outstretched hand. The woman looked to be about thirty, with mousy, marcel-waved hair and a pale face devoid of make-up. She was wearing gold-rimmed glasses. She looked very efficient in her navy blue skirt and white tie-neck blouse, but Jill thought she had a kind, understanding face. 'I'm very nervous,' she confessed.

Joan Sutton took an instant liking to the shy girl. 'There's no need to be,' she whispered. 'I'll look after you. Come on, I'll show you which office you'll be working from. Mr Sedgewick doesn't come in until half-nine, so I'll have time to explain our filing system to you.'

Jill followed closely, too frightened to let her eyes linger on the other girl she could see sitting at a desk in one of the offices they passed. In her heart she was saying a prayer, please God, don't let me make a fool of myself.

Joan Sutton knocked on a door before throwing it open. 'Mr Miles, Miss Bennett is here.'

The young man finished what he was writing before

looking up. When he saw Jill he jumped to his feet. 'Hello, I'm Miles Sedgewick.'

Jill swallowed hard. He must be Mr Sedgewick's son. 'Jill Bennett.'

Joan Sutton was pulling a chair out from a desk at the opposite side of the office. 'This is your desk, Jill, you can put your belongings in a drawer. The files are kept in here,' she pointed to a row of cabinets, 'so you'll be working in here until such time as one of the partners may need you. Now, while you're getting settled in, I'll nip back to my office and finish a letter that urgently needs to be sent out this afternoon. I'll be back in ten minutes.'

When the door closed, Miles smiled across at Jill. 'Welcome to the firm.'

He can't be much older than me, she was thinking, and he's very good-looking. 'Thank you, Mr Miles.'

'Miles will do. And may I say that coming to work in future will be a much more pleasant prospect.'

Chapter Seventeen

'Will yer keep still!' Half a dozen straight pins were clamped between Doreen's lips, muffling her voice. From her kneeling position on the floor she glared up at Jill, who was standing on a kitchen chair. 'How d'yer expect me to get the hem right when yer keep twistin' around?'

'I'm sorry.' Jill stood to attention, her head held high, her back ramrod straight. She had on the dark brown straight skirt Doreen had made for her. It was almost finished now, only the hem to sew when Doreen was satisfied it was even all around. 'You've made a good job of it, Doreen, no one would dream it was home-made.'

'I should hope not!' Doreen scrambled to her feet. 'Turn round slowly.'

Molly sat looking on with interest, fingering the skirt of the dress her daughter had made for her. It was a navy blue cotton, covered in tiny white spots, and she was delighted with it. At this rate, the second-hand Singer treadle sewing machine she'd bought for ten bob four weeks ago would soon have paid for itself. Doreen had certainly lived up to her claims to be a good machinist.

And she could cut from paper patterns as though she'd been doing it for years. In fact, Molly told herself, for a kid not yet fifteen, she was brilliant.

'You can sew the hem yourself, Jill, it's not hard. Just make sure the stitches don't show through.' Doreen was feeling very pleased with herself. It was her turn to be the centre of attention and she was loving every minute of it.

'Come on, Maureen, on the chair.' Doreen slid some pins from a strip of paper. 'Let's see how yours is for length.'

Doreen's friend was a pleasant, happy girl, and Molly had taken to her the first time she'd seen her. But since the machine came, Maureen was at their house every night and there was no peace. If the sewing machine wasn't whirring away, the table was cluttered with paper patterns and the two girls would be laughing and chattering as they cut away at the material. They bought remnants from Blackler's, and could make a dress for about one and six and a skirt for less than a shilling.

'I'll sew it tomorrow night.' Jill draped the skirt carefully over her arm ready to take upstairs. 'I promised Steve I'd go for a walk for half an hour.'

When Jill was out of earshot, Maureen bent down and whispered, 'He's dead handsome, Jill's boyfriend, isn't he? Like a film star.'

Doreen whispered back, 'Keep yer eyes off 'im, Maureen Shepherd! If our Jill doesn't want 'im, I'm next in line.'

Jack was supposed to be reading the *Echo*, but when a smile crossed his face Molly knew he was listening to everything that went on. He looked up and caught her eye, winking as much as to say, 'Some hope they've got.'

At half past nine, Maureen glanced at the clock and sighed. 'I'd better be makin' tracks. Me mam does her nut if I'm not in by ten.'

'I'll walk to the tram stop with yer.' Doreen reached for her cardigan. 'Stretch me legs.'

'Just 'old yer horses, the pair of yer.' Molly pointed to the scraps of material littering the floor, and the paper patterns strewn across the table with reels of cotton and loose pins. 'Who was yer servant before I came along, might I ask? Now get this place tidied up before yer go anywhere. It looks like a muck midden.'

When they'd gone, the place looked more like home. Molly poked the fire into life and drew her chair near. 'Yer can tell winter's on its way, the nights are drawin' in and it's nippy out.'

'When are we goin' to have the place to ourselves again?' Jack asked, turning the page of the *Echo*. 'We always seem to have a houseful.'

'The novelty will soon wear off,' Molly laughed. 'But I hope it's not too soon. Our Ruthie's waitin' for a new dress. I've got to get a pattern when I go to the shops, an' if it hasn't got a sticky-out skirt there'll be blue murder.' She flexed her fingers before holding her hands out to the flickering flames. 'I can't get over our Doreen. For a kid of 'er age she's not half clever with her hands. I remember me ma sayin' Doreen would surprise me one of these days, an' she was right. I'm real proud of her.'

'She certainly made a good job of that dress yer've got on. It looks a treat on yer.'

263

'That's what Nellie an' Mary said. I haven't mentioned it to Doreen yet, but they want me to ask if she'll make them one. They said they'd pay 'er for it.'

'It's a way of making herself a few bob, I suppose.' Jack folded the paper carefully before putting it on the couch. 'Mind you, I don't fancy havin' people traipsing through the house every night, we'd never have any privacy.'

Molly glanced at the paper. 'Anythin' in the *Echo* worth reading?'

'Nowt but trouble,' he said. 'The way things are goin', there'll be another war before long.'

'Oh, ay, Jack, don't say that! The last one was supposed to be the war to end all wars.'

'Mark my words, Molly, the way Germany is building its armed forces up, they're gettin' ready for war. If we can believe the stories that are coming out of Germany, about the way the Jews are being persecuted, that Hitler is a monster. I wouldn't trust 'im as far as I could throw him.'

'He wouldn't try anythin' on with us, though, would he? Surely the man's not that stupid, not after we beat them last time.'

'He's already taken over the Sudeten an' got away with it. Now he's got his troops massed on the border of Austria, and I'll bet a pound to a penny it won't be long before he invades that country.'

Molly stared into the flames. 'If there was a war, you wouldn't be called up, would yer, not at your age?'

Jack shrugged his shoulders. 'I dunno! In the last war they called all the young ones up first, but it wasn't long before men of my age were being conscripted.'

'It doesn't bear thinkin' about.' She ran her hands over her thighs. 'Why do we 'ave to 'ave wars? Why can't we all live together in peace?'

'Because there will always be people like Hitler, love, greedy for power. Right through history it's been the same.'

'I hope to God you're wrong, Jack. Our Tommy's only a kid now, but in a couple of years he'd be old enough for the army.'

Jack cursed himself for taking the smile off her face. Why hadn't he kept his thoughts to himself? 'Don't start worryin' about something that may never happen, love. Hitler's probably got more sense than I'm givin' him credit for.'

'Someone should shoot 'im,' Molly said, grinding her teeth. 'If I 'ad a gun, I'd do it me bloody self!'

Steve laced his fingers with Jill's as they walked down the street. They saw each other every night without fail, sometimes just for half an hour if Jill wanted to wash her hair. Apart from Saturday when they went to the pictures, they would go window shopping or, if the weather was fine, they'd walk through the park. Jill was earning more money than Steve and could have afforded to go to the pictures more often, but knowing how proud he was, she never suggested treating him.

'How did work go today?'

'Smashing! Mr Brown's secretary was off sick so I did all his letters. It's the first time I've worked for him, and he was very nice.' Jill squeezed his hand. 'It made a change from filing all day, that gets very boring.'

Steve tried to keep the words back, but couldn't. 'And 'ow is your Mr Miles?'

'Will you stop calling him "my Mr Miles"?' Jill regretted ever telling Steve about sharing an office with Miles. If she'd known he was going to be so jealous, she would have kept quiet about it. 'We work together, that's all!'

Steve caught her around the waist and pulled her to him. 'I can't help being jealous of him bein' in the same room as you all day.'

'And I'm fed up telling you, there's no need to be jealous! He's a nice bloke, we get on well together, but that's all!'

'Okay, don't bite me head off! I was only kiddin'!' I'm a liar, Steve admitted to himself. I'm as jealous as hell and can't talk myself out of it. 'I can think of nothin' I'd like better than to sit all day just lookin' at you.'

Jill stopped dead in her tracks. 'If you think that's all Mr Miles has got to do, you're crazy! He's training to be a solicitor, being articled I think they call it, and he studies very hard. He's twenty now, and he's still got years to go before he qualifies. So he's got more important things on his mind than sitting looking at me all day, even if he thought I was worth it.'

'He 'asn't got a girlfriend, though, has he?' Steve knew he was going too far, making a mountain out of a molehill, but he couldn't help himself, his jealousy knew no bounds. 'Most men I know his age are courtin' strong.'

'Perhaps he's more interested in making something of himself than he is in courting.' The second the words left her lips, Jill was wishing she could take them back. She knew they had hurt Steve, she could tell by the look on his face, and the last thing in the world she wanted to do was hurt him. 'I'm sorry,' she said, 'I shouldn't have said that. I didn't mean it to sound the way it did.'

'You must 'ave been thinking it, or yer wouldn't have said it.'

'But you keep winding me up, always talking about Mr Miles! I'm your girlfriend, we see each other every night, so why keep harping on someone you don't even know?'

This was the nearest they'd ever come to arguing and Steve knew it was all his fault. If he didn't watch it, keep his feelings under control, he'd lose her. 'I'm sorry, love, I went too far.' He managed a smile. 'Forgive me?'

Jill gazed into his handsome face. 'I'll forgive you where thousands wouldn't.'

'That's my girl! Now, let's go and look in the shop windows, see what we'd buy if we 'ad the money.'

Molly was on her knees scrubbing the front step with a donkey stone, while at the same time holding a conversation with Nellie. 'I'm waitin' for the coalman, he's late today. I don't want to miss him 'cos I want 'im to throw an extra bag in, get a stock up for when the bad weather comes.'

'Good idea, I think I'll do the same.' Nellie leaned against the wall, her arms folded beneath her mountainous bosom. Although it was a cold day, she only had a short-sleeved cotton dress on, with a wrap-around pinny over it. She never seemed to feel the cold, always said she had enough fat on her to keep her warm. 'It's bound to go up a copper or two when the winter comes.'

Molly sat back on her heels, a grin on her face. 'Remember when the kids were little an' we 'ad to count every penny? Many's the time we borrowed a shovelful of coal off each other.'

'Yeah,' Nellie grinned back, 'they were the days. We were happy though, weren't we? Didn't 'ave a ha'penny to bless ourselves with, some days, but we still 'ad a laugh.'

'And the odd fight,' Molly chuckled, putting the donkey stone down and dipping her hands in the bucket of water at the side of her. Wringing out the floor-cloth, she grinned up at Nellie. 'We used to be fightin' over the kids, nearly tearing each other's hair out, and while we were goin' at it, high ding-dong, the kids had made it up and were playin' together.'

'Yeah, the neighbours used to come out an' watch.' There was a tender look on Nellie's face as she gazed down at Molly, now wiping the floor-cloth over the step. 'But we never really fell out, did we? We'd be callin' each other fit to burn one minute, then the best of mates the next.'

Molly threw the dirty floor-cloth into the bucket and struggled to her feet. 'I was all mouth, Nellie! If it 'ad ever come to blows, I'd have been away like a shot. One blow from you an' I'd 'ave been out for the count.'

Nellie screwed her eyes up, squinting down the street. 'Isn't this Ellen?'

Molly picked the bucket up before turning her head. 'Yeah, she's late today, must have been to the 'ospital.'

The smile Ellen raised was an effort. Her head was splitting, as though someone had tied a band around and was slowly tightening it until she felt like screaming. 'Busy, Molly?'

'Yeah, the step was filthy. Mind you, it'll be as bad as ever by tomorrow.' The bucket of water was heavy so Molly set it down before rubbing her hands down the front of her pinny. 'Been to the 'ospital, Ellen?'

'Yes, worse luck.' She pulled a face. 'I was dead chuffed on me way there, 'cos Mr Fletcher from the Maypole asked me to work an extra hour every day. It's a few bob extra every week and I was made up. But I might 'ave known Nobby would spoil it for me, like he's spoilt everythin' since the day I married him.'

Molly and Nellie exchanged glances. They could see Ellen was near to tears and wondered how much more the poor woman could take. 'Molly, put the bucket in the 'all and come an' have a cuppa with me.' Nellie took Ellen's arm. 'You too, Ellen.'

Seated at Nellie's table, Molly moved the aspidistra plant to one side. 'Can't see a thing with that in me way. It's as big as a flamin' tree!'

'Thirty leaves I've got on it now,' Nellie said proudly. 'I'll give yer a cuttin' off it if yer like, Ellen.'

'Thanks, Nellie.' The last thing Ellen needed was a plant, but she wouldn't say no. These two women were the only friends she had, and they'd been so good to her. Like fairy godmothers, they'd looked after her for the last four months. Without them, she'd have lost her sanity.

Molly could see the pain in Ellen's eyes and wondered

how Nobby still had the power to hurt her. 'Well, what's he been up to now?'

Ellen pinched the bridge of her nose, trying to ease the pain in her head.

'I can't make the man out. All the times I've been there, he's never once said a word to me. He stares me out, as though daring me to do something. It was the same today. I sat there for about fifteen minutes, then I couldn't take any more and left.' She let out a deep sigh. 'I was walking down the corridor when the matron called me into her office. Apparently the doctor wants to have Nobby fitted with artificial legs. They said he'd be able to get around on crutches if he 'ad them.' Ellen's fingers curled around the cup, as though taking comfort from the warmth. 'But Matron said Nobby won't entertain the idea. He uses terrible language, she said, and hits out at anyone who goes near 'im.'

'Trust Nobby,' Molly agreed. 'He's 'is own worst enemy. Anyone else in his position would do anythin' to be able to get out of that bed and move around under 'is own steam.'

'There's another man in the ward who lost 'is legs in an accident at the docks. He came in a month after Nobby, but he sits out in a chair by the side of the bed, an' he talks to everyone. He's strapped in, so he doesn't fall out, but he's got a smile for everyone.' Ellen sipped at the tea. 'Matron said he's being fitted with artificial legs an' he's over the moon.'

'Doesn't Nobby talk to the other men in the ward?' Nellie asked. 'Surely to God he must talk to someone?'

Ellen shook her head. 'Not a word to anyone! The only one he talks to is 'imself. Sits there all day, muttering under 'is breath. The other men in the ward feel sorry for me, I can tell. One day, when I was leavin', the man in the next bed called me over. He said not to worry, Nobby was like that with everyone, even the matron and nurses. He said he'd tried for weeks to get Nobby talkin', but he's given it up as a bad job.'

'What happens now, then?' Molly asked. 'Is that what Matron wanted to talk to yer about?'

'I haven't got a clue what's going to 'appen, and Matron only wanted to see me to keep me in the picture. She said Nobby's wounds 'ave healed well, and there's no reason why he couldn't learn to walk on artificial legs if he wanted to. But he flatly refuses to 'ave them, and that's that!'

'Oh, well, if he wants to spend the rest of 'is life in bed, that's 'is own look out,' Molly said. 'Let 'im get on with it.'

'But they're not goin' to keep him in 'ospital all his life, are they? An' I couldn't manage him at home.' Ellen's voice was thick with unshed tears. 'I know it's a sin, but I hate him! I couldn't bear 'im near me, never mind havin' to lift and carry for 'im.'

'When's Corker due home?' Molly asked suddenly. 'Should be any time now, shouldn't it?'

Ellen flushed at the unexpected question. 'I don't know for sure. Some day next week, I think.'

'He'll 'ave a word with the 'ospital.' Molly's head nodded slowly. 'They'll take more notice of a man, tell 'im more.' She lifted her empty cup and stared down into the tea leaves. 'I wish I could read cups, find out what's in store for me.'

'That's bad luck, that is,' Nellie said. 'Yer shouldn't believe in things like that.'

Ignoring Nellie's remark, Molly fastened her gaze on Ellen. 'I know I sound nosy, and it's none of my business, but when yer were young, did yer ever go out with Corker?'

The blush started at Ellen's neck and quickly covered her face. 'Why d'yer ask that?'

'Just curious, that's all,' Molly said, with a shrug of her shoulders. 'Yer can tell me to mind me own business, if yer like.'

Ellen started to fidget. 'I did go out with 'im a few times, yes, but what about it?'

'Was he goin' to sea then?' Molly slapped Ellen's hand. 'Stop pickin' yer nails, yer'll get a whitlow an' then yer'll know about it. Painful flamin' things they are.'

Nellie was leaning her fat elbows on the table, her eyes agog as she waited for Ellen's answer. When it wasn't forthcoming, she nudged her neighbour's arm. 'Well, was Corker goin' to sea when yer were goin' out with him?'

Ellen nodded. 'He was hardly ever home.'

'If he'd had a shore job, would yer 'ave gone out with him proper? Yer know, courted him?' Molly asked.

'I don't know!' Ellen started to pick at the skin around her nails again, then noticed Molly's frown and clasped her hands together. 'I was only eighteen, and he was away more than he was home. You can't court someone who's away six months at a time.'

'An' so Nobby came along an' swept yer off yer feet?' Molly pursed her lips. 'Yer a fool, Ellen. Anyone who turns down a good man like Corker for a stinker like Nobby must be tuppence short of a shilling.'

'I found that out the hard way, Molly. But what's done is done, there's no goin' back.'

Molly had her own thoughts on that, but kept them to herself. 'Yer lucky yer've got Corker for a friend, Ellen, he's one in a million.' She laid her hands flat on the table and pushed herself up. 'I'd better get 'ome and get some work done, otherwise my feller will think I sit on me backside all day.'

Nellie gave her friend a playful push, nearly knocking her off her feet. 'I'll stick up for yer, kid! You tell Jack I said yer don't sit on yer backside all day . . . only half the day.'

It was unusually quiet around the dinner table that night. The arguing and laughter was missing as all ears listened intently to what Molly was saying. When she'd finished, Tommy was the first to break the silence. 'Yer mean, he'd 'ave wooden legs, like Peg Leg Pete?'

Molly tapped her nose. 'Ay, nose fever, just keep yer trap shut. Anythin' yer hear in this house stays in this 'ouse, d'yer hear? If yer repeat one word, I'll break yer flamin' neck for yer.'

'Your mother's right,' Jack said. 'One word to a living soul an' yer'll have me to answer to.'

'I feel very sorry for Mrs Clarke and the kids,' Jill said. 'She must be worried sick.'

'She was daft for marryin' him.' Doreen spoke with

273

her mouth half full. 'He's so ugly an' mean, I don't know what she ever saw in him. She must be blind.'

'Ay, clever clogs, just wait an' see what sort of a husband you get! Yer've got to live with a person before yer know what they're really like.' Molly hadn't mentioned Corker and was glad now she hadn't. In fact, she realised too late she shouldn't have said anything in front of the children. If she'd had any sense, she'd have waited until she and Jack were on their own. 'Nobby was probably all right when they were courtin'.'

Jill was pushing a potato around her plate. 'How does Mrs Clarke manage for money?'

'She doesn't!' Molly said. 'Mind you, she never moans. But I know what she gets, and by the time she's paid her ways she can't 'ave a penny over to buy anythin' for herself or the kids. They never get any pocket money for sweets, an' their clothes are in rags. An' yer must 'ave noticed that Ellen's still wearin' the clothes you an' Mary gave her.'

Silence descended once again as heads were bent over plates. It had taken the plight of their neighbours to make them realise how lucky they were. 'I've got a ball Peter can 'ave,' Tommy said gruffly. 'An' I've got some ollies he can share with Gordon. I'm too big now to play silly games.'

Molly smiled at him fondly. 'Yeah, yer a big lad now, sunshine! Be leavin' school in a few months!'

'I've got a skirt an' blouse Mrs Clarke can 'ave,' Doreen said. 'I've got plenty of clothes now I'm makin' me own.'

Molly's heart was swelling with love and pride. Hers

274

was a family to be proud of. 'Thanks, love, Ellen will be made up.'

Jill was wondering how she could help, then an idea came to her. 'Doreen, if I bought the material, would you make dresses for Phoebe and Dorothy?' She saw the look that crossed her sister's face and hurried on before the refusal came. 'Go on, Doreen, please? I don't think they've ever had a new dress in their lives, and they'd be so thrilled. It wouldn't take you long, you're so quick. If I was as clever as you, I'd make them myself.'

Such praise from a sister she'd always envied had Doreen sitting up straight, a look of pleasure on her face. 'Yeah, okay! But you'll buy the cotton as well as the material, won't yer?'

Jill nodded. 'And the pattern.'

'There's no need to buy a pattern,' Doreen boasted. 'I can use the one we've got. All I've got to do is make a tuck in it.'

There was genuine admiration on Jill's face. 'You were lucky getting that job in Johnson's, you know, Doreen. You've learned something that'll be of use to you all through your life, especially when you get married and have children. I mean, it's not only clothes you can make, but curtains, sheets, everything! As for me, what can I do when I get married? Shorthand and typing aren't going to get me very far.' She grinned. 'Unless I write me shopping list in shorthand, just to amuse meself.'

'Go way, yer've got more brains in yer little finger than I've got in me whole body.' Doreen put her arm around her sister's shoulder and squeezed. 'You're the brains of the family.'

Molly sat with her mouth open. This was the first real show of affection she'd seen between her daughters. Their natures were so different, she'd resigned herself to the fact they'd never be really close. But this little scene had proved her wrong. And to think it had been brought about by Ellen's troubles! It's a funny old world, Molly thought as she pushed her chair back. And if I don't move myself quick, I'll start blubbering like a baby!

Always able to read his wife's mind, Jack collected the plates and followed her into the kitchen. As he expected, tears were glistening in her eyes. He put the plates down on the draining board and held his arms wide. 'Come here.'

Molly went willingly. With her arms around his waist and her head resting on his chest, she sniffed, 'We've got lovely kids, haven't we, Jack?'

He stroked her hair. 'They couldn't be anythin' else, with the mother they've got. Yer've got a heart as big as a week, Molly, an' I'm crazy about yer.'

'Go on, yer daft ha'porth!' She ran the back of her hand across her nose. 'It's you they take after . . . the bestest man in the whole world.'

A discreet cough forced them to break apart. 'I'll help with the dishes, Mam.' Jill rolled the sleeves of her blouse up. 'I'll wash, you dry.'

Jack went to sit in his favourite chair by the fire and picked the evening *Echo* up. He could hear the low murmur of voices from the kitchen and smiled. God was certainly looking after him the night he met Molly. He couldn't imagine a life without her.

Molly picked up a plate and rubbed the tea towel over it. 'Our Tommy's gone next door with the toys, but I've told 'im to keep his trap shut about the clothes. I want it to be a surprise.' She reached up to put the plate on a shelf. 'I've been thinkin', we can't leave the two boys out, they'd be broken-hearted. So for my contribution, I'll nip down to Paddy's market and see if I can get them a decent pair of second-hand trousers an' a shirt each.'

Jill emptied the bowl of water into the sink. 'If you can, get them a jersey each, and I'll pay for them. It was cold when I came in tonight, and they were standing by their door with just their thin shirts on. They must have been freezing.'

'I don't think they feel the cold, love, they're used to it.' Molly hung the wet tea towel on the draining board. 'Ellen hasn't got the money to buy enough coal to keep the 'ouse warm.'

'It's sad, isn't it, Mam?'

Molly moved closer and whispered in Jill's ear, 'It is, sunshine, but I've got a feelin' in me bones that one of these days, things are goin' to start lookin' up for Ellen. An' it won't be before time.'

Chapter Eighteen

Doreen chewed on her food without relish. Her mouth was so dry with nerves, the piece of dumpling she was eating felt like a ball of cotton wool. She glanced at her mother under lowered lids, trying to pluck up courage to ask the question that was burning on her tongue but wouldn't pass her lips. She was the only one at the table; her dad was working late, Jill had gone out with Steve, Tommy was playing with his mates and Ruthie was in bed.

'Yer very quiet tonight.' Molly was eyeing her daughter suspiciously. 'Is somethin' wrong?'

'No!' Go on, Doreen urged herself, get it over with. If you leave it any longer someone will come in and you'll have lost the chance. 'Mam, I've told yer about Mike Grant, haven't I? The boy who works in our place, fixes our machines when they break down?'

Molly nodded. 'I've heard you an' Maureen talk about 'im, why?'

Doreen took a deep breath. 'He's asked me to go to the pictures with him on Saturday.'

'What!' Molly laid her knife and fork down. 'Over my

dead body! Does he know 'ow old yer are?'

'Of course he does! An' there's no harm in goin' to the flicks with him, he's a nice bloke.' Doreen averted her eyes. 'His mate, Sammy, has asked Maureen, so there'd be four of us goin'.'

'Yer mean there would be four if I said yer could go, which I'm not about to,' Molly huffed. 'Fourteen years of age an' going out with a boy, yer dad would 'ave something to say about that!'

'I'll be fifteen in three weeks!' Watch your temper, Doreen warned herself, or you'll rub her up the wrong way. 'Ah, go on, Mam! We'll go to the first house an' be in early, I promise.'

Molly knew now how her own mother had felt when she wanted to grow up before her time but it wasn't without sympathy that she said, 'Even if I said yer could go, yer dad wouldn't agree to it. We've never even seen the boy, know nothin' about him.'

'He knew yer wouldn't like it, said his mother wouldn't let 'is young sister go out with a stranger either. So he's comin' up tonight to ask yer himself.'

That took the wind out of Molly's sails. He can't be that bad, she thought. At least he seems to have a bit of sense. 'How old is he?'

'Him and Sammy are both seventeen.' Now she'd got it off her chest, the churning in Doreen's tummy eased. 'You'd like 'im, Mam, honest!'

'That remains to be seen. An' yer say he's comin' here tonight?'

'I told him to wait at the corner of the street for me. I didn't want him knockin' here and gettin' his head chewed off.' Doreen picked up Molly's plate and placed it on top of her own. 'I'll help yer wash up.'

Molly couldn't keep the chuckle back. 'Yer a crafty little madam, our Doreen. D'yer think I'm so daft I don't know when yer trying to soft soap me? I wasn't born yesterday, nor am I as green as I'm cabbage looking! Offerin' to wash the dishes, for the first time in living memory, I might add, won't get yer anywhere with me, my girl.'

'But yer will see him, won't yer, Mam, please?'

'Yeah, okay! But I'm not promising anythin', mind! We'll have to wait an' see what yer dad says, he's the boss in this house.'

Doreen closed her eyes in relief. Her dad might think he was the boss in the house, but Doreen knew different. She'd seen her mother twist him round her little finger. 'Yer won't make a fool of me in front of Mike, will yer, Mam? Don't forget I've got to work with him.'

Molly poured the kettle of hot water over the dishes in the bowl. 'Is Maureen comin' tonight as well?'

Doreen stood next to the sink, the tea towel ready in her hand. 'No, she's staying in, 'cos Sammy's goin' to see her mam and dad.'

Molly let the water drip off a plate before laying it on the draining-board. 'Well, I'll say this for the boys, they've got good, old-fashioned manners.' She saw Doreen grin and hastened to add, 'Don't think it's all signed, sealed and delivered, kid, 'cos as I've said, it's up to yer dad.'

Jack was eating his meal when Doreen came in. She was

281

followed by a tall, thin boy who seemed to be all arms and legs. He had a pale complexion, fine blond hair, and bright blue eyes that were blinking fifteen to the dozen with nerves. He looked so terrified, Molly felt like mothering him.

'Hello, Mike.' She stretched her hand out. 'Our Doreen's told us all about yer.'

'How d'yer do, Mrs Bennett?' Mike's voice was gruff, and the smile he attempted didn't quite come off. He offered his hand to Jack. 'Pleased to meet yer, Mr Bennett.'

'Same here, son, same here.' Jack had been primed by Molly to be pleasant. If we don't like him, she'd said, then Doreen's not going out with him. But the boy's doing it the right way, asking permission, so let's give him a chance. 'Sit down, son,' Jack waved his fork, 'make yerself comfortable.'

'Thank you.' Mike turned to Doreen, and when she indicated the couch, he sat down. 'I'm sorry to interrupt when yer havin' yer dinner.'

'Think nothin' of it,' Jack laughed. 'I was born in a zoo, so I'm used to eatin' in public.'

'So that's it!' Molly's laugh was loud. 'I wondered why yer were covered in hair and swing from the lamp-posts.' She winked at Mike. 'Married twenty years and now he tells me he's a gorilla!'

Molly could see the tension leaving Mike's body as he sat back on the couch. Poor bugger, he was scared stiff when he came in. Probably thought we were going to eat him. But he's well mannered, and he's got guts. And what's more, I like him, she decided. Our Doreen won't come to any harm with him.

'Doreen said yer want to take her to the pictures on Saturday, Mike,.is that right?' Molly saw him run his tongue over his lips, his face flushed to the colour of beetroot. She felt sympathy for his discomfort and hurried on before he could answer, 'It's all right with me as long as there's four of yez goin', but it's really up to me husband.'

Jack glared at her. Well, if that wasn't dropping him in it! Still, he had to admit the boy seemed decent enough. And he had no doubt that his daughter was well able to take care of herself. Hadn't she fought with the biggest boys in the street and licked them? 'She's to be in by ten o'clock, Mike, so think on. Any later an' that'll be her lot.'

'Ooh, the gear!' Doreen wagged her head from side to side. 'Thanks, Mam, Dad.'

'I'll make sure she's home, Mr Bennett.' There was sincerity in the deep voice that seemed at odds with the tall, thin body. 'Ten o'clock on the dot.'

At the end of the day, with all the children in bed and the house quiet except for the hissing of the coals, Molly put her feet up on the couch. 'Just ten minutes, then I'm hittin' the hay.' She lifted her foot and poked at Jack's arm. 'Two workin' and two courtin'!'

'Oh, come on, love, don't be putting years on them! I know Jill's courting, but our Doreen's a different kettle of fish. She's just findin' her feet, and I've got a feeling Mike's just the first of many. I'm not saying she's a good time girl, but I'll bet this time next year she'll be out flying her kite. She'll get the most out of life before settlin' down, an' I don't blame her.'

'Neither do I, as long as she doesn't bring trouble to our door.' Molly ran a hand through her hair, making it stand on end. 'Time doesn't half go quick, doesn't it, love? It seems only yesterday they were all babies, an' now the two girls are workin' and Tommy leaves school at Christmas. Pretty soon there'll only be thee an' me, and our Ruthie.'

Jack leaned over to smooth her hair down. 'You look like Stan Laurel after he's got Ollie into another fine mess.' He stood up to kiss her brow then fell back into his chair. 'Talkin' about Christmas, it's only about five weeks off, isn't it?'

'Yeah, it's Doreen's birthday in three weeks, then two weeks after it's Christmas.' Molly's eyes lit up. 'I'm not half organised this year, Jack. In fact, I'm so far ahead I'll soon be meetin' meself comin' back! For months now I've been payin' a few coppers each week in the butcher's, the greengrocer's, and the corner shop, so that's nearly all the food paid for. An' I don't owe me club woman very much, so I can get a cheque for clothes an' shoes.'

Jack smiled. 'Got it worked out to a fine art, haven't yer?'

'Yer've no idea what a difference it makes havin' the two girls' wages comin' in every week. When I think of all the years I 'ad to scrimp and scrape.' Molly shuddered. 'Ooh, I'd hate to go through that again.'

'Please God you never will,' Jack said. 'You kept this family going through those bad days, love, and yer've earned every penny yer get now. So go mad, make this the best Christmas we've ever had.'

Molly clasped her hands together and rested her chin on them. 'I've got wicked thoughts in me head, Jack, and try as I may, I can't get rid of them. Remember last Christmas, I was lookin' forward to the first party we'd ever had, an' Nobby Clarke spoiled it for me? Well, may God forgive me, but I keep thinking he can't spoil it for me this year.' Her eyes held Jack's. 'Isn't that wicked of me? I say me prayers, and when I come to the part about forgiving those who trespass against us, the words stick in me throat.'

'Molly, you haven't got a wicked bone in yer body. If anyone is wicked, it's Nobby Clarke. What happened to him was his own fault. He was in a drunken stupor, spendin' money while his wife an' children starved. I have no sympathy for him, only contempt.'

'Ellen won't 'ave much money for Christmas, but at least she won't have the worry of 'im comin' in drunk and knockin' her about,' Molly said. 'An' Tony's givin' her a turkey as a present, so at least they won't starve. Me an' Nellie will 'elp with pressies for the kids, make sure they have somethin' to wake up to on Christmas morning.'

'You haven't mentioned Nobby for a few days. Hasn't Ellen been in to see 'im?'

Molly shook her head. 'Not for a week. I think she's been waitin' for Corker to come 'ome, hopin' he'll be able to find out what's goin' on. She's terrified of goin' in herself in case they say they're sendin' Nobby home. But surely she couldn't be expected to look after him, Jack! She's only the size of sixpennyworth of copper, an' so thin that if she stands sideways yer can't see her!'

'When's Corker's ship due in?'

'He came 'ome this afternoon. I only spoke to 'im for a few minutes, 'cos we were both in a hurry, but he did say he'd be goin' to the 'ospital tomorrow. We'll know more then.'

'How come Corker an' Ellen are so friendly all of a sudden? I didn't think they knew each other that well.'

'Oh, they've known each other for donkey's years!' There were some things Molly had kept to herself. 'He knew Nobby as well, but never liked him. An' yer know what the queer feller was like. All he wanted was 'is boozing pals. So with Corker bein' away at sea all the time, he's never bothered.'

'Turned up trumps now though, hasn't he? Ellen seems to rely on him a lot.'

'Yer can say that again!' Molly slid her legs from the couch, thinking it would be better if she made herself scarce before she was forced into telling more lies. Least said, soonest mended. 'I'm off. An' don't be puttin' yer cold feet on me when yer come to bed, Jack Bennett! Yer wait till I've got the bed nice an' warm, then plonk yer ice cold feet on me!'

'I didn't think you'd noticed,' he laughed.

'Aye, well, now yer know different.' Molly yawned as she opened the living room door. 'If yer feet are cold, keep yer socks on.'

Ruthie laid her head on the table. 'Mam, I feel sick.'

Molly put the pot of tea down and gazed at her daughter with suspicion. It wouldn't be the first time

Ruthie had tried to talk her way out of going to school, but she did look a bit pale this morning. 'What is it, sunshine?' Molly felt the child's forehead and was alarmed to find it burning hot. 'Turn around, sweetheart, an' let yer mam have a look at yer.'

'Don't do that, Mam!' Ruthie protested when Molly lifted her jumper and vest. Tommy was sitting opposite, viewing the proceedings with interest as he chewed on a piece of toast, and his sister was embarrassed that he could see her tummy. 'Stop it, Mam!'

Molly groaned when she saw the tell-tale red marks. 'That's all I need! I think yer've got the measles, sunshine, or the chicken-pox.'

She pulled Ruthie's clothes down. 'No school for you until yer've seen the doctor.' Molly looked at the clock, telling herself it could be worse. At least it would be over by Christmas. 'Tommy, run over to Mary's an' tell her Ruthie won't be goin' to school today 'cos I think she's got the measles.'

He was back within minutes. 'Mary said their Bella's covered in spots, too! She's callin' the doctor out.'

'Blimey! The whole ruddy school must 'ave it! Anyway, the doctor can look at Ruthie while he's at Mary's. Now you poppy off, son, or yer'll be gettin' the cane for being late. But hurry home in case I need some shoppin'.'

Molly brought a blanket and pillow down and made Ruthie comfortable on the couch. 'I'll run up to the corner shop for some bread, sunshine, an' make yer some nice bread an' milk. I'll be as quick as I can, in case the doctor comes.'

But it was two o'clock when the doctor arrived, looking very flustered. 'It's raging, Mrs Bennett,' he said, feeling Ruthie's pulse. 'I've been run off my feet for the last week.' He lifted the little girl's nightdress and nodded. 'It's measles all right. I think half the children in the neighbourhood have caught it.' He pushed a wayward strand of hair from his eyes in a gesture of weariness. 'You know what to do. Keep her in an even temperature, no moving from one room to another, and give her plenty of liquid. Oh, and draw the curtains, keep the light from her eyes.' He swung his bag from the floor. 'Call me out if you're worried, otherwise I'll see her next week.'

Molly came back from seeing the doctor out and stood beside the couch. 'Well, that's you confined to barracks, sunshine! Yer'll 'ave to sleep on the couch, 'cos the draughts in yer bedroom are somethin' chronic.' She put her finger under her daughter's chin and lifted the pixie-like face. 'There's one consolation, at least yer know yer best friend feels as bad as you.'

'Can Bella come and lie on the couch with me?' Ruthie's lip trembled. The prospect of being off school appealed to her, but not if she was going to feel as sick as she did now. 'We're only little, we'd both fit on, easy.'

'Uh, uh, I'm afraid not! Like you, Bella won't be goin' anywhere for the next week or two.' Molly tucked the blanket around her daughter. 'Now, while I see to the dinner, why don't yer have a little sleep?'

Next time Molly looked in her daughter was in a deep sleep, her thumb stuck in her mouth. Walking on tip-toe, Molly crept down the hall and silently opened the front door. While the coast was clear, she'd nip over and see how Mary was coping. Molly had gone through measles, chicken-pox and mumps with each one of hers, but Bella was Mary's only child and she was probably worried sick.

'I won't come in, Mary, 'cos I've left Ruthie asleep. If she wakes up an' finds me gone, she'll scream the 'ouse down. I only slipped across to see 'ow things were.'

Mary was wringing her hands in distress, her eyes red-rimmed from crying. 'She looks so ill, Molly!'

'I know.' Molly rubbed her arms briskly. It was a freezing cold day and she was sorry now she hadn't put her coat on. 'I've been through it all with the other three so I know what to expect. There's an old wives' tale that says "It take three days to come on, stays three days, then takes three days to go away". That's how it spreads so easily. They pass it on during the first three days when they don't know they've got it.' She grasped Mary's arm. 'Don't worry, kid, this time next week they'll both be over the worst. They'll be runnin' around, gettin' under our feet an' eating us out of house an' home.'

'Please God.' Mary's eyes went to the heavens. 'She frightened the life out of me.'

'I'll send our Tommy over when he comes 'ome from school an' he'll get yer messages for yer. But if yer need me, give us a shout.' As Molly turned, she saw Ellen and Corker walking up the street. 'I'll see yer later, Mary, ta-ra!'

Molly put her head inside the front door to listen for signs that her daughter was awake, but everywhere was quiet. So she stood on the step waiting for her friends, thinking what an odd couple they made. Mind you, anyone would look like a midget next to Corker. A man and a half, he was!

'Well, any news?'

'Molly, d'yer mind if I don't stop?' Ellen said. 'I've got to be at work in an hour, an' I want to get the fire goin' for the kids comin' home from school. I don't want them comin' in to a cold house.'

It was Corker who answered. 'You go about yer business, girl, I'll have a word with Molly.'

They watched Ellen put the key in the lock and when she disappeared from view, Corker shook his head. 'That's one woman with more troubles than the rest of us put together.'

'Corker, before I ask yer in, have yer ever had the measles?' Molly saw his startled expression. 'Yer see, our Ruthie's come down with it.'

Corker's laugh started as a low rumble, then grew into a loud guffaw. 'Molly, me darlin', I've had every disease known to man . . . and quite a few not known to anyone.'

'Right, yer can come in then.' Molly held the door while he passed. 'Try not to make too much noise, our baby's asleep on the couch.'

'Let's go through to the kitchen,' he whispered. 'It's best if she doesn't hear what I've got to say.'

While Molly filled the kettle and struck a match over the gas ring, Corker spoke in a low voice. 'We looked in the ward first but Nobby was just the same. Ignored both of us. Seemed to be in a world of his own. So I sat Ellen down in the corridor and went in search of the matron.' He cocked his ear, still no sound. 'I'll keep it brief in case the little one wakes up. The matron called Ellen, then sat us in 'er office while she went for the doctor. When he came he told us that at first they thought Nobby's strange behaviour was a result of the accident, and the trauma of havin' his legs amputated. He said he was firmly convinced that, given time, Nobby's mental state would improve. But there's been no improvement, in fact there's been a deterioration. He's so abusive and violent, the staff can't handle him.' Corker wiped his hand across his forehead. 'They're transferring Nobby to an institution for the insane.'

'Oh, dear Mother of God!' Molly's hand was shaking so badly the cup started to rattle in the saucer she was holding. She put them on the draining board and covered her face with her hands. 'I feel terrible, Corker! I've called that man fit to burn, but never in a million years would I wish this on him.'

'Ellen nearly collapsed in the matron's office. How the hell she's goin' to work, the state she's in, I'll never know,' Corker said. 'She's feeling guilty, blaming herself. Said perhaps if she'd tried harder, she'd 'ave made a better wife.' His laugh was hollow. 'He's beaten her, kicked her, walked all over 'er, and she still thinks it's her fault. I've tried to reason with her, reminded her of what Nobby put her through, but it doesn't seem to sink in.'

'I'll go in to her when she gets 'ome from work.' Molly poured the spilled tea from the saucer into the sink before handing it over. 'When yer come to think about it, it's probably for the best. She could never 'ave managed to look after 'im, not the way he is.

Imagine her trying to lift 'im, wash and dress 'im, seein' to his toileting . . . she'd 'ave been dead in a week! Even if he was the best-tempered person in the world, with the patience of a saint, she'd never have been able to cope.' Molly heard a faint cry from the living room and put her finger to her lips before whispering, 'An' where would the money come from to keep them? She wouldn't be able to leave 'im to go to work.' She poked her head around the living room door. 'Comin' now, sunshine.' She turned back to Corker. 'I really do feel sorry for Nobby, but if he's out of 'is mind, he won't know anythin' about it, an' that's a blessing.'

When Corker walked in behind Molly, Ruthie smiled and tried to sit up. 'I'm poorly, Sinbad, I've got the measles.'

Corker ruffled her hair. 'It's not very nice, is it, me darlin'? I remember getting it when I was your age, an' I didn't half play me mother up, crying and moaning, day an' night. A real big baby I was, not like you. I bet you're not goin' to make a fuss like I did, are you?'

Ruthie shook her head solemnly, her eyes like saucers. She couldn't imagine the big man ever being a baby. 'No, Sinbad, I'm goin' to be a good girl for me mam.'

'That's the spirit!' He smoothed down his hair before donning his cap. 'I'll be in to see you tomorrow an' I'll bring yer a nice slab of chocolate. What's yer favourite?'

'Fry's chocolate cream,' Ruthie said without hesitation. 'It's me mam's favourite as well!'

'You crafty little so-and-so!' Molly laughed. 'Take no

notice of 'er, Corker, she's tryin' to cadge an extra bar for 'erself.'

'When I get home, I'll count me pennies. If I've got enough, and your mam say's yer've been good, I'll mug yer to a large slab.'

Molly saw him to the door. 'That'll keep her quiet. She'll do anythin' for a Fry's chocolate cream.'

'I'll see yer tomorrow, Molly, but don't forget to go next door, will yer? Ellen needs a woman to talk to, she gets embarrassed with me.'

'I'll watch for 'er passing the window, give 'er time to get the kids to bed, then go in. I'll 'ave a go, see if I can get 'er to open up. She'll feel better if she gets it all off 'er chest. As me mam says, a trouble shared is a trouble halved. An' my shoulder will always be there for Ellen to cry on.'

'I know that, Molly, me darlin',' Corker said as he walked away. 'I know that.'

Jack wasn't working overtime that night, so all the family were having their meal together. But Molly wasn't sitting at the table, she was perched on the end of the couch, her plate balanced on her knee. Her eyes kept going to her daughter, who was whimpering and fretful. 'I've got a rice pudding in the oven, sunshine, just for you. I'll put plenty of sugar an' milk on top, an' yer'll really enjoy it.'

Jack turned in his chair. 'You'll not get a wink of sleep if yer stay down here, love, none of the chairs is comfortable. Why not light the fire in the back bedroom and Ruthie can go to bed?'

'Yer must be joking! That fire hasn't been lit for

donkey's years, the chimney will be full of soot!' Molly used one of her hands to push herself up. 'No, I'll stay down here, where I can keep me eye on 'er. It won't do me no harm for a few nights.'

Doreen was round the table like a shot to take Molly's empty plate from her. 'I'll wash up, Mam.'

Molly's eyes became slits. 'Again! Now what are yer after? When you offer to wash up I know it's not out of the goodness of yer heart, so what is it this time?'

Doreen had the grace to blush. 'I wanted to ask yer a favour. Trust our Ruthie to get measles now, 'cos yer'll probably say no!'

'Try me,' Molly said. 'I'm not exactly in the best of moods, but go on, what d'yer want?'

Doreen could feel five pairs of eyes boring into her, all eager to know what was on her mind. She moved from one foot to the other, suddenly wanting to go down the yard to the lavvy. 'I was wonderin' like, if instead of givin' me money for me birthday, like yer did our Jill, could I 'ave a party?'

'Did yer hear that, Jack? Last night it was the pictures, tonight it's a flippin' party!' Molly could feel laughter bubbling inside, then decided she had nothing to laugh about so it must be hysterics. 'What 'ave yer got in mind for tomorrow night, Doreen? A box at the Empire, or is it dinner at the Adelphi Hotel?'

'Only a small party, Mam!' Having got the worst over now, she had no intention of giving up without a fight. 'Just Maureen, Mike an' Sammy. An' our Jill and Steve, if they want to come.'

Molly's change of mind was so rapid she didn't even

know it was happening. To hell with it, she thought, why not? There's so much sadness and misery around, we need something like a party to cheer us up. 'Okay, sunshine, but only on condition that it's not only for youngsters.' She looked around the five disbelieving faces and grinned. 'It goes without sayin' that me and yer dad will be here to chaperon yez, an' yer can invite Nanna and Grandpa, and Nellie an' George too.' After a slight pause, she added, 'And Ellen.'

'Oh, thanks, Mam!' Doreen's face glowed with pleasure. 'Yer an angel.'

'Don't thank me, thank this little one!' Molly bent to rub Ruthie's tummy. 'If it was next week yer'd got the measles, there'd be no party, would there, sunshine?'

'Are yer sure yer can manage it, love?' Jack looked doubtful. 'It's just before Christmas, an' I thought yer wanted to have a few people in then.'

'It won't cost much, Jack, there'll be no booze, only lemonade.' Molly lifted her clasped hands over her head and did a little jig, singing 'McNamara's Band'. 'We don't need to get plastered to enjoy ourselves.' She stopped dancing, her chest heaving from the exertion. 'D'yer know, I've 'ad a right miserable day, what with one thing and another, but now I've got somethin' to look forward to, I feel fantastic! We'll 'ave a little do for Doreen's birthday, and a real jars out knees-up for Christmas.' She clapped her hands in glee. 'Oh, it's good to be alive!'

Chapter Nineteen

Doreen's party wasn't turning out as Molly had hoped. The young ones were sitting on the straight chairs by the table, looking bored stiff. And Molly wasn't surprised, because the conversations going on around couldn't possibly be of interest to them. The men had their heads together talking about Germany and the threat of war, while the women chattered about everything under the sun. What their neighbours were up to, the weather and the price of food. They were hardly topics to interest the youngsters and their faces showed how fed up they were. Doreen was looking really down in the mouth, disappointed that her party was turning out to be a flop.

If we weren't here, Molly thought, they'd soon liven themselves up, make their own enjoyment. The situation called for drastic action. 'Jack, will yer leave Hitler alone for a while? I'm fed up hearing his blasted name!'

He looked up, surprised. 'We're only talkin', love!'

'An' a bloody miserable conversation it is . . . nothin' but war, war, war! I think we should go out for a drink, leave the young ones to enjoy themselves. What d'yer say, Nellie?'

'Good idea!' She understood the message in Molly's eyes. 'My feller hasn't taken me for a drink since Adam was a lad!'

'That's settled then.' Molly didn't bother asking what the others thought. She'd explain when they got to the pub. 'Come on, gang, get yer coats on an' we'll be off.' She pointed a finger at Steve. 'You're the eldest, Steve, so I'm relyin' on yer not to let the others make too much noise. An' if the 'ouse gets wrecked, I'll batter the lot of yez.' She ushered the others out, then turned at the door and gave a broad wink.

'Enjoy yerselves, but don't forget to listen for Ruthie.'

'We will, Mam, honest!' Doreen readily agreed, silently thanking her mother for coming to her rescue. 'We won't make any noise.'

Ellen was waiting outside the door for Molly. The others had walked on, the men leading the way, still talking about the threat Germany was posing, while Nellie and Bridie walked behind, arm in arm. 'Molly, I won't come to the pub, if yer don't mind.'

Molly didn't need telling why. 'Yer won't need any money, Ellen, the men will pay.'

She shook her head, wrapping her coat more closely around her body. 'I'm not goin' anywhere if I can't pay me whack.'

'Don't be so flamin' independent! Can't my feller mug yer to a glass of port if he wants to, for heaven's sake? It's only coppers!' Molly bit on her top lip before trying a different approach. 'He'll be upset if yer don't come, Ellen. In fact they'll all be upset, think yer don't like their company.'

'They won't even miss me, Molly! I'm not exactly the life an' soul of the party, am I?' The confidence Ellen had gained when Nobby was in hospital had left her since he'd been transferred to Winwick Mental Hospital. One day, in a rare show of emotion, she'd told Molly she felt ashamed and thought everyone was talking about her. It was the day she'd travelled all the way to the hospital in Warrington to see him. She'd had to miss the rent to pay the fare and take him a new pair of pyjamas, but as she told Molly, she may as well not have bothered because he didn't even know her. 'You go on, Molly,' she said now, 'don't worry about me.'

'Who the heck's worried? Yer a big girl now, Ellen, yer don't need anyone to worry about yer. But I think yer a bit mean to spoil me party. It's me first bit of pleasure since our Ruthie got the measles.'

Ellen grasped her arm. 'I don't want to spoil yer pleasure, Molly, it's the last thing in the world I'd want to do, yer've been so good to me.'

'Then come on!' Molly took a tight grip on the thin hand and started to pull. 'By the time we get there, the others will be blotto!'

She pulled Ellen through the group of men standing by the bar, to a table in the corner where the others were sitting. 'Where's yer manners, Jack Bennett? Sittin' down while there's ladies standin'! You weren't brought up, yer were dragged up!'

He sprang to his feet. He could see by Ellen's face she didn't want to be there, and guessed why. 'I've ordered yez both a port and lemon, I hope that's all right?'

Ellen nodded. 'Thanks, Jack.'

Perched on a round stool, Molly leaned across the table and stared into her husband's face. 'If I hear the words "Hitler", "Germany" or "war", I'll flatten yer. I'm here to enjoy meself, an' it's nourishment I want, not punishment.'

'Okay, boss!' Jack, leaning to one side so the barman could put the tray of drinks on the table, whispered in Bridie's ear, 'She's a holy terror, that daughter of yours, always laying the law down.'

'Is that right, now?' Bridie smiled. 'Well, it's not meself she gets her temper from, so don't be looking at me.'

'It's this one I got me temper from.' Molly jerked a thumb at Nellie. 'I used to be as quiet as a mouse before I met her. A real lady I was, wouldn't say boo to a goose.'

'Ha, ha,' Nellie roared, 'yer can tell that to the marines, Molly Bennett! It's the other way round, isn't it, George? I was the quiet one, till I met you.'

'Then all I can say is, it's a pity you two ever met!' George said, keeping a straight face. 'What do you say, Jack?'

'Oh, give over!' Molly picked up a glass and handed it to Ellen before reaching for her own. Lifting it high, she said, 'Here's health and happiness to us and all our families.' She looked directly at Ellen. 'Let's forget our problems and look forward to happy days ahead. We've got our health and strength, and, thank God, plenty of good mates.'

An hour later the pub was alive with laughter and singing. Some of the regulars, those with good voices, were coaxed to sing a particular favourite, then everyone would join in the chorus. Molly and Nellie were on their feet, arms around each other's waists, heads thrown back and mouths wide as they sang at the top of their voices, clearly enjoying every minute of it. Even Ellen, after a couple of port and lemons, couldn't resist the odd snatch of a well-known song.

'If anyone asks,' Bridie smiled at her husband as she tried to make herself heard above the noise, 'I'll say I've never seen her in me life before. Sure I never thought I'd see me own daughter standin' up in a pub singing like a fish-wife.'

'It's good to see her enjoying herself.' Bob smiled back into his wife's beloved face. 'What a pity, though, that she didn't inherit your voice.'

A bell sounded, followed by the manager's voice. 'Time, gentlemen, please! Come along now, drink up before I have the police down on me head.'

'D'yez know, I really enjoyed that!' Molly linked arms with Ellen and Bridie as they walked up the street. 'Did me the power of good, just what the doctor ordered.'

'We did notice,' Jack said, walking behind with George and Bob. 'You an' Nellie drowned everybody else out.'

'Oh, there he goes, old misery guts!' Molly slipped her arms free and turned around. She grabbed hold of one of Jack's arms and put it around her waist; the other she held high, in a dancing position. Spinning him around, she started to sing 'Who's Taking You Home Tonight?'. To everyone's amusement, Jack waltzed her up to their front door, finished with a twirl, then bowed from the

301

waist. 'There yer are, girl,' he said in a thick Liverpool accent, 'an' ta very much for the dance.'

'Sure, an' begorrah, 'tis welcome yer are, kind sir.' Giggling helplessly, Molly gasped, 'An' aren't I so drunk I can't get me Irish accent right, even though I've been hearin' it all me life.'

Steve came to the door to see what the commotion was, and called to the others, 'Come an' take a dekko at this.'

Doreen peered over his shoulder. 'Mam, yer drunk!'

'So I am, me darlin', so I am.' Molly struggled to contain her mirth, but it was no good, she felt too happy. 'An' I'm not ashamed to say so, either.'

Jack took her by the arm. 'Inside, love, before the neighbours come out to see what's goin' on.'

Doreen's party went with a swing after that. Molly had them all in stitches with her impersonations of the various singers they'd heard that night. She had their facial expressions and every movement of their arms off to perfection. 'What did that feller sing, Nellie? Yer know the one I mean, Mr Thingamajig . . . oh, I remember now. It was "Won't You Come Home Bill Bailey?".' With a hand covering her mouth, as Molly imagined the posh people did, she gave a slight cough to clear her throat. 'Can we have the best of order for the singer, please, ladies and gentlemen?' She nodded to the treadle sewing machine, pretending it was a piano. 'Will you let me have a note, please?

'Lah . . . lah . . . lah . . . yes, that's it! Now, when I do this,' she waved a hand, 'I'd like you all to join in the chorus.'

Ellen left about twelve o'clock, frightened of leaving Phoebe sitting up on her own any longer. But her flushed, smiling face told how much she'd enjoyed herself. It was two o'clock before the rest of the party showed any signs of breaking up. 'It's way past me bedtime,' Bridie yawned, 'and at my age, I need me beauty sleep.' She kissed her granddaughter. 'It's been a lovely party, so it has, I've had the time of me life.'

'It's time we were all on our way.' Nellie pulled her coat on. 'It's been a great party, Doreen, thanks for askin' us old fogies.'

After seeing her parents and neighbours out, Molly looked sympathetically at Mike and Sammy. 'No trams this time of night, boys, so yer've got a long walk ahead of yez.'

'We don't mind, Mrs Bennett,' Mike said, 'it's been worth it.'

'It certainly has!' Sammy agreed. 'It's been a smashin' night.'

Doreen was as happy as a dog with two tails. The evening had turned out better than she'd dared hope. 'Aren't yer glad yer mam said yer could stay the night, Maureen? Our couch isn't very comfortable, but it's better than that long walk.'

'Yer not joking!' Maureen's pretty face was flushed with excitement. 'I wouldn't fancy walkin' that far.'

'You can sleep with me if you like?' Jill offered. 'It's only a small bed, but we could sleep top and tail.'

'Right, come on, the lot of yez.' Molly started to put the chairs back in their rightful places. 'See the boys out, then yer can discuss yer sleepin' arrangements.'

303

'Goodnight, Mrs B, an' thanks.' Steve put his hands on Molly's shoulders and planted a kiss on her cheek. 'I'll never 'ave a party without you there to entertain the guests. Yer should be on the stage, yer know.'

'Yer mean the landing stage at the Pier Head?' Molly chuckled as she lifted her hands and cupped his face with them. 'With me ukulele in me 'ands, an' a box at me feet for people to throw coppers in?'

'I'd empty me pockets if I saw yer,' Steve said, smiling down into her face. 'In fact, if yer want a partner, I'll carry a box an' collect the money in.'

'We'd make a good team, you an' me, son.' Molly lowered her hands and gave him a gentle push. 'Come on now, all of yez, an' let me an' my feller get to bed.'

The three girls walked down the hall after the boys, but when Jack went to follow, Molly grabbed his arm. 'Don't be a spoil-sport! They don't want you looking on when they get their goodnight kiss.' She gave him a dig in the ribs. 'Yer've got a short memory, Jack Bennett! How would you 'ave liked it if me ma 'ad followed me everywhere? Yer'd never 'ave got to kiss me.'

Jack pulled her close. 'Why should they be the only ones enjoying themselves? Come on, give us a kiss.'

Molly pushed the door of the corner shop open and stopped dead in her tracks. She'd never seen the place so packed. 'What's goin' on, Maisie?' she bawled. 'Are yer givin' the stuff away?'

'Is that you, Molly?' Maisie stood on tip-toe, trying to see over the heads of her customers. 'Come an' give us a hand, will yer? I'm run off me feet.'

Molly elbowed her way to the hinged part of the counter, nodding and winking at faces that were familiar to her. Once behind the counter she slipped off her coat and threw it on top of some boxes. Rolling up her sleeves, she asked, 'Well, what can I do to 'elp?'

'Some of them only want one or two things. If yer'll serve them I can manage the rest.' Maisie's face was flushed, her hair dishevelled. 'If yer not sure of the price, ask me, and yer know where the till is.'

'Right, let's get the show on the road.' Molly smiled at an elderly woman who was moving from one foot to the other. 'Legs playin' yer up, are they, Mrs Dawson? We'll see to you first, shall we? Did yer say six large tin loaves?'

A smile crossed the lined face. 'Those days are long gone, Molly! Only meself to see to now. Just a small cottage loaf and a pound of sugar, please.'

Molly took the sixpence with a twinkle in her eye. 'Now I can get me hands in the till. If yer see me wearin' a fur coat, yer'll know where the money came from.'

Fifteen minutes later the shop was cleared and Maisie's sigh was one of relief and tiredness as she mopped her brow with the corner of her apron. 'Thank God for that! I'm sweating cobs!'

'Where's Alec?'

'The silly beggar tripped over a sack of potatoes and sprained his ankle.' Maisie sliced a piece of brawn, tore it in two and passed half to Molly. 'I haven't had a cup of tea or a bite over me lips since nine o'clock an' me belly thinks me throat's cut.'

'I'll stick the kettle on for yer.' Molly made her way to

305

the back room. She knew the shop inside out and within minutes Maisie was sipping a much appreciated cup of tea.

'Where's Alec now?' Molly asked.

'Sittin' like Lord Muck with his foot propped up on the couch.' Maisie pulled a face. 'He certainly picked a fine time, I can tell yer! All the Christmas cakes and puddings have been delivered and we were going to start making the orders up today, but his little trip 'as put a stop to that! And how I'm going to get the orders delivered, heaven only knows! I can't be in the shop and do the deliverin' at the same time, I've only got one pair of hands.'

'Alec won't be laid up for long,' Molly said to comfort her, 'he'll probably be up an' about tomorrow.'

'Fat chance of that! He's in agony, can't put his foot to the floor or even bear to touch it.' Maisie looked at the end of her tether. 'I'll have to try and get a lad to make the deliveries, someone who I can trust an' can ride a bike. It wouldn't be hard, 'cos I'll put the orders in boxes with the name and address on, and load them into the basket on the bike. And they're all local, easy to find.'

Molly leaned on the counter, an idea forming in her mind. 'Yer'd 'ave to pay them a few coppers, wouldn't yer?'

'Well, yer couldn't expect anyone to do it out of the goodness of their heart, could yer? Of course I'll pay them!'

'I know someone who'd be glad to do it.' Molly nodded her head slowly. 'Someone yer could trust.'

Maisie studied Molly's face for a second, then her lips

curled into a smile. 'Molly, yer'd never cock yer leg over! It's a man's bike, with a crossbar.'

'I wasn't thinkin' of meself, yer daft thing! I was thinkin' of Ellen's boy, Peter! He'd be over the moon to 'ave a few pennies in his hands.'

Maisie gaped. 'But he's only about ten! He'd never manage it, I bet he can't even ride a bike!' Then she saw the funny side. 'He couldn't even reach the pedals!'

Molly wasn't going to tell her Peter was nowhere near ten. 'Wouldn't need a bike,' she said, having worked it all out in her head, 'he could take them in a pram! Mary Watson's got that big pram she 'ad when Bella was a baby, it's only standin' in the yard doin' nothing.'

'Oh, no!' Maisie shook her head vigorously. 'I'd be out of me mind with worry. He's too little, he wouldn't be able to carry the boxes.'

'He's only little, but he's wiry,' Molly said. 'Give the kid a chance, Maisie, try 'im with a small order first. If he can't do it, then there's nothin' lost, but give him a try. Yer know as well as I do, every penny that goes in that house is like sixpence in any other. They're on their uppers, especially now, with Christmas comin' on.'

Maisie blew through her clenched teeth. 'Yer'd get blood out of a stone, Molly Bennett! Playing on me heart strings, that's what yer doing.' The shop bell jangled when the door opened and a customer came in. 'I'll give 'im a try, but be it on your head if anythin' goes wrong.'

Molly was smiling as she struggled into her coat. 'Ta, Maisie, yer won't be sorry, I promise yer.'

Molly hurried down the street muttering to herself, 'Even if I 'ave to push the flaming pram meself, I'll make sure Peter gets the job. If there's a few coppers to be had, they're better goin' in the Clarkes' house than anywhere else.'

'Mary, d'yer know that pram of your Bella's, 'ave yer still got it?' Molly waited anxiously for the reply. If Mary had given the pram away, all her scheming would have been in vain.

'Yes, it's in the yard.' Mary leaned back against the door jamb. 'It's no good, yer know, been out there for ages, in all weathers.'

'It's just the job for what I want it for.' Molly explained quickly, with Mary's eyes growing wider as the story unfolded. 'So yer wouldn't mind lendin' it, would yer?'

'With the best will in the world, Molly, I can't see Peter bein' up to it.' Mary's face showed her doubt. 'Yer can have the pram by all means, but it won't work out.'

'If we don't try, we won't know.' Molly rubbed her hands together. 'But I bet yer a tanner it does.'

Miles Sedgewick glanced across the office at Jill's bent head. As he watched, her hand came up to sweep the long blonde hair back over her shoulders. 'Looking forward to Christmas, are you, Jill?'

'Oh, yes, Mr Miles! I love Christmas, it's my favourite time of the year.' Jill's vivid blue eyes were sparkling. 'I know it sounds childish, but I love the tree, the decorations and the excitement of opening presents. And everyone is so happy and friendly, I just wish it was Christmas all the year round.'

That's the nice thing about her, Miles thought, she's so

open, honest and unaffected. There were no fluttering eyelashes or coy looks. Not like some of the girls he knew. And she wasn't always nipping out to the toilet to comb her hair or renew her lipstick. Not that she needed to, she was so pretty she didn't need any embellishment. 'I suppose you'll be going to lots of parties?'

Jill shook her head. 'Me mam's having some friends in on Christmas night, but that's all. How about you, Mr Miles, what have you got lined up for the festive season?'

'I wish you wouldn't call me Mr Miles, it's so formal!'

'All the staff call you that, and I'm one of the staff. I can't remember to call you Mr outside this office, then drop it in here.' She grinned. 'Anyway, you haven't answered my question.'

This was the opening Miles had been waiting all week for. 'I'm in a bit of a quandary, actually. My father belongs to a gentlemen's club, and once a year they have a dinner when they're allowed to bring their wives or girlfriends. I've been invited this year, but unfortunately I don't have a female companion to take.'

Jill looked surprised. 'Oh, come on, Mr Miles, a man like you must have loads of girlfriends.'

'I hate to disillusion you, Jill, but I haven't! I've been studying so hard for the last few years I haven't had time to socialise.' Miles tapped the end of his pen on the blotting paper pad and watched as the ink spread, making a pattern. He kept his face averted to hide the calculating gleam in his eyes. 'I can't go to the dinner without a companion, so I need someone to take pity on me. I don't suppose you would consider it, would you, Jill?'

She was stunned at the way the conversation had turned. She didn't know how to refuse without offending him. He was, after all, her employer's son, and if the office gossip was right, in a few years he'd be a junior partner in the firm. 'Oh, I don't think so, Mr Miles. You know I have a boyfriend and he wouldn't like the idea of me going out with anyone else.'

But Miles wasn't going to be put off so easily. 'Surely he would understand it was just a favour? It wouldn't be like going out on a date with me, there'll be about a hundred people there. I could pick you up in the car and drop you off again, no harm done.' His brows drew together. 'He's not one of these jealous types, is he, doesn't trust you out of his sight?'

'No, of course not! Steve has no reason not to trust me!' Jill wished someone would come into the office and put an end to this conversation and her embarrassment. 'I'm sorry, Mr Miles, but I'd rather not come. It's not that I don't want to help you, because I really would like to, but you see I've never been out to a dinner before and I don't have anything suitable to wear.'

'Nonsense!' He tilted his head and grinned. 'No matter what you wore, Jill, I bet you'd be the prettiest girl there.' He thought she was weakening, and coaxed, 'Take pity on me in my hour of need, please? You'd be doing me an enormous favour, and I'd be very grateful.'

Jill felt cornered. If she told him Steve would be jealous, it would sound as though she was being big-headed, reading more into his request than there really was. And when you came to think about it, what harm was there in what he was asking? He merely wanted a partner for the evening, nothing more. Just someone to make the numbers up.

Jill crossed the room to the filing cabinet. Her fingers flicked over the alphabetically filed folders until she found the one she needed. Walking back to her desk she could feel Miles' eyes on her and flushed under his gaze.

'Well, Jill?' Miles asked. 'Will you be my fairy godmother, or do I not get to go to the ball?'

She took a deep breath. There were many reasons why she didn't want to go, apart from Steve who she knew would go mad. For a start, she'd have to buy a suitable long dress and evening shoes, things she would probably never wear again. And all the people there would be posh, like Miles and his father were. She'd be terrified of opening her mouth and putting her foot in it.

As Jill searched for an excuse to refuse, an argument raged in her head. Wasn't it a bit mean to refuse to help him out when he'd been so good to her? She remembered when she'd first started in the office and didn't know the ropes, how Miles had always been there to advise and explain. He'd been very patient and she'd have been lost without him because the other secretaries were usually too busy to spend much time with her.

'Will you let me think it over, Mr Miles, and I'll let you know tomorrow?' Jill managed a weak smile. 'I'll have to see what me mam and dad say.' Not for the world would she admit it was Steve's reaction that worried her.

'I'll come and ask them if you like,' he offered. 'Show myself and put their minds at rest. I'll even come and see your Steve, if it would help.'

'No!' Jill said quickly. 'I'll have a word with them tonight. When is it, by the way?'

'Next Friday.' Miles smiled. 'So it wouldn't interfere with your Christmas arrangements.' He lifted his hand and crossed two fingers. 'I'll keep these crossed until tomorrow.'

Jill smiled before opening the folder on her desk. I'll need to do more than cross my fingers when I ask Steve, she told herself. He'll blow his top!

Chapter Twenty

'Ooh, I say, the Bennetts are goin' up in the world!' As Molly leaned across the table it crossed her mind that Jill didn't look like someone who'd been invited out by her boss to a posh dinner dance. 'Where did yer say this do is?'

'I didn't ask because I won't be going.' Jill pulled a face. 'How can I, Mam? I haven't got the clothes for a kick off.'

'I'll make yer a dress!' Doreen offered, feeling green with envy. 'Yer'd be daft not to go, our Jill, I would if I 'ad the chance.'

'It's next Friday, there wouldn't be time to make a dress. Besides, it would have to be something special or I'd stand out like a sore thumb.'

'Yer've got a few bob saved up, buy yerself a nice dress,' Molly said, excitement for her daughter glowing on her face. 'An' a nice pair of silver dancin' shoes with straps.'

'It's not only that, Mam, it's the other people. They'll all talk frightfully far back, like Miles and his dad. I'd feel daft, terrified of opening me mouth.'

Jack had remained quiet, just eating his meal and listening, taking it all in. Now he laid down his knife and fork, and when he spoke his voice was full of emotion. 'Jill, you're as good as anyone, don't ever forget that!' He looked from Doreen to Tommy. 'Don't any one of yer forget it. Because people speak differently, it doesn't mean they're better than yer. It's what you are inside that counts.'

'Yer dad's right, sunshine,' Molly said, her mouth pursed. 'We're as good as anyone.'

'But what about Steve?' Jill's face clouded. 'I don't think he'd be very happy if I went.'

'Steve!' Molly laughed. 'He won't mind! Why should he? Hell, it's only a dinner yer goin' to, an' yer only goin' to help Mr Miles out. What could Steve find wrong with that? Yer see him every night, so one without won't kill 'im.'

'I wouldn't care what Steve thought,' Doreen said. 'It's not as though yer engaged or anythin'. If I 'ad a chance like that, I'd jump at it.'

'What do you think, Dad?' Jill asked, needing some assurance to give her the courage to tell Steve. 'Shall I go?'

'I don't see why not, love,' Jack told her as he cut into a potato. 'But there's a few things I'd like to know for me own peace of mind. Where is it yer going, what time is it on till, and does your Mr Miles understand yer too young to be walkin' home on yer own late at night?'

'Oh, he said he'd pick me up in his car and bring me home again,' Jill said. 'In fact, he said he'd come and see you if you were worried about me going out with

someone you didn't know. But honestly, Dad, you have
no need to worry. He's a nice bloke, and it isn't as
though he's got designs on me or anything. The only
reason he asked me is because he hasn't got a girlfriend.
He's too wrapped up in his studies to be interested in
girls.'

'Will yer be goin' into town to buy yerself a dress?'
Doreen asked. 'If yer are, can I come with yer on
Saturday afternoon?'

'What do you think, Mam?' Jill was still unsure. 'Shall
I go?'

Molly nodded. 'Make the most of it, sunshine, yer
may never get another chance.' She patted her daughter's hand. 'Yer can tell us 'ow the other half live.'

With all her family in agreement, Jill felt easier. As
her mam said, she might never get another chance so
should make the most of it. She turned to Doreen. 'I'll
meet you in town on Saturday. Come straight from work
otherwise we won't have much time to look around. I'll
mug you to a cup of tea and a toasted tea cake in the
Kardomah.'

Doreen rubbed her hands, her face beaming. 'The
gear! Where shall we try first?'

'I sometimes look in Bunny's window in me dinner
hour.' Jill was beginning to feel excited. 'I've never been
inside, but they have some lovely dresses in the window.
There's a tram stop in Lord Street, right by it, so I could
meet you there.'

When Steve knocked, Jill had her coat on ready. Her
mam had said Steve wouldn't mind her going to the

315

dinner, but Jill wasn't so sure and decided it would be better if they were alone when she told him. Her family's support had given her courage, but as they walked down the street, arms linked, her nerve began to desert her. Still, she thought, he's got to be told sometime, so better get it over with.

'Guess what happened today?' Jill began the story with a silent Steve walking beside her. His eyes staring straight ahead, he didn't utter a word until she ended by saying, 'I'm meeting Doreen on Saturday to look for a dress.'

She was expecting moans and protests, but wasn't prepared for his anger. He stopped walking and pulled her round to face him. 'Yer not going!'

'Why not? Me mam and dad said I can.' Jill looked into his face and saw the flared nostrils and the angry red blotches on his cheeks. 'Let go of me arms, Steve, you're hurting me.'

'Not until yer promise yer won't go.'

Jill, gentle by nature, would usually give in rather than argue. But not this time. Steve was being so unfair she wasn't prepared to give in. 'I'm not promising anything, Steve McDonough, so let go of me arms.'

The tone of her voice warned Steve he had gone too far. Releasing her, he hung his head. 'I'm sorry, Jill! I didn't mean to hurt yer, but I don't want yer to go out with that Miles feller.'

'Why not? It's only for one night, for heaven's sake, I'm not going to marry him!'

'Because you're my girl, that's why.' Steve's eyes were pleading. 'Don't go, Jill, for my sake. Yer know I've had a feeling about this Miles bloke for a long time, thought he 'ad his eye on yer. You wouldn't have it, but now I've been proved right. What a lame excuse, sayin' he didn't 'ave time for girls.'

'Steve, you've got a bad mind. And you're not only calling Mr Miles a liar, you're calling me one, too!'

'I don't think you're a liar, but I think yer've been taken in by him. He's pullin' a fast one on yer, can't yer see?' Steve made to take her hand but Jill pulled away. 'Don't do it, Jill, please?'

'I'm not going to stand here all night arguing, Steve,' she said. 'If you're not going to drop the subject, I'm going home.'

Steve stared. Gone was the naive girl he was used to, her place taken by a young woman who was poised and self-assured. He loved her so much it hurt, but he had calmed down enough to realise if he didn't curb his jealousy he was in danger of losing her. If he'd kept a rein on his temper he could probably have coaxed her around, but now all he'd done was rub her up the wrong way. Tomorrow he'd do it differently. 'Okay, I give in. I won't say another word about it tonight, I promise.' He held out his hands, a penitent expression on his face. 'Don't let's fall out, I couldn't bear it.'

'Me neither!' Jill sighed as she linked her hand through his arm. 'Come on, let's go for a walk.'

'Hold the boxes so they don't fall off.' Young Peter Clarke pulled down on the handle of the big Silver Cross pram and pushed it on to the pavement, while his younger brother, Gordon, steadied the pile of boxes.

'Where to now, our Peter?' Gordon wiped his sleeve across his runny nose, leaving a streak of dirt in its wake.

'Number twenty-six.' Peter touched the top box. 'Mind 'ow yer go with that one, it's got eggs in.'

Just then a group of older boys turned the corner. They stopped in their tracks when they saw the Clarke brothers and began to whisper between themselves. Then they walked around the pram, laughing into the frightened faces of Peter and Gordon. 'Where's yer dad, eh? In the loony bin, isn't he?' A lad of fourteen cuffed Gordon across the side of his head while the others chanted, 'His dad's doolally, 'is dad's doolally.'

Peter threw his body across the pram, terrified that if the eggs got broken he'd lose his job. 'Go away an' leave us alone.' He was sorry now he hadn't let Mrs Bennett come with them. She'd been with them on the first delivery, but he'd wanted to do this one on his own. If he did well, the woman in the corner shop said she'd give him a little job to do every week. That meant pocket money every week, something he'd never had. Now these big boys had come along to spoil it. 'Why don't yez leave us alone? We're not doin' yer no harm.'

But the boys were enjoying themselves with such an easy target. Running around the pram, they pulled faces and shouted, 'All the Clarkes are doolally, doolally, doolally!'

So intent were they in terrorising their two victims, they didn't see Corker turn the corner. He took in the scene in a flash, threw his bag on the ground and stood before them, feet well apart.

'Well now, what's goin' on here?' his voice boomed.

'Having a bit of fun, are we?'

The boys stood like statues, not daring to move, hardly breathing. Corker stared them out until in the end the ringleader muttered, 'We were only playin' around, Sinbad.'

'Oh, is that what it was? Well, aren't you the brave ones, eh? Picking on two little fellers who can't fight back. I think yer cowards, so what d'yer say to that? Nobody got a tongue in their head?'

Peter and Gordon were standing upright, their chests bursting with pride, while their tormentors hung their heads in shame.

'Answer me, boys!' Corker roared. 'Unless yez want me to drag yez home an' tell yer mothers how brave yez are!' When there was no reply, he said, 'Perhaps I should put yez across me knee and give yez a thrashing, what d'yer say to that?'

The ringleader craned his neck to look up into the giant's face. 'We're sorry, Sinbad, we won't do it again. Don't tell me mam or she'll batter me.'

There were mumbled apologies from the other lads. The choice between a hiding from their mother or Corker was like choosing between the devil and the deep blue sea.

Corker bent to ask Peter what he was doing with the pram. He listened intently, all the while keeping his eyes on the group to make sure they didn't scarper. He nodded, then straightened up. 'When I turned the corner yez were sayin' someone was doolally. I think it's *you* lot who are doolally, but that's beside the point. What is the point, an' I'd advise yez to keep it in mind, is that Mr

319

Clarke had a bad accident an' is in hospital. While he's there, I promised to be a father to his children, look after them like. So in future, if yer've anythin' to say about the family, say it to me 'cos I'm their dad for the time being. Have yez all got that?'

The boys nodded, eyes downcast, shoes kicking at the paving stones. 'Yes, Sinbad.'

'Well now, seein' as we're in agreement, an' I'm letting yez off this time, I want to ask yez a favour. When I'm away at sea, I want yez to keep an eye open for these two boys, and report to me if any bullies pick on them. Will yez do that for me?'

'Oh, yeah, Sinbad!' the tallest boy said. Another piped up, 'We'll look after them, no one will pick on them when we're around.'

'Good!' Corker held back a smile. 'Poppy off home now, but remember, I'm relying on yez.'

The group split up and sped off in all directions, leaving Corker with a smile on his face. He kept the smile fixed when he gazed down into two pairs of eager eyes, but his heart was full of compassion. Poor little blighters, he thought, just look at the state of them. Their trousers, bought from a second-hand stall at Paddy's market, were miles too big. They reached halfway down thin legs and were kept up by a piece of string tied around the waist. Their jackets had holes in the sleeves, they had no socks on and their shoes were scuffed and worn.

Corker sighed inwardly. 'Well, now, let's sort you two out.'

'We'll be all right now, Sinbad, honest!' Peter felt he

could take the world on now. 'Me an' Gordon can manage.'

Corker understood the boy's need for independence and didn't argue. 'I'll see yez later, then.' He swung his bag over his shoulder. 'By the way, I think yez should call me Uncle Corker. Make things legal like.'

He walked away leaving the two boys happier than they'd ever been in their young lives. Fancy having Sinbad for an uncle! They'd be the envy of all the kids in the neighbourhood.

Doreen jumped from the tram platform and ran to where Jill was standing. 'Been waiting long, our kid?'

Jill shook her head. 'Only a few minutes.' She tucked her arm through her sister's and they crossed over Whitechapel to Bunny's, the big store on the corner. 'Let's go straight to the dress department, then look for a pair of dancing shoes.'

Doreen's eyes were nearly popping out of her head. 'I've never been in 'ere before, it's big, isn't it? Not cheap though, from the looks of things. Yer'd 'ave been better going to TJ's.'

'No harm in looking,' Jill said as they climbed the staircase. 'If it's too dear, we'll try somewhere else.'

Doreen was in her element, her expression one of awe as she studied the dresses on the models dotted at intervals through the huge department. 'Ay, kid, look at this. Seven guineas it is! Blimey, I could make six dresses for that.' Then she began to look through the racks and brought one out that caught her eye. 'This is nice, Jill, an' it's only four pounds.'

321

Jill shook her head at the light green dress. It had frills at the throat and sleeves, far too fancy for her taste.

'Can I help you, madam?' An assistant stood at her elbow. 'Have you anything particular in mind?'

'Not really. I'd like something straight and plain, but fashionable.' Jill smiled at the assistant. 'It's for somewhere special, but I'd like one I could shorten so I could wear it afterwards.'

The assistant looked into her vivid blue eyes and nodded. 'I think I may have something that would suit you.' She walked to a rack and picked out a dress that she herself had admired, but it was far too young a style for her. With the dress draped over her arm, she admitted she was kidding herself. Age had nothing to do with it. It was the bumps and bulges that prevented her even thinking of wearing a fitted dress. She held it up for Jill's inspection and heard the pretty young girl give a sigh of pleasure. The pale blue dress in shot silk was straight and slim, with a high mandarin collar and long narrow sleeves. It was perfectly plain, no decorations whatsoever.

'It's beautiful,' Jill breathed, 'just what I want.' She fingered the material, loving the feel of it. 'It probably costs more than I can afford, though.'

'Four guineas, madam, but worth every penny. It's a real classy dress.' The assistant handed it over. 'Try it on, the fitting rooms are over there.'

Doreen followed closely. 'How much money 'ave yer got, our kid?'

'Six pounds,' Jill whispered back. 'I'd still have enough for a pair of shoes.' She drew aside the curtain which served as a door to the fitting room. 'It's beautiful. I hope it fits.'

While Doreen waited outside, she weighed up the passing customers. All well dressed, wearing fashionable hats and expensive shoes. 'Must all 'ave a few bob,' she muttered under her breath. 'I'd 'ave to save up for a year to buy anythin' from here.'

The curtain parted and Jill stepped out, her face aglow. 'It fits me perfectly, just like a glove. How does it look?'

Doreen was speechless as she gazed at the vision in front of her. She had never realised her sister was so beautiful. The blue was the exact colour of her eyes, and the dress clung to every contour of her body. She looked like one of those mannequins Doreen saw in the paperback books she bought.

Jill's smile dropped. 'Don't you like it?'

'Kid, yer look a knockout! Turn around.'

The assistant had been hovering in the background. Now she came forward with a smile. 'Madam, you look lovely.'

Jill looked down the length of the dress and grinned when she saw the toes of her plain black shoes showing beneath the hem. 'I look a scream in these shoes, but when I've got a pair of silver sandals on, it'll make all the difference.' She turned back to the fitting room. 'I'll take it.'

Half an hour later they were sitting in the Kardomah with a pot of tea and toasted tea cakes in front of them. Jill's new dress and silver sandals were in bags, carefully placed on a chair at the side of them. She had her purse

323

open on her knee and was counting the money she had left. 'I'll have to borrow half a crown off me mam to pay me fares to work. I'm skint, but I don't care, I'm so happy.'

'I'll pay the tram fares home,' Doreen offered, tucking into a toasted tea cake. 'It's only coppers.'

'You will not!' Jill snapped her purse shut. 'It's my treat.'

'Are yer goin' to the pictures with Steve tonight?' Doreen asked. 'If yer are, we'll 'ave to get a move on.'

That one innocent question was enough to diminish Jill's happiness. 'Yeah, we're going to the flicks, but Steve's not very pleased with me, I'm afraid. He said I shouldn't be going out with Miles when I'm supposed to be his girlfriend.'

'But yer not really going out with 'im, are yer?' Doreen ran a hand over her chin where the melted butter from the tea cake had trickled down. 'I mean, yer won't be on yer own with him, there'll be hundreds there.'

'Try telling that to Steve, he just won't listen. Every time I see him he tries to get me to change me mind.'

'Don't give in to 'im!' Doreen didn't have her sister's gentle nature. If she thought something, she came right out with it and to hell with the consequences. 'Start as yer mean to go on, our kid, otherwise he'll rule yer life for yer.'

'He's me boyfriend, and I think the world of him.' Jill felt guilty talking about Steve, but she was glad to have someone to confide in. 'I wish he wasn't so jealous, though, it spoils things.'

'If it was me, I'd tell 'im to take a runnin' jump!' Doreen began to fasten the buttons on her coat. 'Maureen's coming to ours tonight for a game of cards, so we'd better be makin' tracks.' She grinned. 'Yer won't forget yer parcels, will yer?'

'Not likely!' Jill picked up the bags, wishing she had half of her sister's cheek. But you were what nature made you, and there was nothing you could do about it.

The tension between Jill and Steve was almost tangible. She was glad when the picture was over, and as they walked out of the Carlton couldn't even remember what it had been about. Steve had hardly spoken all night, and in the darkness of the picture house had made no attempt to hold her hand. She felt hurt and upset, but also a little angry. Her family had been overjoyed when she'd tried the dress and shoes on, delighted for her. But even though Steve knew she was going into town, and what for, he didn't mention it. If only he'd show some interest, she could have shared her pleasure with him.

Jill was glad when they turned the corner of the street and her home was in sight. She did love Steve, and hated to see that hurt look on his face. But the only way to remove it was by giving in to him, and she wasn't going to, not this time. He was being unreasonable and childish, making a mountain out of a molehill. If helping Miles out for just a few hours was wrong, then her parents would have been the first to say so.

They stood outside her house and still Steve stayed silent. He didn't even meet her eyes, just stood staring down at the pavement. 'I'm going in, I'm freezing.' Jill

325

rooted in her bag for the front door key. 'Will I see you tomorrow?'

She heard Steve's deep sigh before he answered, 'Yes, okay.' She waited a few seconds for her goodnight kiss, but when he made no move she put the key in the lock. 'Goodnight and God bless.'

Jill closed the front door and leaned back against it. She'd never knowingly hurt anyone in her life and it grieved her to see Steve so upset. But if she gave in to him now, she'd never be able to have a mind of her own, never make a decision without first wondering whether Steve would agree with it. When they were married, and she did want to marry him, she'd need some independence, some freedom to make up her own mind about things.

Jill felt her way down the dark hallway to the chink of light showing beneath the living room door. Steve would get over it, she told herself, and perhaps it would teach him not to be so jealous.

She hesitated with her hand on the knob, fixed a smile on her face and threw the door open. 'I'm back, Mam! Ooh, that fire looks lovely, it's freezing out.'

'Are yer comin' in, Corker?'

'No, thanks, Molly, I'm having dinner next door.' Corker saw her raised brows but didn't answer the question he could see in her eyes. Ellen would go mad if she thought anyone knew he'd supplied the shoulder of mutton, and the necessary vegetables and potatoes to go with it. She was busy in the kitchen now, making the first roast dinner she'd had in years. 'I was wonderin' if Jill would sit next door tonight, while I take Ellen out?'

'Hang on a minute while I ask 'er.' Molly bustled back seconds later to say, 'Yeah, she'll be glad to.'

'Thanks, Molly.' Corker made off, saying over his shoulder, 'I'll see yer!'

'Enjoy yerselves!' As Molly closed the door she asked herself what would come of Corker's friendship with Ellen. Did he still have a soft spot for her, or was he just being kind? She shrugged her shoulders, saying softly, 'Only time will tell.'

Jill scribbled a note to Steve, asking did he mind spending the evening in the Clarkes'? She was going to add that if he didn't feel like it, she wouldn't mind sitting in there on her own. But after careful consideration she decided not to. It sounded too much like an ultimatum.

'Run up to Steve's with this note, Ruthie, there's a good girl. And wait for his answer.'

There were butterflies in her tummy as she helped her mother peel the potatoes. What would she do if Steve sent word back that he didn't want to mind the Clarke children? In fact, what would she do if he said he'd finished with her? Jill dropped a peeled potato in the pan of water and reached for another. Oh, why did I ever ask Miles what he was doing for Christmas? she reproved herself. One innocent, stupid question and look at the trouble it's caused.

Ruthie came dashing into the kitchen, a piece of chocolate clutched in her tiny hand. 'Auntie Nellie give me some chocolate, Mam!'

'So I see,' Molly said, shaking her head. 'It's all round yer mouth and on yer coat.'

'What did Steve say, Ruthie?' Jill tried to sound casual.

'Oh, er, he said okay!' Ruthie popped the remaining chocolate in her mouth and sucked on it with a look of pure bliss on her face. 'He'll see yer there at half-seven.'

'Shall we play snakes an' ladders, or tiddlywinks?' Phoebe asked. 'I say snakes an' ladders.'

'An' I say tiddlywinks,' Dorothy said, just to be awkward. 'What do you want to play, Steve?'

'I don't care what we play,' he said. 'Please yerselves.'

'Have yer got a cob on?' Phoebe asked with childish openness. 'Yer don't 'alf look miserable.'

'I've got a headache.' It was no lie, Steve had been suffering a constant headache for days. He knew he was being ridiculous, behaving like a big soft kid, sulking because he couldn't get his own way. But no amount of self-recrimination could alter the way he felt. Lying in bed at night, he tortured himself by allowing images to enter his mind. Images of Jill being held close in the circle of this bloke's arms as they danced. Sometimes the picture was so real, he could see Miles bending to whisper in her ear, his manner possessive. Steve had tried to banish the images from his mind, but they persisted in haunting him and the torment was driving him mad. If Jill loved me as much as I love her, he thought, she wouldn't do this to me.

'We'll play tiddlywinks.' Jill couldn't stand the silence any longer. She emptied the coloured discs out of the box and set the egg-cup in the middle of the table. Then she looked directly into Steve's eyes.

'Phoebe, Steve's telling fibs. He has got a cob on. With me. You see, I'm going out on Friday night, but he doesn't want me to go.'

'Oooh, er!' Dorothy stopped dividing the counters out to stare at Steve. 'Why don't yer want 'er to go?'

Steve ignored the girl's question, his eyes fixed on Jill. 'So yer still going?'

'Yes, Steve, I'm still going,' Jill answered. 'I made a promise and I don't break promises.'

'What about me?' His voice was loud and angry. 'Don't yer care what I think?'

The two young girls rested their elbows on the table, their round eyes going from Jill to Steve. This was more exciting than a game of tiddlywinks.

'You know I care what you think, Steve.' Jill's voice was quiet. 'But this time I think you're in the wrong.'

'Oh, yer do, do yer!' He scraped back his chair. 'In that case, there's nothin' more to be said! I'm goin' home.'

Jill closed her eyes when the slam of the front door reverberated through the house. Tears were stinging the backs of her eyes but she willed them not to fall. She had two curious young faces gazing at her.

'Does that mean yer won't be gettin' married?' Dorothy queried. 'Isn't Steve yer boyfriend any more?'

Phoebe, at eleven years of age, was much wiser. She could see Jill was upset so she remained silent. But there was a sadness in her heart for the two people who had been so kind to her. And she thought they made a lovely couple, like Cinderella and Prince Charming.

Jill sighed, wishing she was sure the words she was about to utter were true. 'Of course he's still me boyfriend! We've just had a falling out, that's all. Everyone has a tiff now and then, but we'll get over it.' She picked up one of the playing counters. 'Come on, let's play. A penny for the winner.'

Chapter Twenty-One

'It was only a thought, Molly me darlin', but I wondered if Jill would like to borrow this to wear tonight?' Bridie asked, as she carefully folded back layer after layer of tissue paper. 'I haven't worn it meself for over thirty years, an' 'tis a shame for it to be lyin' in a drawer, never seeing daylight, so it is.'

As her mother held up the white shawl, crocheted in wool so fine it was as delicate as a spider's web, Molly gasped with pleasure. 'Oh, Ma, I haven't seen that since I was a little girl! It must be as old as me, yet it still looks brand new! Oh, it's beautiful. Our Jill will be as pleased as Punch. She's been worried about what to wear with her dress, 'cos the only coat she's got is the one she goes to work in.'

Jack leaned forward for a closer inspection. 'You made this, did yer, Ma? I've never seen anythin' as beautiful. It must 'ave taken yer ages to make.'

'Aye, son, it did that! Many's the long hour I sat by the fire with me crochet hook goin' like the clappers.' Bridie folded the shawl carefully and laid it back in the tissue paper. 'I only wore it once, when Pa took me to the

Empire. After that, well, what with one thing and another I never had occasion to wear it.' She handed it to Molly, saying, 'D'yer want to take it up to Jill, see if she likes it?'

'Oh, she'll like it, Ma, never fear,' said Molly. 'She'll be over the moon. But I won't take it up, yer can give it her yerself when she comes down. She's been hours gettin' herself ready. Anyone would think she was goin' to see the Queen.'

The door burst open and Doreen, flushed of face, ran in. 'She's comin' down now.'

Jill held her dress up as she came slowly down the stairs in case the hem got caught in the high heels of her silver sandals. Her mouth was dry with nerves and she felt sick to her stomach. Her reflection in the long wardrobe mirror told her she looked good; the dress fitted her to perfection and her long blonde hair was shining like silk. But it wasn't enough to calm the myriad of emotions coursing through her body. Sadness and anxiety because she hadn't seen Steve since the night at the Clarkes' house, worry that her dress wasn't suitable, and fear that she wouldn't know how to conduct herself with people who were of a different class from herself.

She stepped from the bottom stair and smoothed the dress down over her hips. In two days it would be Christmas Eve. Steve was bound to come around then. He wouldn't let Christmas pass without making it up. With that comforting thought, Jill forced a smile to her face and opened the door. She heard silence descend, saw the unsmiling faces and thought, They don't think I look nice. Tears were beginning to form when everyone started talking at once. 'Jill, me darlin',' Bridie said, ''tis a wonderful sight yer are for me old eyes.'

'Oh, sunshine, yer look like a princess.' Molly made no attempt to keep her tears at bay. 'I've never seen anyone as beautiful.'

Jack swallowed hard as he stood up and hugged his daughter. 'I'm the proudest man in Liverpool, love. I bet there'll be no one there tonight to hold a candle to yer.'

Jill looked beseechingly at Bob. 'Grandpa?'

'I think you're as pretty as a picture.' Bob smiled before turning to his wife and clasping her hand. 'As pretty as yer nanna was at your age.'

Molly rubbed the back of her hands across her eyes. Sniffing loudly, she said, 'If yer dad doesn't say the same about me, so help me I'll clock 'im one.'

Jack put an arm around her shoulders. 'Molly, yer still the most gorgeous thing on two legs.'

She gave him a push. 'Yer polished beggar!' She smiled at Jill. 'Turn around, sunshine.'

'Don't yer think she should put some rouge on, Mam?' Doreen was surveying her sister through half closed lids. 'An' more lipstick?'

'No!' Jill tutted impatiently. 'If I took any notice of you, I'd be done up like a painted doll!'

'Yer don't need it,' Bridie said. 'Hasn't the good Lord given yer a complexion like peaches and cream?' She took the shawl from its wrapping and held it out. 'Would this be any use to you?'

Jill opened the shawl, her eyes full of wonder. 'Oh, Nanna, it's absolutely beautiful! Where did you get it?'

'She crocheted it 'erself,' Molly said before Bridie had

a chance to open her mouth. 'An' it's just the thing for tonight. With that draped round yer shoulders, yer'll bowl 'em over.'

'Here, let me do it.' Bridie took the shawl and moved behind her granddaughter. 'Let it hang low across yer back, don't put it around yer neck like a scarf. Then, over the tops of yer arms and let the sides hang down. That's 'ow the posh ladies wear them.'

Jill walked to the sideboard, liking the feel of the long skirt as she moved. She picked up an evening bag covered in silver sequins and held it between both hands. 'Mrs Watson lent me this, Nanna.'

Bridie nodded, remembering the days when she hid at the top of the stairs in the big house so she could watch the ladies of fashion arrive. 'Just what was needed to complete the picture.'

Jill glanced at the clock. 'Mr Miles should be here any minute, I'd better run down the yard first.'

'Me and yer granda will be on our way before he comes.' Bridie stood up and kissed Jill's cheek. 'Wouldn't want 'im to think he was under inspection, would we now? But enjoy yerself, sweetheart. We'll be thinking about yer, so we will.'

Bob kissed his granddaughter before pulling his cap on. 'Yes, have a lovely time and come an' tell us all about it tomorrow.'

Jill paced the floor, her fingers playing nervously with the sequins on the evening bag. 'Me nerves have gone, Mam! I'll probably make a fool of meself and faint on the Adelphi steps.'

'Don't act so daft!' Molly straightened a cushion for the umpteenth time. It wouldn't do to have the place looking untidy when Jill's boss came. Thank goodness Ruthie had gone to bed without a murmur and dropped off to sleep almost at once. Doreen had gone to Maureen's and Tommy was out playing, having strict instructions not to come in before eight o'clock. 'Just remember what yer dad said, yer as good as anyone.'

'And better than most,' Jack said, nodding his head. 'In fact . . .' The knock on the door brought seconds of silence then he asked, 'Shall I go?'

Jill's face drained of colour. 'I'll just nip to the kitchen, make sure my hair's all right.'

Molly watched her daughter disappear, pulled a face at Jack, then said, 'I'll let 'im in.'

'Hello, Miles, I'm Jill's mother.' She held out her hand and kept the smile firmly in place even though her heart had done a double take at the sight of the man standing before her. Talk about a toff! His overcoat was open, showing the black evening suit, white starched shirt with pleats down the front, and black dickie bow. And looking past him, Molly could see his black, shiny and very expensive-looking car. She didn't know much about cars, didn't see many in their street, but she knew enough to realise this one had certainly cost a few bob. What a field day the neighbours must be having, she thought. I bet every curtain in the street is twitching right now. 'Come in, won't you?'

Jack stood up. 'Pleased to meet yer.'

'It's my pleasure, sir.' Miles' fingers played with the fringe of the white silk scarf hanging loosely round his neck. 'Is Jill ready?'

'She won't be a minute.' Molly pointed to the couch. 'Won't yer sit down?'

'No, I won't, if you don't mind. I spend my life sitting down.'

Molly sat on one of the wooden dining chairs. Suit yourself, she thought, Mr High and Mighty. He was a fine-looking man, there was no getting away from that, but short on smiles and friendliness. She watched his eyes roaming around the room, taking in the worn furniture and scuffed lino, and if that wasn't a look of distaste on his face she'd eat her hat.

Miles made no effort to make conversation and the silence was becoming uncomfortable. Jack shifted in his chair, racking his brains for something to talk about. It was difficult to talk to someone who looked as though there was a bad smell under his nose, but for Jill's sake he forced himself to smile and ask, 'The Adelphi, isn't it?'

'Yes, we're dining in the French restaurant then moving to the ballroom. Should be a very enjoyable evening.' Miles lifted his hand to glance at his gold watch. 'I say, is Jill nearly ready? I don't want to arrive when everyone is seated.'

Molly was about to say 'Now wouldn't that be just too bad!' but bit the words back. Instead, she shouted, 'Jill, hurry up, sunshine!'

The kitchen door opened and Jill walked in. 'Hello, Miles.'

Molly was watching his face and had the satisfaction of seeing the aloof expression change to one of utter surprise. 'Jill! I say, you look absolutely stunning! Quite breathtaking!'

'Thank you, Miles.' Her head held high, Jill walked across the room, the dress clinging to every curve of her slim figure as she moved. 'I won't be very late, Mam, but don't wait up.' She kissed Molly's cheek before turning to Jack. 'I've got me key, Dad, so you don't need to worry.'

Miles cupped her elbow. 'No, old chap, you need have no fears for your daughter whilst she's in my care. I'll protect her with my life.'

Molly preceded the couple down the hall and pulled the door open to reveal a sight that brought a look of horror to her face. Dozens of kids, her son included, were swarming around the car which was standing in the light given out by the gas lamp. Grubby hands were running over the paintwork, playing with the windscreen wipers and headlights, while curious eyes peered through the windows at the luxurious interior. 'Hey!' Molly shouted, stepping out into the street and clapping her hands. 'Scram, the lot of yez!'

Within seconds there wasn't a soul in sight. 'I'm sorry about that,' she apologised, 'but they're only kids.'

Miles was inspecting the car. 'I just hope the ruffians haven't broken anything.'

'They're kids, not ruffians.' Molly's voice was tight. 'The only damage yer'll find is fingerprints.' She would have said a lot more but held her tongue because of Jill. She watched Miles help her daughter into the passenger seat before rounding the car to the driver's door.

'Goodnight, Mrs Bennett.' He inclined his head before taking his seat behind the wheel, then turned to Jill to ask if she was comfortable, before setting the car in motion.

Molly waved until the car was out of sight, then made her way back into the house. Standing in the middle of the room, she put her hands on her hips and wiggled her bottom. 'Oh, lah-de-dah-de-dah! There's no flies on us, we're a proper toff and no mistake!'

'Now, Molly, give the lad a chance, we hardly know him!' Jack said. 'He was probably nervous.'

'Oh, ay, Jack Bennett, if yer think that, yer as thick as two short planks! Honestly, talk about a snob!' Molly walked to where Miles had stood and gazed around the room, the same look of distaste on her face that she'd seen on his. 'Did yer see the way he looked at our furniture? Must 'ave thought he was really slumming it tonight.' She suddenly burst out laughing. 'And the posh voice on him! I don't know where he got plums from, this time of the year, but 'is mouth was full of the bloody things! If he'd spoken any further back, we wouldn't 'ave heard him.'

'Molly, the lad can't help the way he was brought up.' Jack had been making excuses in his mind for Jill's boss, but what Molly was saying was what he really thought. He grinned broadly. 'He is a bit of a drip, isn't he?'

'A drip? He's a ruddy torrent!' Molly pulled a chair towards the fireplace. 'I don't envy our Jill one little bit. A night in 'is company would drive me round the bend! Give me Steve any day.'

'That reminds me, I haven't seen him for a few days,' Jack said. 'Is he ill?'

Molly shook her head. 'They've fallen out. He got a cob on with her 'cos he didn't want her to go tonight.'

'Oh, dear, so that's it? Still, he'll get over it.' Jack leaned forward to poke the fire, lifting the coals to let a draught through. 'They'll be as thick as thieves in a day or two, you'll see.'

'I hope so, I'm very fond of Steve. He'd make ten of the bloke that's just gone out of 'ere.'

'Don't tell our Jill that, love, 'cos we might be wrong about him. She's always said how good he's been to her, always helpful and friendly. We might be misjudging him.'

'Aye, an' pigs might fly!' Molly held her hands out to the fire. 'There's no heat from this coal, it's all flamin' slate. Wait till I get me hands on Tucker, I'll marmalise 'im, givin' me rubbish like this!'

Jill stood in the foyer of the Adelphi Hotel, her eyes wide with wonder. She didn't know places like this existed. Gleaming chandeliers, marble floors and pillars, heavy velvet drapes and lots of lush green plants. And all the women passing, their hands resting elegantly on their partners' arms, were expensively dressed and heavily perfumed. They were dripping in jewellery, and it certainly hadn't come from Woolworth's.

When Miles came back from depositing his overcoat in the cloakroom, he asked, 'Would you like to go to the powder room before we go upstairs?'

'No, thank you.' Jill smiled nervously. 'I'm fine.'

Miles held his arm out. She's more than fine, she's an absolute dream, he thought. He noticed the looks of admiration on the faces of the men they passed, and felt very proud. He'd always thought Jill was one of the prettiest girls he'd ever met, but tonight she was more than pretty. With her head held high, her long blonde hair fanning her shoulders, a dress that showed off her slim figure to perfection and her naturally graceful walk, Jill was a beauty.

Although she kept her eyes straight ahead as they walked up the wide staircase, she was drinking in all the splendour. She wanted to remember every little detail so she could tell her family. Oh, how she wished they could see it for themselves.

They stood at the entrance to the French restaurant until a waiter came to lead them to their table. It was for a party of eight, and six of the seats were already occupied.

Miles' father jumped to his feet when they neared the table, followed by the other two men. 'My dear Jill, you look charming.'

'Thank you, Mr Sedgewick.' She felt a thrill of pleasure at the expression of astonishment on his face, and when he introduced their friends, she smiled in acknowledgement. But her mind was in too much of a whirl for their names to register.

Miles held her chair out for her, and when she was seated the other men followed suit. Miles sat next to her, and on her other side was his mother. The wine waiter had been hovering near the table. Now he rushed to fill their glasses. 'I hope you like champagne, Jill.' Miles lifted his glass and whispered softly, 'Here's to us and an enjoyable evening.'

Jill had never tasted champagne before and was unprepared for the bubbles that tickled her nose. But the taste wasn't unpleasant and she managed to empty the glass without making a fool of herself. The wine had a calming effect and she was soon relaxed enough to join in the conversation and laughter without worrying about dropping her h's. She found Mrs Sedgewick a friendly woman with a great sense of humour, and all through dinner it was she who kept everyone amused.

Jill had only ever drunk port and lemon before, and her mam always made sure it was more lemonade than port. So after two glasses of champagne, when she started to feel light-headed, she refused a further refill. The dinner seemed to go on forever, with so many courses Jill lost count. And the food was rich and plentiful, like everything else, particularly the cutlery. She'd had a shock when she'd seen the six knives and forks, but simply watched Miles and followed suit.

'Would you like to take a menu as a memento?' he asked, when the meal was finally over.

Jill shook her head, feeling embarrassed. She would have loved one to show her family, but it would seem childish, as though she'd never been anywhere before. She hadn't, of course, but there was no need to tell everyone she was as green as a cabbage.

'Do take one, Jill!' Mrs Sedgewick smiled. 'We're all taking ours. You see, my dear, we women only get asked to join the gentlemen once a year, so we need something to remind us we still have a husband.'

Jill smiled back as she picked up the thick white menu. Most of the gold writing was in French, but it would be nice to show her mam and dad.

When Miles led Jill through the heavy glass doors to the ballroom she felt she was walking into a wonderland. Huge chandeliers hung from the ornate ceiling, small tables were set around the sides of the room, and high potted palms surrounded the small stage at the far end of the room where an orchestra was playing.

'Would you like to dance, Jill?' Miles pulled a face. 'I must warn you, though, I don't dance very well. I've got two left feet.'

'That makes two of us,' she said. 'I'm hopeless.'

They stood for a while, watching the dancers already on the floor. Then Miles said, 'I'm sure we could do as well as some of them. I'm willing if you are.'

Why not? Jill asked herself. Tonight is a one off, I'll never get the chance to dance at the Adelphi again. 'Don't say I didn't warn you!'

Miles held her stiffly at first, too engrossed in getting his steps right. Then gradually he relaxed, enjoying the feel of the slim figure in his arms, and held her closer.

Sitting at one of the small tables, Evelyn Sedgewick nudged her husband's arm. 'What a delightful girl, Edward! She's an absolute darling, don't you agree?'

He nodded. 'She's a good worker, capable and efficient. Always got a smile on her face, but never pushy or gushing. I've always thought she was a pretty little thing, but tonight is like seeing a flower coming into full bloom.'

'Is Miles smitten with her, d'you think?'

Edward chuckled. 'Don't start match-making, my darling. Let things run their course.'

'I do worry about Miles though,' his wife said. 'He spends far too much time studying, never has any fun. It's about time he found himself a nice girl.'

'And you think Jill is that girl?'

Evelyn ran her fingers over her newly waved hair. 'She would be an asset to him.'

'Here they come,' Edward said under his breath. 'Don't interfere, darling. Whatever will be, will be.' He smiled as Jill and Miles approached the table. 'Had enough?'

Miles grinned, looking very happy. 'We managed the waltz, but the quickstep is far too intricate.'

Evelyn patted a chair at the side of her. 'Sit down, Jill, it's much less tiring to watch.'

She sat down with a sigh of relief. 'These sandals are new and they're rubbing my heels.'

'Oh, you poor dear,' Evelyn sympathised. 'Slip them off for a while.'

'Uh, no thanks. If I take them off I'll never get them on again.'

'I could always carry you.' Miles leaned forward, resting his elbows on his knees. 'Be your knight in shining armour.'

While Jill was shaking her head, Evelyn raised her brows at her husband. The gleam in her eyes told him she thought Miles was on the right track.

'You must bring Jill to lunch one day, Miles,' she purred, 'we'd love to see her again.'

'Why don't you ask her yourself, Mother?' Miles wasn't too pleased. His mother was a manipulator, always planning things so they would go the way she wanted. His father was to blame, he gave her everything she asked for. Miles was glad she liked Jill, but knew the girl well enough to know if she was pressed too hard she would back off. He wanted to give her time to get to know him, let things drift along slowly. That way he might stand a chance with her. And tonight he knew he definitely wanted that chance.

Evelyn raised her eyebrows. It was unusual for her son to answer so sharply. But she'd made up her mind and wasn't going to be put off. 'How about it, Jill? Would you come to lunch one day?'

'Perhaps after Christmas,' she answered evasively. 'I'll talk to Miles about it.'

'Don't forget, my dear,' Evelyn laid her fingers, with their long red-painted nails, on Jill's arm, 'because I'll look forward to seeing you.' Jill smiled, but her mind was telling her she'd be back with Steve by then, so there was no chance of her going anywhere for lunch.

Miles glanced at his watch. 'It's time I got you home, Jill. Remember your father said eleven at the latest.'

She wasn't sorry. She'd enjoyed the evening, seen so many things she'd never seen in her life before and probably never would again. As her mam would say, she'd seen how the other half lived. But it was over now, and she wanted to get back to her family. She knew her mam and dad would wait up for her, and was looking forward to telling them all about it. 'Goodnight, Mr and

Mrs Sedgewick, and thank you for a lovely evening. I've really enjoyed myself.'

'Don't forget, I'm expecting you to visit us.' Evelyn brushed a kiss against Jill's face. 'Make it soon.'

The car stopped outside the Bennetts' house at exactly eleven o'clock. 'Right on time,' Miles said, before sliding from his seat and hurrying to open the car door for Jill. 'You see, I'm a man of my word.'

'Thank you, it's been lovely.' Jill held out her hand. 'Goodnight, Miles.'

He took her hand between his own. 'It's been my pleasure. Perhaps we can do it again some time?'

'Perhaps.' Jill withdrew her hand. 'I'd better go in, I know me mam and dad will be waiting.' She saw Miles' face coming closer and twisted her head to one side so his kiss landed on her cheek. 'Goodnight.' She slid the key in the lock, opened the door and stepped inside without a backward glance.

Neither of them had noticed the figure standing in the darkness of the entry on the opposite side of the street. Steve flattened himself against the wall and didn't emerge until the noise of the car engine had faded away. Then he left the shadows, devastated by what he had seen. He'd been standing there for half an hour, hoping for a chance to talk to Jill. To tell her he was sorry and make it up with her. He'd missed her so much in the last few days, couldn't get her out of his mind. And he'd waited in the cold and darkness to tell her he'd been a damn' fool and was sorry.

He had been perished with cold during his long wait,

but as he crossed the street his hurt and anger made him forget the cold. Oh, I've been a fool all right, he thought, but for different reasons! She said she was only going to help her precious Mr Miles, and even though I didn't want her to go, I believed her. But you don't let somebody kiss you unless you want them to.

Steve let himself into the house quietly. All the family were in bed and he mounted the stairs gingerly, not wanting to wake them. His younger brother Paul was snoring softly as Steve undressed before slipping between the icy sheets. Clasping his hands behind his head, he stared at the ceiling, knowing he was in for another sleepless night. His mind in a turmoil, he tried to tell himself to forget about Jill. If it was somebody with money and a fancy car she wanted, then let her have them. The words came easily to him, but he knew that abiding by them wasn't going to be so easy. When you'd loved a person for years you couldn't just erase them from your mind as though they had never existed.

Molly sat with the menu in her hands, a comical expression on her face. 'I can't understand a word of it!'

'It's in French, Mam! I couldn't understand it myself, so I just said I'd have what Miles was having.' Jill slipped her shoes off and sighed with relief. 'I didn't know what I was eating half the time. They don't cook like us.'

'Well, it's been an experience for yer, love,' Jack said. 'I've got to my age without seein' half of what you've told us about.' He gave a low chuckle. 'The nearest I've ever got to the Adelphi was passing it on a tram.'

'How many of those . . . what did yer say they were,

chandeliers or somethin' . . . how many were there?'
Molly was trying to picture the hanging lights that Jill
said had about twenty bulbs on each of them.

'About five in the main ballroom,' Jill told her. 'And
they were enormous.' She spread her arms wide. 'Each
one of them must have been as big as this room.'

'Yer don't say!' Molly smiled across at Jack. 'When
yer win the pools, love, I'll 'ave sixpennorth of what our
Jill's had tonight.'

Jack returned her smile. 'If I win the pools, love, yer
can have a shilling's worth. There'll be no expense
spared.'

'I'm glad I've seen it,' Jill said, rubbing her aching
feet, 'but I wouldn't want to live like that all the time.
Everyone was very nice, especially Miles' mam and dad,
but they're not like us, not down-to-earth.' She suddenly
got a fit of the giggles. 'Dad, can you imagine me mam
with long red fingernails, hair all waved, face thick with
make-up, and puffing on a cigarette through a long
holder?'

Molly gasped, 'They never do!'

'Not all of them, but quite a lot.'

'Well, I never! They sound more like the kind yer see
down Lime Street than toffs.' Molly whistled through
her teeth. 'We live a very sheltered life, Jack, don't
know what's goin' on in the world.'

'I don't particularly want to, love, I'm quite happy
with my little lot.' There was tenderness in his eyes. 'I
wouldn't swap what I've got for all the money in the
world.'

'Me neither, I'm quite happy the way I am,' Jill said,

347

bending to pick up her shoes. 'D'you mind if I go to bed? I'm dead beat.'

'No, you poppy off, sunshine. It's a good job it's Saturday tomorrow and yer can 'ave a lie in.' Molly put her head to one side and winked. 'If I think of somethin' I've forgotten to ask yer, I'll write it down in me head and ask yer tomorrow. Like 'ow many roast potatoes did yer get?'

Oh, I do love you, Mam, Jill thought, mentally comparing her mother to Mrs Sedgewick, with Miles' mother coming a poor second. 'Sleep well, both of you. Goodnight and God bless.'

Chapter Twenty-Two

'Have yer got all yer shoppin' in now, Molly?' Nellie McDonough asked as she trudged up the street with her friend, her wide hips swaying from side to side. 'Yer haven't got to go out again, 'ave yer?'

'No, thank goodness.' Molly stopped to take a deep breath. 'I know it's Christmas Eve, but I've never seen the shops so packed. Some of them were buyin' enough to feed a flippin' army!' She put one of the carrier bags on the ground and held out her hand for Nellie's inspection and sympathy. 'Look at that! The blasted string has cut right into me flesh an' it's not half sore.'

Nellie grinned. 'That's the best of 'aving plenty of fat on yer, it cushions the pain.'

Molly stooped to pick up the bag. 'I'm glad our Tommy went for the tree this mornin', and the butcher's sendin' me turkey home with Ellen. I couldn't face goin' out again, me feet are givin' me gyp.' When they reached her front door she jerked her head. 'Will yer come in an' have a cuppa, Nellie? I think we both deserve one, an' ten minutes isn't goin' to make that much difference.'

'What about Ruthie? Aren't yer goin' to pick her up?'

Molly shook her head. 'No, Mary said not to worry about 'er, she's not in the way. Bella's got 'er own bedroom an' they play up there as good as gold.' She raised her arm, her face screwed up with the effort of lifting the heavy bag. 'Be a pal, Nellie, an' get the key out of me pocket, will yer?'

Molly made a bee-line for the kitchen and dropped the bags and parcels on the floor. 'Thank God for that! Now we can 'ave a quiet sit down before the mad rush starts.'

Leaving her shopping by the door, Nellie sank heavily on to the couch. 'Ellen's smashin', servin' behind that counter,' she shouted through to the kitchen where she could hear Molly filling the kettle. 'I didn't think she 'ad it in her.'

'Tony said she's a Godsend,' Molly shouted back. 'He said we did 'im a favour that day, when we talked him into takin' her on. He's full of praise for 'er, said he doesn't know how he ever managed without 'er.'

'She's certainly opened my eyes.' Nellie's chins did a little dance as she nodded her head. 'Different woman altogether than she was this time last year.'

'Yer can say that again!' Molly came through carrying two cups of steaming tea. 'No saucer, Nellie, I've no time for niceties.'

'That's all right, girl!' Nellie's legs were spread wide, revealing the elasticated legs of her pink, fleecy-lined knickers. 'I'm not a visitor, I'm yer mate.'

Molly sat by the table, her hands around the cup that possessed only half a handle. 'Corker's still home, so him an' Ellen are comin' tomorrow night. With you an' George, me ma and da, Maisie and Alec, and our

Doreen's friend, Maureen, we'll 'ave a houseful.' For a few seconds she gazed at the tea leaves floating on top of the tea, then looked across at Nellie. 'Is your Steve comin' with yer?'

'Don't ask me!' Nellie rested the cup on the arm of the couch. 'When I told 'im he'd been invited, he just stared through me. I don't know what happened between 'im and Jill, but he's walkin' around like a flamin' wet week!'

'He fell out with 'er 'cos she went to the Adelphi the other night,' Molly told her. 'Which was daft really, 'cos she only went to make the number up. Our Jill hasn't said anythin', but I know she's upset. She thinks the world of Steve.'

'An' he thinks the sun shines out of her backside, always has. So what's got into 'im, I don't know. He's cuttin' off his nose to spite his face, the stupid nit.'

'They're only kids, we were probably the same at their age. Yer can't put an old head on young shoulders,' Molly said. 'But I hope it blows over, 'cos I've always thought your Steve was the right one for our Jill.'

'It'll blow over, don't worry. Me an' George used to fall out every night, but he always came round the next day, cap in hand.' Nellie held her cup out. 'Take this off me, will yer? It's a blasted work of art tryin' to get off this couch.'

Molly was grinning as she put the cup on the table, then held her two hands out. 'Here, get hold of these an' I'll pull yer up.'

'I need one of those cranes they 'ave at the docks.' Nellie shuffled to the edge of the couch. 'Now, all together, one . . . two . . . three . . . up she comes!'

Molly carried Nellie's shopping down the hall. 'I'll see yez about half-seven tomorrow night, God willing. An' try and get your Steve to come, eh? One of them 'as got to make the first move, but I don't think it'll be our Jill, she's too stubborn.'

'She shouldn't 'ave to,' Nellie said, holding on to the door frame as she lowered herself down the step. 'Always let the feller do the running, that's what I say.'

'An' I agree with yer.' Molly handed the bags over one at a time. 'I'll see yer tomorrow, Nellie, ta-ra.'

The room was pitch dark and the house silent but Ruthie had been wide awake for hours, praying for someone to wake up and realise it was Christmas morning. All she could think of was the wooden hoop she'd seen sticking out over the top of her mother's wardrobe. It was something she'd always wanted but couldn't have because her mam said she was too young. But Father Christmas had brought her one this year and she couldn't wait to try it. She could see herself running down the street, hitting the wooden circle with her hand to make it go faster. Doreen slept on the outside of the bed, Ruthie by the wall. The only way she could get out without waking her sister was by crawling down to the bottom of the bed. She thought for a while, then the picture of the hoop flashed through her mind and she decided it was worth a try.

'Hey, where yer goin'?' Doreen sat up in bed, rubbing the sleep from her eyes. 'Get back in, yer little tinker, it's the middle of the night!'

'I'm goin' downstairs to see what Father Christmas 'as

brought me.' Ruthie was feeling her way to the door when two hands gripped her and tried to pull her back. 'Leave me alone, our Doreen, or I'll tell me mam on yer.'

'There's no need to, I can hear for meself.' Molly stood framed in the doorway, a lighted candle in her hand. 'In fact, yer've probably woken the whole flamin' street! D'yer know it's not seven o'clock yet?'

'Ah, ray, Mam!' Ruthie wailed. 'Let me go down, please.'

Molly sighed. 'Stop that racket or Father Christmas will hear yer an' come an' take all yer presents back.' Her mind was torn between five grown-ups wanting to sleep, and one child who didn't. It didn't take her long to decide. Christmas was a time for children, and God knows, they weren't children very long. 'Okay, you win.' Molly stuck her head out of the door and shouted, 'Wakey, wakey! Everybody out!'

There were grunts and groans, but soon the tiny landing was crowded. Holding on to Ruthie's hand, Molly led the way down the stairs. And seeing the look of wonder in her baby's eyes when she saw the presents all wrapped in colourful paper set out on chairs, and the stockings hanging from the fireplace, Molly told herself that was all the reward she needed. There was nothing in the world more beautiful to see than the innocence on the face of a child who still believed in Father Christmas and fairies.

Two hours later, when the noise and laughter had died down, Molly asked, 'Well, are yez all happy with yer presents?'

353

'Ooh, yeah!' Tommy was holding his new long trousers to his waist, measuring them for length. 'These are the gear, Mam, an' me new shirt an' shoes.'

'Yer can wear them today, then they're goin' away till yer go for that interview at yer dad's works next week.'

Doreen gave her mother and father a big hug. Her presents had been a handbag and gloves to match, plus lipstick and chocolates. 'Thanks, both of you. I'll be a real swank now.'

'Me too!' Jill stood in front of them, holding a matching necklace, bracelet and ear-rings in nickel silver. She bent to kiss her parents. 'They're beautiful.'

A wave of sadness swept over Molly. Jill had joined in the laughter and merriment as the presents were opened, but to Molly's ears the laughter was hollow and the merriment forced. And she knew Steve was at the bottom of her daughter's unhappiness. There'd been no card from him, no attempt at reconciliation.

'I'm glad yer like them, sunshine,' Molly said, thinking all was not lost. Perhaps he'd come tonight with his mam and dad. 'If yer ever get to wear yer long dress again, they'll look nice with it.'

'Oh, I don't think I'll be wearing that again.' Jill turned away. 'I'll get our Doreen to shorten it for me.'

Doreen was at her side in a flash. 'I'll buy it off yer.'

'Oh, you're not soft, are yer?' Molly huffed. 'Let Jill hang on to it. Yer never know, somethin' might crop up an' she'll need it.'

'Can I interrupt for a minute?' Jack glared at Molly. What a time to be fighting over a dress! 'We haven't said thanks for our presents.' He held up the box containing a light blue shirt and maroon tie. 'There'll be no flies on me tonight. Thanks very much, I'm made up with them.'

'And my underskirt is very ooh-lah-lah.' Molly grinned broadly. 'Remind me to do the Highland Fling tonight, so everyone can see the lace on the bottom of it.'

'Mam, can I go out an' play with me 'oop?' Ruthie stood in front of Molly, the wooden hoop hanging from her neck. It had been the first thing she'd made a bee-line for, and she wouldn't let go, even when she'd been opening her other presents. 'Just outside the door, Mam, please?'

'It's too cold, sunshine,' Molly said. 'Play in the hall with it.'

The rosebud lips pouted. 'Ah, Mam, don't be a meanie, there's no room out there!'

'Do as yer mam tells yer, Ruthie,' Jack said. 'Anyway, no one is going anywhere until all this mess is cleared up, so get cracking.'

Molly stretched her arms wide. 'I feel more like flyin' than starting work. But if we all pull together we might manage an hour's shut eye this afternoon. Ruthie, you an' Tommy help yer dad tidy up in here while Jill and Doreen give me a hand. They can do the potatoes and vegetables while I make some cakes for tonight.'

Three doors away, Nellie was confronting her son. 'Are yer comin' with us tonight or wha'?'

Steve's face was like thunder. 'Mam, how many times 'ave I got to tell yer, I'm not going! Why d'yer insist on harping on it?'

'Because I can't make yer out, that's why! Yer actin' like a flamin' schoolboy instead of a man!' Nellie's face was mutinous. 'I thought Jill was supposed to be yer girlfriend, so what's happened?'

'She's not me girlfriend any more, is that good enough for yer?' Steve was angry with himself because it still hurt to think of Jill.

'No, it's not good enough for me!' Nellie folded her arms and met his eyes head on. 'Yer've been potty about the girl since yer were in short pants, so how come yer've changed all of a sudden?'

'That's my business,' he replied. 'It's got nothin' to do with anyone else.'

'Oh, but it has! Molly is me best mate, an' she's bound to wonder what's goin' on. What do I tell her?'

'Mam, will yer just leave it! Tell 'er anythin' yer like, I couldn't care less.'

'So it's not only Jill yer've fallen out with, it's 'er mam, as well!' Nellie was getting angrier by the minute. 'I always thought yer liked Molly Bennett.'

All the fight went out of Steve. 'I do like Mrs Bennett, she's a smashing woman. But I'm not goin' out with her daughter any more, Mam, so don't keep on about it.'

'Have yer told Jill yer've packed her up, an' why?'

Steve shook his head. 'She knows why.'

'If it's all to do with this Adelphi lark, then it's about time yer grew up, Steve McDonough. Yer actin' like a flamin' two year old.'

Steve walked away without answering. He could forgive what his mother called the Adelphi lark, but he couldn't, and never would, forgive the kiss.

★ ★ ★

Jill's tummy was in knots as the visitors started to arrive. If Steve really wanted to make it up with her, accepting the invitation to the party was one way of doing it without denting his pride. And she'd be truthful with him, tell him how much she'd missed him and that she'd never do anything again that would upset him.

When Molly went to answer a knock on the door and Jill heard Nellie's voice, she clasped her hands together, fixed a smile on her face and said a silent prayer.

Molly held her hand out for Nellie and George's coats. 'Steve not comin', then?'

Nellie shrugged out of her coat. 'No, he sends his apologies but he'd already promised to go to a mate's.'

Jill could feel all eyes on her, but her smile never wavered. 'I'll take the coats up, Mam.'

'Put them on our bed, sunshine, and try not to make a noise goin' up the stairs,' Molly said without meeting her daughter's eyes. 'Ruthie was so tired I don't think a bomb would wake her, but best not to take any chances.'

Jill climbed the stairs, biting on the inside of her lip to keep the tears at bay. It was pitch dark in the front bedroom, and after feeling for the brass knob at the end of the bedpost, she sat down with the coats still draped over her arms. With no one to witness her sadness she asked herself why she had ever agreed to go to that stupid dinner. She should have listened to Steve when he said he didn't want her to go. If she had, he'd be sitting downstairs right this minute waiting for her with that special look in his eyes and a wide, welcoming smile on his face.

Jill gulped in an effort to move the lump that was forming in her throat. Rubbing her hand up and down the material of Nellie's coat, she whispered, 'But he's not downstairs, he's gone to his mates. He prefers their company to mine now. I've lost him, and it's all me own fault.'

Then a voice in her head asked, Why was it your fault? Ye gods, it wasn't as though you'd gone out on a date with Miles. He's just a friend, that's all! If Steve's packed you up because of that, then he couldn't have loved you as much as he said he did.

Jill nodded her head in agreement and started to question the justice of the whole affair. She'd done nothing wrong, so why was she blaming herself? It seemed to her now that Steve must have wanted to finish with her and was using this as an excuse. Well, if that was what he wanted, then good luck to him. She certainly wasn't going to run after him!

Jill jumped when she heard her mother's voice floating up the stairs. 'What's takin' yer so long, sunshine?' Molly called. 'I'm waitin' for yer to give me a hand with the eats.'

'Coming, Mam!' Jill laid the coats down on the bed and took a deep breath, determined she wasn't going to let Steve spoil her night. But as she put her hand on the banister rail, she asked herself why, if she didn't care, she felt as though a door had been slammed in her face? And why was her heart so heavy?

Molly was waiting at the bottom of the stairs. She eyed her daughter anxiously before taking her by the arm. 'Give Doreen a hand to pass the sarnies round, there's a good girl, while I make the tea.'

For the next few hours Jill put on the performance of her life. She helped with the food, refilled glasses as soon as they were empty, sang with gusto and laughed loudly at Sinbad's jokes and Doreen's interpretation of the Charleston. She looked as though she didn't have a care in the world.

Molly caught Jack's eye and leaned forward to whisper in his ear, 'Who's she tryin' to kid?'

'Mam!'

Molly turned to see Ruthie clinging to the door frame rubbing the sleep from her eyes. 'Ah, did we wake yer up, sunshine?'

'Can I stay down, Mam?' The rosebud mouth quivered. 'I'm frightened in the dark on me own, in case Old Nick comes.'

'I'll take her up.' Jill took her sister's hand. 'I'm tired anyway, so I'll get into bed with her. Our Doreen can sleep in my bed.'

Molly opened her mouth to protest, then realised Jill was glad of the excuse to escape. 'Are yer sure?'

She nodded. 'Goodnight, everyone.'

After a chorus of goodnights, the room was silent until they heard the click of the bedroom door closing. Then Bridie sighed softly. 'Young love can be very painful at times, so it can.'

'Yer know the old saying: True love never runs smooth.' Jack passed his cigarette packet around. 'By this time next week it'll all be forgotten and they'll be as thick as thieves again.'

★ ★ ★

Nellie turned the key in the lock and pushed the front door open. 'The light's on, George, someone must still be up.'

Steve looked up from the book he was holding. 'Hi-ya.'

'You're back early.' Nellie threw the bunch of keys on the sideboard. 'I thought yer were stayin' at yer mate's?'

'I changed me mind.' Steve closed the book that had been open at the same page for the last half hour. He leaned forward and put it on the table. 'The house was packed, we were jammed in like sardines. So I decided to come 'ome and get some sleep.'

'Yer should 'ave come with us,' George said, pretending he didn't know anything was amiss. 'We've had a great time, haven't we, Nellie?'

'Always do when we go to Molly's. An' that Sinbad is a scream. Me throat's sore with laughin' at his jokes.' Nellie's eyes were lost in folds of flesh as she chuckled. 'That one about the parrot had me doubled up.'

George flashed her a warning glance. Sinbad's jokes were a bit near the knuckle and not for the ears of youngsters. Even he had waited until Molly's children were in the kitchen making tea before telling the one about the parrot. 'He's a real comedian, is Sinbad.'

'I'm makin' a cuppa.' Nellie eyed her son. 'D'yer want one, Steve?'

'No, ta, Mam, I'm goin' to bed.'

Nellie waited for a few minutes then closed the living room door. 'I can't make 'im out! There's something fishy about the whole thing, if yer ask me. Him and Jill are as close as two peas in a pod one minute, then all of a sudden he won't even mention her name!'

'Don't interfere, Nellie, let 'im sort it out himself,' George said. 'But if he carries on like this he'll lose her, an' then he'll be sorry. He'll not find a nicer girl than Jill if he lives to be a hundred.'

Steve lay on his back staring at the ceiling, his hands clasped behind his head. He'd never felt so miserable in his life. When he'd set off for his mate's house it was with a determination to enjoy himself. His friend, Joe, had told him there would be plenty of girls there and he intended to get a click with one of them. But it hadn't worked out that way. Oh, there were pretty girls there all right, and he could have had his pick, they'd hung around him like flies around a jam jar. And he had tried flirting with a couple of them, even kissed them, but they aroused no feeling in him, he just didn't find them attractive. The trouble was, he found himself comparing them to a girl with long blonde hair, vivid blue eyes and a smile that could make his heart do somersaults.

Steve punched the pillow before turning on his side. 'I've got to forget Jill Bennett, he told himself. She let me down once, she'll not get the chance to do it again. And I'll make sure no other girl gives me the run around. Once bitten, twice shy. From now on I'm going to play the field, look after number one. Love them and leave them, that'll be my motto, and to hell with everyone.

Four doors away, Jill lay on her side, an arm tucked around her baby sister whose even breathing was the only sound in the room. Doreen hadn't come to bed yet, and Jill was hoping she could drop off to sleep before her outspoken sister came up and started to ask questions. She'd gone over the events of the past week so many times her head was splitting. First she'd blamed herself, then Miles. But it was ridiculous to lay the blame at his door. After all she had a tongue in her head, all she'd had to do was say no.

As her eyelids became heavy with sleep, Jill finally admitted that it was nobody's fault. The truth, which she hadn't wanted to accept, was quite simple really . . . Steve just didn't want her any more.

Sleep came over her in waves, and Jill's last thought was that he should have had the guts and the good manners to tell her to her face. After courting for two years, she deserved that much.

Chapter Twenty-Three

Her legs swinging to and fro beneath the chair, Ruthie ran a finger over the dolly mixtures lined up on the table. 'Eeny, meeny, miney, mo, this is the one that's got to go!' Her finger came to a stop on a pink, heart-shaped sweet and she tutted in disgust. This wasn't what she wanted at all. It was the red jelly with sugar coating she had her eye on and that was two sweets away. Her tongue came out of the side of her mouth, as it always did when she was concentrating. Then she sat up straight, a smile on her face and a solution in her mind. Start at the other end, that was the answer. But once again she was thwarted as she came to the end of the ditty and her finger was still two sweets away from the elusive jelly for which her mouth was watering.

Molly glanced up from her ironing, saw the look of disgust on her daughter's face and grinned. 'That's what yer get for eatin' all the jellies first,' she called through from the kitchen. 'Yer shouldn't be so greedy.'

Ruthie glared, her legs swinging faster. 'I'll mix them all up again, then it'll come out right, you'll see.'

There was a pounding on the front door and Molly put

the flat iron down on the ring and turned the gas off. 'This'll be the rent man.' As she hurried through the living room, picking up the rent book from the sideboard as she passed, she warned, 'Don't move from that chair, d'yer hear? If yer touch the iron it'll burn the fingers off yer.'

Ruthie watched her mother disappear, a cunning look on her pixie-like face. She'd do it this time, now there was no one watching. 'Eeny, meeny, miney, mo, stick the baby on the po, when it's done, wipe its bum, eeny, meeny, miney, mo!' Success! Her tongue came out to receive the jelly, and she hummed with pleasure as her heels banged against the bottom of the chair.

'Good morning, Mr Henry!' Molly passed the brown rent book over. 'Did yer 'ave a nice Christmas?'

'Yes, thanks.' Mr Henry's father owned most of the houses in the street and his son had been collecting the rent since Molly moved in. He took the pound note from inside the book and placed it carefully in the back compartment of the leather bag that hung from his shoulder. 'Christmas Day was hectic with all the family around as usual, but yesterday was nice and quiet.'

'Same here.' Molly leaned against the door jamb and folded her arms. 'Is it true that the Culshaws did a moonlight flit on Christmas Eve?'

Mr Henry finished marking the book, then, as he handed it back, gave a wry smile. 'The house is as bare as Old Mother Hubbard's cupboard. They've cleared everything out.'

'Our Tommy told us there was a horse and cart outside on Christmas Eve, but I was so busy I didn't pay much heed.' Molly pulled at the lobe of her ear. 'I'm sorry about that, they were a nice family. It must 'ave been serious to do a flit like that, without tellin' anyone. They've lived here for as long as I can remember.'

'Money problems.' Mr Henry rifled through the coins in his bag to give Molly her change. 'I think she owed a lot.'

'Yeah, well, I can understand that. Her 'usband's been out of work for years. But surely it wasn't bad enough to do a bunk without even tellin' her neighbours? I think that was a bit mean.'

'Molly, she owed me three months' rent, and from what I've heard this morning, she was up to her neck in debt to everyone. Coalman, milkman, corner shop . . . you name them, she owed them.'

'Poor bugger!' Molly felt sad. 'She was a nice little thing, and the kids were always polite. I wasn't that keen on him, though, he was a lazy so-and-so. Always moanin' that he couldn't get a job, but if yer ask me, he never even tried.'

'Well, the way things are going everyone will have a job soon whether they like it or not.' Mr Henry adjusted the strap on his shoulder. 'The way I see it, there'll be a war before the year's out.'

Molly jumped to attention. 'Oh, don't you start, Mr Henry! It's all my Jack talks about! The last thing he said before he went out this morning was, "You mark my words, Molly, as sure as eggs is eggs, there's goin' to be a war." '

'Well, I hope we're both wrong, but I firmly believe Mr Chamberlain has had the wool pulled over his eyes.

Hitler's built up an army that can take on anyone, and I think he intends to take over the whole of Europe, us included. And unless we stop dithering and prepare for war, we'll be caught with our pants down.'

'It doesn't bear thinkin' about,' she said. 'Why the 'ell doesn't someone bump that Hitler off?'

'Let's hope they do.' Mr Henry looked at his watch. 'It's time for my morning cup of tea. Miss Clegg will wonder what's keeping me.'

That brought a smile to Molly's face. 'Yer know, if I didn't know better, I'd think there was somethin' goin' on between you two. Every Monday morning, without fail, yer pay her a visit. A cup of tea is yer excuse, but what goes on behind those closed doors is anyone's guess.'

Mr Henry grinned as he turned to cross the street. 'Molly, evil comes to he who evil thinks.'

'Oh, aye!' she called after him. 'Well, I'm as evil as they come, but I can't get a handsome man to come to my 'ouse for tea every week.'

Mr Henry knocked on Miss Clegg's door before answering, 'Keep trying, Molly, you never know your luck in a big city.'

'Tell Victoria I'll be over after, for a few tips.' There was a smile on Molly's face as she closed the door, but it faded as she made her way down the hall. All this talk of war was enough to give you the willies. Surely the last war was enough to make men think twice before starting another? Mind you, she thought as she struck a match to light the gas under the iron, by all accounts that Hitler wasn't a man . . . he was a flaming lunatic!

★ ★ ★

'You're very quiet today, Jill.' Miles filled his fountain pen from the bottle of Quink on his desk. 'Was Christmas a disappointment to you, or are you worn out with all the parties?'

'A bit of both, actually.' She smiled. 'It'll take a few days to get back to normal.'

'Tell me about your presents.' Miles laid down his pen. 'What did Steve buy you?'

Oh dear, Jill thought, what do I say to that? Pretend all is well, or tell the truth? Better to be honest, Miles was bound to find out sooner or later. 'As a matter of fact, Steve and I are not friends any more.'

Miles crossed his arms and rested them on the desk, a look of concern on his face. 'Oh dear, I am sorry to hear that. What brought this about?'

'It was just one of those things.' Jill wasn't prepared to elaborate. 'We had a disagreement, and that was that!'

'You fell out over Christmas! I thought it was supposed to be the time of goodwill to all men? Jolly bad timing, don't you think?'

'If you're going to have a disagreement with someone, timing hardly comes into it.' Jill shuffled the papers on her desk. 'If you don't mind, Miles, I'd rather not talk about it right now. I've got some letters to get through before lunchtime.'

'I'm so sorry, I have no right to pry into your private affairs. Just tell me to mind my own business.'

'Oh, I didn't mean it that way!' she said. 'I know you weren't being nosy. But I do have to get these letters ready for your father to sign before he goes to lunch.'

'Well, how about coming out with me for a spot of lunch?' he asked. 'Away from the office, we could talk to our heart's content.'

'Oh, I couldn't do that!' Jill's heart pounded as she searched frantically for an excuse. 'I'm, er, not dressed to go to a restaurant.'

'Then we won't go to a restaurant.' Miles gave her a crooked grin. 'Not a posh one, anyway. There's the Bradford Hotel in Tithebarn Street, they do light lunches.'

'Thank you for asking, Miles, but I don't think it would be a good idea. What would the other girls think? Going out with the boss's son, I'd be the talk of the office!'

'Nonsense! We're not beholden to them!' Miles raised his brows. 'Is that just an excuse, Jill?'

She gazed down at her hands. Why shouldn't she go out for lunch with him? He was nice, easy to talk to, what harm was there in it? After all, she was free now, no boyfriend, no ties. 'As long as you don't mind being seen with me in my scruffy coat, I'd like to have lunch with you.'

'Oh, I say, jolly good!' Miles grinned like a young boy who'd been offered a treat. Running a hand through his hair, he pushed his chair back. 'I'll go and tell Father. I usually have lunch with him and his colleagues, but it's so boring. All they do is discuss the various cases they're dealing with.'

Jill watched the door close behind him and wondered if she was doing the right thing. Not that she'd had much choice in the matter, she could hardly have refused point blank. Anyway, she didn't have to justify her actions to anyone now, so why make a big issue out of it?

When they turned the corner of Castle Street they were met by the full force of the bitterly cold wind blowing in from the Mersey. Jill shivered, wrapping her coat more closely around her. With the wind whipping her hair, eyes watering from the cold and teeth chattering, she forced her long slim legs to move quicker to keep in step with Miles.

'You'll soon be warm,' he said, his hand cupping her elbow as they crossed a busy main road. 'A glass of sherry will do the trick.'

'I'm not old enough to go in a pub,' Jill reminded him. 'I'm not seventeen yet.'

'It's an hotel, dear, not a pub.'

Jill glanced sideways, wondering whether to be ashamed of her ignorance or worried about the endearment. Then she decided she couldn't care less about either.

'Here we are.' Miles held the door open and Jill could feel the warmth as she stepped inside. 'Let me take your coat.'

Jill sat down and looked around with interest. The atmosphere was quiet but friendly. And it was lovely and warm.

'A glass of sherry before we eat?' Miles saw the doubt on her face and bent towards her. 'Go on, be a daredevil.'

Jill laughed at his expression. 'Oh, all right, but don't blame me if I don't get any work done this afternoon.'

During the meal she became more talkative and outgoing. Her face was animated as she told him about the antics of her family and friends, and Miles thought she'd never looked so pretty. No, not pretty, he corrected himself, Jill was beautiful. He had refrained from asking about Steve in case she withdrew into her shell, but as the clock on the wall ticked away, and their lunch hour was nearly over, he knew he'd never have a better chance to ask the question he needed an answer to. He'd always been attracted to Jill, but with Steve around he knew he'd never be in the running. Now he wanted to be sure the coast was clear for him to make his play.

'That was most enjoyable.' Miles pressed the table napkin to his lips. 'Mind you, the company had a lot to do with it.'

'Thank you.' Jill smiled. 'The meal was lovely.'

'Now, while there are no distractions, can I ask what happened between you and Steve?'

Caught unaware by the question, Jill blushed. 'I told you, we've fallen out.'

'I hope I wasn't in any way responsible? It didn't have anything to do with the Adelphi, did it?'

'Yes,' Jill answered truthfully, 'it had a lot to do with it. Steve didn't want me to go, and I thought he was being childish.' She lowered her eyes. Why did it still hurt so much to talk about Steve? 'Anyway, it's over and done with, so can we change the subject, please?'

Miles put his hand to his heart. 'I promise not to mention it again. Now, I'll get our coats.' He walked to the cloakroom with a smile on his face and a spring in his step.

★ ★ ★

'You're late tonight.' Molly stepped aside to let Ellen pass. 'I thought yer'd gone straight home.'

Ellen had taken to calling in to Molly's every night on her way home from work, just for a five-minute chat. 'There was a lot of extra work to do tonight. What with Christmas Eve bein' mad busy, we didn't get a chance to clean up properly.'

Molly glanced at the clock before sitting down. 'Jack must be working overtime. Not that I'm complainin', mind, 'cos the money comes in handy. I'm in debt up to me eyeballs, buyin' presents I really couldn't afford. Still, it only comes once a year, thank God!'

'My kids 'ad the best Christmas they've ever had,' Ellen said. 'Thanks to Corker, he's been marvellous.'

'Gone away now, hasn't he?' Molly couldn't figure out the relationship between Ellen and Corker. It was a mystery to her.

'Only for two weeks. He's doin' short trips now, just to Holland and Belgium, places like that.'

'Ay, did yer hear about the Culshaws doin' a flit?' Molly shook her head, she still couldn't believe it. 'I wonder where they've gone? Poor buggers, I believe they owed everyone. I just hope they're not livin' rough, no one deserves that.'

'Molly, there but for the grace of God go I,' Ellen said. 'Only in my case it wasn't God who saved me from bein' thrown on the streets, it was you an' Nellie.'

Jill came in from the kitchen where she'd been rinsing through a few of her undies. Her face looked troubled. 'The children won't be walking the streets, will they?

Surely someone has to find them a place to live.'

Knowing how much Jill worried, Molly made light of it. 'Of course they won't be walkin' the streets, yer silly nit! They'll 'ave had a house ready to move in to.'

Jill gave a sigh of relief. 'I'm going up to clear my drawers out, see if anything wants washing.'

'No developments between her and Steve?' Ellen asked, when Jill was out of earshot.

'Not a dickie bird! I'm disappointed in Steve, thought he had more sense than he's showin' now. An' if he's not careful he'll miss the boat, 'cos she went out with her boss today, for lunch.'

'Go way!' Ellen looked suitably impressed. 'Fancy that now!'

'I don't blame 'er,' Molly said, 'no point in hangin' around till Steve gets over his sulks.' But Molly didn't really mean what she said. She still thought the world of Steve and was saddened by the whole sorry mess. He and Jill were made for each other, and the sooner they made it up the better. 'Anyway, Ellen, any news of Nobby?'

She shook her head. 'I haven't been to see 'im for weeks. I can't afford the fare, Molly, it takes me all me time to manage as it is.'

Molly studied her neighbour's face. 'Yer look worn out, Ellen. It's too much for yer, doin' two jobs.'

Ellen leaned forward and touched Molly on the knee. 'I've got some good news for yer, and that makes a change, doesn't it?'

Molly sat up straight, her eyes eager. 'Blimey, Ellen, I couldn't half do with some good news! What is it?'

'Tony's offered me a full-time job.' Ellen's thin face shone with a beaming smile. 'I'm givin' me notice in at the Maypole tomorrow.'

Molly fell back in her chair. 'Well, that *is* good news! Oh, Ellen, love, I'm so happy for yer.'

'It's an extra pound a week in me purse, Molly, and that pound will make all the difference. We still won't be well off, of course, but I won't be skint on a Saturday after I've paid me ways, like I am now. And for the first time in their lives, I can give me kids a penny pocket money.' She clapped her hands together. 'Tony's been ever so kind to me. I don't need to start in the mornings till a quarter past nine, so I can give the kids their breakfast and get them off to school.'

'D'yer know, Ellen, it's been a miserable bloody day for me, what with worryin' about the Culshaws and everyone sayin' there's goin' to be a flippin' war. But you've bucked me up no end, yer really have. I'm so pleased for yer, I feel like doin' a little jig.'

They heard the front door open and Doreen came in, dragging Ruthie by one hand and holding the wooden hoop in the other. 'This one was playin' on the main road, Mam!'

'What!' Molly jumped to her feet, sending the chair crashing against the table. 'You little faggot, you! How many times 'ave yer been told not to go out of the street?' Molly took the hoop from Doreen and dropped it behind the sideboard. 'Right, that stays there until yer learn to do as yer told. Just you wait till yer dad gets home.'

'Ah, ray, Mam, don't tell me dad.' Ruthie began to jump up and down, and it was then Molly noticed the tell-tale signs on her daughter's socks.

'Yer've wet yer knickers! Five years of age, an' yer've wet yer knickers!' She rolled up her sleeves. 'Right, that does it! In the kitchen for a wash, then it's bed for you, me lady.'

Ellen stood up, trying to keep her face straight. 'I'll make meself scarce, Molly.'

'Okay, Ellen, I'll see yer.' Molly winked broadly as her neighbour passed. Then, as she looked down, she was just in time to see Ruthie kick Doreen's leg. 'It's all your fault, our Doreen, you're a clat-tale-tit, that's what you are.'

Doreen's hand came up to swipe her sister, but Molly caught it in mid-air. 'That's enough! If there's any smackin' to be done, I'll do it.'

Doreen glared at her sister. 'It's a damn' good hidin' she wants.'

'Ay, ay, less of the language, if yer don't mind, madam!' Even as Molly spoke, she thought, I'm a fine one to talk about language when mine would put the devil to shame. 'Your dinner's in the oven. See to it yerself while I get this one sorted out.' Taking Ruthie by the ear, Molly dragged her through to the kitchen, ignoring the screams which were more from anger than pain. 'Now, where's that scrubbing brush?'

Molly was a good story teller and she fitted her actions to her words. She had gone over the events of the day and now had Jack chuckling as she described the look of horror on Ruthie's face when the scrubbing brush was produced. 'She really thought I meant it!'

'Yer should 'ave used it on her, she's a . . . a . . .' Doreen tried to find words that would convey her feelings without provoking a telling off for using bad language. 'She's a hard-faced little brat.' She lifted her leg. 'Look at the bruise where she kicked me.'

Molly rolled her eyes to the ceiling. 'Would yer like me to remind yer of some of the things you used to get up to at her age? Compared to you, she's an angel.'

'How come I always end up gettin' the dirty end of the stick?' Doreen demanded. 'What about our Jill?'

Jill lifted her hands. 'Leave me out of it, I haven't opened me mouth yet.'

'Can we stop this bickering, please?' Jack intervened. 'I know I was laughing before, and the way you tell it, love, it was funny. But our Ruthie playing on the main road isn't something to laugh about. If her hoop ran in front of a tram or bus, she'd run after it without thinkin', and she could be killed.'

'Oh, I think she's learned her lesson,' Molly said. 'I told her a little white lie, said if she promised not to do it again, I wouldn't tell you. So don't let on yer know, and you two keep yer traps shut.'

Doreen wasn't about to argue because she had something to ask and didn't want her parents in a bad mood. She waited till her dad had settled in his chair with his cigarette lit and the *Echo* opened on his knee, and her mam was busy darning one of his socks.

'Mam, have yer ever heard of Connie Millington's dancing school in Merton Road?'

Molly pulled the thread through before looking up. 'No, why?'

'Me an' Maureen were thinkin' of going there, you know, to learn how to dance properly.'

'What sort of a place is it?' Molly asked. 'It's not a dive, is it?'

'No, of course not!' Doreen was heartened that there hadn't been a blank refusal. 'Some of the girls in work go, an' they said it's a big house and Connie Millington teaches all the dances . . . quickstep, slow foxtrot, rhumba, tango . . . everything! And it's only sixpence to get in.'

'I'll think about it.' Molly lowered her head, then raised it to look across at Jill. 'Wouldn't you like to go?'

Jill pulled a face. 'No, I don't think so. I've got two left feet, I'll never make a dancer.'

Doreen pulled on her bottom lip. If she could persuade her sister to go, there'd be no opposition from her parents. 'Anyone can learn to dance if they're taught properly. Come on, our kid, give it a try. Even if yer only go the once, just to see.'

Their eyes met and Jill could see the path Doreen's thoughts were taking. The last thing she wanted was to go to a dancing school, but would Doreen be allowed to go without her? 'What d'you think, Mam?'

'It's up to you, sunshine! Nothin' ventured, nothin' gained.' Molly smiled. 'Who knows? Yer might turn out to be another Ginger Rogers!'

'Some hope! This Connie Millington would have to be good to make a dancer out of me.'

'Suit yerself.' Molly knew Jack was listening and

wondered whether, as man of the house, he should be consulted. But she knew he'd soon butt in if he didn't agree. 'If you go, then Doreen can. Otherwise she's not on. I'm not havin' a girl of fifteen walking home on her own in the dark.' She saw Jack's nod of approval. 'There's some queer folk walkin' the streets late at night.'

Doreen kicked Jill under the table. 'Come on, our kid, say yer'll come with us.'

'I don't have much choice, do I? But don't expect me to be as eager to learn as you. If I want to sit like a wallflower, then let me.'

With her looks, unless all the blokes are blind, there's not much chance of her being allowed to sit like a wallflower, thought Doreen, but she kept her thoughts to herself. Now she'd got what she wanted, she had no intention of rocking the boat. And she certainly wasn't going to tell her parents that Mike and Sammy would be there. 'How about tomorrow night, kid?'

Jill's mouth gaped in surprise. 'Tomorrow! I didn't know you intended to go so soon! I thought you meant sometime in the future.'

Molly spoke before Doreen had time to open her mouth. 'Not goin' anywhere tomorrow night, are yer, sunshine? Then get out an' enjoy yerself. Yer don't want to be sittin' in every night with two old crocks like me an' yer dad.'

Molly was telling her daughter not to hang around waiting for Steve. If he wanted her he'd soon come running when he knew she was going out enjoying herself. 'Yer've got plenty of nice clothes to wear, so there's no excuse.' She started to rumble with laughter. 'After two lessons, I expect yez to be able to teach me and yer dad how to trip the light fantastic.'

Jack scratched his chin. 'Now that conjures up a vision to delight the eye, I'm sure.'

Chapter Twenty-Four

'You two go on your own.' Jill hung back when they reached the large Victorian house which had a board outside advertising the Constance Millington Dancing Academy. Shy by nature, the thought of walking into a room full of strangers was giving her the jitters. 'I'm not fussy about learning to dance anyway!'

Doreen gave Maureen a look and they each cupped an elbow of Jill's and hurried her up the path. 'Yer not backin' out now!' Honestly, Doreen thought, our Jill's so shy she can be a right pain in the neck sometimes. 'If yer don't want to dance, just sit an' watch.' She put a hand in the small of her sister's back and pushed her through the front door.

The room they entered was large, two knocked into one. It had a wooden floor with chairs placed around the sides. As Jill looked around with interest her eyes alighted on Mike and Sammy, sitting opposite the door. She turned to Doreen, her voice angry. 'You sly thing! Why didn't you tell me your friends were coming?'

'What difference does it make?' Doreen shrugged her shoulders. 'It's a free world, isn't it?'

'Let's sit down,' Maureen said, 'I feel like one of Lewis's dress dummies standin' here.'

'I'm sitting down, and staying put.' Jill walked to the far end of the room. 'I'm annoyed with you, our Doreen.'

But Connie Millington wasn't allowing anyone to stay put. She took the first timers to one end of the room, leaving the experienced dancers with her partner. 'I'll take you through the basic steps of the waltz, ladies first, then the gents.' She walked to the opposite side of the dance floor and turned her back on them. 'Now, watch my feet. Starting with the left foot. One, two, three, one, two, three.'

Doreen nudged Maureen. 'It looks easy, doesn't it?'

Before Maureen had time to reply, Connie was telling them to stand up. 'Now try it. Just watch my feet and do as I do. Left foot back, right foot back and to the side, then left foot over so your feet are together.' She went through the routine several times until she was sure they had the hang of it. Then she told them to sit down and called the boys over. 'It's the same for you, except you'll be leading so you start with the right foot.'

When Jill saw the blushes and the antics of some of the boys she began to feel better. At least she wasn't the only one with two left feet. And it was easy, really, even their Ruthie could have done it.

But it was a different story when Connie put a record on and told them to take their partners. The one, two, three was easy when you were doing it alone, but trying to fit your steps in with a partner was a very different kettle of fish. And the gangling youth who had made a bee-line for Jill had huge feet that kept getting in her way. He was blushing furiously as he apologised each time he stepped on her feet. She was glad when the record finished.

'Take a break,' Connie said, 'then we'll try again. Those are the three main steps of a waltz. When you've mastered them the rest will come easy. But some of you are as stiff as boards, you'll have to learn to loosen up.'

'Ay, it's the gear, isn't it?' Doreen had been up with Mike and she was well pleased with their performance. 'Easy, peasy.'

Maureen agreed that she and Sammy hadn't done badly either. But Jill was busy rubbing her feet. 'I'll be black and blue tomorrow! That bloke spent more time on me feet than he did on the floor.' She wrinkled her nose. 'His breath smelled terrible, too. If I see him coming towards me again, I'm going to do a bunk.'

But when the record started another boy claimed Jill and he was much lighter on his feet. She found their steps matched perfectly, and although both were stiff and unsure, she felt she was holding her own.

Connie watched the couples with an eagle eye, telling one boy to lift his feet up, another to relax. 'Listen to the beat . . . one, two, three . . . now move your feet in time to it.'

The three steps took them all in a straight line to the end of the dance floor where they all bumped into each other, giggling with embarrassment and wondering how to turn around and dance back the way they'd come. In the end, flat-footed and clumsy, the boys pulled their

381

partners around, muttering under their breath, 'One-two-three, one-two-three.'

When the music came to an end, Connie told them to sit down and watch while she and her partner went through all the steps of a waltz which they would be learning during future lessons. Once they'd mastered the waltz, she said, they'd go on to the other dances.

Jill thought she had never seen anything so beautiful as Connie and her partner swept across the floor, their slim bodies in perfect harmony, rising and falling to the music. Poised swaying on their toes, spinning on their heels, floating effortlessly across the floor, it was sheer magic to watch. Jill remembered someone using the expression 'poetry in motion' and it fitted the dancing couple better than anything else she could think of.

'I'm goin' to learn to dance like that,' Doreen said with confidence. 'Then I'm goin' to proper dances, like the Rialto and the Grafton.'

'Yeah, me too!' Maureen wasn't going to be left out. 'An' see her dancing shoes? Well, I'm goin' to get a pair like that, with high heels.'

'Take your partners now,' Connie said, 'and we'll go through the basic steps again. Then we'll show you one or two of the easy spins. Don't worry if you can't get it right, you can't expect miracles from one lesson. You can practise at home, using a chair as a partner.'

At a quarter past ten Jill reminded Doreen they'd promised not to stay out late. 'I think we'd better be making tracks.'

'Ah, ray, kid!' Doreen protested. Mike and Sammy

had come to sit with them after the interval, and they'd think she was a baby having to be home at a certain time. 'Just another half hour.'

Jill shook her head. 'I promised me mam to get you home early. Otherwise she won't let you come again.'

The threat did the trick, but Doreen wasn't too pleased as she stood up. 'It's ridiculous! Just when I'm gettin' the hang of it!' She turned to Maureen. 'Are yer comin'?'

'Uh, uh!' Maureen grinned. 'Me mam said I could stay as long as Mike an' Sammy saw me home.'

This fuelled Doreen's anger. Reaching under the chair for her handbag, she said, 'Just wait till I get home. I'm goin' to remind me mam I'm workin' now, I'm not a baby.'

But walking to the bus stop, her arm linked through Jill's, Doreen's temper mellowed. She knew if she said one word to her mother, her dancing days would be over. And she did want to go to Millington's again. She wanted to learn how to dance properly, be another Connie Millington. 'Did yer enjoy it, kid?'

Jill could read her sister's mind like a book. And she knew that next week she'd be cajoled into accompanying her to the dancing academy again. But it hadn't been that bad, in fact she'd quite enjoyed it. 'Yes, it was fun. At least I know me left foot from me right now.'

They laughed and chatted all the way home, and Doreen was in a very happy frame of mind when they let themselves into the house.

'Well, how did it go?' Molly leaned forward to switch the wireless off. 'Can yez dance the light fandango now?'

'It was brilliant!' Doreen ran out to hang her coat on the hallstand, coming back with a beaming smile on her face. 'We can do the waltz, can't we, kid?' She reached for Jill's hand. 'Come on, let's show them.'

Jill shrank into the corner of the couch. 'Not likely!'

Molly took Doreen's side. 'Come on, sunshine, don't be so flamin' miserable. We've been listening to a murder play on the wireless and it scared the life out of me. I could do with cheering up.'

Jill looked at her father, and when he gave a broad wink of encouragement, she stood up. 'Oh, all right! But nobody dare laugh, okay?'

'Yer'll 'ave to move yer chair, Mam,' Doreen said. 'We need lots of room.' She put her hand on Jill's waist and lifted her arm. 'I'll be the feller. Now, I put me right foot forward, you put yer left foot back.'

But leading was very different from being led, and Doreen kept standing on Jill's feet. At first she blamed her sister, then the lack of space, and finally the absence of music to keep time to. Her face set in determined lines, she happened to glance up and saw the tears of laughter running down her mother's face. She glared for a second, then saw the funny side. Dropping Jill's hand, she doubled up with laughter. 'Not much like Ginger Rogers, eh, Mam?'

Molly ran the back of her hands across her eyes. 'Well, love, even she 'ad to start somewhere. She wasn't born with a pair of dance shoes on 'er feet.'

'Well, there's one dance I can do.' Doreen looked smug. 'One of the girls in work 'as been showin' me, in our dinner break.'

'Gettin' a demonstration, are we?' Jack asked, sitting back enjoying himself. 'This is as good as goin' to the pictures any day! Sittin' in the best seats, too!'

'I'll go round with the hat after.' Doreen grinned. 'Mam, you hum that song they do the Charleston to. And move out of the way, 'cos I've got to kick me legs about.'

'We've seen yer do the Charleston,' Molly said. 'I thought we were goin' to see somethin' exciting.'

'Yer've never seen me do it like this, Mam, so move out of the way and start humming.' Doreen pushed the table back towards the sideboard, giving herself plenty of space. Then she moved to the middle of the floor and started an exhibition that at first stunned her audience, then had them leaning forward, their eyes bright with surprise and appreciation. Her feet twisting in time to Molly's humming, Doreen moved her shoulders up and down and kicked out one shapely leg after the other. Holding her hands either side of her face, her fingers spread and wiggling while her hips swayed, she put on a fine performance.

While Molly watched her daughter with surprise and enjoyment, she imagined her dressed in one of those short shimmy dresses with a fringe on the bottom, and a velvet band around her forehead with a feather sticking out of it. Just like she'd seen them on the pictures. She's good, Molly thought, no doubt about that!

'Ooh, that's enough, Mam.' Doreen leaned on the table gasping for breath. 'I'm puffed out.'

'I wish I could do that!' Jill was full of appreciation. 'It was really marvellous!'

385

'It certainly was,' Jack said, with more than a hint of pride in his voice. 'If I'd had the energy, I'd 'ave joined yer.'

'Yer need more than energy, love, yer need the know-how.' Molly glanced from Doreen to Jill. How different my two daughters are, she thought, different as chalk from cheese. But I love the bones of both of them. 'Reminded me of when we used to do the Black Bottom, Jack, d'yer remember? Except when we did that, we used to come 'ome with our backsides black an' blue.'

'Can I go again next week, Mam, please?' Doreen begged. 'I really want to learn to dance properly. Yer should see the way Connie Millington dances. It's so graceful, isn't it, our kid?'

Jill nodded. 'It was a treat just to sit and watch.'

'Are you goin' again, Jill?' Molly asked.

'Yes, I'll go with her,' Jill said, keeping her eyes away from her sister. 'But could we stay out a bit later, Mam? It's a bit daft having to leave so early.'

'As long as yez come home together, we don't mind, do we, Jack?'

'As yer said, love, as long as they come home together.' He lit his last cigarette of the day. 'I wouldn't want Tilly Mint here comin' home on her own.'

'Ah, ray, Dad!' Doreen said angrily. 'Anyone would think I was about ten years of age!'

'Don't answer yer dad back, my girl!' Molly said. 'An' while yer learnin' to dance, there's other things yer should be learnin'. One, never push yer luck when yer on a winning streak.'

★ ★ ★

'Hi-yer, Nellie!' Molly opened the door wide and jerked her head. 'Come in quick so I can put the wood in the hole. It's cold enough to freeze the you-know-whats off a brass monkey.'

'Oh, that looks a treat.' Nellie stood in front of the roaring fire rubbing her hands. 'Did yer get a letter about us havin' electricity put in?'

'Yeah, great, isn't it?' Molly pulled two dining chairs nearer the fire. 'Park yer carcass an' get a warm.'

The wooden chair creaked under Nellie's weight. She pulled her dress up over her knees and sighed with pleasure as the warmth spread up her legs. 'I'm made up we're gettin' the leccy, 'cos it's a lot cleaner than gas. But I 'ope they don't start while the bad weather's on. D'yer remember when they did yer ma's? They 'ad the front door open all the time, in an' out like a flamin' yo-yo the workmen were.'

'It'll be ages before they get to us, they're bound to start at the top of the street first.' Molly rattled the poker between the bars of the grate and the flames roared up the chimney. 'That's better! I went down the yard for a jimmy-riddle, an' the seat was like ice. Haven't been able to get warm since.'

'I came to see how Tommy got on? Did he get the job?'

Molly's shoulders did a little jig. 'Yep! Starts next Monday.'

Nellie grinned. 'Yer won't know yerself with three wage packets comin' in, girl. Yer'll be livin' the life of Riley!'

'What about yerself? You've got three workin' as well!'

'Yeah, I know, don't bite me head off!' Nellie stared into the flickering flames. 'It's nice not havin' to worry about where the next penny's comin' from, but yer know somethin', girl? I sometimes think we had more fun when we 'ad nowt. We seemed to 'ave more to laugh at in those days.'

'I know what yer mean, Nellie, I often think about the old days.' Molly folded her arms and crossed her legs. 'But we shouldn't complain 'cos we're doing better. There's many a folk would swap places with us. And we can still have a laugh. Yer should 'ave been here last night, yer'd 'ave laughed yer head off.'

'Why, what did I miss?'

'Our Jill and Doreen went to a dancin' class.' Molly told her story before pushing her chair back and giving Nellie the benefit of her impersonation of Doreen doing the Charleston. 'Honest to God, Nellie, she was good. She can be a real hard clock at times, but she's got plenty of personality. Not a shy bone in 'er body, not like our Jill.'

'I still can't get over what's happened between our Steve an' your Jill,' Nellie said, looking glum. 'I'd 'ave bet money on them two gettin' married.'

'I haven't given up hope,' Molly said. 'They'll get together again, I feel sure.' Her eyes slid sideways. 'D'yer know, I haven't seen hide nor hair of your Steve for weeks. Never even seen 'im in the street, goin' to work or comin' home.'

Nellie tutted. 'I'm beginnin' to think the silly sod's got a screw loose. He comes in an' out the back way now, an' the only reason I can think of is that he doesn't want to bump into Jill.'

'There yer are, yer see!' Molly gave her friend a gentle dig on the arm. 'If he didn't care for her, why would he do that? There's more to this than meets the eye, an' I wish I knew what it was. If I could get 'im on his own, I'd ask him.'

Nellie bridled. 'D'yer think I haven't? But every time I ask him, he just glares at me. Honest, if looks could kill, girl, I'd be a dead duck.'

'I'll give it another week or two, an' if things are still the same I'll think of some way to get them together.' Molly took the tongs from the companion set, picked out a large piece of coal from the scuttle and placed it in the middle of the fire. 'Even if they 'ave a blazing row an' decide they've finished with each other, at least things will be out in the open.'

Nellie's tummy started to shake with laughter. 'Are yer goin' to get a big hat for their weddin'?'

'If our Jill was marryin' Steve, I'd buy a hat as big as a flamin' cartwheel.'

Nellie pursed her lips. 'Yer've got me there, girl! I can't for the life of me think of anythin' bigger than a cartwheel.'

Molly grinned. 'My hat will be so big, we could both get under it. How would that suit yer?'

Nellie's smile faded. 'Molly, if our two kids ever marry, I'll be that happy I'll go down to George Henry Lees an' buy the dearest 'at they've got. One with flowers round the brim an' a big silk bow at the back.' She gripped Molly's arm and levered herself up. 'Sittin' here won't get me washin' done, so I'd better be on me way. Don't bother comin' to the door, I'll bang it after me.'

Molly cupped her friend's face in her hands and kissed her cheek. 'Yer me best mate, Nellie, an' I love yer.'

Nellie's smile re-appeared. 'All of me?'

'All of yer,' Molly said. 'Right down to the last ounce.' She patted a chubby cheek. 'If I don't see yer later, I'll slip up in the mornin' when Ruthie's gone to school. Ta-ra for now.'

Miles sat back in the swivel chair, his fingers tapping his desk top. 'Did you enjoy it?'

'Yes, it was worth it just to see how graceful ballroom dancing can be.' Jill anchored her hair behind her ear. 'And we had a good laugh when we got home. Our Doreen can be so funny sometimes. She takes after me mam for that. They've both got a marvellous sense of humour.'

'Have you ever been to the ballet, Jill?'

'No.' She shook her head. 'One of our teachers in school was a real lover of ballet and she used to tell the class about the marvellous dancing and the stories behind them. Some of them are quite sad, aren't they?'

'As a matter of fact, they're performing *Swan Lake* at the Empire next week,' he said. 'I heard Mother saying she would like to go. You really should make the effort, Jill, you would appreciate it.'

'I'd love to go, but I've no one to go with.' A smile spread slowly across her face. 'I can just see our Doreen's face if I asked her to come to the ballet with me. She'd think I'd gone barmy.'

'Why don't you let me take you?' Miles half closed his eyes, adding, 'I may be going myself anyway.'

Jill took time to answer. She'd love to go to the ballet, but there were other things to consider. 'Thanks, Miles, but I think not. The girls all gave me sly looks when we went out to lunch the other day, I don't want to give them anything else to gossip about.'

He had been racking his brains for an excuse to ask Jill out, and when she'd brought up the subject of dancing he thought she'd handed him the opportunity. He certainly wasn't going to let office gossip spoil his plans. 'Does it really worry you, what they think? Can't two young people be friends without having to be concerned about what bad-minded gossip-mongers think?'

'It's all right for you.' Jill wrinkled her nose. 'You're not the one being accused of trying to get well in with the boss's son.'

'That is absolutely ridiculous!' Miles' face was flushed with anger and frustration. 'I will not have my life ruled by typists who have nothing better to do than tittle-tattle! If you wish to go somewhere, and I would be delighted, as a friend, to take you, it is of no concern to anyone else! Don't you agree, Jill?'

'Well, yes, put that way of course I agree.' You can't argue with logic, she thought. If we want to be friends, and that's all we are, what's it got to do with Mr Pearson's or Mr Brown's secretaries? I really would love to see *Swan Lake*, and there's no one else to take me.

'So you'll come?'

'Yes, please.'

'Good!' Miles smiled before picking up the telephone and dialling a number. 'Will you come in, Miss Sutton? I have the papers ready for you now.'

Jill exchanged smiles with Joan Sutton before bending her head over the letter she was working on. She heard Miles explaining what typing was required, sensed Joan turning to leave the office, then heard Miles' voice. 'Oh, Joan, just one second, please.'

'Yes, Mr Miles?'

'You go to the ballet, don't you?'

Jill lifted her head when she heard the question. What on earth was Miles up to?

'Yes,' Joan said, 'as often as I can. I'm going to the Empire next week, as a matter of fact, to see *Swan Lake*. I've seen it several times, but never cease to be thrilled by it.'

'I'm trying to persuade Jill to come with me next week, but I'm having a hard time.' Miles pushed his chair back and crossed his long legs. 'You try and persuade her for me. Convince her she'd enjoy it.'

When Joan turned to look into Jill's startled eyes, her intuition told her the predicament the young girl was in. She too had heard about the gossip from one of her colleagues and had immediately rooted out the offenders and given them a severe talking to. 'Oh, you must go, Jill! You would really love it! It would be such a shame to miss the opportunity.'

Jill gulped, then managed a weak smile. 'I suppose you're right.'

Joan, her back to Miles, winked. 'I'll be looking forward to hearing what you think of it.'

When the office door closed behind Joan, Miles threw back his head and laughed. 'That should solve your problem.'

He is very attractive when he laughs, Jill thought. In fact he's nice in every way. Polite, attentive, and he treats me like a lady. I'd be a fool not to go out with him. The alternative would be to sit at home moping, with everyone feeling sorry for me.

'Don't book for Wednesday,' she said, ''cos I've promised to go dancing with our Doreen.'

'The ballet!' Molly's jaw dropped. 'I've never known anyone go to the ballet. Always thought it was only for toffs.'

'Oh, don't be daft, Mam!' Now she'd got it off her chest, Jill didn't care what anyone thought. 'I'm going, and I'm not a toff.'

'It's for cissies!' There was a look of disgust on Doreen's face. 'Men prancin' round the stage in them tight trousers. Yuk! It's enough to put yer off yer dinner.'

'The world would be a sad place if we all thought alike,' Jack said, noting Jill's growing distress. 'I wouldn't mind goin' meself, if I 'ad the money. Yer can't criticise somethin' yer've never seen, now can yer?'

'No, you can't,' Jill said, grateful for her father's support. 'Joan Sutton said it's brilliant, and she's not a snob.'

Tommy had been listening with interest. He was fond of both his sisters, even if they did get on his nerves sometimes. But if he had to take sides, it would be with Jill. Their Doreen was well able to take care of herself. He leaned his elbows on the table. 'When I've been workin' for a while, an' I'm in the lolly, I'll mug you an' me mam to the ballet, Dad! Might even go meself, just for a look-see, yer know, see if I like it.'

The two men of the house taking a stand behind Jill made Molly realise she should have shown more pleasure in her daughter's news. She was going places none of them had ever had the chance to go, seeing something of the good things in life. As a mother, she should be glad to see her daughter getting on, having some fun in life. After all, why should she sit around waiting for someone who might never come? Even if that someone was the one person Molly knew was made for her daughter.

'Yer'll be twenty-one before yer in the money, son, so we'll 'ave a long wait.' Molly ruffled her son's hair, causing him to pull a face and move out of reach. He was starting work on Monday, didn't his mam realise he was too big now for that sort of thing? 'But I won't forget, mind! In seven years' time me an' yer dad will be off to the ballet, paid for by our dear son.' Laughter gurgled in her throat. 'With our luck, yer'll probably up an' get married before we get the chance to feel the benefit of yer money.'

'An' I don't think!' Tommy's lip curled in disgust. 'I'm not gettin' hitched until I'm old . . . twenty-five at least! I'm goin' to enjoy meself first. If there's a war, I'm goin' to join the army an' see the world.'

Molly banged her fist down on the table, sending the plates and cutlery flying in all directions. 'If anyone mentions that word again, I'll throttle them, so help me. D'yer hear? There's not goin' to be a flamin' war!'

'Molly,' Jack said, calmly, 'the noise you're makin', next door will think the war's already started . . . in here!'

Chapter Twenty-Five

'This'll be for you, Jill,' Molly shouted up the stairs as she went to answer the knock on the door. 'Put a move on!'

'Won't be long, Mam!' she shouted back. 'Five minutes.'

Molly hesitated for a second with her hand on the latch. It wasn't like her to take a dislike to someone she'd only seen the once. And if push came to shove, and she was honest with herself, she couldn't really say why she disliked the poor bloke. He was probably very nice in his own way, but she couldn't help wishing it was another face she was going to see when she opened the door.

'Jill won't be long.' The smile stayed fixed on her face, hiding the surprise she felt inside. Miles was done up like a dog's dinner. His hair was sleeked back with just enough brilliantine to keep it in place, and underneath the heavy overcoat she could see he was wearing evening dress and bow tie.

Good grief, Molly thought, that's put the cat amongst the pigeons. Our Jill's planning to wear a skirt and blouse, hardly the thing to walk out with someone dressed up as fancy as a tailor's dummy in Lewis's window. She held the door wide. 'Are yer comin' in?'

'I won't if you don't mind,' Miles said, his eyes on the gleaming car standing by the kerb. 'I'll wait for her in the car.'

'I'll tell her to put a move on. You won't mind if I close the door, keep the draught out?'

'Of course not.' Miles knew he wasn't making a good impression, but he wasn't having every scruffy kid in the neighbourhood climbing all over his car again.

Molly closed the door and her eyes at the same time. 'God forgive me, but I'm never goin' to take to him,' she muttered before making for the stairs and climbing them quicker than she ever had. She threw the bedroom door open and gasped, 'Yer'd better get changed, sunshine, His Nibs 'as got his best bib an' tucker on.' She saw the questioning look in Jill's eyes. 'Evening suit, bow tie, the lot! You name it, he's got it on.'

Jill sat on the edge of the bed. 'Oh, no! I never thought to ask Joan what to wear, I just assumed it would be like going to the pictures.'

'Think again, sunshine, and get changed on the double. He's waitin' in the car, wouldn't come in.'

'I've got nothing to wear!' she wailed. 'I can't wear that blue dress again, he'll think I've got nothing else!'

'Just calm down,' Molly said, her chin in her hand. 'What about that nice lilac dress? It's plain, an' yer could wear yer necklace and bracelet to set it off. An' the ear-rings.' She pulled her daughter from the bed. 'Come on, just do the best yer can.'

While Jill was slipping her dress over her head, Molly

opened a drawer of the tall-boy. 'Here yer are, yer nan's shawl is still here. Wrap that over yer shoulders an' yer'll look a treat.'

Leaving Jill rushing round the bedroom, Molly plodded heavy-footed down the stairs. She closed the living room door behind her and leaned against it. 'I don't think I'll ever take to that feller. He wouldn't come in, preferred to wait in 'is car. An' God knows what the neighbours will think, 'cos he's done up like a flamin' penguin!'

'Molly, for heaven's sake, don't start! It's not often I go against yer, but this time I've got to 'ave me say.' Jack ran his hands through his hair, a worried look on his face. 'If our Jill hears yer, it'll only upset her, so not a word, d'yer hear? It's her life, an' if she likes 'im then that's the main thing. Just don't interfere, that's all.'

'Okay, okay!' Molly moved from the door. 'I'll keep me trap shut an' not say a word to her. But I'm tellin' yer now, an' time will prove me right, he's not the one for our Jill.'

Doreen was standing in front of the mirror combing her hair. She had parted it down the side to see if it suited her, but after turning her head and viewing it from all angles, decided it looked better parted down the middle. Tapping the comb on the palm of her hand, she asked, 'What did happen between our Jill and Steve? I never heard nothin' about them havin' a row.'

'Your guess is as good as mine,' Molly answered. 'The whole thing is a flamin' mystery. An' if yer ask me, although she 'asn't said anythin', our Jill's as flummoxed as we are.'

'I saw Steve tonight, gettin' off the tram.' Doreen went back to combing her long blonde hair, her pride and joy. 'Next time I see 'im, I'll ask him what happened.'

'Yer will not!' Molly said indignantly. 'If yer mention it to him, he'll think Jill put yer up to it, tryin' to get round him. An' although I'd love to see them back together, I don't want 'im to think she's pining for him. Let him come back of 'is own accord.'

'Hush!' Jack lifted a warning hand just as Jill burst through the door.

'Do I look all right?' She did a twirl for their inspection. 'It's the best I could do.'

'Fit for a King, yer look, sunshine.' Molly smiled encouragement. 'The jewellery doesn't half set the dress off.'

'You look lovely, lass,' Jack said. 'But you'd better hurry. The young man will be frozen, sittin' out there all this time.'

Serves him right if he is frozen. Molly's thoughts were dark. If he wasn't so stuck up, he could have been sitting in front of a nice warm fire.

Jill blew a kiss. 'See you later.'

Doreen hurried to the window and moved the curtain aside. She hadn't seen this Miles yet, and she was curious. 'Blimey! The state of 'im an' the price of fish!'

'All right, nose fever, that's enough!' Molly raised her eyes upwards. 'Come away from there before he sees yer.'

'Ay, he's some toff, isn't he? Yer should 'ave seen the way he opened the car door for our Jill an' fussed over 'er. He looks like George Raft, only he's taller an' nicer lookin'.'

'Huh!' Molly snorted. 'Fine clothes don't mean a thing, it's what's inside that counts.'

'Well, he looks a bit of all right to me,' said Doreen, going to collect her coat. 'An' plenty of money from the looks of things.'

'Anythin' in trousers looks all right to you,' Molly called after her, 'particularly if the trouser pockets 'ave got money in.' She undid the knot in the ties of her apron. 'I think I'll slip round to me ma's for an hour. Listen for Ruthie, will yer, love? An' when Tommy comes in, tell him to be quiet when he goes upstairs.'

Jack made a grab for Molly's arm and pulled her down on his knee. 'Yer can go out on two conditions. First, give us a kiss. Second, bring a bag of chips in with yer.'

Laughing, Molly planted a noisy kiss on his mouth. 'Yer a proper seven bellies, you are! How can yer be hungry after the dinner yer've just eaten?'

'I'm not hungry, love, it's just that I fancy eatin' some chips straight from the paper. They never taste the same from a plate.'

Molly gave him another kiss before standing up. 'As long as that's all yer fancy.'

Jack listened to make sure Doreen had gone out, then grinned. 'Yer never know yer luck, love! I might just fancy something else later.'

'Oh, aye!' Molly said, struggling into the arms of her coat. 'I come second to a bag of chips now, do I? Yer certainly know how to flatter a woman.'

Jack chuckled. 'If I'm on a promise, yer needn't bother with the chips.'

Molly turned at the door and studied his smiling face. 'For the life of me I don't know why, but I love the bones of yer, Jack Bennett.'

'Skip the chips, Molly,' he called after her retreating back. 'We'll start with the dessert.'

'Well, now, this is a surprise, so it is!' Bridie turned down the wireless. 'I wasn't expectin' visitors tonight.'

Molly bent to kiss her. 'Listening to *Bandwagon*, are yer, Ma?'

Bridie nodded. 'It's very funny. Me an' Da have been laughin' our heads off, haven't we, Bob?'

He pulled a chair forward for his daughter. 'Arthur Askey and Richard Murdoch are a scream. The things they come out with would make a cat laugh.'

'Put it up higher, Ma,' said Molly, slipping her coat off and hanging it over the back of the chair. 'I could do with a good laugh.'

For the next quarter of an hour Molly laughed so much the tears were running down her cheeks. She had seen Arthur Askey on the pictures and in her mind could imagine the changing expressions on his face. A little man wearing horn-rimmed glasses, he was nothing to look at but, oh, he was dead funny.

When the show finished Molly's arms were wrapped around herself. 'I've laughed that much I've got stitches in me side.'

'I don't know where they get the ideas from, week after week,' Bob said, wiping his eyes on a spotlessly clean white hankie. 'I can never remember one joke, never mind reeling them off like they do.'

Bridie switched the wireless off. 'There's nothing much on now until the news, so we'll have a nice cup of tea. An' I did some baking today, so yer can have a piece of that jam sandwich cake yer like so much.'

Molly heard the tap running as she turned to her father. 'One of these days I'll get me ma to show me how to bake. My cakes either turn out as hard as rocks or they drop in the middle. There's a knack . . .' She leaned forward suddenly, her eyes narrowed into slits. Her father was sitting back with his eyes closed, his face drained of colour. 'What's wrong, Da?'

'I feel a bit breathless.' Bob rubbed a hand over his chest. 'I'll be all right in a minute, just a bit of wind.'

'That's what yer get for laughin' so much,' Molly said, trying not to panic. She didn't like the look of her father at all. His face was a terrible colour and he was having a lot of trouble breathing.

Bob suddenly fell forward in the chair, both hands clutching his chest, his face screwed up in pain. Molly ran to kneel in front of him. 'What is it, Da?'

'Terrible pains, lass.'

'That's never wind, is it, Da?'

Bob didn't answer as the pains grew in intensity and had him gripping the wooden arms of the chair. When he looked at Molly she could see fear in his eyes. 'We'll get the doctor, Da, just in case. Better be on the safe side.' She patted his knee before scrambling to her feet. 'Don't worry, yer'll soon be all right.'

Molly told herself to be calm, not to let her mother see

401

how worried she was. But she couldn't put the colour back in her cheeks or the smile on her face. And Bridie only had to take one look at her to know all was not well. Her voice anxious, she asked, 'What is it?'

'Da's not feeling well.' There was no way Molly could soften the blow, there wasn't time. 'I think we should get the doctor.'

Bridie pushed her daughter aside and rushed into the living room. Bob was sitting with his head back and his eyes closed. 'Oh, dear sweet Jesus.' Bridie made the sign of the cross before kneeling in front of the man she loved more than life itself. She took one of his hands between hers and stroked it gently with her thumbs. In all the years they'd been married Bob had never been ill. Now she tried to be strong even though she wanted to hold him close and shed the tears that were building up behind her eyes. 'Molly's going for the doctor, me darlin', and we'll have yer as right as rain in no time, so we will.'

Molly grabbed her coat. 'I'll run round to Maisie's and use her phone, it'll be quicker.'

'Don't be long, love.' There was pleading in Bridie's eyes. Don't leave me on my own, they were saying, I'm frightened.

'I'll be there an' back before yer know I've gone,' Molly promised. And she ran as though her life depended on it, praying with every step.

Maisie and Alec were alone in the shop when Molly burst in, tears streaming down her face. Leaning on the counter, she panted, 'Me da's ill. Ring for the doctor, Maisie, please. Yer know the address. Tell 'im it's urgent.' She straightened up. 'I'll 'ave to get back to me ma, I can't leave her on her own. Anythin' happens to Da, it'll be the death of her.'

Maisie was already on her way to the stock room where the phone hung on the wall. 'I'll make sure the doctor gets the message, Molly. An' if there's anythin' else I can do, let me know.'

'Thanks, Maisie, an' Alec. I'll see yez. Ta-ra.'

Molly was turning the corner of her mother's street when she remembered Jack. She stopped briefly to mutter, 'Oh, aren't I stupid? I should 'ave asked Maisie to give 'im a message. Still, it's too late now to turn back.' She set off again, half running, half skipping. 'I'll ask Ma's neighbour Katy to go for me. She's a good soul, she won't mind. An' if Tommy's in, please God, Jack will come round like a shot. The Lord knows I could do with him here right now.'

'I've never been so glad to see anyone in me life, Doctor!' Molly closed the front door quietly. 'Da's in a bad way. He's doubled up with pains in 'is chest, can hardly get his breath.'

John Whiteside had been the family doctor for as long as Molly could remember. He was a pleasant man, tall and well-built with a shock of white hair, ruddy complexion, twinkling blue eyes and a strong, square jawline. He was sixty-five but looked a good ten years younger. He put his hand on Molly's arm. 'Now get a grip of yourself. It might just be a bad attack of indigestion your father's got, or he's eaten his food too quickly. We'll soon find out. Take Bridie into the kitchen while I examine him.'

Bridie tried to shrug her daughter's hand off, but Molly wasn't going to stand any nonsense. She had enough sense to know that the sight of her mother crying wasn't going to do her father much good. She couldn't do anything about it before because she couldn't leave him on his own, but now the doctor was here it was a different matter. Putting a hand under each of her mother's arms, she lifted her bodily and carried her through to the kitchen. 'Now just cut that cryin' out, Ma, d'yer hear?'

'I can't help it, lass! I love him so much it grieves me to see him like that.' Bridie reached for the tea towel to dry her eyes. 'I wouldn't want to live if anythin' happened to him.'

There was a light knock on the door. 'Molly!'

She exchanged glances with her mother. The doctor had been very quick, was that a good sign or a bad? She poked her head around the door. 'Yes, Doctor?'

'I'd like your father in hospital. I'm nipping back to the surgery to ring for an ambulance.'

Bridie tried to push past, but Molly was too quick for her. 'Stay there, Ma, yer only goin' to make things worse.'

'He's my husband, an' I want to know what's wrong with him! Why are yer sending him to hospital, Doctor?'

John Whiteside raised a hand to silence her. 'Because I think that is the best place for him. He'll be in better hands than mine. I'm only a general practitioner, not a specialist. It may be nothing to worry about, but I can't take that chance.' He stepped into the kitchen and partly closed the door behind him. In a low voice he said,

'There's nothing you can do for him until the ambulance comes, except give him a drink if he asks for one. And keep calm, Bridie, do you understand? He is not to be excited or upset under any circumstances.'

She squared her shoulders and sniffed up before nodding. 'Can I sit with him now?'

'Yes, and Molly can see me out.' On his way through the living room, the doctor bent to look into Bob's face. 'It'll do you good to get away from these women for a while, have a few pretty nurses running around after you.'

Bob gave a faint smile. 'I've already got a pretty woman.'

The doctor smiled back. 'So you have, you lucky man! Anyway, I'll slip in and see you in hospital tomorrow. When I ring for an ambulance, they'll tell me which hospital you'll be going to.'

Molly stood on the top step. 'Not good, is it, Doctor?'

'Heart attack, Molly, I'm afraid. And before you ask me, I don't know how bad it is. It all rests in the hands of God.' The doctor pulled his coat collar up against the wind. 'I'll tell them it's an urgent case and the ambulance should be here within the half hour.'

Molly watched until the car turned the corner and was about to close the door when she heard her name called. She saw Jack bounding up the street and ran to meet him. Throwing her arms around him, she cried, 'Oh, thank God yer've come.'

Jack hugged her before holding her at arm's length. 'Maisie came and told me. Then when I was halfway here, I met Katy from next door. She's on her way back

405

now, I ran on ahead of her.'

'It's a heart attack, Jack, the doctor's just left to ring for an ambulance. Me ma doesn't know, an' I think it's best if we don't tell her.'

'Well, you'd better get a hold of yerself, Molly, 'cos yer shakin' like a leaf.' Jack put his arm around her. 'If Da thinks we're worried, it'll rub off on him an' make him worse. So try and act normal.'

Jack being there had a calming effect on everyone. He talked about everyday things, like the weather and what had happened at work that day. Even when Bob was caught in the grip of pain and clutching his chest, it was Jack's soothing voice which helped him through. 'They'll give yer something in the hospital to take the pain away, Da. Have yer as right as rain in no time.'

Bridie had pulled a chair next to her husband's and sat stroking his hair. She felt stronger now Jack was here, he was a great comfort. And because he was saying what she wanted to hear, she believed him when he said Bob would soon be better.

It was when the ambulance came that Bridie showed signs of cracking up. Seeing her beloved Bob being carried out on a stretcher was almost more than she could bear.

'I'll go with Ma,' Jack said. 'They won't let three of us go in the ambulance.'

'No!' Molly cried. 'I want to go with him, he's my father!'

'I know, love, but it's better for everyone if I go. No one knows what's going to happen, and Bridie might need help. Far better for me to be there to answer questions and such like.' Jack saw Molly's face cloud over and held her close. 'If Ma breaks down, you'd do the same. An' that wouldn't help anyone.'

Molly nodded into his shoulder. He was right. While she could be strong when helping neighbours and friends, it was a different matter when it came to her own family.

'I'll have to go.' Jack gave her one last hug. 'Can't keep the ambulance waiting any longer. You go home and wait there for me. As soon as there's any news, I'll either ring Maisie's or come home.'

Chapter Twenty-Six

Miles took his eyes off the stage to steal a glance at Jill. She was sitting perfectly still, her eyes wide and her lips slightly parted, totally absorbed in the story unfolding on the stage. She was in a world of her own, oblivious to him and everyone around her. If he spoke, he doubted she would even hear him.

Miles smiled contentedly. She's an absolute angel to take out, he thought. Gets so much pleasure out of everything. Looks like an angel, too, with her pretty face and blonde hair. She stood out even amongst the diamonds and furs of the other women around them. Didn't reek of perfume either, unlike the woman sitting on the other side of him who obviously wasn't content with just a dab on her wrists and behind her ears.

Miles was jerked abruptly from his thoughts by the applause of the audience and the closing of the curtain for the interval. He heard Jill give a soft sigh of pleasure and reached to take her hand in his. 'There's no need to ask if you're enjoying yourself.'

'Oh, I really am! I know now why Joan is so hooked on ballet.' Jill's eyes were dreamy. 'To be able to dance so beautifully, it really is a gift.' She was very much aware of his gentle stroking of the hand he held, but was so happy she didn't feel any embarrassment. It was just his way of sharing the enjoyment of a perfect performance.

'Would you like to go to the bar for a drink?' he asked. 'It's probably crowded, but I'm quite good at pushing myself to the front.'

Jill wrinkled her nose. 'I'll go if you really want to, but I'm not that keen.'

'In that case we won't bother,' Miles said, then bent his head to whisper in her ear, 'We'll sit here and pull everyone to pieces, shall we?'

'We will not!' Jill grinned. 'Only women gossip.' She pulled her hand free and took the top off the box of chocolates Miles had brought for her. It was the biggest box of chocolates she'd ever been given, and it had a big bow of blue ribbon on the lid. Make a nice bow for our Ruthie's hair, she thought as she handed the box to him. 'Would you like one?'

Miles shook his head. 'Not for me, thanks. Take them home and give the family a treat.'

Jill lowered her head quickly. He might not have meant to sound condescending, but that's the way it came over. As though her family only ever got chocolates as a special treat. She chose a coffee cream and popped it into her mouth, telling herself she was being bad-minded. Miles wouldn't mean it the way she'd taken it, he wasn't like that. But inside Jill's head the niggle of doubt persisted, taking away some of the pleasure she'd been feeling. She chatted with Miles, but was glad when the bell went to warn drinkers in the bar that the interval was over and they should return to their seats.

The lights dimmed, the curtains parted, and within minutes Miles was forgotten as Jill's emotions were stirred by the beauty and sadness of *Swan Lake*.

'That's me mam at the door, and our Doreen.' Jill leaned forward in the car seat. 'There must be something wrong. Mrs McDonough's there too.'

Miles still had his foot on the brake when Jill opened the car door and jumped out. She saw a figure detach itself from the group and walk quickly away, and her heart skipped a beat as she recognised Steve. It was the first time she'd seen him for weeks, but with her instinct telling her there was something very wrong, she didn't allow herself the time to feel hurt or sad that the very sight of her would send him away.

'What's wrong, Mam?'

Molly was leaning against the wall, a cardigan slung across her shoulders and Nellie McDonough's arm around her waist. 'Yer grandad's had a heart attack, he's been taken to 'ospital.' Molly wiped her eyes with a sodden handkerchief. 'Yer dad went in the ambulance with yer nan, an' we're waiting' for them to come back with some news.'

'Oh, Mam!' Jill threw her arms around her mother's neck and began to cry. To think she'd been sitting in the theatre, enjoying herself, and all the time her beloved grandad was ill.

Nellie McDonough prised Jill's arms loose. 'Don't take on so, girl, yer mam's bad enough as it is!' She

411

threw Jill a warning look. 'I've told 'er he'll be all right.'

'But they should be back by now!' Molly's voice was choked. 'They've been gone for hours!'

Miles had been standing by the car. Now he came forward. 'Would you like me to run you to the hospital, Mrs Bennett?'

'I don't know which 'ospital he's in, I never thought to ask the ambulance men,' she cried. 'I wasn't thinkin' straight, I was that worried.'

'You could ring the nearest hospital,' Miles suggested. 'They'd tell you if he's been admitted.'

'We're not on the phone.' Jill felt angry having to admit it. What with the chocolates and now the phone, he probably thinks we're as poor as church mice.

'Walton Hospital is the nearest, he's probably been taken there.' Miles held Jill's arm. 'It's only a five-minute run, Jill. If your mother would like me to, I'll make enquiries.'

She sighed, ashamed of herself. It wasn't fair to take it out on Miles, it wasn't his fault. She glanced at her mother in her floral pinny and scruffy bedroom slippers, then at Nellie in her wrap-around apron and dinky curlers showing beneath the scarf she had tied under her many chins. A wave of tenderness swept over Jill. The two women had been mates for as long as she could remember, sharing all each other's joys and sorrows. She'd seen them at each other's throats, fighting over the children, then the next minute they'd have their arms around each other, laughing their heads off. That sort of friendship you couldn't buy if you had all the money in the world.

Jill turned back to Miles. He looked so out of place in his evening clothes she felt sorry for him. You couldn't hold it against him because he spoke posh, it was the way he'd been brought up. It didn't mean he had no feelings, didn't care. He was kind enough to offer them help when he didn't have to. That showed he was kind and caring.

'Thanks, Miles.' In an impulsive gesture, she took his hand. 'I do appreciate your offer, and I'm sure my mam does, but I think it's best if we wait for me dad to come home. He might be on his way and you'd only pass each other.'

Miles squeezed her hand. 'I'll leave you then. If I stay I'll only be in the way. Hopefully I'll see you in work tomorrow.' He walked towards Molly. 'I do hope your father will be all right, Mrs Bennett. If there's anything I can do, you only have to ask.'

'Thanks, son, that's nice of yer.' Molly stuck her hand out. 'Goodnight and God bless.'

Jill walked around the car with Miles. As he opened the door, she said, 'Thanks for taking me to the ballet.'

'I'm just sorry the night had to end this way.' He slid into the driver's seat. 'If you're not in work tomorrow, I'll call around in my lunch hour to see if I can do anything to help.'

'Thanks, Miles.' Jill waited until he'd switched the engine on, then waved as the car moved off.

'He seems a nice enough young feller,' Nellie said. 'Bit too posh for the likes of me, but his heart's in the right place.'

'Mam, I've made a pot of tea.' Doreen stepped into the street and took her mother's arm. 'Come on, yer'll

413

get yer death of cold standin' here. I've put coal on the fire an' it's roaring up the chimney. Come 'ed, get a warm.'

Molly seemed reluctant to move, so Nellie gave her a push. 'Yer know what they say about a watched pot, girl, it never boils. I bet yer any money that as soon as we go in, Jack and Bridie will turn up with good news.'

'Are yer comin' in, Nellie?' There was pleading in Molly's voice. Her friend was strong and sensible, and that's what she needed right now.

'Yeah, I'll wait with yer.' Nellie's hips touched each side of the wall as she waddled down the hallway. 'They should be back any minute.'

'Look, it's one o'clock,' Molly said. 'You lot will 'ave to go to bed or yez'll never get up in time for work.'

'I want to wait until me dad and me nanna come home.' Doreen's bottom was numb with sitting in the hard chair for hours on end and she grimaced as she changed position. 'I've waited this long, I might as well hang on till they come.'

'Me too!' Tommy scowled. 'I want to know 'ow me grandad is.'

'I'm not askin', I'm tellin' yez!' Molly said firmly. 'You only started work on Monday, me laddo, yer can't afford to walk in late on yer third day or yer'll get the sack. So up the stairs with the lot of yez, an' don't argue.'

'I'll stay up, Mam,' Jill said. 'I'll take the day off if need be.'

'That's not fair!' Doreen cried. 'If she's not goin' to bed, then I'm not either.'

'Ay, ay!' came Nellie's voice from the depths of Jack's armchair. 'Yer mam's got enough on 'er plate without you two startin'! Jill won't 'ave any pay docked if she stays off, but youse will. So behave yerselves an' poppy off.'

The pair looked so disappointed, Molly took pity on them. 'Look, I know yez are worried about Granda, but I promise I'll wake yer if there's any news. How's that?'

Doreen raised her eyebrows. 'Promise?'

'Yes, sunshine, I promise.'

'Okay, come on, Tommy.'

When they'd gone, Jill borrowed her mother's cardigan to go down the yard for coal. 'Better keep the fire going, they'll be cold when they come in.'

'Take the torch an' pick out a few big pieces,' Molly said. 'They'll last longer.'

When they heard the kitchen door close, Molly turned to Nellie. 'Your Steve disappeared quick, didn't he? When the car drew up he vamoosed into thin air.'

'I don't know what's come over 'im.' Nellie's chins moved in the opposite direction to her shaking head. 'Whatever it is, seein' Jill with the queer feller isn't goin' to help.'

'But at a time like this, yer'd think he'd forget whatever it is that's botherin' him. He was fond of me da, was Steve.' Molly heard Jill open the back door and raised her hand. 'Shush, here she comes.'

It was two o'clock when Molly heard the sound of a car, and rushed to the window to pull back the curtain. 'They're here, Nellie, came 'ome in a taxi.' She flew down the hall with Nellie and Jill close on her heels.

Bridie was swaying on her feet as Jack paid the taxi driver, and Molly rushed to take her arm. 'Come on, Ma, let me help yer.'

'I feel that weak I can hardly stand,' Bridie said as she was led down the hall. 'It's been the worst day of me life, so it has.'

While Molly lowered her mother gently down on to the couch, she said over her shoulder, 'Put the kettle on, Jill.'

His face grey with worry and fatigue, Jack leaned on the sideboard. 'We don't know.' He answered the question in Molly's eyes. 'Da's in intensive care. He's holding his own at the moment, that's all they'll say.'

'He's goin' to be all right,' Molly said, not allowing herself to think otherwise. 'He's a strong man, is Da. If he's holdin' his own, he'll pull through.'

'I wanted to stay at the hospital in case he asked for me.' Bridie had cried so much in the hours she and Jack had sat in the hospital corridor, there were no more tears left to shed. 'But they wouldn't let me.'

'It wouldn't have done any good, Ma.' There was love and pity in Jack's eyes as he looked at the woman he had seen age ten years in the last six hours. 'And you need some sleep if you're to go to the hospital first thing. Yer must be as tired as me, an' right now I could sleep on a clothes-line.'

'But he might take a turn for the worse, an' I won't be there!' Bridie's hands were gripped tight, the knuckles white. This was the first time in their long married life that she and Bob had been apart, and she felt lost without him. 'My place is by his side.'

416

'If they'd thought it likely he would take a turn for the worse, they'd 'ave let yer stay,' said the ever practical Nellie. 'So it looks hopeful to me, don't yer think so, Jack?'

'I've been tryin' to tell her that,' he said wearily, 'but she won't listen.'

'You get a few hours' sleep, Bridie, an' yer'll feel much better. Everythin' looks ten times worse when yer tired.' Nellie could feel her scarf slipping back and pulled it forward, over her forehead. 'I'll see to Ruthie in the mornin', an' Molly can go to the 'ossie with yer.'

Jill saw the look of doubt on Bridie's face and stepped in. 'Mam, I'll kip down here and me nan can have my bed.'

'There yez are, all sorted out.' Nellie's face did contortions as she tried to lever herself up. In the end she gave a grunt of disgust and held her hand out to Molly. 'Give us a hand, girl, will yer? Otherwise we'll be 'ere all night an' no one will get any sleep.'

Jill was washed and dressed when Jack came down, the table was set ready for breakfast and the bread board was piled high with thick slices of bread ready for toasting. There was a bright fire burning in the grate, too. 'Good morning, Dad!'

Rubbing the sleep from his eyes, Jack squinted. 'Have you been up all night, love?'

'I tried to sleep, but I couldn't stop thinking about me grandad, wondering how he is.'

'I left Maisie's phone number at the hospital, so they'd 'ave got in touch if his condition had worsened. The doctor said if he can get through the next few days there's a good chance he'll pull through.' Jack's mouth stretched wide in a yawn. 'I feel as though I've been put through the mangle. I'll get a swill in cold water and wake meself up.'

Molly came bustling in, tying the cord of her dressing gown. 'What a performance, tryin' to wake Tommy' an Doreen without disturbin' me ma and Ruthie. If they're not down in five minutes I'll go back and drag them down.' Her eyes went from the table to the bright, welcoming glow of the fire. 'Oh, thanks, sunshine, yer a real pal.' She picked up the bread board and made a dash for the kitchen, where Jack was washing himself at the sink. After striking a match under the grill, she placed two pieces of bread on the toasting tray. 'Yer'll 'ave to move if yer want to clock in on time, Jack, we're running late.'

He shivered as he reached for the towel hanging on a nail behind the door. 'The water's flamin' freezing.'

'Yer should have boiled a kettle,' Molly said, turning the toast. 'Yer can't wash properly in cold water.'

There was a commotion on the stairs and Molly tutted with anger. 'They're makin' enough noise to waken the dead. Keep yer eye on the toast while I sort them out.' She walked through to see Doreen and Tommy fighting in the hall, each trying to get through the living room door first. 'Knock that off before I flatten the pair of yez! Actin' like bloody two year olds.'

Brother and sister glared at each other, then Tommy took advantage of the brief lull in hostilities and charged through the door. 'She's a pain in the neck, she is.'

'Oh, aye!' Molly stood with her hands on her hips, ready to do battle. Then as quickly as her temper had flared, it receded. Her nerves were frayed this morning, due to worry and lack of sleep, and the others must feel the same 'cos they all adored their grandad. So she contented herself with saying, 'Yer both a pain in the backside,' before dashing back to the kitchen to see to the breakfast.

It was a mad rush, and Jack was still struggling into his coat when Molly opened the front door for him. 'Get yer skates on, Tommy,' he shouted, 'or we'll miss the tram.'

'You run on, Dad, I'll catch yer up.'

Jack gave Molly a quick peck on the cheek. 'I hope yer've got good news for me when I get 'ome. Give Da my regards, won't yer, an' tell 'im I'll see him on Saturday.'

Molly nearly fell off the top step as Tommy charged past. 'Me too,' he shouted as he ran to catch up with his father. 'That's if they'll let me in.'

Molly watched them running down the street and thought how alike they were. But the way Tommy was growing he'd be taller than his dad. He was only fourteen and they were nearly the same height now.

Doreen was sitting eating her breakfast when Molly came in rubbing her arms briskly. 'Wrap yerself up well when yer go out, it's perishing.'

'I'll wrap me woolly scarf over me head an' around me neck,' Doreen said. 'That'll keep me as snug as a bug in a rug.'

Jill placed a plate of toast on the table. 'I've made a

fresh pot of tea, Mam, so sit down and relax for five minutes.'

Molly pulled a chair out, sighing. 'I'm not 'alf dreadin' goin' to the hospital. I wish today was over.' She reached for the piece of toast with one hand and the jar of jam with the other. 'I've said more prayers in the last twelve hours than I 'ave in a whole year.' Resting her knife on the plate, she raised her eyes to the ceiling. 'I hope You were listening, God.'

'Grandad's going to be all right, Mam,' Jill said, 'I just know he is.'

'Of course he is!' Doreen was licking jam off her fingers as she pushed her chair back. 'I bet when yer get to the 'ospital yer'll get a nice surprise.'

'Please God.'

They didn't see Da yesterday, Molly thought, didn't know how bad he was. But there was no point in worrying them now, better wait and see how things were first. 'It's time you were on yer way, Doreen, or yer'll be late.'

'I'll rinse me hands first, they're all sticky.' She flinched as the cold water trickled over her fingers and wished they had hot running water, like Maureen did. She was lucky, was Maureen, their house had a bathroom, too.

When Doreen turned the tap off, the sound of Jill's voice drifted through to the kitchen and she cocked her head to listen.

'Mam, why did Steve walk away last night when he saw me?'

'I couldn't tell yer, sunshine, he was there one minute

and gone the next!' Molly was talking through a mouthful of toast and her voice was muffled. 'I can't make 'im out, and neither can Nellie!'

'But I've never done anything bad enough for him to snub me like that!' It was unusual for Jill to raise her voice, but she did now. 'If he doesn't want to be my boyfriend any more, why doesn't he just say so? If he'd come right out with it, I would understand and we could still be friends.'

'Sunshine, if I knew what was wrong with 'im, I'd tell yer, but your guess is as good as mine. It'll all come out in the wash one day, but until then I've got other things on me mind.' Turning her head, she bawled, 'Doreen, what the blazes are yer doin'?'

'Coming, Mam!' Doreen moved like a streak of greased lightning. In sixty seconds flat she had her coat on, a scarf wrapped around her head, and was pulling on a pair of woollen gloves as she fled down the hall. 'Ta-ra, see yez tonight.'

'It'll take a good one to get the better of that little madam.' Molly closed her eyes and sighed. 'I'd better wake Ma or she'll 'ave me life. But I'll tell yer this for nothin', sunshine, I'm worried stiff.'

'Mam, not long ago I remember you saying to someone, "Never trouble trouble, till trouble troubles you".' Jill leaned forward and stared into her mother's face. 'Why don't you follow your own advice?'

'Easier said than done, that's why.' Molly pushed herself up, every bone in her body aching. 'Are you goin' in to work today?'

Jill nodded. 'I'll go in today, but if you need me, I'll

stay off tomorrow.' She wouldn't have thought twice about staying off, but didn't want Miles calling around in his lunch break, like he'd said he would. Her mam had enough on her mind without worrying about what the place looked like.

'Are yer goin' out with Miles, steady like?'

'No, we're just friends! He's very nice, and I like him, but that's all there is to it.'

'Just the way it should be at your age.' Molly pushed the chair back under the table. 'Now I'd better wake me ma, she wants to be at the 'ospital for nine. An' Nellie will be here soon to pick Ruthie up.'

'I can only allow one in, I'm afraid.' The matron stood in the corridor, her voice and manner abrupt but not unkind. 'Mr Jackson is very poorly and we can't have him getting excited.'

'You go in, Ma, and I'll wait out here,' Molly said. 'And don't let 'im see yer worried.'

'Only a few minutes, Mrs Jackson, no longer, because the doctor is due on his rounds.' The matron turned to Molly, her manner unbending a little. 'If there's any improvement in your father's condition, perhaps you can see him for a few minutes this evening.'

Bob was in a side ward on his own, and Bridie hesitated outside the door to compose herself. She was in turmoil, but was determined to put a brave face on for her husband's sake. Taking a deep breath, she pushed the door open.

'Hello, me darling.' Bridie took hold of the hand lying outside the bed covers. Bob looked so ill, his face the colour of the white sheets, she felt like taking him in her arms and loving him back to health. Bob's eyes fluttered open and a weak smile crossed his face. 'Hello, sweetheart, it's so good to see you.'

'It won't be long before yer home again.' Bridie bent to kiss his cheek. 'Matron said you're doing fine, so she did.'

'I miss you.' A lone tear trickled from Bob's eye, down his cheek and on to the pillow. 'I love you so much, sweetheart, I'm nothing when I'm not with you.'

Please God, don't let me cry, Bridie prayed silently. Make me brave enough to carry this off. 'I miss you too, Bob Jackson, so you'd better hurry up and get well again. I slept at Molly's last night, but I miss me own bed and you lying next to me.'

He squeezed her hand. 'Molly's good, she'll look after you.'

'Molly and her family are the best in the world and I love them all dearly. But they're not you, me darling, you are my whole life.' Bridie was fighting hard to keep the tears back. Time enough to cry later. 'So bear that in mind an' get yerself better.'

'I'll try, sweetheart, I promise.' Bob felt so weak it was an effort to keep his eyes open. But he wanted to feast them as long as possible on the face of the woman he loved so much it hurt. 'You look after yourself, and stay with Molly until I come home.'

Bridie didn't hear the door open and jumped when she heard the voice of the matron beside her. 'Time's up for today, Mrs Jackson, we don't want to tire your husband.'

'I can come in again tonight, can't I?' Bridie asked,

her eyes flitting nervously from the matron to Bob. 'At visiting time?'

'You can come in any time.' The matron had been warned in no uncertain terms by Molly not to mention that Mr Jackson was on an urgent note.

'When your husband is transferred to the big ward you'll have to stick to visiting times, but while he's here, you can come any time. However, I would suggest you leave it until this evening. The doctor will have seen him twice by then.'

Bridie bent to kiss Bob on the lips. Because of the presence of the matron, it was a fleeting kiss, but it conveyed all she felt in her heart. 'I love you,' she said softly, 'and I need you.'

Bob lifted a hand to stroke her cheek. 'I love you too, my beautiful Irish colleen.'

Nellie, Bridie and Ellen sat around Molly's table, cups of tea in front of them. 'What time d'yer want to go, Ma?' Molly asked. 'D'yer want me to come with yer, or will yer wait for Jack?'

'I'll go on me own, so I will,' Bridie said. 'You've had a busy day and Jack's been working. It's too much for either of you.'

'Don't act so daft!' Molly banged her cup down. 'Yer don't think we'd let yer go on yer own, do yer?'

'Well, I would like some company,' Bridie admitted, running her finger around the rim of the cup. 'I don't relish the thought of goin' on me own, not just yet. When he's on the mend, I won't mind.'

'Yer won't 'ave to go on yer own, ever!' Nellie said.

'If they'd let us in, the whole street would love to see Bob.'

Bridie smiled at the big woman. Big in body, she thought, and big in heart. 'I know yer would, Nellie, an' I'm grateful to all of yez.'

'Corker's home, he came in the shop to see me.' Ellen could say Corker's name without blushing now, especially in front of these people who were her friends. 'He got a shock when I told 'im about Mr Jackson. Wanted me to ask when he could go in to see 'im.'

'Corker will probably call here, so I'll explain things to 'im,' Molly said. 'Da might be well enough to see 'im before he sails again.' She screwed up her eyes. 'I've just thought on! How come yer home so early?'

'Tony knew I was worried about yer dad, so he let me go. Said he'd do the cleaning up himself.'

'That was nice of him,' Bridie said. 'Everyone's so good.'

'That husband of yours is a popular man,' Nellie said, her chubby face creasing, 'as well as a handsome one.'

All heads turned when they heard the key turning in the lock. Jill came running in, her face flushed. 'I got off early and Miles ran me home. He's outside, Mam, can he come in?'

There was a mad scramble. 'Oh, dear God, just look at the place,' Molly said, collecting the crockery off the table while Nellie, without being asked, pushed papers under cushions before grabbing the brush from the companion set and sweeping the hearth.

'Mam, there's no need for all that!' Jill said. 'He only wants to know how me grandad is.'

Molly's eyes swept the room. It would have to do, he could like it or lump it. 'Ask him in.'

Doreen jumped from the tram and wrapped the scarf tightly around her neck. I wonder how me grandad is? she thought as she walked briskly towards home. She crossed her two fingers, muttering, 'Please let him be all right.'

Then, through eyes watering from the cold, Doreen saw a familiar figure walking ahead of her. 'Steve!'

He turned, lifted his hand in greeting, then waited for her to catch up. 'How's things?' he asked.

'I wouldn't know.' She laughed. 'Me mind's frozen.'

'Yeah, it's not half cold, isn't it?'

Thoughts were whirling around in Doreen's head. Should she bring the subject up, or not? She knew their Jill was upset and hurt because of Steve, and it wasn't fair. He'd just dropped her like a hot potato, no reason or excuse. And her sister deserved better than that.

'What happened to you last night, Steve? Yer just walked away without even a by-your-leave.'

'There was something on the wireless I wanted to listen to.' He stared straight ahead.

'Don't give us that, Steve McDonough! D'yer think I came over on the banana boat! It was our Jill, wasn't it?'

Steve glanced sideways for a second. 'Just leave it, Doreen.'

'Will I heckers-like! One minute yer've only got eyes for each other, all lovey-dovey, then yez can't even bear the sight of one another! What went wrong?'

'It's a long story, kid, so forget it.'

They'd reached the end of their street, and Doreen pulled him to a halt. 'If yer talk quick, it won't take long. An' I promise I won't say a word to anyone . . . not even our Jill.' With a gloved finger, she made a cross over her heart. 'Scout's honour.'

Steve leaned against the wall, pulling the collar of his donkey jacket over his chin. 'As long as yer don't tell anyone.'

Chapter Twenty-Seven

'Hello, Molly, me darlin!' Corker's massive arms encircled Molly's waist and lifted her off her feet. 'Pack yer bags and let's run away, yer know we belong together.'

'Put me down, yer big daft ha'porth.' Molly didn't think she had a smile in her, but who could resist this giant of a man with his ruddy face creased in a grin and his blue eyes twinkling? 'You can come in, but yer'll 'ave to excuse the place, it's a tip. I've only just got back from the 'ospital.'

'So I believe, I've just been talkin' to Nellie.' Corker went to stand in front of the couch, his seaman's cap in his hand. Screwing his eyes up, he tossed the cap, sending it sailing across the room to land neatly over the vase on the sideboard. 'How is the old man?'

'Ay, you, less of the old man!' Molly gave him a none too gentle push and the springs of the couch pinged as it took his weight. 'My da's not old, he's . . . he's . . . just not young any more.'

'How is he?'

'Just the same.' Molly pulled a chair round to face him. 'They let me in to see 'im this morning, just for a few minutes. I think he looks terrible, but the sister said his condition was stable, whatever that's supposed to mean.'

'It means exactly what it says.' Corker brought a packet of Capstan Full Strength out of his pocket and lit up before continuing, 'If he keeps that up for the next few days, he'll pull through. The same thing happened to a mate of mine, and we all thought he was a goner. But he's still alive an' kicking, an' that was five years ago. Surprised us all, he did.'

'Ooh, I hope so, Corker.' His words were like music to Molly's ears. 'I don't know what me ma would do if anythin' happened to him. She's been staying here, but this mornin' she said she wanted to go home. I tried to put her off, but she wasn't havin' any. All her memories are in that little house, all Da's things, an' she said she wanted to be near them.'

'D'yer know, Molly, your parents 'ave got the happiest marriage I've ever known.' Corker blew a circle of smoke in the air and scratched his beard as he followed its progress towards the ceiling. 'They're like a couple of youngsters, in love and don't care who knows it.'

'Don't start me off, Corker, or yer'll have me bawlin' me eyes out.' But Molly was glad he'd come, he was like a tonic, just what she needed. 'Anyway, how long are yer home for?'

'Just a week. I'm hoping to get Ellen's livin' room decorated before I go back, brighten the place up a bit. Right now I'm off into town to meet a couple of me ship-mates. I promised to have a few jars with them in the White Star . . . that's a little pub off Mathew Street.

It's a sailors' pub an' yer hear some yarns down there, believe me! Not for a lady's ears, they'd make yer hair curl and bring a blush to yer cheeks. But I'll not stay long, I want to make a start on the room. If I can get it stripped today, I can start papering tomorrow.'

'Ellen's a changed woman, isn't she?' Molly picked a hair off her cardigan and leaned forward to throw it in the fire. 'I can see now what yer meant when yer told us how she was years ago. She takes an interest in her appearance now, got more confidence.'

'It was Nobby made her what she was, treatin' her like a skivvy and knocking her around. And the poor kids suffered, too. Little mites had a dog's life with him.' There was anger in Corker's voice. 'But all that's changed now, and they're startin' a new life. They're warm, well fed and they've decent clothes on their backs. Ellen does wonders with the money she has coming in, but there's no man to do the things a man ought to do. That's why I thought I'd decorate the house, brighten the place up a bit.'

'Any word of Nobby?' Molly asked. She never mentioned him to Ellen for fear of upsetting her.

'Not since I went with Ellen to see him at Christmas. It's a terrible place, bars on the windows and all the doors locked.' Corker threw his cigarette stub in the grate. 'Mind you, all the patients in there are tuppence short of a shilling, and some of them are very violent. Like Nobby, they 'ave to be locked up. He didn't even know us so I've told Ellen not to go again.'

'We've got no money but we do see life, eh, Corker?' Molly sighed. 'I can't help feelin' sorry for the poor man, but I'm glad Ellen's shut of him. He'd have put her in an early grave.' She put a hand over her mouth to stifle a yawn. 'Excuse me, but I'm dead beat. Hardly any sleep, hospital twice a day with me ma and me mind full of worry. Not the best ingredients for a happy life, eh?'

'Give it a week, Molly, an' I bet yer'll be feeling different. A lot can happen in a week.' Corker stood up. 'I'd better be on me way. But I'll knock later tonight to see how things are.'

'How's your mother, Corker? I haven't seen much of her this last few days?'

'Oh, she's fair to middling, thanks, Molly. I think havin' me home more often makes her feel better. But the way things are goin', I'll be back on the long hauls before long. There's a war brewing, and if it hasn't started before the year's out, I'll eat my hat.'

Molly groaned. 'Oh, don't say that, Corker!'

'Yer got to face facts, Molly, no good burying yer head in the sand. Hitler's made a fool of Chamberlain an' everyone else who wanted to believe in his "peace in our time". Peace be blowed! Hitler and his fat, strutting side-kick Mussolini are all geared up for war. Those small countries don't stand an earthly, and if we don't buck our ideas up, we'll be fightin' with broom handles.'

'Well, they're not gettin' any of my family,' Molly said as she followed him to the door. 'Not bloody likely, they're not!'

Corker turned, his bushy eyebrows touching his hairline. 'Molly, me darlin', if a war starts, d'yer think anyone will have a choice?'

★ ★ ★

'You're early!' Molly nodded at the clock on the mantel-piece. 'That thing hasn't gone haywire, 'as it?'

'No, that's the right time.' Jack smiled. 'I got off half an hour early 'cos you looked like a wet rag this morning. It's too much for yer, going to the hospital twice a day, what with Ruthie and the housework to see to. So I thought I'd give yer a break and go with Ma tonight.'

Molly moved quickly to hug him. 'Yer a little love, Jack Bennett, that's what yer are. An' I'll take yer up on it, 'cos I don't only look like a wet rag, I feel like one.'

'Can I go to see Granda?' Ruthie was sitting at the table in her night clothes, ready for bed. 'Let me go, Mam, please?'

'Not tonight, sunshine, yer can go when Granda's a bit better. Next week, perhaps.'

'Is the dinner ready?' Jack asked, struggling with the stud in the back of his collar. 'I don't want to keep Ma waiting.'

'I've got it on a low light ready for the girls, they're due in any minute.' Molly pinched his cheek between finger and thumb. 'You get yerself washed and changed while I dish yer dinner out.'

Jack was sitting down to his meal when Doreen came in, her face glowing from the cold wind. 'Yer early, Dad!'

'I got fed up, so I clocked off,' Jack said, hiding a smile as he cut into a piece of liver. 'Thought I'd go to the pub for a few pints.'

'Take no notice . . .' Molly broke off as Jill appeared

in the doorway. 'Well, everyone arriving together, that makes a change.'

'I've only just got in,' Doreen said, unwinding the woolly scarf from her neck. 'It's a wonder yer didn't see me walkin' up the street.'

'Miles drove me home.' Jill lowered her eyes as she pulled at the fingers of a glove. 'He's outside, Mam, waiting to hear how grandad is. Will it be all right to ask him in?'

Molly didn't look too happy. 'Can hardly refuse, can I?'

'Of course you can ask 'im in,' Jack said, noting Molly's expression. 'Can't leave the lad out in the cold.'

Molly opened the sideboard cupboard to get out one of her best cups and saucers. Never rains but what it pours, she thought. I can do without visitors right now.

'Sit down, son,' Jack said with a welcoming smile. 'Have a cup of tea to warm you up.'

'I won't sit down if you don't mind, Mr Bennett.' Miles stood just inside the door. 'And thank you for offering, but I won't have a cup of tea. Mother will have my meal ready and she doesn't like me to be late.' He shifted from one foot to the other. 'How is your father, Mrs Bennett?'

Doreen leaned against the sideboard weighing Miles up while her mother answered his question. This was the first time she had seen him close up and her inspection was thorough. He doesn't half dress nice, she thought, cost a few bob that overcoat. Nice dark grey suit, white shirt and light grey tie. Certainly no shortage of money there! Doreen narrowed her eyes. He was nice-looking

434

all right, but his face lacked character. His lips were too thin and his chin weak.

Doreen smiled and nodded as Miles bade them all goodnight. No, she decided firmly, he's not good enough for our Jill. Not a patch on Steve.

'Not goin' out tonight, Doreen?' asked Molly. She'd pulled the couch round to face the fire, and was sitting back with her legs stretched out towards the warmth. 'Not often we 'ave the pleasure of your company, so yer must be skint.'

'Saving me money.' Doreen gave a broad wink. 'I'm goin' straight into town on Saturday with Maureen, to buy some material. We're makin' ourselves long dance dresses.'

'Ooh, are yez now! The state of you!' Molly slipped her shoes off and sat wiggling her toes. 'And where, pray, are yer goin' to wear these dresses?'

'Don't know yet! We want to go to Millington's a few more times to learn to dance proper, then we might try the Grafton, or even the Tower Ballroom in New Brighton.'

Jill had been sewing a ladder in her stockings, now she lifted her head. 'They do wear long dresses at the Tower, I've seen them going in.'

'Oh, when was that, sunshine?' Molly asked.

'It was a while ago, when I was going out with Steve.' She went back to her sewing, wishing she'd thought before opening her mouth.

Molly and Doreen exchanged glances. Molly shook her head in warning and changed the subject. 'What sort of material are yer gettin' for this posh dress of yours?'

'Have to wait an' see what they've got. We need four yards, so we won't be able to afford dear stuff.' Doreen addressed Jill's bowed head. 'What colour d'yer think I'd suit, Jill?'

'You can have my long dress if you want, I don't suppose I'll ever wear it again.'

'No, I want to make me own.' Doreen gave her mother a sly wink. 'Besides, what's to stop you comin' with us an' wearing yer dress? Yer don't half look nice in it, an' it's a shame to leave it hangin' in the wardrobe doin' nothing. The moths will get at it if yer not careful.'

'We'll see.' Jill broke the cotton off with her teeth then surveyed her handiwork. 'It's a good job the ladder was at the top, at least it won't be seen.'

'D'yer feel like a walk, our kid?' Doreen asked casually. 'Just round the block.'

Molly was about to ask if she'd gone crazy, wanting to walk out on a freezing cold night. But there was something about Doreen's face that stopped her. That little madam is up to something, she thought. There's method in her madness. Whatever it is, though, she'll never get our Jill out in this weather.

Jill looked up. 'Is this a joke?'

Doreen shook her head. 'Just down to the main road, look in a few shop windows, then back. It'll break the monotony and blow the cobwebs away.'

Much to Molly's surprise, Jill nodded, and a few minutes later the sisters were walking down the street, arm in arm. 'D'yer like this Miles?' Doreen asked. 'Is he yer boyfriend?'

Jill laughed. 'No, don't be daft! I've only been out with him a few times.'

'But d'yer like him?'

'I like him, yes, he's a nice bloke.'

Doreen was thoughtful for a while. 'Has he ever kissed yer?'

'No, of course not!'

'Never?'

'No!'

'I don't believe that! He seems dead keen on yer! Are yer tryin' to tell me he's never even tried?'

'If it makes you happy, then he did try once. It was the night we went to the Adelphi.' Jill started to giggle. 'We were standing outside our house, and when I saw his face coming towards me I twisted me head. His kiss landed somewhere in the region of me ear. He's never tried since.'

So that's what happened, Doreen thought. A silly, stupid trick pulled by our 'nice' Mr Miles, and look at the trouble it's caused. He's nice all right, and I don't think! He knew Jill was courting, it was a lousy trick to try and pinch her off Steve.

Doreen found herself getting mad because there was nothing she could do about it. Hadn't Steve sworn her to silence?

Jack came home while the girls were out. He made straight for the fire and spread his hands in front of the flames. 'Sister said there's a slight improvement in Da's condition. But she said not to build our hopes up, though, 'cos he's still very poorly. The next few days are critical.'

Molly closed her eyes. 'That's somethin' though, thank God. Did they let yer in to see 'im?'

'Just for a minute. He sends his love to you and the kids.' Jack cocked an ear. 'It's very quiet, where is everyone?'

'The little one's in bed, Tommy's up in Ginger's, and the two girls have just gone for a walk.' Molly smoothed the front of her dress. 'Don't bite me head off, but I've got to ask. An' I want the truth, Jack Bennett, no messing, d'yer hear? I want to know what yer really feel about this Miles feller?'

Jack rubbed the side of his nose, torn between loyalty to his daughter and his true feelings. 'I'm not very keen, but then I'm not the one goin' out with him.'

'Not keen? I think he's a flamin' snob! He's been here about six times an' 'as never sat down, not once mind yer, an' he won't even 'ave a cup of tea! He seems gone on our Jill, but he doesn't want to know us, that's for sure. We're not good enough for 'im, I suppose. I was that flamin' mad tonight, I felt like standin' in front of him, tugging me forelock, doin' a curtsy, then lifting me two fingers up to him.'

'Molly, yer can be very vulgar at times.' But Jack was shaking inside with laughter. He knew exactly how she felt because it was hard going trying to hold a conversation with Miles. It was obvious he didn't want to be in the house, and the excuse that he was interested in Bob, well, that just wouldn't hold water. The top and bottom of it was he had his eyes set on Jill and was trying to worm his way into her good books. 'Let's hope it blows over. She's not soft, she knows what she's doing.'

He waited till the girls and Tommy were in, then said he was off to bed. 'I need me beauty sleep.'

'I won't be far behind yer, love. I just want to put some things on the maiden and put it in front of the fire.'

Jill and Tommy said they were tired, too, and followed their father up the stairs, leaving Doreen alone with her mother. 'It's time you were in bed, sunshine.'

'Yeah, I'm goin' now.' Doreen picked up her bag, got halfway across the room and stopped. She was in a quandary. Should she tell her mother or not? She'd promised not to tell a soul, but if there was any way of getting Jill and Steve back together, surely it was worth breaking a promise for. She needed someone to tell her what to do, and who better than her mother?

'Mam, if I tell yer something, will yer promise not to breathe a word to anyone? It was told to me in confidence, so by rights I shouldn't be tellin' yer. But I want to ask yer advice.'

Molly opened the maiden up and set it near the fire. 'If it's a secret, sunshine, then perhaps yer'd better keep it to yerself. Yer know I've got a mouth as big as the Mersey Tunnel. Never did 'ave the brains to think before I open me gob.'

'Keep it to meself, even if it's about our Jill an' Steve?'

'Now yer've put me on the spot, haven't yer?' Molly sat on the arm of the couch, chewing on her bottom lip. 'Okay, I promise.'

Doreen told her word for word what Steve had said, and how she'd got it out of him. Then came Jill's version of what really happened.

'My God, yer a crafty little faggot!' But there was

admiration in Molly's voice. 'Talk about Sherlock Holmes, you'd 'ave solved the case before he'd lit his flamin' pipe!'

'What shall I do, Mam?'

'Ooh, I don't know, sunshine.' Then Molly tutted, shaking her head. 'How bloody stupid can yer get? Why the hell didn't Steve open 'is mouth, tell Jill to her face? That way, he'd 'ave found out the truth.'

Molly was silent for a while, then she let out a long sigh as she stood up. 'Let's leave it for a few days, see how Grandad gets on. I'm not thinkin' straight right now, but when me mind's more at rest, I'll put me thinkin' cap on an' see what we can come up with.'

'Yer won't give me away, will yer, Mam?' Doreen was anxious. 'It's all that Miles' fault, yer can't blame Steve. I like him, an' I don't want 'im thinking I go round telling tales.'

'My lips are sealed, sunshine, so don't be worryin'. But let's get to bed now, I'm nearly asleep on me feet.' Molly put her arm around Doreen's waist and squeezed. 'Yer did well, love, an' who knows? Yer little bit of detective work might just change the course of history.'

Chapter Twenty-Eight

Jill glanced down at her watch. Half past nine and Miles hadn't turned in yet. This was unusual because his father was strict when it came to his son being treated like any other member of staff. Perhaps he's caught the flu? she thought. There's certainly plenty of it around. Nearly everyone in the office is coughing and sneezing. She read through the last paragraph of the letter she was typing, turned the page of her note-pad to check the dictation, then her fingers started to fly over the keys of the typewriter. Poor beggar's probably tucked up in bed with a hot water bottle. Still, rather him than me!

But the Miles who walked into the office at eleven o'clock looked far from ill. In fact he looked extremely fit and very pleased with himself. After dropping his briefcase at the side of his desk, he pulled his chair out and grinned across at Jill. 'Did you wonder where I'd got to?'

'I imagined you in bed with a running nose and a hacking cough.' She returned his grin before adopting a stern voice. 'I hope you have a good reason for being late, Mr Sedgewick! Explain yourself, please?'

He swivelled the chair from side to side. 'Keep it under your hat, but I've been for an interview for a job.'

Jill's brows rose in surprise. 'You mean you're leaving here?'

'It's not certain yet, but the interview went well.' Miles tapped his fingers on the desk top. 'It was Father's idea. He seems pretty certain there'll be a war, and if he's right, I'd be one of the first to be called up. So he arranged an interview for me with the Ministry of Defence. If I'm accepted, it will mean I'm in a reserved occupation and will be exempt from call up.'

A frown crossed Jill's face. That wasn't fair, surely? Why should Miles be treated differently from anyone else? What about all the young men who didn't have the protection of being in a reserved occupation? Didn't have a father who could wangle a safe job for them?

Miles mistook her silence for sadness, that she'd miss him if he left. 'The only drawback to the job is that I won't be working with you. But the office is only around the corner, I'll still be able to see you every day.'

Jill needed time to marshal her thoughts into some sort of order. She felt angry at the injustice, remembering the saying: It's not what you know, but who you know. But to blurt out her initial reaction was only going to cause ill feeling, so she played safe. 'I'll have to get on with my work, Miles, can we talk about it another time?'

'How about over lunch?'

'Not today, thanks. I've promised our Doreen to look for a dress pattern for her and it may mean trying a few shops to get one I think she'll like.'

Miles' disappointment showed in his drooping mouth.

'That means waiting until Monday, unless you'll let me take you out one night. Will you, please?'

'I'm sorry, but with worrying about Grandad, I'm not in the mood for going out.'

Miles swept his briefcase from the floor, his selfish streak rising to the fore. What difference would it make to the old man if Jill went to the pictures or a dinner dance? If he was going to die, he'd die no matter what. But he had the sense to keep his thoughts to himself. Their relationship was progressing nicely, no good would come from rocking the boat at this stage. 'I understand, Jill,' he lied, 'we'll leave it until Monday.'

That night, sitting around the dinner table, Jill asked, 'Dad, what does a reserved occupation mean?'

Jack swallowed before answering. 'Well, it means in time of war anyone working behind the scenes. Those whose jobs are important to the war effort are exempt from military service.' He eyed his daughter. 'Why?'

'Miles went for an interview today, for a job with the Ministry of Defence. His father had arranged it.' Jill could feel all eyes on her, but for once she didn't try to defend Miles. 'He said if he gets the job he won't be called up.'

'Oh, aye?' Jack lowered his head to hide his feelings. Least said, soonest mended.

But Molly had no such inhibitions. 'What!' she bawled, her face red with anger. 'Well, that's not bloody fair! My God, money talks all right! Why should he be any different from all the other poor sods who 'ave no

443

choice? I don't think it's right, an' I'll tell 'im to his face if I ever see 'im!'

'It was his father's idea.' Oh, lord, what have I done? Jill asked herself. If Miles shows his face here again, me mam will make a holy show of him. But I agree with her, it's not fair.

Tommy spoke through a mouthful of potato. 'He's a coward, that's what he is. A flippin' cissy boy.'

'That's enough, son.' Jack pointed his fork. 'It's a free country and everyone can do as they wish.'

'That's the whole bloody point, isn't it?' Molly raged. 'It's a free country because a lot of men lost their lives to make it free! Ooh, me blood's boiling now.'

'If there is a war, I'm goin' to join up when I'm old enough.' Tommy, too young to understand the horrors of war, could see himself dressed in a soldier's uniform, with a gun at the ready. A hero, defending his country. The prospect filled him with excitement. 'They won't need to call me up.'

'You keep yer trap shut an' get on with yer dinner.' Molly was beside herself with rage and Tommy's remarks were like throwing oil on to the flames. Her son, not yet fifteen, talking about joining up, while the high and mighty Mr ruddy Miles was skulking off to make sure his own hide was safe. Where was the justice in that?

Jack could see the fast rise and fall of his wife's chest and the patches of red on her cheeks. 'That's enough, love, there's no need to get yerself in such a state. And anyway, aren't you the one who's always saying there isn't goin' to be a war?'

Molly was silent for a while, trying to control her feelings. When she spoke her voice was calmer. 'That's not the point, is it? It's the principle of the whole thing.'

Doreen had kept silent, chewing her food slowly. She'd been right in her summing up of Miles, he was weak. But she wasn't going to add her twopennorth to the row that was upsetting her mam so much. It was time to change the subject. 'How much do I owe yer for the pattern, Jill?'

'You don't owe me anything,' she said, grateful for the timely interruption. 'It was only sixpence, I'll mug you to it.'

'Ooh, thanks, kid.' Doreen's hair fanned her face as she leaned sideways to pick up the pattern from the arm of the chair. 'I'm made up with it, it's just what I'd 'ave chosen meself.' She passed the packet to her mother. 'Do you like it, Mam?'

Molly made a gallant effort. 'It's lovely, sunshine.' She gazed at the sketch on the front of the packet. The dress was fitted to the waist, then fell in soft folds to the model's ankles. It had a round scooped neck and short wide sleeves, gathered in at the elbow by two bows. 'It looks a hard pattern though, d'yer think yer can manage it?'

''Course I can!' Doreen bragged. 'I've done harder than that in work.'

'That's what I like about you,' Molly pulled a face, 'yer so modest.'

'If I don't blow me own trumpet, no one else will.' Doreen gave her father a conspiratorial wink as she began to collect the empty plates. 'I take after me mam, don't I, Dad?'

'D'yer know, I've been racking me brains, wondering who yer reminded me of.' The plate Jack handed over was so clean it looked as though it had just been washed. 'Yer've solved that puzzle for me.'

'Ho, ho, very funny.' Molly gave him a playful clip over the ear. 'I'm the comedian in this 'ouse, so just watch yerself.'

When Molly came home from the hospital on Saturday night it was with a smile on her face. 'Da looks a lot better. He's sittin' up, his voice is stronger an' he said he feels fine. Sister said they're pleased with his progress and very hopeful. He's not out of the woods yet, not by a long chalk, but things are lookin' brighter.'

'That's a relief.' Jack had been reading Ruthie a bedtime story. The little girl was curled up on his knee, her thumb in her mouth, her eyes drowsy. 'I'll just finish "Simple Simon", then I think a certain person will be ready for bye-byes.'

Molly surveyed the state of the room with dismay. Everywhere she looked there were bits of paper and material. 'Oh, my God! I warned yer about the mess, Doreen, now get it cleared, quick!'

Maureen moved as though she'd been shot out of a gun. 'I'll pick the bits up, Doreen, while you clear the table.'

'I'll help.' Jill got down on her knees and held her hands out. 'Pass the bits to me, Maureen, and I'll put them on the fire.'

'What's the hurry?' Doreen asked, carefully folding the pieces of material that had been cut out and were still pinned to the pattern. 'There's no one comin', is there?'

'If yer ever bothered listenin' to me when I talk to yer, yer'd 'ave heard me say that Corker has asked yer dad and Mr McDonough to go for a drink with 'im. An' Nellie an' Ellen are comin' here for a jangle. So get crackin', Doreen, an' less of the lip.'

Doreen was disappointed. She had hoped to have all the dress cut out tonight, then she could have started tacking the pieces together tomorrow. 'I suppose you want us out of the way, too?'

'Yer suppose right, sunshine.' Molly thought she'd never seen anyone move as quick as Maureen. In no time at all the floor was as clean as a whistle. 'If yer ask yer dad nicely, he might mug yez to the pictures.'

Doreen cheered up. 'Will yer, Dad?' When Jack nodded, she gave Maureen a slap on the back. 'We can go an' see Clark Gable on the Broadway, isn't that the gear?'

'Mam, I don't have to go out, do I?' Jill tilted her head, her blue eyes pleading. 'I don't feel like moving.'

'It won't be very exciting for yer, sunshine, listenin' to three old cronies gossipin'.'

'I don't mind,' Jill said. 'I can always read a book or something.'

'Suit yerself, but don't say I didn't warn yer.'

Doreen and Maureen linked arms for warmth as they walked briskly down the street. 'I hope we don't 'ave to queue up,' Maureen said, 'it's too flippin' cold to stand around.'

'I know, me feet are freezin' as it is.' They turned into the main road and Doreen spotted a bus in the distance. 'Come on, run for it.'

There was only one person at the bus stop and he was stepping on to the platform as they approached, shouting to the conductor to wait for them.

'Come on, girls, yer'll be late for yer dates.' The conductor grinned, showing a line of yellow teeth. He blew into his cupped hands then rubbed them together for warmth. 'Two good-lookin' girls like you, I bet yez 'ave loads of fellers after yez.'

Doreen had got her breath back by this time. 'We do all right,' she said airily. 'Is there room on top?'

The conductor nodded. 'Yeah, there's only one bloke up there. Bus is nearly empty. Most people 'ave got more sense than to come out on a cold night like this.'

'Shall we pay yer now, save yer climbing the stairs?' Doreen handed over a threepenny joey and a penny piece. 'Two, please.'

The conductor threw the coins into the leather bag at his side before turning the handle of the ticket dispenser strapped to his waist. As Doreen listened to the creak of the handle and the click as the tickets rolled out, she was reminded of the time their Tommy had been given a bus conductor's set for Christmas. He'd driven them all mad with it, asking them to sit on chairs and pretend they were passengers on a tram. They'd give him a button, he'd click a ticket out, then walk around the room shouting, 'Fares, please! Next stop Great Homer Street.'

He was devastated when the cheap toy broke, but the rest of the family breathed a sigh of relief.

'Hold on to yer tickets,' the conductor shouted after them as they clambered up the stairs. 'There's an inspector on this route an' he's a right tartar.'

Maureen was first up the stairs and she made straight for the front seat. 'Got the bus to ourselves except for a feller sittin' at the back.'

Doreen was about to sit down when out of curiosity she glanced over her shoulder. 'Steve!' Without any more ado, she grabbed her friend's hand. 'Come on, let's sit by Steve.'

'Where are you two off to?' He leaned an elbow on the back of their seat. 'Got dates, have yer?'

'Nah, we're off to the flicks. Me dad mugged us to get us out of the way.' Doreen banged her feet together to get the circulation running. 'Are you meetin' someone?'

Steve shook his head. 'I'm goin' to a mate's house for a game of cards, nothin' else to do.'

'Come to the Broadway with us! It's better than playin' flippin' cards.'

'Doreen!' Maureen gasped. This was her sister's ex-boyfriend, surely she wasn't setting her cap at him? 'Don't embarrass Steve!'

Doreen and Maureen usually told each other everything, but there was one secret Doreen had no intention of sharing. At least not yet. 'Don't be daft! Steve's not embarrassed, are yer, Steve?'

'Don't worry, Maureen, I'm used to her.' Steve smiled, hiding the hurt he felt. Doreen was growing so much like Jill, just looking at her was like a knife turning in his chest. 'She couldn't embarrass me if she tried.'

'Will yer come with us then?' Doreen asked. 'Go 'ed, I dare yer! Keep us company.'

'Oh, all right!' There was method in Steve's generosity. Perhaps Doreen would mention Jill, tell him how she was, if she ever mentioned him. 'But behave yerselves.'

Doreen's face beamed. 'We've got a feller, Mo! We'll share 'im, eh, an arm each?'

Molly pushed the table back against the sideboard. 'Yer can pull the couch right round now, Nellie, in front of the fire.'

'Shall I give yer a hand?' Ellen asked. 'It's heavy.'

'No, I can manage.' And to prove it, Nellie put her backside to the heavy couch and it slid forward with ease. 'It's the way yer hold yer mouth, Ellen.'

Molly came through from the kitchen with three glasses in her hand. 'It was thoughtful of Corker to bring us these bottles of stout. Even took the tops off in case we couldn't manage.' She started to pour the dark brown liquid into the glasses, stopping at intervals for the froth to subside. 'I don't know what you're goin' to have, Jill, unless yer fancy some lemonade.'

Jill was sitting in a chair by the window, *Pride and Prejudice* open on her knee. 'It's all right, Mam, I'll make meself a cup of tea later.'

Molly passed glasses to Nellie and Ellen before sitting down. 'This is nice, isn't it? Should do it more often.'

'Yeah, it's just the job.' Nellie always sat down with her knees pressed tightly together for decency. But after a while they parted company, for comfort. Tonight she was wearing pale blue knickers, and the further her legs parted, the more of her knickers she showed. But Nellie wasn't one to worry about a little thing like that. She took a sip of the stout, leaving a moustache of froth on her top lip. 'Pity Corker isn't 'ome all the time, we'd get rid of our fellers more often.'

'How's the room lookin', Ellen?' Molly asked. 'Corker said he's only got the border to put up.'

'I told 'im not to bother,' Ellen's eyes darted from one to the other, ''cos I'm thinkin' seriously of moving.'

The silence that followed Ellen's bombshell was so deep you could have heard a pin drop. Then Molly realised she was holding her glass sideways and the stout was trickling on to her dress. 'Look what yer've made me do, Ellen, yer silly nit! Fancy comin' out with a thing like that!'

'I wasn't joking, Molly, I mean it!' Ellen glanced to where Jill was sitting, but the girl had her head bent, to all intents and purposes reading. 'I've been thinkin' of it ever since . . . ever since . . . you know, ever since Nobby's accident.'

Nellie tried to lean forward, but her stomach was in the way so she had to content herself with raising her voice. 'What the 'ell d'yer want to move for? I thought yer were gettin' on fine!'

'Oh, I'm doin' all right, thanks to Tony and you two. But I think I should get away for the children's sake. They 'ave to put up with a lot from the kids round here an' at school, about their father bein' doolally.' Ellen took a sip from the glass. 'I thought if we started afresh, somewhere where no one knows us, it would be better for them.'

451

Molly watched the flames in the fire for a while, considering whether to say what she thought, or to mind her own business. But her feelings were too strong to ignore. 'Has Corker got anythin' to do with this?'

Ellen blushed. 'Corker! What's he got to do with it?'

'Ellen, we've known each other too long to mess around. I think Corker's got a lot to do with it! Be honest now, if it wasn't for him, yer wouldn't be thinkin' about moving, would yer?'

'I don't know what yer mean! It's got nothing to do with Corker!'

Nellie made another attempt to lean forward, but to no avail. So she pulled Ellen back until she was sitting on a level with her. 'Come off it, Ellen, we weren't born yesterday, yer know. I understand about the kids, but they're only young, they'll live it down. I agree with Molly, there's got to be another reason. An' if we're right, then yer want yer flamin' bumps feelin'.'

Ellen shifted uneasily. She looked so uncomfortable, Molly felt sorry for her. But things had to be said for her own good. 'Ellen, it's me an' Nellie yer talkin' to, not a couple of strangers. We only want what's best for yer.' Molly took a long drink before setting the glass down on the table. 'Correct me if I'm wrong, but this is the way I see it. You an' Corker are friends, he comes to your house, does jobs for yer and takes yer out. Perhaps he wants to be more than friends, but that's nowt to do with anyone. I think you're afraid that if yer stay here, tongues will start waggin', and yer'll be labelled a loose woman. Am I right, or am I wrong?'

'We are only friends, Molly, honest! We've never

done anythin' to be ashamed of!'

'Ellen, I wouldn't give a toss if yez were livin' tally! An' neither would anyone else round here! Yer deserve a bit of happiness in yer life, an' so do the kids. An' Corker's a good man, they don't come any better than him. Am I right, Nellie?'

'I agree with everythin' yer've said, girl!' Nellie nodded her head vigorously. 'No one expects yer to live like a plaster saint, Ellen, not with the way Nobby is! Yer've got plenty of friends here, girl, so think hard 'cos yer might move away and live to regret it.'

Molly noticed Jill had given up all pretence of reading, and was sitting up straight, listening to all that was being said. That's right, thought Molly, you listen, sunshine, because part of what I'm going to say applies to you as well as Ellen. 'Yer've lived here a long time, Ellen, you know everyone and everyone knows and likes you. I've never heard a soul say anythin' but good about yer. Stay with what yer know, Ellen, yer own kind of people. Stay in yer own backyard.'

By the time Molly had finished, the tears were rolling down Ellen's face. 'Molly, I wouldn't half miss you an' Nellie, yer like me own family. I've been at me wits' end wonderin' what to do for the best.'

'The best thing yer can do is to stay put.' Nellie was having trouble with the lump that had formed in her own throat. 'Just forget all this nonsense about movin', an' get on with life. Believe me, nobody would give a tuppenny toss if Corker moved in with yer, lock, stock an' barrel. In fact yer'd be the envy of every woman in the street.' Nellie sniffed, rubbing the back of her hand across her nose. 'So are we agreed that yer not goin' anywhere, Ellen Clarke?'

Ellen nodded, afraid that if she opened her mouth, no words would come.

'Right, then, that's settled!' Nellie passed her empty glass to Molly. 'Fill it up to the brim, girl, an' let's get some life into this here party.' She was watching the brown liquid rise in the glass when she suddenly burst out laughing.

Molly looked up in surprise. 'What's got into you, yer daft ha'porth?'

'Yer can't half talk well, girl!' Nellie chuckled. 'I particularly liked that bit about stayin' in yer own backyard. It sounded real good, just one sentence that said it all! "Stay in your own backyard". Yeah, I'll 'ave to remember that, might come in useful one day.'

I hope a certain other person remembers it, too, Molly thought as she passed Nellie's drink over. The grass isn't always greener on the other side.

Chapter Twenty-Nine

Doreen ran her hands over her slim hips. 'D'yer think it needs takin' in a bit?' She'd spent the whole day tacking her new dress together and was now showing off in front of her mother and sister. 'Another inch, d'yer think?'

'It's tight enough,' Molly tutted. 'Any tighter an' yer won't be able to breathe.'

'I think it's just about right,' Jill said. 'It's hard to tell until the hem's been turned up because the skirt's trailing on the floor. When the hem's done, it'll hang better.'

Jack wasn't being asked his opinion, being a mere male, but he thought Doreen looked lovely. The soft green shade went well with her blonde colouring, and the style was perfect for the slim figure just starting to blossom into womanhood. He had two lovely daughters, no doubt about that. They were alike to look at, but had different natures. Jill was the more gentle of the two, would walk backwards to avoid a fight. Mind you, she took after him for that, he'd do anything for a quiet life. But Doreen was more outgoing, quicker with her tongue, just like her mother.

Thinking about Molly brought a frown to Jack's face. She hadn't been herself for the last week, and he couldn't make her out. The sparkle had gone from her eyes, her sense of humour was in short supply and her temper easily roused. He'd pulled her up about it a few times but she fobbed him off, saying she was worried about her father. But Da was slowly getting better, so why were the worry lines on her face getting deeper?

'Can I get the sewing machine out, Mam?' Doreen asked. 'I'm dying to see it finished.'

'If I said no, yer'd have a right miserable gob on yer, so go 'ed. But no mess, mind yer, I've just cleared up.'

Doreen went into the kitchen to change into her blouse and skirt. When she came back with the green dress over her arm, there was a look on her face Molly knew only too well. Her daughter was after something. Molly didn't have long to wait.

'Mam, can I go to the Grafton on Saturday night, with Maureen? I can wear me new dress.'

'I wondered what was comin',' Molly said. 'Who else is goin'?'

'Mike and Sammy,' Doreen looked to her sister for support, 'an' you'll come, won't yer, Jill?'

'I don't think so.' Jill shook her head. 'I'm not as good a dancer as you and Maureen. And if Mike and Sammy are there, it would mean me playing gooseberry.'

'Yer'll never be able to dance if yer never try,' Molly said gruffly. 'Don't want to stay in every night, do yer? Get out an' enjoy yerself while yer can.'

This unexpected support brought a smile to Doreen's face. 'We wouldn't leave yer on yer own, yer know that!

An' yer can wear yer blue dress.'

'I agree with yer mam, love,' Jack said, 'get out and enjoy yerself. And yer won't be short of partners, that's a cert.'

'Oh, all right.' Jill tossed her head. 'But only if me mam says we can stay out late. I don't fancy dragging you off the dance floor before you're ready to leave.'

'As long as you're with 'er, we don't mind if yer a bit late gettin' home, do we, Jack? Say half-eleven at the latest?'

'Yippee!' Doreen was over the moon. So far, so good.

The house was quiet, all the children were in bed, and Jack was lighting his last cigarette before going upstairs. This was the time of day he looked forward to. The only time he and Molly could enjoy each other's company without interruption. He threw the spent match away and studied his wife's face as she gazed into the fire.

'Now tell me what's eating yer? And don't tell me it's because yer worried about Da, 'cos I'm not thick.'

Molly stared him out for several seconds, then shrugged her shoulders. 'Okay, you asked for it. Don't know why I'm keepin' it to meself, anyway, 'cos it's as much your worry as it is mine.' A half smile crossed her face. 'Oh, boy, are you in for a shock!'

Jack leaned forward, his voice impatient. 'What is it, for heaven's sake?'

'I should 'ave started me monthly curse after me da went in 'ospital, but it didn't arrive an' still hasn't.'

It took a while for it to sink in, then Jack laughed. 'It

wouldn't be the first time you've been late, it's happened loads of times.'

'Jack, I've been a day or two late, but never over ten days. I didn't tell yer before because I thought it was the shock of me da that did it, upset me whole system. But I can't go on thinkin' that, it would be stupid.'

He fell back in his chair. 'Yer don't think yer in the family way, do yer?'

'What else am I supposed to think? We sleep together, we make love, that's all yer need to make a baby.' Molly clicked her tongue against the roof of her mouth. 'There's no need to sit there lookin' sorry for yerself, you're not the one in trouble, it's me! And I'm worried stiff!'

'Oh, love, I'm sorry.' Jack went to stand behind her chair and wrapped his arms around her. 'I hate to see you like this. But you could be wrong, yer know. With all the upset it could be delayed reaction.' He kissed the top of her head. 'Give it another week. If nothing's happened by then go an' see the doctor.'

'I don't want another baby, Jack, not just when we're gettin' on our feet.' She tilted her head back to gaze into his eyes. 'I know it sounds wicked an' selfish, but I couldn't start all over again with nappies an' bottles, I'm past that now.'

'Molly, yer might be worryin' for nothing. Give it a bit more time and try not to worry. Whatever's to be will be, an' we'll face it together when the time comes.' He rested his cheek against her head. 'I love you, Molly Bennett.'

Molly twisted her head to face him. There was a smile

on her face as she asked, 'Facing things together means sharing things, doesn't it? So I'll have the morning sickness if you'll 'ave the big tummy. How does that suit yer?'

'I'd go through the whole lot for yer if I could, yer know that.'

Molly moved his arms from around her neck. 'If yer could, we'd be in the money! Think how much the *News of the World* would pay for a story like that!' She began to chuckle. 'I can just see the headlines: MAN IN LIVER-POOL FIRST EVER TO BECOME PREGNANT. Yer'd be the talk of the wash-house!'

On Friday night, Molly was waiting for Jack to come in. 'Will you go to the 'ossie with Ma, love, I want to go to the doctor's.'

Jack had no need to ask why, he'd seen the worry lines on his wife's face grow deeper each day. 'Yes, of course I will. I'll hurry me dinner down, have a swill and get round there as soon as I can.'

'Are you sick, Mam?' Jill asked, her face anxious.

Tommy came back from the hall after hanging his coat up. 'What's up with yer, Mam?'

'Nothin' to worry about,' Molly told them. 'Me tummy's upset, that's all. I must 'ave eaten somethin' that didn't agree with me.'

'I'll come to the surgery with yer, Mam.' Doreen pushed her empty plate away. 'Keep yer company.'

'Don't be daft, I don't need a nursemaid! I only want him to give me somethin' to settle me tummy. I'll be there an' back before yer know it, an' I expect to find the dishes washed an' the room tidy.'

There were four people in the surgery when Molly got there, so she had to keep her patience in check till her name was called.

Doctor Whiteside looked up from the papers on his desk. 'Well, you're a stranger, Molly! Is it anything to do with your father?'

'No, it's me that's in lumber.' She didn't give herself time to be embarrassed, just blurted out the reason for her visit.

Doctor Whiteside was grinning by the time she'd finished. 'You're not expecting me to be able to tell you whether you're pregnant or not, are you, Molly? It's much too soon for that. You'll have to come back in a few weeks and I'll examine you.'

'Could it be the shock of me da that's caused it to be late? I've heard that can happen.'

'Yes, it could be.' The doctor laced his fingers together and spread them out on the desk. 'How old are you, Molly?'

'Thirty-nine, why?'

'Has it ever crossed your mind that you could be in the change of life?'

Molly squinted at him. 'At thirty-nine! I'm not old enough to be in the change of life!'

'Molly, there is no special time for it! I know people think it only happens to women in their forties, but it's not true. I have a patient, a young woman of twenty-two, and she is going through the change. Such a case is rare, but I've mentioned it to prove that there is no age limit.'

'Well, I never!' Molly rubbed her forehead. 'So that's

why me periods have stopped?'

'I didn't say that, Molly, I just said it's a possibility. And usually they don't just stop like that,' the doctor snapped his fingers, 'they can be irregular for years before they finally stop altogether.'

'Doctor, I could kiss you.' Molly leaned forward on her chair and smiled. 'Yer've taken a load off me mind.'

'Molly, I didn't say you weren't pregnant! That's something I can't say with any certainty until I've examined you in a few weeks.'

·'No, but yer've given me a three to one chance. I could be in the family way, it could be the shock, or it could be the change of life.' Molly scraped her chair back. 'They're better odds than the ones I came in with. Now I only need to worry eight hours out of the twenty-four.'

Doctor Whiteside burst out laughing. 'Molly Bennett, you are incorrigible.'

'Does that mean I'm past the post? Well, I've been called worse things than that, Doctor.' She held her hand out. 'Thanks. And take a good look at the smile on me face, 'cos if I'm back in a few weeks for an examination, that smile will be missing.'

On Saturday night, when Bridie called for Molly to go to the hospital, the two girls were getting ready for their big night at the Grafton.

'Oh, 'tis grand yer both look,' Bridie said. 'As pretty as any film star I've ever seen. Turn around, so I can tell Grandad all about the pretty dresses yer have on.'

'Aren't they a pair of beauties?' Jack was so full of pride he was near to tears. It was hard to believe that these two beautiful young ladies standing before him were the two skinny kids who used to run down the street to meet him coming home from work.

'Doreen made 'er own dress, Ma, isn't she clever?' Molly, her troubles forgotten for the moment, was beaming with pride and pleasure. 'If they don't get a click tonight, I'll eat me hat. At least I would if I 'ad a hat.'

'Oh, how I wish yer grandad was here to see yez.' Bridie's voice was choked. 'He'd be that proud, so he would.'

'They'll dress up for 'im when he comes 'ome, won't yer, girls?' Molly slipped her arms into her coat. 'A special fashion show, just for him.'

Tommy came through from the kitchen where he'd been getting washed. He bent to kiss Bridie, whispering in her ear, 'Sloppy pair of beggars.'

'Away with yer now!' She tapped his cheek. ''Tis proud of yer sisters yer should be.'

'Oh, I am, Nan, I am!' Tommy gave a wink before escaping to the privacy of his bedroom. Girls were a flipping nuisance, he thought. All they were good for was hogging the mirror over the fireplace when he wanted to comb his hair, chattering away when he was trying to read the paper and stinking the house out with their scent. Give him his mates any day.

Bridie knocked on the door of the side ward before pushing the door open. 'Oh, merciful God, he's not here!'

Molly pushed her out of the way. Sure enough the

room was bare. The bed had been stripped and the bedside locker cleared of the flowers and Da's favourite photographs. 'Wait in the corridor, Ma, while I look for the sister.'

Molly had only gone two steps when the sister came hurrying towards them, the smile on her face easing the pain in Molly's chest. 'Your father's been moved into the big ward. Come with me, I'll take you to him.'

'Praise be to God,' Bridie whispered, making the sign of the cross as they trotted to keep up with the brisk walk of the sister. 'Sure, didn't I get the fright of me life?'

'Me too!' Molly admitted. 'But it's good news, Ma, isn't it? Shows he's on the mend.'

They turned into a big ward and right away Bridie spotted her beloved husband sitting up in the fifth bed down. Breaking into a run, she flew to his side.

Molly reached for the sister's arm and pulled her to a halt. 'Let them have five minutes on their own, shall we? Me ma got a terrible shock when she saw the empty room where he's been since he came in. Thought somethin' terrible had happened.'

'I understand.' The face beneath the starched cap smiled. 'When she was in this morning the doctor hadn't been on his rounds, and although we thought he was being moved, we weren't sure.'

'It's a good sign, isn't it?' Molly asked. 'It must mean he's getting better.'

'The doctor must think he's better to have moved him to this ward. But I can't tell you anything about your father's condition, you'll have to ask the doctor or Matron.'

'Could I see the matron now, d'yer think? I'd like a word with her on me own, find out what the situation is.'

'I'll see if she's in her office. Go and say hello to your father, and I'll come for you when I find her.'

Bob's eyes lit up when Molly approached the bed. 'Hello, lass.'

She bent to kiss him. 'Yer lookin' great, Da, healthier than any of us! I bet yer glad to be in here with other men to talk to.'

Bob nodded. 'I did get a bit fed up in that room on me own. But I'm all right now. And yer ma's been cheering me up, telling me about the girls.'

Molly saw the sister standing at the bottom of the bed. 'I won't be a minute, Da, I'm goin' to see the matron, ask when we can expect yer home.'

'I'm not going anywhere, lass.' Bob winked as Molly followed the sister to the matron's office.

'What did she say, Molly?' Bridie was linking arms with her daughter as they walked down the long hospital path. 'I know what yer told Da, but what I want is the truth.'

'Like I said, it'll be a few weeks before he's allowed home.' Molly was searching in her mind for words that would tell her mother, without upsetting her, what she had to know. 'He'll never be the same as he was, yer know that, don't yer, Ma? He'll have to take it very easy for the rest of 'is life.'

'Molly, me darlin' girl, I'm not stupid. I know Da will never be the same, know he'll probably never work again. But don't yer see, I don't care! We've got a bit of money put by, we'll manage. I'll go out and scrub floors if need be! All I ask out of life is to have the man I love by my side, because without him I'd be lost. And I'll make sure he takes life easy. He's looked after me since the day we met, now it's my turn to look after him.'

'You won't be on yer own, Ma, 'cos don't forget we all love 'im, too!'

Sitting on the bus, Molly had a sickly feeling in her tummy. It's all the flaming upset, she told herself. What with one thing and another, the last few weeks have been a nightmare. But when she stepped off the bus and felt a warm dampness between her legs, she thought she knew what the sickly feeling meant. 'Ma, I'm dyin' to go to the lavvy, I'll have to make a dash for it. Will you be all right if I leave yer to walk home on yer own?'

'Of course I will! Go on, you be on yer way.'

Molly gave her a quick peck. 'I'll see yer tomorrow. Ta-ra!'

Jack was sitting in front of a glowing fire reading the *Echo* when Molly burst in. 'Where's the torch, Jack?'

He blinked rapidly. 'What d'yer want the torch for?'

'To go to the lavvy! Where the 'ell is it?'

Jack held his box of matches out. 'Take these! Yer don't usually take the torch down the yard with yer.'

'What I usually do, an' what I'm doin' now, are two different things.' Molly was already in the kitchen going through the drawers. 'I've seen the flamin' things somewhere,' she muttered, 'but where?' Then her hand touched the round case of the torch. 'I've got it!'

Jack put the paper down, looking puzzled. What was all the excitement about? Molly had never made a fuss about going down the yard before. He was still trying to figure it out when she appeared in the doorway, beaming from ear to ear. 'What's goin' on, Molly?'

'D'yer want the good news first, or the bad news?'

Jack was nonplussed. She was up to something, but what? There was only one way to find out. 'I'll have the bad news first.'

Molly straightened her face and pressed her hand over her heart. 'I'm sorry, but you're not going to be a father.'

'Go way, are yer sure?!'

'Hang on a minute, there's more bad news.' Molly went into her Greta Garbo pose. The back of her hand on her forehead, she said in a low, sultry voice, 'You'll have to treat your wife with kid gloves, she's going through the change of life.'

It was all too much for Jack. He doubled up with laughter, thinking it didn't matter if she was having him on, it was so funny! 'Molly,' he chuckled, 'will you ever grow up?'

'Seein' as how I'm in the change of life, I must be well grown up, Jack Bennett, so watch it!'

He wiped the tears away. 'Is it true? Yer not havin' a baby, and you're in the change of life?'

'Yes, my love, it's all true.' Molly was so relieved she felt as though she was floating on air.

'I'm made up, love, honest I am.' Jack breathed a loud sigh of relief. 'I didn't say too much to yer 'cos yer were worried enough, but I didn't relish the thought of another baby. Not in this house anyway, because we're cramped enough as it is.' Then he remembered. 'What's the good news?'

'Well, yer not goin' to be a daddy, that was one piece of good news. The other is, me da's been put in the big ward.' Molly slipped her coat off and threw it on the couch. 'Mind you, there's good and bad news about me da. He'll be comin' home in a few weeks, all being well, but he's goin' to have to take things easy for the rest of 'is life. He won't be able to work again, no lifting or stretching, no stress or worry – oh, there's loads of things Matron told me, but I'll make us a cuppa first, then tell yer all about it.'

The three girls put their cloakroom tickets in their bags and walked through the door to the ballroom. Mrs Wilf Hamer's band was playing a quick-step and the dance floor was crowded. 'We'll never find anywhere to sit,' Jill said, wanting to hide away and just watch the dancing.

'Stop moanin',' Doreen told her, 'we'll find somewhere when the dance is finished.' Her eyes were scanning the crowds around the floor. Then she spotted the group she was looking for. 'I won't be a tick.'

She was gone before Jill and Maureen knew what was happening. 'Well, I like that!' Maureen said. 'Where's she buzzed off to?'

Doreen pushed her way to the far side of the room where Mike and Sammy were standing with Steve. 'Hi, fellers!' She did a twirl. 'Like me dress?'

'Yeah, I sure do!' Mike stared in admiration. 'Yer look great!'

'You and Sammy stay here a minute, I want a word with Steve.' Doreen pulled a protesting Steve to the very back of the crowd. 'I'm goin' to tell yer something, but if

467

yer let on to our Jill I've told yer, I'll never speak to yer again. Will yer promise?'

'Seeing as how I don't see Jill, there's not much chance of me tellin' her, is there?'

'Jill's here.'

Steve felt as though someone had punched him in the stomach. 'In that case, I'm leaving.' He started to walk away, then turned back. 'You planned this, Doreen Bennett, an' I'll never forgive yer.'

Doreen grabbed his arm. 'Yer as stubborn as a mule, Steve McDonough, an' I don't know why I'm botherin' with yer. But unless yer want me to scream the place down, yer'll listen to what I've got to say. After that yer can please yerself for all I care.'

Doreen got back to her place just as the dance ended and the couples were walking back to their seats. 'You're a fine one, I must say.' Maureen glared. 'Fancy walkin' off like that!'

'I'm back now, Moanin' Minnie.' Doreen was waiting for the floor to clear so she could see if Steve had left as he'd threatened. But no, there he was, staring over at them. She felt Jill give a start. 'What's wrong, our kid?'

'Steve's here.' Jill turned. 'I'm going home.'

'Oh, no, yer not!' Doreen gripped her arm. 'He only lives three doors away, for heaven's sake! Yer bound to bump into 'im sometime, yer can't keep running away. Just pretend he's not here.'

Mike and Sammy joined Steve, their eyes on the girls. 'Three best-lookin' girls in the place,' Mike said.

'They sure are!' Sammy agreed. 'We'll get Doreen and

Mo up for the next dance before someone else claims them, eh?'

'What about you, Steve?' Mike asked, his face innocent. 'Will you get Jill up?'

Steve didn't answer because he didn't hear. His eyes were glued on Jill, a longing in them that was matched only by the longing in his heart. She'd been in his thoughts every day, his dreams every night. But she was even more lovely than he remembered. He didn't see anybody else, just this vision in blue. After what Doreen had just told him, he realised what a stupid, jealous fool he'd been. It would serve him right if she never spoke to him again.

The band started to play 'Night and Day', a dreamy slow fox-trot. Mike and Sammy were already halfway across the room when Steve saw a man walking in the direction of the girls. He was going to ask Jill to dance! Steve moved quicker than he'd ever moved. He ran across the floor, getting to Jill just ahead of the man who already had his hand out ready to ask her to dance. 'Will you have this dance with me?'

Jill glanced at the stranger's hand, then Steve's. Her head told her to reach for the stranger's hand and ignore Steve, as he'd been ignoring her for the past few weeks. What does he take me for? she asked herself. Does he think I'm just someone he can pick up and throw down when the mood takes him? He's got a cheek! But when she looked into the familiar face beneath the mop of dark brown hair, at the strong square jaw, the hazel eyes and the dimples in his cheeks which would deepen when he smiled, her heart overruled her mind.

'I'm sorry.' Jill smiled at the tall dark stranger before walking into Steve's open arms.

'Yer know I can't dance, don't yer?' Steve's heart was fluttering with nerves. For a minute there, he'd thought she was going to turn him down. And he wouldn't have blamed her, it was only what he deserved.

'That makes two of us.' It was so good to be in his arms again, Jill didn't care if they never moved off the one spot. 'We always had two left feet.'

Steve pulled her closer and crooned in her ear, ' "Night and day, you are the one".' His voice broke. 'Jill, Jill, I'm so sorry.'

She moved back and their eyes locked. 'Why, Steve?'

'Because of my stupid jealousy.' He would never break the promise he'd made to Doreen. 'I couldn't bear the thought of yer goin' out with that feller from where yer work. The thought of 'im touchin' yer was enough to drive me mad.' He held her so tight she could hardly breathe. 'An' when I saw his car, I knew I couldn't compete with him. Could never give yer the things he could.'

Oh, Steve, Jill thought, don't sell yourself short. You don't speak posh, don't have fancy clothes or a big shiny car, but you have far more to offer than Miles will ever have. You have strength and compassion, humour and a capacity for loving that he'll never know because of the way he's been brought up. I feel sorry for him, really, because he's missing so much in life. Daft things, I suppose, like sharing a bag of chips on the way home from the pictures, or running hand in hand for the tram.

She nestled her head on Steve's shoulder. There was

only one man for her, always had been. And as her mam would say, he was right in her own backyard. 'I was your girlfriend, Steve,' she said softly, 'you should have trusted me. I never wanted anyone else.'

'I love you, Jill.' He kissed her cheek. 'Always have, always will.'

'And I love you, Steve McDonough.'

'Come on, let's get out of here.' Steve led her off the floor. 'There's so much I want to say an' I want to be on me own with you.'

'But what about the others? They'll wonder where we've gone.'

'No, they won't.' Steve grinned down at her. 'Your Doreen will know what's happened. She's the one that planned this. Got us both here without tellin' either of us the other one was coming.' He pulled her towards the cloakroom. 'She's crafty, is your Doreen, but if yer still goin' to marry me, I'll be glad to 'ave her for a sister-in-law.'

Molly heard the knocking on the door and looked at the clock. 'Who the heck's callin' at this time of night? It's turned ten o'clock!'

'I'll go.' Jack started to get up. 'It's probably someone wanting change for the gas meter.'

'No, stay where yer are,' Molly pushed him down, 'I'll go.'

When Molly opened the door and saw the young couple standing there, her mouth gaped. They had their arms around each other, and as she was to tell Jack later, she'd never seen two happier faces in her life.

471

'Hello, Mrs B,' Steve said. 'Am I welcome?'

'Oh, son, yer more than welcome.' Molly laughed with happiness as she held the door wide. She couldn't believe it! Without warning, a picture of Doreen flashed through her mind. I bet that one's had a hand in this, she thought. And God bless her if she has, 'cos it's just what I needed to fill my cup of happiness to the brim.

Molly hugged Steve first, then her daughter, smothering their faces in kisses. 'Go on in, I'm dyin' to see Jack's face when he sees yer.' She pushed them down the hall, closed the front door, waited until she heard Jack's shout of pleasure, then raised her eyes to the ceiling. 'Thank You, God, for answering me prayers. I'll be back to You again tomorrow over me da, but just for now, thank You for this day.'

A selection of bestsellers from Headline

LIVERPOOL LAMPLIGHT	Lyn Andrews	£5.99 ☐
A MERSEY DUET	Anne Baker	£5.99 ☐
THE SATURDAY GIRL	Tessa Barclay	£5.99 ☐
DOWN MILLDYKE WAY	Harry Bowling	£5.99 ☐
PORTHELLIS	Gloria Cook	£5.99 ☐
A TIME FOR US	Josephine Cox	£5.99 ☐
YESTERDAY'S FRIENDS	Pamela Evans	£5.99 ☐
RETURN TO MOONDANCE	Anne Goring	£5.99 ☐
SWEET ROSIE O'GRADY	Joan Jonker	£5.99 ☐
THE SILENT WAR	Victor Pemberton	£5.99 ☐
KITTY RAINBOW	Wendy Robertson	£5.99 ☐
ELLIE OF ELMLEIGH SQUARE	Dee Williams	£5.99 ☐

All Headline books are available at your local bookshop or newsagent, or can be ordered direct from the publisher. Just tick the titles you want and fill in the form below. Prices and availability subject to change without notice.

Headline Book Publishing, Cash Sales Department, Bookpoint, 39 Milton Park, Abingdon, OXON, OX14 4TD, UK. If you have a credit card you may order by telephone – 01235 400400.

Please enclose a cheque or postal order made payable to Bookpoint Ltd to the value of the cover price and allow the following for postage and packing:

UK & BFPO: £1.00 for the first book, 50p for the second book and 30p for each additional book ordered up to a maximum charge of £3.00.
OVERSEAS & EIRE: £2.00 for the first book, £1.00 for the second book and 50p for each additional book.

Name ....

Address ....

....

....

If you would prefer to pay by credit card, please complete:
Please debit my Visa/Access/Diner's Card/American Express (delete as applicable) card no:

Signature .... Expiry Date ....